Sea Robber

TIM SEVERIN

✳

Sea Robber

MACMILLAN

First published 2009 by Macmillan
an imprint of Pan Macmillan Ltd
Pan Macmillan, 20 New Wharf Road, London N1 9RR
Basingstoke and Oxford
Associated companies throughout the world
www.panmacmillan.com

ISBN 978-0-230-70971-3 HB
ISBN 978-0-230-70972-0 TPB

1 3 5 7 9 8 6 4 2

A CIP catalogue record for this book is available from
the British Library.

Map artwork by Neil Gower

Typeset by SetSystems Ltd, Saffron Walden, Essex
Printed in the UK by CPI Mackays, Chatham ME5 8TD

Visit *www.panmacmillan.com* to read more about all our books
and to buy them. You will also find features, author interviews and
news of any author events, and you can sign up for e-newsletters
so that you're always first to hear about our new releases.

Sea Robber

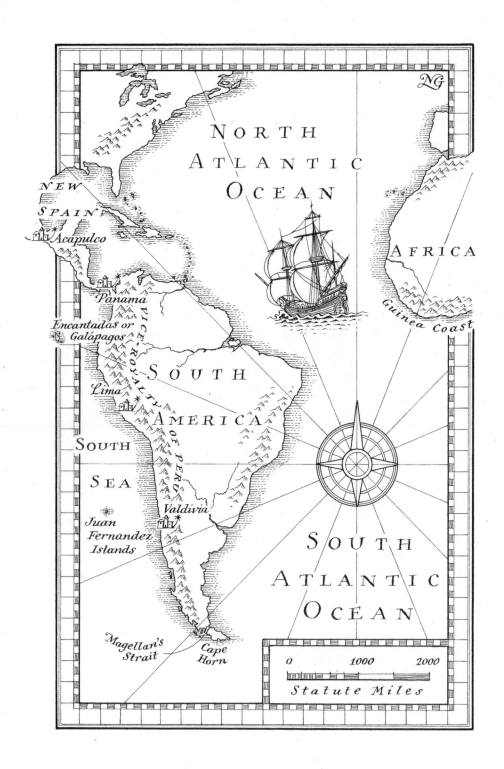

NORTH ATLANTIC OCEAN

NEW SPAIN

Acapulco

Panama

Encantadas or Galápagos

Lima

SOUTH

SEA

Juan Fernandez Islands

VICE-ROYALTY OF PERU

SOUTH AMERICA

Valdivia

Magellan's Strait

Cape Horn

AFRICA

Guinea Coast

SOUTH ATLANTIC OCEAN

| 0 | 1000 | 2000 |

Statute Miles

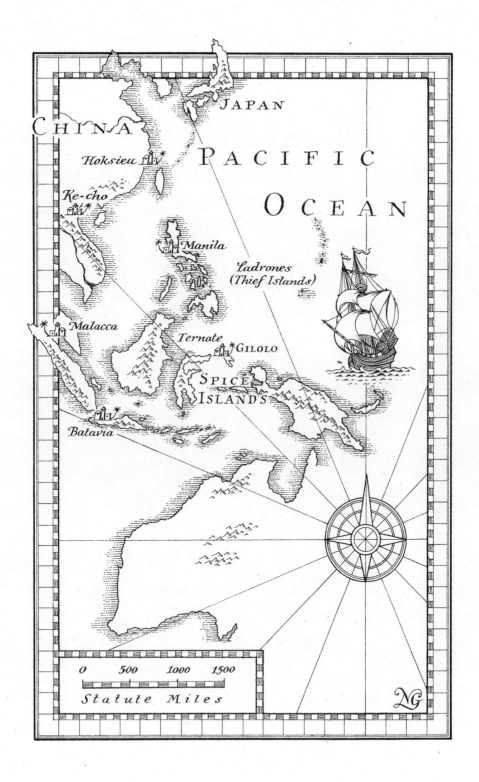

JAPAN

CHINA

PACIFIC

Hoksieu

OCEAN

Ke-cho

Manila

Ladrones
(Thief Islands)

Malacca

Ternate

GILOLO

SPICE
ISLAND'S

Batavia

0   500   1000   1500

Statute Miles

NG

ONE

IT WAS NUMBINGLY HOT, even in the shadow of the fort.
Hector Lynch felt his shirt sticking to his back despite the
afternoon sea breeze, which stirred the shrivelled tips of the
fronds of palm thatch over his head. From where he sat he had
a fine view of the anchorage. The lean-to was built against the
fort's seaward wall, and the wind carried the sound of the surf.
There was a constant rumble as waves crested and broke on the
long expanse of dirty yellow beach. At a distance the regular
lines of crashing foam were hypnotically beautiful. Their brilliant
whiteness contrasted with the translucent jade-green of the sea
behind them. But, up close, he knew from experience that the
surf was a menace. The advancing walls of water churned and
tumbled and threatened to overturn any small boat that risked a
landing. That was why the five ships waiting to take on cargo
stayed moored half a mile out to sea. They were secured safely
in ten fathoms of water, anchors firmly lodged in good holding
ground. Yesterday a longboat had attempted a landing through
the surf and been thrown upside down. A man had drowned,
his corpse eventually pulled from the water by one of the local
fishermen whose canoes were better able to deal with the
breakers.

Hector looked down at the ledger book open on the rough

plank table before him. It was hard to concentrate in the stifling heat. 'Cutlasses, carbines, musketoons, amber beads, crystal beads, rough coral, small shells called cowries,' he read. These were what the slave dealers expected. This was the Guinea coast, and the *Carlsborg*, which had brought him and his three friends to West Africa, was waiting with the other ships to complete her human lading. Her supercargo, who normally kept the accounts, had died of breakbone fever the previous week, and Hector had been charged with drawing up an inventory of goods remaining for barter.

A movement out to sea caught his attention. A launch was putting out from one of the anchored ships and heading towards the beach. Either the oarsmen were very confident or the surf had abated a little. He watched the boat approach the area where the waves began to heap up, and there it paused. He could see the coxswain standing in the stern, scanning the backs of the waves, waiting for the right moment. Hector thought he heard a shouted command, almost lost beneath the roar of the surf. A moment later the rowers were digging their blades into the water, urging their boat forward to catch the sloping back of a wave. Then they rowed flat out, riding just behind the crest as it rolled towards the beach. The final twenty yards were covered in a frothing welter of foam. The launch, still on even keel, was cast surging up the beach. Two men leaped out and grabbed hold of the gunwale to prevent their boat being sucked away in the backwash. A small crowd of natives came running to help manhandle her farther up the beach.

The beaching had been neatly done. The half-dozen men who had landed began walking across the sand, heading towards the fort.

Hector turned back to his ledger. What on earth, he wondered, were the 'perputtianes and sayes, and paintradoes'? Maybe these were Danish words. The supercargo had written his other entries in English, though both the *Carlsborg* and the fort belonged to Det Vestindisk-Guineiske Kompagni, the Danish

West India-Guinea Company. Perhaps someone in the fort would be able to translate.

An eddy of the breeze along the foot of the fortress wall brought a whiff of some foul smell. It was the stench of stale sweat and human waste combined with the sickly-sweet odour of rotting fruit. It came from iron grilles set low in the wall, almost at the level of the sandy ground. Behind the metal bars lay the 'storerooms', as the dour Danish commandant called them. Hector tried not to think about the misery being suffered by the inmates crammed in the heat and semi-darkness, awaiting their fate. Hector, still barely into his twenties, had himself spent time as a slave in North Africa. Kidnapped from his Irish village by Barbary corsairs, he had been sold in the slave market of Algiers. But he'd never been exposed to such vile conditions. His owner, a Turkish sea captain, had valued his purchase and treated Hector generously. Hector shifted uncomfortably on his bench at the memory. To please his master, he'd agreed to convert to Islam and be circumcised. He had since abandoned all religious faith, but he still recalled the shocking pain of the circumcision.

The memory of Algiers made him look across at his friend, Dan. They'd first met in the slave barracks of Barbary and eventually gained their freedom. Dan was seated across the table, his mahogany-coloured face bent over a sheet of parchment as he concentrated on drawing a picture. He had tied his long black hair in a queue so it would not interfere with his pen and coloured inks. Dan did not appear much affected by the heat. He was a Miskito Indian from the Caribbean coast, where the summers could be almost as hot and humid.

'What's that you're drawing?' Hector asked.

'A bug,' answered Dan. He lifted an upturned wooden bowl on the table by his elbow, and Hector had a glimpse of a huge beetle. It was the size of his fist, its shell a vivid yellow-orange with black stripes. 'I've never seen anything like it before,' Dan said. 'In the jungle back at home we have plenty of bright shiny beetles, but nothing nearly as big, or quite this colour.' He clapped the cup back over his captive before the insect could escape.

'I hope the captain is quick in filling his quota,' observed Hector.

'Let's hope there's a war upcountry. That'll bring plenty of prisoners for sale,' observed Dan bleakly. A week ago the *Carlsborg*'s commander had set off inland with a party of sailors. He intended to buy his human cargo directly from the local chiefs, because the stock of slaves held in the fort had already been promised to other ships.

Hector found Dan's remark callous until he remembered that the Miskito themselves were notorious slavers. They raided the neighbouring tribes and took men, women and children.

He was about to change the subject when a mocking voice behind him drawled, 'If it isn't young Lynch, and poring over a book as usual.'

Hector turned in his seat and looked into the cynical gaze of a man of middle age who, despite the heat, was wearing a smart coat of bottle-green serge with a lace jabot tied at his neck. It took Hector a moment to recognize his former shipmate John Cook, whom he'd last seen off the coast of South America on the buccaneering raid that had nearly led to Hector's execution. Judging by the motley collection of rough-looking seamen behind him, Cook still kept the same raffish company.

'Still with your Indian friend, I see,' drawled Cook. Hector remembered him as ruthless, yet astute, quick to seize an opportunity or to save his own skin. He and a number of the other buccaneers had deserted the South American expedition when they judged the risks of being caught and executed by the Spanish colonists were getting too great.

'How did you manage to escape the thief-takers in London? I'd heard you were on the wanted list,' said Cook. He treated Hector to a twisted smile.

Hector didn't answer. Cook was referring to his arrest for

piracy the previous year. He had escaped the noose, but had been advised to leave the country.

'And that other friend of yours, the big man? I'd have expected him to be here.'

'If you mean Jezreel,' Hector replied warily, 'he's out on our ship. He's watchkeeper for the day.'

'Which ship is that?' enquired Cook, squinting against the glare as he looked out to sea.

Belatedly Hector realized Cook and his companions were the same party of sailors he'd just seen come ashore in the launch. 'The big merchantman, flying the Danish flag.'

'A fine vessel. She looks well armed.'

'Thirty-six guns.'

'Hmm . . .' Cook looked impressed. He turned to face Hector. 'But a ship is only as good as her crew. I didn't know Jezreel was a sailor. He's more at home in the ring, cutting capers with his backsword, isn't he?'

'The *Carlsborg* is short-handed. Her captain headed off with half the crew to find a source of prime slaves. There are few to be had here at the fort.'

'I wouldn't know about that,' said Cook. 'We haven't yet had time to pay our respects to the Governor. Not that we'll be staying very long.'

'What brings you here?' Hector asked cautiously. Something about Cook and his companions made him suspicious. They didn't look like merchants interested in trade. 'What happened after you and the others left us off Peru?'

Cook looked vague. 'It's a long story. Some of us found regular work back in the Caribbean. A few gave up the sea altogether. More recently my friends and I got an offer. A group of investors asked if we might try a roving commission . . .' His voice trailed off. He chewed his lip as he gazed out at the anchored ships, a thoughtful look on his face, and glanced down again at Hector and said, 'So you've become a mere book-keeper.'

'Our supercargo died of breakbone. I've been asked to take over temporarily.'

'It's good to meet a former shipmate. If you've got a spare moment, perhaps you can show me around.'

Grateful for an excuse to put aside the ledger, Hector got to his feet and led Cook around the side of the fort, heading towards the main gate. The rest of the shore party stayed behind in the shade of the lean-to. As Hector left, he heard one of them ask Dan if he knew where they could find some palm toddy as their throats were dry.

'I'm elected captain for the venture,' said Cook casually.

His remark confirmed what Hector had already begun to suspect. Only buccaneer crews chose their captains by popular vote. Merchant crews obeyed officers appointed by the owners. Cook was tactfully letting it be known that he and his men had returned to buccaneering. They'd gone back to a life of sea thievery.

'You wouldn't care to join us, would you?' asked Cook softly. 'I seem to remember you've some medical knowledge that could come in handy, and your friend is an excellent striker.' The skill of the Miskito Indians at harpooning fish and turtles was greatly valued among buccaneers. It fed hungry crews.

Hector muttered something about having to consult his companions, but his reply seemed only to encourage Cook.

'I'm sure that Jezreel would be more than welcome. And the Frenchman who was usually in your company – what's his name?'

'Jacques.'

'Yes, Jacques. I can still taste the pimento sauce he made for us when we were off Panama.'

Cook was pressing his point very strongly, Hector thought to himself. He decided to pry a little further. 'You're not planning to return to the South Sea, are you?'

'We called in here to pick up wood and water. It'll be a long voyage, south and west across the Atlantic, then through Magellan's Strait and along the coast of Peru. But it's the route that will bring us there undetected.'

Hector's mind raced. He was desperate to reach Peru and track down a young Spanish woman, Maria. At his trial for piracy the prosecution had relied on her evidence for his conviction, and when Maria had retracted at the last moment, the case against Hector collapsed. She had returned to South America, and Hector had devoted himself to finding her again. He was deeply in love with her. He could picture her face and quiet smile, hear the sound of her voice, and – in scenario after scenario – rehearsed the moment when he might stand before her again and tell her of his feelings. At least half a dozen times each day he read the letter she had smuggled to him after the trial, though it was falling to pieces along the folds. He knew the words by heart. 'I cherish every hour that we spent together,' she had written. 'You will always be in my thoughts.' His burning dream was to hold Maria close, feel her respond and know that she wished to share his future, however uncertain that might be.

Here, unforeseen and very tempting, was the perfect chance for him to reach Peru directly and find her. If he stayed with the *Carlsborg*, the best he could hope for was to arrive in the West Indies. Then he would still have to make his way over-land across Panama and onward. If the Spanish discovered his identity during this journey, nothing would save him a second time from being tried for piracy and found guilty. Then it was prison or the garrotte.

'Which is your ship?' he asked Cook cautiously.

They had passed along the length of the fort's wall and were about to turn the corner below the eastern bastion, losing sight of the anchorage. Cook paused for a moment and pointed. 'There, anchored just astern of your Danish ship. That's our vessel. We've decided to call her the *Revenge*.'

He gave Hector a meaningful glance and it occurred to the

young man that Cook and his colleagues were seeking retribution for the defeats inflicted on them during their raids into the Pacific. Hector's initial excitement deflated abruptly. Maria was Spanish, and he had no desire to go fighting the Spaniards again.

Also, as he observed the *Revenge*, Cook's ship looked ill suited for such an ambitious enterprise. She was shabby and seaworn, and much smaller than the *Carlsborg*. He doubted that she carried more than eight cannon, and he wondered how successful the *Revenge* would be against colonial shipping in the South Sea. The Spanish vessels would be far better armed. On the whole, he'd be wiser to stay with the *Carlsborg*.

They resumed their walk along the foot of the fortress wall with its massive grey and white stones. Glancing up, Hector saw a Danish sentry watching them incuriously from the battlements. The man had draped a chequered cloth over his head to keep off the sun and was looking bored. Standing guard on a slaving fort was dull work. There was little risk of attack from the outside, so the task was more like being a prison warder. What mattered was to prevent a rebellion and escape by the slave inmates.

The main gate stood open, and they turned in. Ahead, the principal compound was an open expanse paved with brick that radiated the heat back so that the air danced. On their right were the slave holes, dreaded for good reason. Hector had been shown them briefly and the sight had left him sickened. The slave holes were the size and shape of large bread ovens and just large enough for one man to be thrust inside. Then the door was locked. Once incarcerated, the victim was left to broil until the captors decided that he risked dying of suffocation. Often they preferred to pull out a corpse. The slave holes were used for punishment to maintain discipline.

An African was standing beside the flight of steps leading up to the commandant's office. His billowing robe of yellow striped with red served to emphasize his muscular bulk, and he must have stood at least six and a half feet tall. A three-cornered black cocked hat, edged with silver braid and decorated with a cluster of drooping ostrich plumes, was placed squarely on his head, and in one hand he held his badge of office, a long, elaborately carved staff. With the other he was fanning himself with a delicate Chinese fan. As the two white men approached, he looked them up and down in a calculating manner. His fleshy face was marked with tribal scars and the whites of his eyes were discoloured and bloodshot. Judging the visitors to be unimportant, the chief deliberately turned away.

'Vicious-looking bastard,' commented Cook under his breath.

'He's probably from the Akwamu tribe. One of their chiefs. They control the immediate area around the fort . . . and drive a very hard bargain when it comes to selling their neighbours,' Hector explained.

'That's not all they have to sell. Look at those teeth.' Cook had spotted a pile of elephant tusks piled in one corner. His covetous tone made Hector wonder for a moment if the buccaneer captain dared to think of plundering the fort. But he dismissed the idea immediately. Cook had far too few men to risk an attack.

They walked on across the compound. There were very few people to be seen, only the native chief and a trio of Danish soldiers. Tunics unbuttoned, they lounged in the shade of some arches that led to the dormitory for the garrison.

'I'm curious to see where the slaves are kept,' said Cook. The slave pens lay directly ahead, behind a row of stout iron-bound doors on the far side of the compound. Hector had never visited the holding pens before, but the *Carlsborg*'s quartermaster, a man experienced in the slave trade, had told him that the fort was designed for smooth handling of the human contents. A brick-lined passageway pierced the outer wall and led directly from the pens to a gate overlooking the beach. When the time came to load the *Carlsborg*, the slaves would be chained together in batches, led down the passageway, and marched straight to

9

where boats were waiting to run a shuttle service out to the ship. Hector had asked whether the *Carlsborg* had enough boats for the task, and was told the local fishermen made a handsome living by hiring out themselves and their canoes as transport.

The iron-bound doors were locked. With no one to give them any directions, the two men climbed a wooden stairway to an upper floor and came to a small door, which was ajar. Entering, they found themselves in a long corridor, which ran almost the full width of the building. After the blinding glare of the compound, it took a moment for Hector's eyes to adjust to the deep gloom inside. The rank stench he'd smelled earlier was now so strong he had to swallow hard to stop himself gagging. In the opposite wall of the corridor he could make out the outline of a small, heavily barred window. Dimly he was aware of more windows on either side, where the gallery stretched away into the darkness. He stepped up to the window and peered in. He was looking down into a dungeon. From a height of a dozen feet it was difficult to see much of what was immediately below him, but from what he could see the dungeon appeared to be about fifteen paces square. The only source of light and air was a row of three tiny windows on the far wall. They were set close to the ceiling and revealed a curved vault roof of dressed stone. Nearly all the light fell on the far end of the dungeon. There the floor was thickly covered with humans. They sat on the flagstones, their heads bowed, arms clasped around their knees. A few had somehow found space to lie down. His nose told him they had no latrine, and he wondered how such a dense mass of humanity could be fed and given water. Immediately below where he stood the light was so poor it was difficult to distinguish individuals. They coalesced into one shadowy, intertwined mass. Eerily, the only sound was an occasional cough or a low moan. A sense of quiet, hopeless resignation exuded from this thick carpet of humanity. Hector was appalled.

Cook, his face only inches away from Hector's, peered into

the dungeon. Hector briefly caught the scent of perfume that he was using. 'A bachelor's delight,' Cook breathed wonderingly. Puzzled for an instant, Hector suddenly comprehended his meaning. Several of the captives in the dungeon had sensed they were being observed. They had raised their heads and looked up towards the spyhole. Hector could just make out their faces and the occasional gleam of an eye. Every one of them was a woman. This was a dungeon exclusively for female slaves awaiting shipment.

'De er alle solgt,' said a husky voice. A Danish gaoler was standing in the corridor, a few paces away. He tapped his chest with one hand.

Hector stepped back from the window. He remembered from the supercargo's ledger that 'solgt' meant 'sold'. The Dane presumed they were potential slave buyers examining the sale stock.

'How do you feed the prisoners?' Hector asked. He pointed to his mouth and pretended to eat and drink, then gestured towards the dungeon. The gaoler imitated the process of picking up a long-handled shovel, loading the blade and thrusting it between the bars.

'Like feeding animals,' muttered Cook.

'Kom!' The Dane made it clear that they should leave. He escorted them back to the door at the head of the stairway and closed it behind them.

'I've seen enough,' said Cook as they walked back across the compound. They passed a blacksmith's workplace. Instead of horseshoes, there were heaps of chains and ankle rings. Cook stopped. Hanging from a row of hooks were several long, thin metal rods.

'That's what the gaoler meant when he touched his chest,' he said. 'Those rods are branding irons. I saw them used to mark wild cattle in the Caribbees. When the slaves are sold, they're branded on the breast to show who their new owner is.'

He paused, as if a thought had occurred to him. 'That

Frenchman, your friend, has a brand on his cheek, as I
remember?'

'Yes,' answered Hector. 'The letter G. It stands for "galérien". It was burned on him when he was convicted in France
and sent to the royal galleys. But the mark hardly shows when
he has a tan.'

'Perhaps you'd ask him if he could come across to the
Revenge later this evening and meet one of my crew – another
Frenchman. He's also an ex-convict and speaks very little
English. He's very sick, and likely to die. Another case of
Guinea fever. Perhaps your Jacques can have a few last words
with him?'

'Jacques is out on the *Carlsborg*, with Jezreel. They're on the
same watch.'

'Then why don't I bring you and your Indian friend out to
your ship on the *Revenge*'s launch so that you can ask Jacques
if he'll do me this favour? I'd appreciate it.'

Hector hesitated. Cook's offer somehow rang false, but he
couldn't define why. The buccaneer persisted.

'When does Jacques have to go back on watch?'

'Tomorrow. He and Jezreel have the morning watch. Dan
and I will be joining them.'

'Sounds as though you all stick together. Just like the old
days.'

'That's true.'

'Then it's settled. I'll see you and Dan on the beach around
sunset and bring you back out to the *Carlsborg*.' Cook straightened the lace at his neck and brushed a speck of dust off the
sleeve of his coat. 'Lynch, think over my offer about joining the
crew of the *Revenge*. Meanwhile I had better pay my respects to
the commandant.'

He turned away and went towards the Governor's office.

TWO

'Jacques should have been back by now,' said Jezreel. It was the following morning and the first glow of the sunrise was defining the horizon. In the dim light the former prizefighter appeared even more of a Goliath than usual as he leaned on the rail and gazed aft to where the *Revenge* was anchored a hundred yards astern of the Danish slaver. The previous evening the Frenchman had gone across to Cook's ship. But he hadn't returned as yet.

'I can't understand what's keeping him,' said Hector anxiously. He was on anchor watch with Jezreel and Dan aboard the *Carlsborg*. The *Revenge* had been a black, ill-defined shadow during the night. Now her outline was becoming clearer, the masts and spars taking shape against the sky. Hector usually enjoyed this early hour. It was the coolest part of the day, and there was little to do but track the passage of time as the stars disappeared one by one until only the brightest remained. He and his companions had been assigned to the foredeck where their task was to check the ship didn't override her anchor cable. Should that happen, they were to alert the officer of the watch and, with the help of the two Danish sailors who preferred to stay on the aft deck, they were to hoist a jib or a staysail to trim the angle of the vessel to her mooring.

'Where's our petty officer?' asked Jezreel.

'He went below ten minutes ago,' answered Dan.

'Probably seeking his bottled comfort.' The petty officer in charge of the watch, an elderly Dane by the name of Jens Iversen, was a notorious tippler. His clothes reeked of alcohol and tobacco.

'Jacques will lose a day's pay over this,' observed Dan. Iversen was a very zealous employee of the Company. He would consider it worth reporting Jacques' lateness to the *Carlsborg*'s captain so that even the paltry sum of a deckhand's daily wage could be trimmed from the vessel's operating costs.

Dan cocked his head on one side. He had heard something. 'Sounds like the *Revenge* is lowering a boat. Maybe that's Jacques on his way back now.' He went to the starboard rail and leaned out so that he could see more easily down the length of the ship. The squeal of blocks came clearly over the water. A few moments later there were shouted orders, then several blasts on a whistle.

'That's odd,' observed Hector. 'It's more like a ship getting under way. Dan, can you make out what's happening?'

A shift of wind caught the *Carlsborg* so that the Danish vessel swung on her cable, obscuring Dan's view. He crossed the deck and looked aft again towards the *Revenge*. Now there was enough daylight to see considerable activity on the other ship. Men were aloft on her spars, others were climbing to join them, and a larger group of seamen was clustered on her main deck. They were bent over and moving slowly in a circle.

'They're raising anchor,' Dan exclaimed.

'Then where's Jacques?' Hector asked, a note of alarm in his voice.

'Maybe they're just shifting their anchorage,' said Jezreel. He was also at the rail, eyes fixed on the smaller vessel.

'They are setting too much sail for that.'

As they watched, the *Revenge*'s anchor emerged dripping

from the water. The men on her yards unloosed the sails, the canvas flapped and filled.

Hector was struck by how clumsily Cook and his crew handled their ship. There was a muddle on the foredeck. One corner of the lower forecourse had wrapped around itself, and the sail was being untwisted. Also the mizzen spar was canted at the wrong angle and needed to be lowered and rehoisted into position. Instead of forging ahead, the *Revenge* began to fall back, partially out of control and crabbing sideways through the water. It was all very unseamanlike and in sharp contrast to the skill shown by her launch crew when they'd come ashore through the surf the previous day.

Hector was more and more agitated by Jacques' absence. He feared the Frenchman might be below deck on the *Revenge* sleeping off a hangover, completely unaware the ship was getting under way. Or perhaps he'd decided to join the buccaneer crew? Cook had seemed keen to recruit him. But, Hector told himself, Jacques would never accept Cook's offer without first consulting his friends. Besides, Jacques had left his favourite cooking utensils, his batterie de cuisine, aboard the *Carlsborg*. He would not leave the ship without taking his simmering pans and skimmers, the bake kettle in which he made excellent loaves, even at sea, and the splendid collection of spices he had acquired on his travels and jealously hoarded in a locked box, its interior neatly compartmented like an apothecary's chest.

'What a foul-up,' said Jezreel, watching the disarray aboard the *Revenge*. 'Can't imagine how they think they can sail her through Magellan's channel.' Earlier Hector had told him of Cook's proposed journey.

Slowly the crew of the *Revenge* got their vessel under some degree of control. She began to move forward, and a ripple appeared under her bow. Hector watched the two masts swing into line, then open up again as her helmsman set her on course. He saw that the *Revenge* was intending to pass close to windward of the anchored Danish ship and this, he thought despairingly, might give Jacques a final chance to return to the *Carlsborg*. He might be able to jump overboard and swim.

Hector left the foredeck and hurried down to the waist of the slave ship. This was where the *Carlsborg*'s smallest tender, the little cockboat, was stowed. He was going to ask Iversen for permission to launch it. Jacques was a weak swimmer at best.

The petty officer had reappeared on deck. Now he was standing at the taffrail with the two Danish sailors and watching the *Revenge* get under way. The scornful expression on his face left little doubt what he thought of the incompetence of the *Revenge*'s crew.

Perched on the bowsprit of Cook's ship, two deckhands were trying to throw a loop of rope around an anchor fluke so that it could be hauled up and made fast. But they were making a mess of it. Twice they cast the rope, and twice they missed. The third time the rope passed under the anchor, but the man who was meant to catch the free end mistimed his snatch. He lost his grip, swivelled around the bowsprit and hung perilously at arm's length, feet kicking in thin air, until he heaved himself back up. The rope splashed uselessly into the sea. His clumsiness drew a mocking guffaw from the Danish spectators, their laughter loud enough to be heard by the hapless sailor.

Hector looked anxiously for Jacques. But he was nowhere to be seen. The *Revenge* was gathering pace, setting out on her voyage.

A sudden shout from the *Carlsborg*'s stern deck made Hector look in that direction. Iversen had his hands cupped around his mouth and was calling out. He waved an arm. For a moment Hector thought he was bidding a farewell. But then the Dane gesticulated again, more urgently, and it was clear he was signalling to the other ship that she was coming too close and must stand clear.

Neither the captain nor the helmsman aboard the *Revenge*

appeared to have heard the warning cry, nor were they conscious of the danger. Their vessel maintained course.

The Danish petty officer shouted again, more loudly this time, roaring at the top of his lungs.

'Maybe they'll skim by us so close that Jacques can jump across and rejoin us,' said Jezreel hopefully. He had appeared at Hector's elbow.

'I don't think so. No one handles a ship that neatly.'

The shouts and yells had brought the *Carlsborg*'s first mate on deck. He was tousled and dishevelled and still wearing a nightshirt. The moment he saw the danger, he turned and ran back down to his cabin and reappeared with a speaking trumpet in his hand. Putting it to his lips, he bellowed another warning to the *Revenge*.

By now Cook's ship was fifty paces astern and steadily closing the gap. It was also obvious that the wind and current would not allow her to pass the *Carlsborg* on her windward side. The *Revenge* had to change her original course and pass downwind.

The first mate shouted again, red in the face with anger. This time the captain of the *Revenge* must have heard him, for Hector saw Cook wave acknowledgement. Then he turned towards his helmsman and Hector heard him shout clearly, 'Hard to starboard, you fool.'

Hector saw the helmsman fling his weight on the helm and put it to port, the wrong direction.

'What a dolt,' exclaimed Jezreel.

But Hector had spotted Jacques. The Frenchman was standing at the foot of the *Revenge*'s foremast, stock-still and staring towards the *Carlsborg*. Beside him stood a man Hector did not recognize. He was holding a pistol to Jacques' head. The tableau was clearly visible, and was meant to be. With a sickening lurch, Hector understood exactly what was happening.

So too did the *Carlsborg*'s first mate. He turned on his heel

17

and bolted for his cabin, his nightshirt flying out behind him. A moment later he reappeared, a pistol in one hand and a bunch of keys in the other. He screamed at the Danish sailors to look out for their lives as he darted past them towards the arms chest placed beside the helm. It was there in case an uprising by the slave cargo had to be suppressed with weapons. Inside were loaded muskets and a pair of the newfangled blunderbusses.

The officer unlocked and flung back the lid, and began frenziedly pulling out the guns. He thrust them into the hands of his Danish compatriots. Then, looking around in desperation, he saw Hector and his two friends still standing by the cockboat. Gathering up three more guns, he darted across the deck and pushed the weapons into their grasp. 'Skyde. Skyde,' he commanded breathlessly and pointed towards the oncoming ship. 'Shoot. Shoot.'

From his vantage point at the *Carlsborg*'s rail, Hector looked down and saw armed sailors crouched on the *Revenge*'s foredeck. They were waiting to leap on to the larger vessel. Flat explosions of musket shots told him the Danes had opened fire, but he couldn't see where their bullets struck. He felt the weight of the musket in his hands, thumbed back the lock and brought the weapon up to his shoulder as if to use it. But he already knew he wouldn't pull the trigger while Jacques was held hostage. Instead he swung the muzzle of the gun menacingly, pretending to seek a target, and found himself staring over the gun's sight at Cook. The buccaneer captain had moved forward to stand next to Jacques. Cook glanced up and must have seen Hector, for the buccaneer gave a sly smile and raised a finger to his forehead in a sarcastic salute.

The *Revenge*'s bowsprit was now so near that it was about to spear through the *Carlsborg*'s stern windows. At the last moment the buccaneer helmsman gave a deft touch, which laid his vessel alongside the stern quarter of the bigger ship with a grinding crash. A pair of light grappling hooks flew through the air and caught on the *Carlsborg*'s side rail. A moment later Cook's men swarmed up.

There was the bang of a musket, then another. The Danish sailors had reloaded and were shooting downwards. Hector saw one of the buccaneers slip and fall back, tangling with one of his comrades. The two men tumbled back on to the *Revenge*'s foredeck. But the assault did not waver. Several musket balls whizzed past Hector's head, fired from below by the boarders, but he ignored them. Deliberately he lowered his weapon. He was aware that neither Jezreel nor Dan had fired, either. The three of them had left the defence of the *Carlsborg* entirely to the Danes.

On the poop deck the first mate was cursing, a steady stream of oaths. He had discharged his pistol and was scrabbling in the arms chest, trying to find a blunderbuss. A few paces away the two Danish sailors had dropped their guns and stood helplessly, looking on. Beside the helm Iversen clutched his side, blood oozing through his fingers.

The first mate found his weapon and turned, ready to use it, when a shot rang out. He grunted abruptly and a bright crimson stain appeared on the front of his nightshirt. For a moment he stood there, bewildered, took a half-step backwards until he came up against the open lid of the arms chest. As he toppled over, the lid slammed shut beneath him and his body lay across it for a moment, before sliding to the deck, dead.

There was a sudden, still silence and the overpowering acrid smell of gunpowder. Hector hadn't seen who had fired the fatal shot, but already the first wave of the *Revenge*'s boarding party – half a dozen men – were taking control of the poop deck. They relieved the two Danish sailors of their muskets and ordered them forward. A buccaneer put his arm around the shoulders of the wounded petty officer and helped him down to the main deck. The first mate's body was pushed to one side, and a man whom Hector took to be the *Revenge*'s sailing master stepped up to the helm and began tentatively working it from side to side, trying it out.

At least two dozen more men from the *Revenge* were clambering up to the deck of the slaver. In their sea-stained smocks and wide breeches and broad-brimmed hats, they could have passed for the crew of any honest vessel. There was nothing to mark them out as sea bandits. Hector looked into their faces closely, trying to identify anyone among them who had sailed with him in the South Sea. He thought he recognized one or two, but it was impossible to be sure, for they pushed past him without a word. Unlike the chaotic departure of the *Revenge*, which had been a sham to lull their Danish victims, Cook's men went about their business briskly and with barely a command spoken. Some took up position by the companionways and hatches, and as the sleepy crew of the Danish slave ship appeared, they faced the muzzles of their captors' guns and quietly surrendered. A larger group of the buccaneers dispersed about the ship, checking sheets and braces, looking up at the spars, climbing into the rigging, searching out capstan bars, and then stood ready, waiting for orders.

By Hector's estimate only half an hour had passed from the time Dan had heard the first sounds from the *Revenge* as she began to get under way. In that interval Cook's men had captured a ship almost half as big again as their own and with three times as many cannon, and had done so without loss to themselves. They were complete masters of the *Carlsborg*.

Finally Cook himself came aboard with Jacques. The Frenchman looked crestfallen. 'There wasn't much I could do,' he muttered to Hector. 'I was hustled under hatches the moment I came aboard the *Revenge* last night. Shut up all night in the cable locker, where I couldn't be heard.'

Cook called down to the men still on the *Revenge*. They were to cast off and resume course. The buccaneer captain turned and glanced at the musket Hector still held, cocked but never fired. 'That was sensible of you. I didn't imagine you could bring yourself to shoot at your old comrades.'

'Where are you taking this ship?' Hector asked. He had an uncomfortable feeling that Cook's plan was more devious than first appeared.

'As I told you yesterday,' said Cook casually, 'we head for the South Sea by way of Magellan's Strait. But aboard this fine vessel rather than our worn-out tub.'

'And the *Carlsborg*'s crew? What are you going to do with them?'

'We'll turn them loose in the *Revenge*'s longboat as soon as we are safely clear.'

'I trust you'll allow me and my friends to go with them.'

Cook treated Hector to an oily smile. 'If that's what you want. But it's not what I would advise. If I were a Dane who had witnessed the capture of my ship, I would think maybe you and your friends had a hand in it.'

'Hector, we'll not be welcome back at the fort,' cut in Jezreel. 'We did nothing to fight off the attack.'

'I couldn't have expressed it better myself,' observed Cook sardonically. He smoothed the lapels of his immaculate green coat before adjusting the lace at his throat.

Hector made one last attempt to regain the initiative. 'I'd prefer if you gave us the cockboat so that we can head off on our own. Try to reach one of the English forts.'

Cook seemed amused. 'Maybe you would make it, maybe not. I wouldn't fancy falling into the hands of someone like that Akwamu chief we saw yesterday. You could be treated very nastily.'

Hector was conscious his three friends were looking at him, waiting for his lead.

'Do we have another choice?' he asked.

'The offer I made yesterday still stands. I'll recommend to my crew that all four of you join our company. They must vote on it, as you know. That's the custom. But I'm sure they'll vote in favour.'

'My friends and I have had our fill of buccaneering,' said Hector stubbornly.

'Then, in view of our long-standing acquaintance and how helpful you've been in the capture of this fine ship, I'll inform the crew that I'm willing to take you on, even if you haven't signed articles. That way you'll be free to leave the ship whenever you wish.'

Yet again Hector sensed that Cook was being dangerously subtle. 'What would be our duties on board?' he enquired cautiously.

'Work the ship, stand watches, that sort of thing. Also I need a navigator who has already been around the Cape.'

'But you're heading through Magellan's Strait.'

'True. But I'm a cautious man, and if we have problems there, we'll need to have an alternative route. When you left the South Sea last time, you came around the Cape, so I believe.'

Hector hesitated, still unwilling to commit himself when Jezreel intervened again. 'Hector, I think we should accept Cook's offer. At least until something better comes along.'

'I don't fancy taking my chances among the black men,' agreed Jacques.

Hector looked across at Dan. He was always level-headed. Dan gave a rueful smile. 'I'm with Jezreel and Jacques. We go to the South Sea aboard this ship. Besides, Hector, it will bring you closer to Maria, and we'd be happy to see that.'

Hector felt a surge of gratitude. He hadn't realized his friends were aware of his longing to find Maria again. He'd no idea that his desire was so obvious.

'All ready,' called the sailing master from the poop deck.

'So is it settled between us?' asked Cook. There was a glint of triumph in his eyes.

Hector nodded his agreement.

Cook raised his voice so that he could be heard throughout

the ship. 'Time to move off. Remember, be slow and calm, as if the *Carlsborg* is simply heading down the coast to visit another trading post, and the *Revenge* is going with her.'

He grinned wolfishly as he turned back to face Hector. 'We don't want the fort mistaking us for pirates stealing Company property.'

'I blame myself for telling you that her captain was away with half his crew,' said Hector.

Cook shrugged. 'I'd probably have found out for myself, from gossip among the canoe men. But I only decided finally to take the *Carlsborg* when you told me you and your friends would be on watch at dawn. The ideal time to capture a ship, and an opportunity I couldn't ignore.'

'And you counted on our loyalty to Jacques.'

'Of course.'

'What if the Governor raises the alarm when he sees the *Carlsborg* sail off before her captain has returned from the interior?'

'Yesterday, after our little tour of the fort, I called in at the Governor's office. I told him that my visit had made it clear there was a shortage of slave stock locally, so I would be taking the *Revenge* farther down the coast to trade.'

'And he believed you?'

'Naturally. He saw us as we left the slave pens. I took care to add that I would recommend to the *Carlsborg*'s first officer that he sail in company with me for a day or so, if he wished to pick up a few extra slaves. He would be able to return in time for her captain's arrival.' Cook gave a mirthless grin. 'Before the Governor realizes the *Carlsborg* is overdue, I propose to make her vanish.'

With that, Cook walked away.

Hector slid a hand into his pocket and fingered Maria's letter once again. His mind was in a tumult. Already he was calculating how many weeks it might be before he saw her again, and he felt a surge of happy anticipation at the thought that every mile the *Carlsborg* sailed would bring him closer to her. Yet he knew that he was also putting everything at risk by arriving on the coast of South America with a crew of ruffians whom the Spaniards considered barbaric pirates. He promised himself that at the very first opportunity he and his friends would abandon such unwelcome company.

THREE

THE LANDFALL off the broad entrance to Magellan's Strait was both disheartening and confusing. The weather, hazy with frequent rain showers, made for poor visibility, and the tide, flowing out of the Strait, created an ugly current of at least six or seven knots, which was more than the ship could manage. The only land in sight was a low barren island, a dismal yellowish-brown, a cable's length to starboard. A single black albatross, which had followed the vessel since early morning, was now gliding over the boulder-strewn beach, searching for food.

As he stood by the helm, Hector glumly set aside any hope that this was where he and his friends might be able to leave the ship.

'Not much of a place, is it?' observed William Dampier morosely. As navigator, he was responsible for the landfall. Hector had always liked him. Long-faced and lugubrious, Dampier had sailed on the previous South Sea raid. He'd admitted to Hector that his real reason for voyaging with the buccaneers was not to win plunder, but to have the chance to observe and record the natural world. He kept notes of whatever caught his interest, whether plants or animals or local people and their customs, tides and the weather, and wrote his observations on scraps of paper, which he kept dry in a stoppered bamboo tube. Now he had a chart in his hand and was trying to identify exactly where they were.

'It would help if we knew our latitude more accurately,' he muttered.

'Little chance of that. This overcast looks set,' Hector observed.

There was sharpness in the air, a chill that had been increasingly noticeable these past few days. Hector was wearing a thick jacket and a heavy scarf purchased from a shipmate. The sultry warmth of the Guinea coast was a distant memory. Behind them lay 4,000 sea miles from Africa, covered in little more than six weeks.

'Our first snow,' muttered Dampier, shaking the chart to dislodge a flake that had drifted down on it.

'What do you think? Should we attempt the Strait?' The question came from Cook, who had joined them by the helm.

'We'll be sailing into dirty weather,' replied Dampier. Ahead of the ship, the sky was turning a menacing blue-black as if a great bruise was slowly spreading up from the horizon. Flickers of sheet lightning lit the underbelly of a cloud bank forming in the far distance. To emphasize Dampier's warning, a sudden gust of wind made the vessel heel abruptly, causing all three men to stagger and lose their balance.

'Are you confident this is the entrance to the Strait?' Cook asked.

'As sure as I can be, with such poor charts,' answered Dampier.

Cook chewed his lip. Hector had noticed the same habit when the captain had been thinking about stealing the *Carlsborg*.

Away to the south an expanse of blue-grey water was already churning into white caps. Turning to Hector, Cook asked, 'You've been the other route, around the Cape. What did you think of it?'

'We were travelling in the opposite direction and were lucky. We had an uneventful passage.'

'Nothing like the fierce storms we hear so much about?'

'Fresh winds, no more than that.'

'Our ship swims better than most.'

Hector agreed. The Danish West India-Guinea Company would find it difficult to recognize their stolen vessel. After Cook and his men had turned their prisoners loose in the *Revenge*'s longboat, the buccaneers had set to work with saws and axes and chisels. The *Carlsborg*'s high poop deck had been ripped out. Next, the forecastle was dismantled. Anything that might slow the vessel in a chase or make her cranky in bad weather was discarded. Deckhouses were knocked down, top-masts shortened, twenty of her cannon lowered from the main deck and repositioned where once there had been a half-deck for stowing slaves. Gun ports were cut. Very soon the tall, stately merchant ship was transformed into a low, lean predator. When all was ready to receive them, the stores and supplies were shifted out of the *Revenge*, and the carpenters went back aboard their former home with their mauls and axes and smashed great holes in her lower strakes. The *Revenge* sank within an hour and left no trace.

In a final flourish the buccaneers chose a new name for their ship. At Cook's suggestion, they called her the *Bachelor's Delight*.

'We'll find it hard to beat up into the Strait,' commented Dampier. A heavier flurry of snow swept across the water towards them. Hector shivered despite his warm clothing.

Cook made up his mind. 'Then let us trust in the *Delight*. We'll not use the Strait, but go around the Cape. That way we avoid bad weather here, and there's less chance the Spaniards will detect our arrival.' He patted Hector on the shoulder. 'And you, young man, can give us the benefit of your experience.'

Dampier handed Hector the chart. The tip of the continent,

the Land of Fire, was drawn in uncertain outline. Large spaces had been left blank. Various islands and channels had been added in such a way that they looked suspiciously like guess-work. Hector placed his finger well below the final cape.

'To be safe, we should go here, to fifty-eight degrees, before we turn to the west.'

'But there we risk meeting ice islands.'

'Better than running into cliffs,' grunted Dampier.

✳

COOK'S DECISION appeared to be a good one. For the next ten days the skies remained cloudy and the temperature con-tinued to fall, but the crew of the *Bachelor's Delight* had an easy time. With a favourable breeze on her quarter, the ship pressed forward through a sea that teemed with whales, seals and penguins, and there was scarcely any need to trim the sails.

'Not long before we are in the glorious Pacific,' gloated Jacques. He had emerged from the galley where he had been concocting a stockfish broth. Prone to seasickness, he was relieved to have a steady deck beneath his feet.

'We don't know what the currents are doing. They might be pushing us off-course,' observed Hector uneasily. The weather seemed too settled and favourable. He looked question-ingly at Dan, who had been watching a small school of dolphins for the past half-hour. The animals had been cavorting energet-ically, close beside the ship. Now they had moved farther out and were showing themselves less often. Oddly, though, the sound they made as they emptied their lungs was just as loud.

'They know a storm is brewing. They are warning us,' said Dan.

'Then they would be better off speaking with our captain,' said Jacques, who was sceptical of sea lore. Hector, however, respected Dan's opinion. Like many of his people, the Miskito had an uncanny ability to read sea signs.

Making his way to the quarterdeck, Hector found Cook

already making preparations for heavy weather. The mast stays were to be doubled, and the anchors brought inboard to reduce the strain when the vessel pitched in a head sea. All the remaining deck cannon were to be sent down into the hold of the ship to increase stability.

Shifting the heavy guns was delicate, dangerous work and it took almost the entire day before the artillery was safely stowed and lashed, the covers over the deck hatches doubled, and the storm canvas brought up from the sail lockers. 'Your Indian friend was right,' said Cook. Sinister black clouds were stacking up ahead of the ship, and the sea had turned an ominous, sullen grey. A succession of steep, hollow swells was building. Each time the ship sank into a trough, Hector had the feeling that the ocean was mustering its strength, waiting to unleash its full power. 'Tell our cook to prepare hot food while he still can,' Cook ordered, 'I fear we are in for a long blow.'

By nightfall the first violent squalls were striking. They came out of the south, sudden angry blasts of wind that buffeted the *Bachelor's Delight*, sweeping away anything that hadn't been securely fastened down. Jacques could be heard cursing in the galley, as his largest cauldron tipped, slopping out the soup and dousing the cookhouse fire. The ship's crew were experienced mariners, and a sense of foreboding settled over them as they listened to the steadily rising sound of the wind.

By midnight it had shifted and was coming out of the west, the direction in which they had hoped to progress. It moaned ceaselessly in the rigging as it rose to a full gale. The advancing swells heaped higher until they began to break, tumbling forward in lines of broken water. Sail was reduced to a minimum as the *Delight* rode out the onslaught. It took four men to manage the helm and steer the ship so that she sidled across the ranks of waves. Soon the seas became so steep that the vessel lay back at an alarming angle as she rose, then tilted and plunged forward as the crest passed under her and the bowsprit plunged deep into the water.

'Thank God we're not aboard the *Revenge* now,' Dampier shouted to Hector above the roar of the wind. 'She would have shaken to pieces.'

The two men were on the quarterdeck at daybreak, taking turns as members of the watch and trying to shelter from the constant spray whipping into their faces. There was an unexpected curse from one of the helmsmen. 'Spritsail's gone. Can't hold her steady,' he roared. Looking forward down the length of the ship, Hector saw that the tiny sail set on its own small spar far in the bows had been torn away. It no longer served to help balance the ship's steering.

'Bo'sun, take two men and see what can be done,' yelled Cook above the din as the helmsmen struggled to keep the vessel heading safely into the oncoming waves.

Moments later Hector found himself alongside Jezreel, struggling forward to reach the crippled sail. Hand over hand, he pulled himself along one of the ropes rigged for the safety of those moving about the heaving deck. A rogue wave swirled over the gunwale and he clung on tightly as the surge of water dragged at his legs, trying to sweep him overboard.

They reached the wreckage of the spritsail and its spar where they lay across the bow. The boatswain was an ex-fisherman named Evans and had a lifetime of experience in dealing with such situations. One look at the waterlogged tangle and he tugged a knife from his belt and began to cut through the ropes. Hector knelt beside him and followed his example. 'Hang on,' bellowed Jezreel as the ship lunged forward, driving into a roaring mass of water that submerged Hector entirely.

He held his breath and gripped tightly to the damaged sail, waiting for the ship to rise. The water poured off him, and he was free once more to saw away with his blade at the sodden cordage. Half a dozen times the bow dipped, and the sea sluiced over him, before he felt the knife cut right through and the tangle of sail and spar and rigging begin to shift. Still on his knees, he slid back out of the way to allow the wreckage to drop overboard. Beside him Jezreel gave another warning cry. But it was too late. A loose rope wrapped itself around the boatswain's ankle and, as the ruined spritsail went over the side, it dragged the sailor with it. There was a despairing shriek, and Hector had a glimpse of Evans' white face as he looked up towards the ship.

The *Bachelor's Delight* was barely moving forward through the water. Her motion was only a tremendous, wild swoop and heave as she rode out the seas. Just yards away, the spar and spritsail stayed afloat. Evans swam, his head above water. His sea coat of oiled canvas had trapped the air and ballooned and was floating like a glistening bladder around his shoulders. Hector rose to his feet and fled back towards the quarterdeck. 'Man in the water,' he shouted, pointing. The helmsmen had already seen the accident. Several sailors were at the rail, trying to throw ropes to the floundering man. But the ropes fell short, and for the space of several minutes the wretched boatswain lay floundering in the water, one leg pinioned within the flotsam, still swimming strongly. But with each succeeding wave he gradually drifted away in the gale. The gap was growing wider and wider.

'Can't bring her up any more into the wind,' bawled the chief helmsman. 'The steering doesn't answer.'

Appalled, the remaining members of the watch could only gaze on as Evans was swept slowly out of view. Another two or three minutes passed and he could no longer be seen among the spume and spray.

'Even double earrings didn't save him,' muttered a grizzled sailor, turning away from the rail, his face hard-set. Evans had worn gold hoops in both ears in the common belief that an earring would save a sailor from drowning.

'We still have ourselves to worry about,' barked Dampier. 'The wind's picking up. The storm isn't yet at its worst.'

As he spoke, the mizzensail shredded above his head. The canvas split into a dozen sodden rags, which thrashed back and forth, cracking like whips. Then they ripped loose and whirled away downwind. The bolt rope that had edged the sail lasted only a moment longer, before it too disintegrated and vanished. The gale increased to a hurricane. It raged out of the west, screaming through the rigging, and by mid-afternoon the seas had grown higher than anything even the most experienced sailor on board had witnessed. Solid walls of water reared up and loomed over the labouring ship. The *Bachelor's Delight* lay under bare poles, scarcely managing to stay afloat. She rose to each wave, staggered as the crests struck her and skewed sideways. It was suicidal now to try to reach the foredeck. Again and again the sea washed over her, thundering along the deck in a swirling mass and bursting its way under the hatch covers. From there it poured below, adding to the water leaking in through the seams as the *Delight*'s hull flexed in the raging sea. Four men at a time, the crew took their turn at the wooden handle of the ship's pump and desperately tried to stop the level of water rising in the footwell. They knew that if they failed, the *Delight* would founder.

For the rest of that day and all through the following night, the ordeal continued. The wind veered into the north-west, driving the vessel even farther south. As she wallowed and rolled, her crew had little respite. Those off-duty huddled in the noxious darkness below decks amid the smell of vomit, damp and excrement, for it was no longer safe to go on deck to relieve oneself, and the men used the bilges as their latrine. Hector wedged himself in his cot and took refuge in thoughts of Maria. They helped him blot out the pounding of the waves against the hull, the sudden gushes of water cascading through her deck leaks and the creaking and groaning of the timbers. He conjured up the moment he had first seen her as she stepped from the cabin of a captured Spanish merchantman two years earlier. She had been plainly dressed in a long-sleeved brown gown with a collar of white linen, her nut-brown hair loose. He recalled her small, neat hands clasped in front of her in a gesture of exasperation. She was travelling as companion to the wife of a powerful colonial official, so she had stayed in the background, but his glance had kept returning to her. He found her remarkably attractive with her wide-set, dark eyes, regular features and a lightly freckled complexion the colour of dark honey. She radiated a quiet intelligence, which he found intriguing. Just once their gaze had met, and he'd felt a surge of admiration as he recognized that Maria was unafraid, even when faced with a gang of lawless buccaneers. Now, as the *Delight* swooped and shuddered in the storm, Hector pictured her courage and defiance and was more certain than ever that he had to find her and tell her that he was in love with her.

By dawn on the second day the storm was easing enough for the exhausted crew to emerge and attend to the needs of their ship. They knotted and sliced damaged ropes, tightened slack shrouds and drove home extra wedges where the masts had begun to work loose. Jacques got a fire going in the galley and had boiled up some hot soup when a maverick swell shook the vessel and capsized the cauldron yet again. This time Jacques slipped on the greasy spillage and, falling heavily, dislocated his shoulder. Hector bound the arm in place with strips of sail canvas. Then Dan and Jezreel carried the Frenchman below. The crew had to make do with plain food and, as the wind rose again, chew on cold biscuit and gulp down brandy to sustain themselves.

Accurate navigation was impossible. Scudding clouds obscured the sky, and when there was a brief glimpse of the sun or the stars, the heaving, rolling deck and a horizon broken with a jumble of swells made it impossible to take an accurate sight. Cook and Dampier could only guess the ship's position and speculate how much progress had been made.

The ship was being driven farther and farther south – that was evident. One gale succeeded another, with scarcely a lull of a few hours between them. The temperature fell even further. The squalls carried more and more snow. On the seventh day a blizzard reduced visibility to nothing more than a white blur. By then a permanent glaze of ice had formed on masts and rigging. Everything was encased in a thin slick of ice, and it became dangerous to climb the rigging or move about on deck. The men's hands froze and lost all feeling. Several had finger-nails torn away without even noticing as they worked the ship. They counted themselves lucky. One man slipped from an icy yard and fell, smashed like a broken doll, dead.

It seemed like a miracle when, after two weeks of this ordeal, the sky cleared and at dawn they had a gentle breeze in their favour. At last it was possible to set the larger sails and resume their voyage. On the quarterdeck Dampier took a reading with his backstaff, gave a slight grunt of surprise and handed the instrument to Hector.

'Just to be sure, what do you make of it?'

Hector measured the sun's angle for himself, and after the two men had consulted the almanac, they agreed that the *Delight* now lay a full degree farther south than they had thought.

'Well, there's no fear of us striking a reef if we head west from here,' Dampier remarked. Like the others, he looked haggard. His eyes were red-rimmed, his hair dirty and matted with dried salt, and the hand that held the battered chart was little more than a claw, stiff with cold.

'Just as long as we stay well clear of those monsters,' said Jezreel. In every direction they could see floating ice islands. Some were huge, white shining blocks, their cores deep aqua-marine and vivid blue. Others were low and flat, covered with a mantle of snow and barely showing above the water. After the noise and turmoil of the storms, the ice islands had a strange, alien quality. They were motionless, silent and ghostly.

Dan had said nothing. He was standing at the starboard rail, gazing intently at the largest of the ice islands about half a mile ahead. 'What are you staring at?' Hector asked.

'A ship,' replied his friend.

Perplexed, Hector looked more closely. The ice island was

shaped like an enormous wedge. One end was a blunt cliff, sheer and spectacular, perhaps sixty feet in height. From there the surface of the ice sloped down in a series of irregular ridges and spurs to a low shelf at the opposite end, scarcely above water level. Here a barely perceptible swell could be seen swirling over the submerged ice ledge.

'At the lower end, do you see it?' Dan pointed.

Hector put up a hand to shield his eyes. The glare of the sun reflecting from the ice was dazzling.

'That darker patch,' said Dan.

Hector turned to Cook. 'Could we steer towards that ice island over there?' he asked. 'Dan thinks there may be something on it.'

As the *Delight* came closer, the dark object Dan had seen took shape. Stranded on the ice was indeed the wreck of a small ship. She lay at a slight angle, her bow tilted up, as if she had been run on to the ice at speed. Her forward third was buried in what appeared to be a snow bank, and her stern still projected into the sea. A shattered stump was all that remained of her single mast. One side of the hull had burst open. A tangle of damaged rigging hung draped over one side. Rime and ice had coated the entire vessel, so that she seemed like a fly that had been caught and embalmed by a spider.

The entire crew lined the rail as the *Delight* glided past the extraordinary sight. No one spoke. All were unnerved by the melancholy spectacle.

'Maybe there's someone still aboard,' said Hector.

Cook snorted in disbelief. 'Not a chance. That ship is a graveyard at best.'

'At least let me check. There may be something to salvage,' Hector begged.

'Very well, but we won't waste time. You have an hour, no more.' He turned and shouted an order that the sails were to be brailed up.

Hector hurried to the cockboat, and within minutes Jezreel

was rowing him and Dan towards the wreck. With a final powerful stroke he propelled the little boat right up on to the ice so that Hector and Dan could step out, dry-shod.

'Jezreel, stay here and be ready to pick us up. We won't be long,' Hector said over his shoulder as he and his friend crunched their way through the frozen snow alongside the stranded ship.

She was a bark, less than half the size of the *Delight*. There was no name on her stern to identify her, and any flag or distinguishing mark had long since gone.

'How do you think she got here?' Hector asked.

'I'd say she ran on the ice by accident, in the dark and during a gale,' Dan answered.

'Then what happened to her crew?'

'There's only one way to find out.' The Miskito scrambled in through the gap where the hull had split. Hector followed cautiously.

The interior of the hull was dimly lit by shafts of light falling through ragged holes where the deck above them had fallen away. Inside was a jumble of debris – broken planks and barrels, anonymous bundles and crates, scraps of cloth. It was difficult to be sure what anything was because everything was coated in ice or half-buried in small drifts of snow that had accumulated.

Moving cautiously, the two men picked their way through the rubbish to a companionway that led up to the deck. Dan brushed away a thin scattering of snow, which lay on the steps of the companionway. His breath steamed in the shaft of light from the open hatch above.

'I doubt we'll find much. Whoever was on board left with what they could salvage.'

He mounted the steps and called down, 'All the ship's boats are missing. The vessel was abandoned by the survivors.'

Hector followed him up on to the deck and looked around. There was little to see. The vessel was bare.

'Dan, go forward and search,' he said. 'I'll try aft. There must be some clue as to why the vessel is here.'

The slant of the wreck made it awkward to clamber up on to the quarterdeck, and he was obliged to haul himself up by a side rail, using both hands. Again he found nothing of interest. The vessel had been stripped.

He was descending carefully to the main deck when he heard a shout from Jezreel. He was gesturing towards the *Delight* and calling out that they should hurry. Hector looked across the water and could see men on deck, bracing the yards around. Cook was preparing to sail on.

Hector was on the point of abandoning the search when he noticed a low, narrow door under the midships rail. He guessed that it must lead to the captain's cabin. He tested the door, but it was either jammed by ice or the frame had warped. Hector put his shoulder to the panel and gave a hefty shove. The door grated open and he peered inside. The cabin was tiny, no more than eight feet square and with a roof so low it would have been impossible to stand upright. Even in the gloom Hector could see that the room was bare of furniture except for a narrow bunk along the far wall, a small stool tipped over on its side and what looked like a rumpled coat dropped on the floor. On second glance Hector saw that what he had taken as a discarded coat was the carcass of a gaunt, hairy dog. It had dark brindle markings and was almost the size of a small calf. It lay curled up, its lips drawn back to show the teeth, and rigid in frozen death.

Outside Jezreel called again, urging him to come on, but something prompted Hector to step across to the narrow bunk. In it lay the stiff corpse of a man. The icy conditions had preserved the cadaver. Only his face and one hand were visible. The rest of the body was concealed under a blanket that the dead man must have drawn up around his neck to try to keep out the cold. He looked to have been about fifty years old, with a few wisps of grey hair, and there was a scar across the bridge of his nose that might have been left by a sword cut. Like the dog, the man's lips were drawn back in a grimace, and the cheeks had fallen in. If he had not died of cold, he had perished of starvation.

The light in the cabin was very poor. Hurriedly Hector looked around, hoping to see some papers, a chart, something that might yield information about the vessel. There was nothing. He reached down to pull the blanket further up and cover the dead man's face. In doing so he dislodged the man's hand, which clutched at the edge of the cloth. There was a faint clinking sound, and Hector saw that the dead man had been clutching a small medallion at the moment of his death. Very gently he reached out and turned the medallion. Its surface was worn. One side was so smooth he could see nothing. But on the other face he could just make out what looked like a bird, perhaps a hawk, and around it a wreath of leaves. He pulled at the medallion, thinking to take it out into the daylight and examine it more closely. But it was attached to a chain around the dead man's neck, and Hector felt he risked becoming a grave robber. Instead, he eased the blanket up to cover the corpse's face. Then he turned to leave.

Dan was already coming towards him, slipping and sliding along the sloping deck. 'Better hurry,' he called. 'I don't doubt that Cook will leave us here if we stay any longer.'

Hector looked out towards the *Bachelor's Delight*. One corner of the main-course was already being let loose. Soon the ship would get under way.

The two men ran across the snow to where Jezreel was waiting. He had already turned the boat's stern to the ice so that the two men could jump aboard, and as soon as they had joined him, he began to row with quick, powerful strokes.

They caught up with their ship just as she was gathering pace, and scrambled on to her, out of breath as the crew hoisted in the cockboat.

'You took your time, so what did you find?' demanded Cook. He was angry at the delay.

'Very little. The vessel probably ran on to the ice in a storm. She was too badly damaged to be refloated, so her crew took the boats and all that was useful and set off.'

Cook scanned the expanse of sea around them. 'Then I doubt they survived.'

'It must have been a year ago, maybe more,' said Dan.

'She was a Spanish ship?'

'Probably,' said Hector.

'No charts we could use?'

'Nothing. I found what I think was her captain. He died in his bunk. My guess is that he chose to stay behind, for whatever reason.'

'This is a dreadful place, and the sooner we get clear of it, the better,' admitted Cook. He had shed his usual self-confident manner and looked sombre. 'From now on, we post two men at all times in the maintop on the lookout for ice. And I don't care how cold it is, or how much wind there is. If necessary we draw lots for who goes up there.'

No one contradicted him or questioned his order. As the *Bachelor's Delight* sailed onwards, the crew were noticeably subdued as they went about their tasks. From time to time they cast furtive glances over the stern. It was as if they had encountered a horrific nightmare, which they knew they would be unable to forget. Hector could only wonder how much longer – whether months or years – the two corpses would continue to drift on the current with a ship for a coffin and an ice island as their catafalque.

FOUR

THE SKIN RASHES broke out a week later – dark-red blotches tinged with purple. They appeared first on the chest and then spread to the lower body, and they itched incessantly. The victims complained of muscle pains and violent, prolonged headaches. Initially there were just a handful of isolated cases, but quickly the malady spread to nearly one-third of the crew. The affected men felt lethargic and listless and could barely drag themselves about the vessel. The worst cases were too feeble even to clamber up on deck. They stayed slumped in their berths, scratching at the inflamed eruptions on their skins.

'It's ship fever,' announced Cook. He had called a meeting to discuss the situation. Anyone with medical knowledge – including Hector and Dampier – had gathered in the captain's cabin.

The quartermaster, a tight-mouthed Manxman, spoke up for the crew in general. 'We must get ashore as soon as possible. We've been at sea for too long.' A seasoned mariner, he was familiar with the dangers of ship fever. If the sickness intensified, it could reduce an entire crew to wraiths, unable to work their vessel. The only known cure was to set the invalids on land and wait until the fever disappeared.

Cook turned to his navigator. 'Dampier, how far to the nearest refuge?'

Dampier looked even more doleful than usual. He gestured vaguely at the chart spread on the table before them. 'I am uncertain as to our exact position. The mainland is best avoided. If we encounter the Spaniards in our weakened state . . .' His voice trailed away.

'Then we steer for Juan Fernandez and restore ourselves there,' said Cook firmly. Several of those present knew the island of Juan Fernandez from their previous venture in the Pacific. Uninhabited and 400 miles off the coast of South America, it was seldom visited by Spanish patrols.

'Juan Fernandez is at least three weeks away,' warned Dampier.

'So we must hope the fever does not take a stronger grip,' replied Cook brusquely.

Hector intervened, 'If I may make a suggestion . . .'

'Yes, what is it?' Cook snapped. He had been made irritable by the run of bad luck – heavy weather and now an outbreak of sickness.

'My friend Jacques tells me he observed the same illness in the Paris prisons.'

'And, as an ex-gaolbird, what does he suggest?' Cook allowed a sarcastic edge to creep into his voice.

'The prison doctors ordered all the cells washed with vinegar and the convicts' bedding to be aired. I've noticed most of our fever cases are among those who sleep in the forward hold, where it's airless and full of lice and vermin. Could we not allow in additional light and air to that area of the vessel?'

The quartermaster was adamantly opposed. 'It's warm down there and the rats aren't no trouble at all. We'd block up any openings the moment they were made.'

'I have a better solution,' said Cook tartly. 'Issue three pints of burned rum for every man who presents himself for work. That should get them out on deck.'

It was an effective solution, even if it failed to cure the sickness. The *Bachelor's Delight* slowly clawed her way north, with her depleted crew often half-fuddled. Hector, however, heeded Jacques' experience, and the four friends brought their own bedding up on deck. Despite the cold, drizzly weather they were anxious to spend as little time as possible in the stuffy, noxious accommodation. They were witnesses, therefore, to an event that no man aboard could have foreseen, though many had heard it rumoured.

It happened shortly after midnight on the sixty-eighth day of their voyage. The *Delight* was making steady progress with a moderate breeze. The faint light of a new moon showed the small regular whitecaps covering the sea around her. Earlier in the day Dan had declared this was a sign that the vessel was finally moving out into the open ocean.

'Seems we're due for a drenching,' observed Jezreel, looking to windward. A line of thick, black clouds was beginning to blot out the stars in that quarter, and there was an occasional faint rumble of thunder.

'Mon Dieu, not another storm. We've had more than our share,' said Jacques with a groan.

'No,' Dan assured him. 'If that was an approaching storm, we'd be feeling the swells already. It's no more than a patch of bad weather and should pass over quickly.'

The black line advanced rapidly and, with the *Delight* already under reduced sail, there was nothing to be done but wait for the deluge. Hector and his friends gathered up their blankets and retreated to the shelter of the small overhang under the break of the quarterdeck.

They did not have long to wait. All of a sudden a broad sheet of lightning lit up the sea about half a mile ahead. This was followed by a tremendous clap of thunder. Moments later the downpour rushed upon them. It was a wild torrent, the raindrops bouncing off the planks to a height of several inches. At times the rainfall was so intense Hector felt it was becoming difficult to breathe. Dazzled by the lightning, he could barely see a couple of yards in any direction. Again and again the lightning flashed through the deluge, and the thunder was so loud that it seemed to vibrate the deck beneath his feet. The intervals between flash and sound became shorter and shorter until the centre of the storm was directly overhead. In the brief moments when the sky lit up, Hector could see that the surface of the sea was beaten flat by the strength of the downpour. The tops of the waves were gone. Instead the ocean looked like a vast river, speckled and glistening and flowing by as the ship moved forward.

Then, as abruptly as it had begun, the deluge stopped.

Jacques sucked in his breath in surprise and seized Hector by the elbow.

'Corposants,' he exclaimed, pointing upwards.

A ghostly blue-white light had appeared at the mastheads. A pale luminous spike, as long as a man's arm, was extending straight into the black sky from the tip of each spar. These spikes of light gave off an unearthly glow, which pulsated erratically – now bright, now fading and growing dim, only to become bright once again. After about a minute of this eerie display, Hector felt Jacques' grip on his elbow tighten. The Frenchman indicated away to one side. Dozens more points of light had begun to spring up. This time they were growing from the ends of all the cross-spars, parallel to the sea. They too varied in intensity. Finally, in concert with what had gone before, strands of the same spectral light began to glow along the rigging, flickering and dancing in an unearthly rhythm.

'What in God's name causes that?' demanded one of the helmsmen in a hushed voice.

No one answered. Everyone on deck was gazing upwards, their awestruck faces strangely illuminated.

The *Delight* sailed forward, seemingly suspended on the ink-black sea and outlined in a nimbus of unnatural fires. The phantom lights were miraculous. They burned, but consumed nothing. For perhaps five minutes the eerie display continued until, for no apparent reason, the ethereal signs began to diminish. They sank lower and lower until they were barely visible. Then they vanished.

'I thought I heard a hissing sound,' said Jezreel. He stepped out from shelter and peered up at the masts, as if expecting to find something burned or blackened.

At that instant there was an enormous, deafening bang, far louder than anything that had gone before. From ahead, out of the darkness, flew a series of bright, blazing projectiles. Yellow and white, they were like huge sparks thrown out by some enormous log that had split in the hearth. They came whizzing through the air, straight at the ship. Hector, too astonished to react, could only gape as they hurtled past. Later he would swear that he felt the wind of their passage. The air was filled with a sharp, burning smell and he recognized the stench of sulphur. He was still recovering from his astonishment when a second massive thunderclap seemed to take the air from his lungs. Again the blazing projectiles shot towards him out of the black night like a salvo of deadly fireworks. Forewarned this time, he ducked down, his ears ringing from the explosion.

There was the shortest pause, a moment's calm and, as he straightened up and looked forward again, a dozen or so large globes of light came hurtling silently through the air. Each light ball was about the size of a man's head. This time their colour was a peculiar deep blue, which changed to violet as the globes came closer. They were moving at an unnatural speed and yet Hector had time to track their progress. Most passed harmlessly on either side of the ship, safely out over the water. But four or five of them came aboard. The first skimmed along the windward rail, then vanished over the stern. Another blinked out the moment it collided with the foremast. But two of the blazing fireballs appeared to drop downwards, land on the deck and roll along its length.

Hector and his friends stood rooted to the spot as the apparitions skittered towards them. Hector felt a tingling sensation all over his body, a massive jolt, and then the fireballs were gone. Once again the air smelled of sulphur and this time there was a sharp taste on his tongue. It was as though he had licked a tarnished spoon.

'God's cannon fire,' said a deep voice. It was Jezreel. He had described it very well. A battery of heavy artillery fired at close range and directly at them could not have equalled the assault of sound. The blazing sparks were like fragments of burning wads shot from the muzzles of huge cannon. Hector realized that he was shaking.

'Is everyone all right?' he asked into the darkness.

'I think so,' said Jacques. 'I've heard of corposants and St Elmo's fire. But no one warned me about balls of lightning.'

Hector's sight had yet to recover from the dazzling flashes. He squeezed his eyelids tight shut, then opened them, hoping to clear his vision. Something dark, little more than a shadow, was rising from the deck. He recognized Dan getting back on his feet.

'Are you hurt, Dan?' he asked.

There was a short pause before the Miskito replied. 'One of those fireballs knocked me down.' There was a moment's silence, and then he added, 'I don't seem to be seeing so well.'

'That blaze was enough to blind anyone . . .' began Hector before he realized that in all the time Dan had been his friend, he had never known the Miskito striker voice any sort of complaint. He stepped across to where his companion was standing. In the dim light he could just make out that Dan was gently rubbing both his eyes. 'What do you think is the trouble?'

'Everything is dark and blurred.'

Hector reached out and gently pulled his friend's hands

away. 'Let me check. Maybe you need time to recover from the glare of the lightning.'

It was too dark to discern very much. Hector could only distinguish the contours of the Miskito's face, the shadowed hollows of his eye sockets. 'Better wait until dawn. Then we'll be able to judge.'

*

IT WAS AN ANXIOUS few hours. Dan sat quietly on the deck, his head leaning back against the rail and his eyes closed. He said not a word, and it was left to Hector to worry what might have happened to his friend. The Miskito possessed the keenest eyesight of anyone he had ever known. At sea he was always the first to pick out the tiniest speck on the horizon, whether it proved to be a sail or a landfall. On land he noticed tiny changes in detail and identified objects that others failed to see. It was a gift that made his friend such an acute observer and was the foundation of his skill in painting and drawing. The thought that Dan had now lost his sight, and would no longer be able to hunt with gun or harpoon, was too gloomy to contemplate.

Gradually the sky lightened and the tracery of the rigging of the ship took shape. 'Dan, what can you see now?' he asked.

The Miskito, his head still leaning back, might have been asleep. He opened his eyes and gazed up. There was a long silence. Then he said quietly, 'Everything is still blurred.'

Hector's spirits sank. Crouching down beside his friend, he said, 'Dan, look straight at me.'

The Miskito, his face expressionless, opened his eyes so that Hector could stare into them. The black pupils and the dark-brown irises appeared normal. 'I can see nothing wrong. But you have to rest your eyes. I'll fetch a bandage.'

As Hector went below to bring a strip of cloth from his seaman's chest, he noticed a new atmosphere among the men. They were more cheerful, exchanging jokes and banter. Even the fever invalids were more animated than before.

'You'd have thought they might feel some sympathy for your misfortune,' he commented to Dan as he returned and prepared to wind the bandage around his friend's head.

As usual, the Miskito took the situation calmly. 'Why should they have much care for us? We are still outsiders. Latecomers who joined in Guinea. They'll be more pleased that the appearance of St Elmo's fire is a sign of good luck.'

'It didn't bring you much good luck . . .' Hector broke off. Dampier had appeared on deck and was walking across to join them.

'What's the trouble?' the navigator asked. There was concern in his voice.

'Dan was laid low by one of those fireballs last night. It seems to have damaged his sight,' Hector explained.

'In both eyes?'

'Yes.'

'Then there's a good chance he'll recover. I've known men who received a sudden blow on the head, and went blind. They got their eyesight back in a short while. Not like those blockhead sea captains who go blind in one eye from staring at the sun too long whenever they take a sight.'

A hail from the masthead interrupted him. The lookout was shouting down excitedly that there was a sail in the distance, off the port bow. There was a rush to the rail as the crew tried to get a glimpse of the stranger. Those invalids who could manage to stand upright staggered to where they could hang on to the lower shrouds and look towards the distant speck of sail. One hopeful blackguard gave a great whoop. 'Let's catch that ship and see what she's worth,' he roared.

'Now they're sure that St Elmo's fire brings good fortune,' said Dan wryly.

Above them, Cook was at the quarterdeck rail, calmly directing the deck watch to trim the sails.

'What about our cannon? Do we bring them up from the hold?' called a voice.

'There's not enough time and we are short-handed as it is,' Cook snapped. 'We leave the cannon where they are, and make out that we are a peaceful merchant ship seeking to exchange news. No one yet knows we are in the Pacific.'

'The prospect of plunder is even better than burned rum for inspiring a crew,' muttered Dan. 'Hector, if I'm to wear this bandage, you'll have to tell me what is going on.'

Men were scurrying down to their berths and bringing up their weapons, hastily unwrapping pistols and cutlasses from the oiled cloths in which they had been stored for the passage round the Cape. There was much clicking and snapping as the buccaneers checked their musket flints were throwing off sparks.

'Vessel's turning towards us. Seems to want a meeting,' shouted down the lookout.

'Sailing right into our jaws,' exulted a buccaneer as he scrabbled among the contents of his cartridge box.

'Tell me what the newcomer is like?' Dan asked Hector quietly.

'Looks to be some sort of merchant ship. Maybe a trifle smaller than us. I think I see some deck armament. At a guess, sixteen guns . . .'

'What's his flag?'

'Can't see. He's sailing straight towards us,' Hector answered. He glanced aft. From the *Delight*'s mizzen now flew a huge yellow and red flag. 'We've hoisted Spanish colours,' he told Dan.

The quartermaster was cursing and chivvying a number of the invalids, telling them they were too sick for action and he wanted as few people as possible to be visible on deck so as not to arouse the stranger's suspicions.

'You there,' he said to Dan. 'Get below. A blind man is no use to us.'

'If Dan goes below, so do I,' Jezreel growled. 'There's more risk in that stinking space than out here on deck.'

The quartermaster glared angrily at the big man, then turned away. Jezreel was known to be good in a fight.

Some time later Dan asked, 'How close is the stranger now?'

'About half a mile,' Hector answered. 'And eager to speak with us. He hasn't run out his guns.'

There was an air of suppressed excitement as men from the *Delight*'s crew crept to their positions. They crouched behind the bulwarks with their muskets, grapnels and boarding axes. Hector was reminded of the day Cook's buccaneers had taken the *Carlsborg* by surprise.

Cook called out his final instructions. 'We'll get only one chance. The moment we are alongside, you board and take that ship before they realize we are sickly and short-handed.' He looked down at where Hector was standing.

'Lynch, come up here,' he called.

'I would prefer to stay beside my friend if there's to be any fighting,' said Hector.

'Then bring him up with you.'

Hector took Dan by the arm and led him up the companion ladder to the quarterdeck, where they joined Dampier and Cook. The captain was rubbing his hands together in anticipation and looking pleased with himself. 'I doubt the stranger suspects anything. He takes us for a Spaniard. He's due for a surprise.'

'What do you want me to do?'

'I believe you speak fluent Spanish.'

'My mother was from Galicia.' Hector wondered how much Cook remembered from the last South Sea raid, when the young man had often acted as interpreter.

'I want you to play the captain for a few minutes. When we get within speaking range, tell the stranger we're newly arrived from Spain and looking for a pilot.'

'And what if I'm asked about our intended destination?'

'Say that we're on our way to join the Armada del Sur, the

South Sea Fleet. That will account for the fact that we look more like a warship than a merchantman.'

By now the other ship was barely a hundred paces away, and had still not shown a flag. A man whom Hector took to be her captain was standing at the rail with a speaking trumpet in his hand.

Moments later the stranger came up into the wind and backed her topsails. Slowing to a halt, she waited for the *Delight* to approach within hailing distance.

'Could be a trap. Maybe she has guns in a lower tier and is keeping the gun ports closed,' said Dampier nervously. 'She could be ready to serve us out.'

'Quiet,' growled Cook in a low voice. 'Hold her there,' he said to the helmsman, who spat over the lee rail, then pushed the tiller over.

The *Delight* also lost way and came to a stop. The two ships lay quietly, barely a pistol shot apart, their crews eyeing one another.

Hector took a deep breath. Putting a hand on Dan's shoulder and pressing downwards, he murmured, 'Dan, sit down out of the line of fire, just in case there's trouble.'

'Let them speak first,' cautioned Cook in a whisper.

The captain of the other vessel raised the speaking trumpet to his lips. 'Saludos!'

Hector cupped his hands around his mouth. 'Saludos,' he replied.

'Qué nave es usted?'

'He wants to know the name of our ship,' Hector relayed to Cook in an undertone.

'Tell him we are the *Santa Rosa* from Seville, and ask him who he is.'

'*Santa Rosa* de Sevilla. Y usted?'

There was a noticeable delay before the captain of the other vessel replied. But already Hector knew something was wrong. In a low, urgent voice he told Cook, 'That's no Spaniard.'

'What do you mean?' There was a sudden note of alarm in Cook's voice.

'His accent's wrong.'

Cook gave an angry snarl. 'We've been fooled.' He spun on his heel and snapped at the steersman, 'Bear away.' Raising his voice so that his men waiting on the main deck could hear him, he shouted at them to make all sail.

It was several moments before his order took effect and the sails filled and the gap between the two ships began to grow wider. In that interval there was confusion aboard the *Bachelor's Delight* – shouted commands for the yards to be braced round, the noise of running feet, grunts of effort from men hauling on the sheets, the clatter of canvas bellying out, and all the time the buccaneers waited for the first salvo from the stranger to come crashing aboard. The men who had been hidden behind the bulwarks stood up, levelled their muskets and loosed off wild shots at the other vessel. From across the water came similar uproar as the strangers' vessel also got under way in a hurry.

'Stop firing. Tell the men not to shoot,' someone was shouting. Seated on deck and with the bandage over his eyes, Dan was trying to make himself heard above the commotion. 'Stop firing,' he repeated. 'The other ship is English.'

Cook's head snapped round. 'What do you mean, English?' he demanded.

'They're English, I tell you. They are speaking English.'

'How do you know?'

'I may not be able to see so well, but my hearing's fine. I can hear them giving commands in English.'

For a moment Cook looked disbelieving. Then he said, 'There's one way of finding out.' Turning to the quartermaster, he said, 'Pull down the Spanish colours and hoist an English flag.'

The quartermaster ran to follow his instructions. He fumbled at the halyard, and soon the English colours floated at the mizzen peak.

By now the *Delight* had begun to move, slanting away from the danger and showing her starboard quarter towards the strangers. They could clearly see her new ensign.

Moments passed, and then a matching flag was run up at the stern of the other vessel.

'What's she doing in these waters?' Cook exclaimed. 'Wear ship and pass close. But reload and be ready to fire.'

The *Bachelor's Delight* checked her flight, reversed course and once again the two ships approached one another, but this time like two wary mastiffs poised for a fight. Cook stood on the rail, holding on to a shroud, and bellowed in English, 'What ship are you?'

'*Cygnet* out of Bristol.'

'And a right stupid lot of bird-brained buggers too,' called someone from the waist of the *Delight*.

A wave of relieved laughter washed over both ships.

✳

FIFTEEN MINUTES LATER the *Cygnet*'s commander was climbing up the *Delight*'s side while his grinning boat crew exchanged banter with Cook's buccaneers leaning over the rail.

'I am Charles Swan,' said the new arrival, stepping across to shake Cook by the hand. The *Cygnet*'s captain was an affable man of middle age, dressed in a faded blue coat and grubby buckskin breeches. His face would have been unremarkable – watery blue eyes and regular, slightly chubby features – but for the fact that his eyebrows and the stubble of close-cropped hair were so pale as to be almost invisible. By contrast, his skin was sunburned a harsh and painful shade of pink.

'Swan, did you say? Then I take it that you had a hand in the naming of your vessel,' said Cook with a half-smile. He was regarding the other man with baffled caution.

'That's correct. I own a tenth share. Calling her the *Cygnet* was an act of self-indulgence,' conceded Swan. He seemed naively unaware of how close he and his ship had come to being attacked and looted.

'It is unusual to meet an English ship in this region.'

'I'm here with a licence to trade with the Spanish in Peru, a licence granted to me by the Duke of Grafton.'

'You've come here to buy and sell,' exclaimed Cook. His eyebrows shot up, he was so astonished.

Swan appeared not to notice. 'Exactly. Our two countries are at peace, and His Grace the Duke saw an opportunity for mutual commerce.'

He nodded towards the north-east horizon. 'Over there in Chile the colonists are paying exorbitant charges for goods brought out from Spain and trans-shipped across Panama. Aboard the *Cygnet* we have a cargo of iron goods and fine woollen cloth, which we should be able to sell to great advantage, having much less cost of freight.'

Cook was almost lost for words.

'But surely you are aware that the Peruvian Viceroy forbids all trade with foreigners?'

'That is why I did not hoist any colours on your approach,' answered Swan amiably. 'I am aware of the antipathy between the two nations. I thought the English flag might attract an unprovoked attack. Equally, if I had hoisted a Spanish flag, I might later be accused of sailing under false pretences. No nation likes to see their emblem borrowed without a by-your-leave.'

Cook shook his head in amazement. 'I wish you and the Duke luck with your venture. But don't be surprised if you meet with disappointment.'

'What about you? What brings you here?' asked Swan, though it must have been clear from the number of armed ruffians on deck that the *Delight* was not a peaceable merchantman.

'We proceed to Juan Fernandez,' said Cook. 'We had a difficult passage around the Cape.'

'I preferred Magellan's Strait. The transit took more than

two weeks and was challenging – frequent gales, no depth for anchoring, fog and mist – but we got through,' answered Swan. He sounded a little smug.

'And now where are you headed?' asked Cook as he deliberately changed the subject.

'I thought to try Valdivia first. It is the closest town on the coast. I wish to begin my trading there.'

Hector, who had been listening to the conversation, saw his chance.

'Excuse me, Captain Swan,' he interrupted. 'Would you need an interpreter for your commercial negotiations?'

Swan's eyes lit up as he recognized the young man. 'You are the person who called out to us in Spanish. Indeed, I took you to be a Spaniard. I fear my own efforts at the language were all too clumsy. Unfortunately my factor – a most excellent speaker of Castilian – died at sea some weeks ago. So yes, I do require a trustworthy interpreter.'

'Then I am willing to act for you.'

Swan's watery blue eyes looked enquiringly at Cook. 'Are you able to let this young man go?'

'He has not signed articles, so he can do what he wants,' Cook answered curtly.

Hector decided to press home his advantage. 'I am travelling with three friends. Perhaps they also could join me on your ship? One of them is a fine cook.'

Swan beamed with pleasure. 'It sounds as if I am getting a real bargain.'

'Not entirely,' Cook responded sourly. 'You'll be taking on a blind man.' He nodded towards Dan, still standing nearby with a bandage across his eyes.

Swan was about to speak when Hector intervened. 'My friend's eyesight may soon return. He was partly blinded during a lightning storm last night, but he can still see a little.'

Swan held up a hand and stopped him. 'He too may join the

Cygnet.' Then, unexpectedly he added, 'I too have been similarly afflicted.'

And without further explanation he began to take his leave of Cook.

✳

THE RIDDLE OF Captain Charles Swan's last remark was solved on the way back to his ship with Hector and his friends in the *Cygnet*'s launch. The captain groped in his pocket and pulled out a pair of spectacles. Each lens was the colour of freshly cut slate. Swan placed them on his face, carefully hooked the wire loops around his ears, then tied a leather thong behind his head to hold them securely. For a moment Hector was reminded of a blind beggar, his sightless eyes hidden behind black glass. But on looking more closely, he realized that he could still discern the captain's eyes, though dimly.

Swan anticipated his reaction. 'Vanity precludes me from wearing them on meeting strangers. All too often they think they are dealing with an unfortunate.'

'Maybe there are times when it is useful to conceal your eyes,' Hector ventured.

'A shrewd observation. It's said that in China the judges wear such spectacles in court so that their thoughts are hidden until they deliver judgement.'

'But that's not why you wear them?'

'Bright light, especially when reflected off the sea, hurts my eyes. Like your friend here, it sometimes damages my vision, leaving me half-blind for hours at a time.'

'You were never struck by a fireball, nor stared at the corposant?'

'Indeed not. The doctors tell me that my condition is often found among those whose hair has little colour. Wearing these spectacles reduces the risk and discomfort.'

Hector twisted in his seat and took a last look at the

Bachelor's Delight. He would miss a few of her crew, in particular the navigator William Dampier, who was a thoughtful and intelligent man. But John Cook was not to be trusted. He was an outright bandit of the sea, and his men were no better. Hector was not sorry to be leaving them.

FIVE

AFTER THREE WEEKS in Swan's company Hector had grown accustomed to seeing two smoky dark lenses fastened to his captain's face whenever the sunshine was bright. Now Swan was squinting through them into the early-morning glare as he looked forward over the *Cygnet*'s bow. It was a clear, bright day and they had arrived on the coast of Chile with the first hint of an onshore breeze filling the ship's sails as she glided gently into the entrance of a deep gulf. The low headlands on either side were shrouded with a dark mantle of scrub and native forest, and the hills behind them appeared wild and desolate. If the chart had not shown that the town and port of Valdivia lay within the gulf, Hector would have thought the land was uninhabited.

'Unless I'm mistaken, there's some sort of building by that white mark where the trees have been cut back,' said Swan.

The identity of the building became obvious some minutes later when a cloud of grey smoke burst from it, quickly followed by the sound of a cannon shot.

'Surely they can see our flag?' exclaimed Swan, disappointment in his voice. Hoisted at the *Cygnet*'s main topmast was an enormous white sheet, which the captain had hoped would be accepted as a token that his ship came in peace.

Without waiting for an order, the steersman put the helm hard over and the vessel sheered away from the gunfire. Even as he did so, there was another cannon shot, this time from a concealed battery on the opposite shore. The splashes from the cannonball were clearly seen as it skipped across the surface of the sea a hundred paces ahead of the ship.

'We must make our intentions even plainer,' said Swan. 'Let fly the fore-topsail as a signal that we wish to parley. Then brail up the courses.'

The *Cygnet* crept along, barely a ripple under her forefoot, while her crew watched and waited. After a while a guard boat could be seen putting out from the beach in front of the nearest fort and heading towards the waiting ship.

'Lynch, this is when your knowledge of Spanish can be put to good use,' said Swan. 'I will write a letter for you to carry to the Governor of Valdivia explaining that we come to trade, and providing a list of our merchandise. If he lacks a competent translator, you can make our intentions plain.'

'Should I mention that you have a licence from the Duke of Grafton?'

Swan shook his head. 'No. The Governor may never have heard of the Duke. Say instead that we intended to make for the East Indies by way of the Cape of Good Hope, but met with such heavy weather that we were obliged to turn around and go westabout. Our stopover here is a chance matter.'

Hector thought such a far-fetched tale was unlikely to be believed, but he made no comment. All that mattered to him was to get ashore and begin in earnest his search for Maria. The smuggled note she'd written to him on the day she'd saved his life told him of her expected return to Peru and her employment with Doña Juana, whose husband Don Fernando de Costana had been promoted to the Audiencia, the ruling council. The Governor of Valdivia should surely know the whereabouts of such a prominent colonial official.

Within moments of Swan disappearing into his cabin to write his letter, word of his plan had spread throughout the ship, and a worried-looking Jacques emerged from his galley and came to speak with Hector. 'Mon ami, you should not go on your own,' said the Frenchman.

'I'll be all right. You stay behind with Dan and Jezreel,' Hector assured him. Day by day Dan's damaged eyesight had improved, though the Miskito still found it difficult to see clearly objects at a distance.

'Jezreel can look after Dan,' said Jacques stubbornly. He wiped his hands on a rag to get rid of a smear of soot.

'Lynch will manage very well on his own,' insisted Swan, overhearing their conversation. He had reappeared with a folded and sealed paper in his hand.

By now the guard boat was within hailing distance. Hector climbed up on the rail and waved the note in the air. 'A letter for the Governor,' he called in Spanish. The guard boat was a small piragua rowed by what looked like half a dozen fishermen. In the stern sat two uniformed soldiers and a young man of about Hector's own age, wearing an officer's red and white sash, who appeared to be in charge.

'I wish to speak with the Governor of Valdivia. I have a letter to him from our captain,' repeated Hector, shouting at the top of his lungs.

After a short hesitation the boat crew bent to their oars, and Hector was climbing down into the piragua, which shoved off as quickly as if the *Cygnet*'s hull was hot to the touch.

'My captain wishes to open commerce. We were on our way to the East Indies by way of the Cape of Good Hope, but bad weather forced us to turn back and take the westward route,' said Hector after he'd introduced himself. The explanation sounded even lamer than before.

'I am Ensign Luis Carvalho,' said the young man. His mournful dark eyes set in a long, narrow face regarded Hector with open disbelief. 'My uncle—' He corrected himself, 'the Governor wishes to know by what authority you bring your vessel to Valdivia.'

'If you will take me to the Governor, this letter will explain everything,' Hector answered.

The ensign glanced back over his shoulder. 'Your ship may anchor where she is. There is good holding ground. Valdivia is some distance from here and it will be at least two hours before we get there, even with the flood tide under us.'

For the first part of the journey Carvalho sat stiff and silent, leaving Hector to watch the passing scenery. His initial impression of a land barely touched by humans was confirmed. Beyond a shoreline of granite rocks began virgin forest, and after so many weeks at sea he could smell the resin of pine trees. The nearer hillsides were the first in a series of dark, sombre ridges, which extended to a far cordillera, its crest marked by a thin band of snow. Everything was on a vast scale, empty and brooding.

Closer to hand, the waters of the gulf teemed with wildlife. A flock of squabbling seabirds chased a shoal of anchovies directly into the path of the piragua. The gulls dived repeatedly as fish rose to the surface, and once or twice Hector had a quick sighting of a sleek, black fin when a dolphin came up from below, feeding on the same shoal, driving them back towards the birds' greedy beaks.

After about a mile, where the channel skirted around a low green island, he noted a third defensive fort being built on a bluff. There was a web of scaffolding and the ant-like figures of workmen toiling on the battlements, which were already formidable. Hector wondered if this was something it was intended that he should see.

Ensign Carvalho leaned forward. 'The Viceroy sends us the best military engineers, who have had their training in Spain. He is determined Valdivia is secure from attack, whether by land or from the sea. His Majesty in Madrid takes a close interest. He has declared that he intends to protect the southern flank of his possessions here in Chile, as he has done in Barbary.'

The mention of Barbary gave Hector the opening he needed. 'I spent some time at the court of the Moroccan Emperor.'

Carvalho's eyes lit up with interest. 'Is it true that he employs Spanish officers?'

'I made several good friends among his Spanish cavalrymen. Thanks to one of them, I managed to escape from the imperial household.'

'It's strange that some of my countrymen are willing to serve a foreign potentate, a man whom my King regards with such suspicion that he builds castles to protect his realm from him.'

'Sometimes it is wiser to adapt to changing circumstances,' said Hector, hoping the ensign would pick up the hint.

Fortunately the Spanish ensign had a thirst for tales of exotic adventure, and for the rest of the journey he plied his visitor with questions. Hector found himself describing his days in the service of a Turkish corsair operating out of Algiers and how he had been taken prisoner by the French, working first in the royal galley yard in Marseille and later chained to the oar bench until he was shipwrecked on the coast of Morocco. Discreetly he said nothing of the time he had then spent as a buccaneer in the Pacific, and he made no mention of his search for Maria. He judged it was a topic that would require careful introduction.

By the time the little piragua reached the landing stage at Valdivia, the atmosphere between himself and the ensign was relaxed and friendly.

It was clear that a great deal of money had been spent on Valdivia. An imposing defensive wall had been built of massive cut stone, with bastions at each corner, a ditch, and embrasures for cannon and musketeers. Beyond the city gate, the city planners had laid out wide streets and numerous plazas. But, as Hector walked up the main avenue with Carvalho and the two soldiers, he had the impression that the town had yet to fulfil its ambitious design. The roadway itself was unpaved, many of the subdivisions were empty plots that had not yet been built upon, and several large public buildings of brick and stucco had been left half-finished. There were surprisingly few people to be seen. Those he did encounter were going about the everyday business of any small town: mothers with their children picking over the local produce at food stalls or sorting through barrows heaped with second-hand clothes, idlers gossiping on street corners, a few tradesmen carrying their tools on their way to work. He supposed the occasional passer-by with lank black hair, a broad high-cheeked face and wearing a long fringed cloak of animal skin was from the local Indian tribe. He saw no evidence of any unusual prosperity and wondered if Captain Swan would be disappointed in his hope of lucrative commerce. As far as Hector could tell, the bulk of the goods being offered for sale were farm tools and cords of firewood.

They reached the main plaza and arrived before a tall double-fronted building. Set over the main doorway was a stone slab carved with Spain's royal coat of arms. They entered, and Carvalho asked Hector to wait while he went ahead to find his uncle the Governor and inform him of their arrival.

Hector had expected some delay before he was granted an interview. But in less than five minutes Carvalho was ushering him through the building and out into a pleasantly shaded walled courtyard at the rear. It was a very informal scene. Trellised across the far wall was a luxuriant climbing plant with deep-green leaves and star-shaped blossoms of a delicate purple. Rose bushes grew out of half a dozen large earthenware pots arranged on the flagstones. From one corner came the sound of trickling water where a stone spout dribbled into a small pond covered with water lilies. Seated beside a low table was a small, grey-haired man neatly dressed in an old-fashioned dark-velvet doublet and knee breeches. He was peeling an apple. To add a further touch of domesticity two large, hairy dogs lay dozing at their master's feet.

'This is Señor Hector Lynch. He brings the letter from the foreign ship,' explained the ensign. Turning to Hector, he said, 'May I introduce my uncle, Don Alonso, the Governor of Valdivia.'

Without rising from his chair and still holding the apple, the small man looked up at Hector with bright interest. Hector was reminded of the sharp scrutiny of a blackbird disturbed while foraging.

'Tell me about your vessel,' said the Governor affably. He made no effort at formality.

'The vessel is the *Cygnet* from Bristol. Her captain, Charles Swan, wishes to trade.'

'Bristol is in England, is it not?' The Governor dropped a curl of apple peel on a blue and white plate on the table beside him, and carefully began to cut himself a slice from the fruit.

'Yes, in England.'

'Your captain knows that we are forbidden to trade with foreigners?'

'He was on his way to the East Indies . . .'

The Governor interrupted with a wave of his paring knife. 'Please, Señor Lynch, my nephew has already told me of this fable. We can dispense with it, as no one believes it.'

Hector coughed and began again. 'Captain Swan is genuine in his desire for peaceful trade. He has written you this letter, which explains everything.' He held out the sealed despatch from Swan. The Governor took it, prised open the seal with his fruit knife and unfolded the parchment. Belatedly Hector realized that Swan would have written it in English. It was unlikely Don Alonso would be able to read the contents.

The Governor barely flicked his eyes over the writing before returning the parchment to Hector.

'My nephew tells me that you have excellent Castilian. Please be good enough to read out what is said.'

Hector began to translate. 'To His Excellency the Governor of Valdivia, greetings . . .'

'Yes, yes,' interrupted Don Alonso with a sigh. 'Leave out the compliments. Just give me the gist of the contents.'

Hector quickly ran his eyes down the page. He decided it was best to proceed straight to Swan's request that the ship be allowed to enter harbour, and then read out the list of goods he had for sale.

When he had finished detailing the last of the inventory – apparently the *Cygnet*'s cargo included a stock of black-velvet caps, serge, silk, ribbons and knives – Hector paused. The Governor instantly picked up on the hesitation.

'What else has your captain to say to me?' he asked.

Hector cleared his throat. He was shocked by what Swan had written in the final paragraph of his letter. Reluctantly he continued, 'Captain Swan wishes to inform His Excellency that an English pirate ship is cruising in this area,' he said. He was stunned by Swan's perfidy.

The Governor settled himself more comfortably on his chair. 'Please read out to me your captain's exact words.'

Hector had to concentrate as he delivered an accurate translation of Swan's treachery. 'The captain writes: "I feel it is my duty to report that two weeks ago in latitude fifty I encountered a vessel, the *Bachelor's Delight*. The vessel is armed with thirty-two guns and sails under a false flag. Her captain, one John Cook, is English. I suspect him of being a bloody and known pirate. He claimed to be en route for the island of Juan Fernandez, but is clearly seeking plunder."'

Hector stopped reading and raised his eyes from the despatch. The Governor regarded him thoughtfully.

'I see from your expression you find it shameful that your Captain Swan is so eager to open trade that he informs against his own countrymen,' observed the Governor quietly.

There was a short silence. Then Don Alonso spoke as if Swan's disloyalty was of no importance. 'Señor Lynch, some of those trade goods on board the *Cygnet* could be of interest to our merchants. We have not received a supply ship for several months.' The Governor turned to his nephew. 'You say that the ship has anchored in the mouth of the gulf?'

'Off the Niebla battery,' answered the young man.

'Then send word to the fort that she may remain there. I will consult the merchants of the Consulado and discuss which goods we might buy and what we may offer in exchange.' Addressing Hector, he added in a friendly tone, 'Perhaps you will be kind enough to pen a note to Captain Swan to advise him that we are prepared to consider his proposal. My nephew can carry the message back to the ship tomorrow morning.'

Hector allowed himself a quiet sigh of relief. Everything had gone more smoothly than he had dared to hope. Now was the moment to find out about Maria.

'I will be happy to write such a letter. Meanwhile . . .' he deliberately left the sentence unfinished.

'Yes? Is there anything I can do?' asked the Governor. His tone was solicitous.

Hector took a deep breath. 'Would you be able to tell me where I might find His Excellency Don Fernando de Costana? He was formerly the Alcalde of the Real Sala del Crimen of Paita, but I believe he has been advanced to a higher office.'

As the words left his mouth, Hector felt a twinge of anxiety. He sensed a very brief, subtle change in the Governor's manner. It lasted only a heartbeat, but a shadow flickered across the little man's features.

'You know Don Fernando?' enquired the Governor.

Hector was ready with his reply. 'A member of his household is a distant relation on my mother's side.' It was a lie, but a plausible one.

The Governor appeared to be distracted by the blade of his paring knife. He was turning it this way and that, as if to catch the glint from the sun.

'Of course I am familiar with the name and reputation of the Alcalde. But I have never met him. I will be glad to make enquiries and try to learn his whereabouts.'

He put down the knife and smiled. 'Señor Lynch, it is too late for you to return to your ship. I will arrange for a room to be prepared so that you can stay overnight. And if you would be my guest at dinner this evening, I would be honoured. Meanwhile I'll leave you in the capable hands of Ensign Carvalho.'

The little man rose to his feet and murmured to the two dogs. They rose, stretched and followed their master into the main building, leaving Hector with the uneasy feeling there was something he'd failed to notice.

'I'm glad my uncle has taken a liking to you, Hector,' said Carvalho, leading the way indoors. 'You'll find he is kindhearted and sincere. He's been a parent figure to me ever since my own father died two years ago.'

He brought Hector to a room that was evidently a clerk's office. There was a desk and writing materials, and Hector spent a few moments writing a report to Captain Swan explaining the satisfactory outcome of his visit. Then, after handing the note to Carvalho, he followed the ensign upstairs to find a bedroom ready for him. Already laid out were fresh clothes, and a tub of hot water stood in the adjoining bathroom. After Carvalho had taken his leave, Hector stripped off and lay soaking in the tub, wondering how long it would be before the Governor would have news of Maria's whereabouts. At length, grateful to be getting rid of nearly three months' accumulation of grime and sea salt, he heard a knock on the door and a servant summoning him to dine with the Governor.

He descended the staircase to find Don Alonso waiting in a small side room, where a table had been laid for two people. 'Ensign Carvalho has already gone to contact the members of the Consulado,' said the Governor genially. 'So this evening the two of us will be dining alone. I don't often have visitors, and never before someone who has sailed around the Cape.'

The meal was excellent, a dish of small, succulent oysters followed by delicious beef, and the easy-going, convivial Governor did most of the talking: Valdivia suffered from being very distant from the seat of government in Lima; there had been difficulties with the local Indian tribe, the Mapuche; early hopes of finding silver and gold had been dashed, but there was ample lumber and a potential trade in cattle; it was his intention to make sure the city flourished . . . and so on.

As the evening progressed, Hector found that he grew more and more drowsy. Partly it was the reassuring sensation of being back on dry land after so many weeks at sea. Partly it was the effect of the local wine. It had a slightly resinous flavour, which the Governor assured him was an acquired taste, even as he refilled their glasses yet again. By the time the dessert was served – a concoction of apricots, quince and whipped cream of which Jacques would have been proud – Hector could barely keep his eyes open. The Governor, noting that his guest was growing sleepy, summoned a house servant to escort the young man safely to his room. Hector climbed the stairs, undressed and fell gratefully into bed.

✳

HE AWOKE with a start. His head was aching from the wine, and his eyelids were gummed together. From the angle of sunlight flooding in through the narrow window, he judged it was nearly midday. He rose and found his borrowed clothes where he had dropped them. His own shirt and breeches were missing, and he supposed that they had been taken away for washing. A tray of food had been placed on a table near the door, and he gratefully ate the bread and fresh fruit. A pleasant surprise was the small jug of chocolate. The fact that the drink was barely warm told him how badly he had overslept. He washed and dressed and went to the door.

He was surprised to find it locked. Crossing the room, he leaned out of the window. Below was the courtyard where the Governor had interviewed him the previous afternoon. But there was no one about. Puzzled, he went back to the door and tried it again. It did not budge. Thinking that whoever had brought the tray of food had locked it by mistake on leaving, he banged on the door with his fist and called out, hoping to attract someone's attention. There was no response. He returned to the window and tried shouting out of it. The only result was that one of the Governor's large, rangy dogs loped around a corner and gazed up at his window. Then the creature turned and padded away, ignoring him. Hector sat down on the bed to decide on his course of action.

The door was solidly constructed from a dark, heavy timber. The hinges were of forged iron and opened inwards. He couldn't see how he'd be able either to force the door open or smash through the panels. He checked the window. It was possible to squeeze through, but then he'd be faced with a thirty-foot drop to the flagstones of the yard. There was no handhold, or even a bush to break his fall. He was still sufficiently uncertain of his situation not to want to be found lying in the courtyard with a twisted ankle.

The wisest course was simply to wait and see what happened. He stretched out on the bed and stared at the ceiling.

After a while he thought he heard movement. Someone came quietly to the door and stood outside. He lay still and quiet. A moment or two later he heard the person tiptoe away, then the creak of the stairs. The silence returned.

It was well into the afternoon when he finally heard firm steps approaching the door. There was the rattle of a key in the lock and, when the door swung open, Hector was on his feet, ready to face whoever was there. In the doorway were the same two uniformed soldiers who had escorted him the previous day.

'What's happening?' he asked, both puzzled and angry.

'Come with us,' was the flat answer.

Flanked by the two guards, he was taken down the stairs to the entrance hall and along a passageway to large double doors, which opened into what was clearly a council chamber. At its centre stood a long, well-polished table flanked by a score of chairs with ornately carved backs. The whitewashed walls were hung with formal portraits, including one of the Spanish king. In one corner of the room was an altar surmounted by a large crucifix.

But the sight that held his immediate attention was the figure of Jezreel. His friend stood next to one of the tall windows, the light falling full on him. His wrists were bound in front of him, his shirt was ripped so that it hung off his back and there was a blood-stained bandage around his neck. The enormous ex-prizefighter regarded Hector with an expression of both relief and exasperation.

'Jezreel!' Hector burst out.

'Ambushed,' grunted Jezreel. He had a badly swollen right eye, and his lip was cut.

'Your friend is extremely difficult to subdue,' murmured Don Alonso. Hector swung round to find the Governor standing quietly to one side of the room. 'The intention was to capture your ship, Señor Lynch. But we failed.'

The Governor's manner was as friendly and gracious as he'd been at dinner the previous evening. By contrast his nephew, standing beside him, looked less at ease.

'You said you were willing to trade,' said Hector heatedly.

The Governor allowed himself an apologetic smile. 'Impossible, I'm afraid. The Viceroy's edict is quite clear on that subject.'

'Then why ask me to write to Captain Swan?'

Don Alonso made a slight dismissive gesture. 'The note proved to be unnecessary. In the event, Luis here was able to attract a boat ashore from Captain Swan's ship by wearing your clothes and standing where he could be seen.'

'It fooled me,' growled Jezreel. 'I thought it was you and volunteered for the launch to get you. They jumped us the moment we set foot on the beach.'

'But for the bravery of your friend here, the ambush would have succeeded,' confessed the Governor. 'He held us off long enough for the rest of his party to get away in their boat. My men claim they shot and wounded several of the pirates as they fled.'

Hector's thoughts were in turmoil. 'But the *Cygnet* is a genuine merchant ship. You could have refused to trade and merely turned her away. There was no need to attack.'

The Governor shook his head sadly. 'Señor Lynch, I was dealing with pirates.'

'You have no proof of that.' Hector was despondent.

'I had all the proof I needed from the moment you asked for the Alcalde.'

Hector didn't understand. 'Don Fernando de Costana?'

'Señor Lynch, you underrate the machinery and intelligence of our government. In Valdivia we may be at the farthest end of the viceroyalty, but everyone knows of the Alcalde and how his wife was kidnapped at sea. We have been told to be on our guard, to keep watch for the culprits. Little is known of them, but for the man who acted as their interpreter when negotiating the ransom. He is described as being about twenty years old, with dark hair, eyes possibly hazel or light brown, courteous and well educated, and speaking excellent Castilian with a slight trace of a Galician accent. You should be flattered.'

Hector felt light-headed and foolish. He was dismayed that his past had been uncovered with such apparent ease.

'What's happened to the *Cygnet*?' he asked.

'She put out to sea the moment the launch returned to her. Unfortunately she was out of range of the batteries.' The Governor sighed. 'Now I have to deal with two pirate vessels in the area, maybe more. I have no ships capable of tackling them. That is why I'd hoped to capture the *Cygnet* and turn her against the other.'

Hector tried to gather his thoughts. The *Cygnet* was gone, taking Dan and Jacques with her. He and Jezreel were in the hands of the Spanish authorities, and his identity was known. His situation could hardly have been bleaker.

'What will you do with Jezreel and me?' he asked.

The Governor spread his hands in a gesture of sympathy. 'Officially I can have you tried as pirates now, and executed if found guilty. Yet last night, over dinner, I found it difficult to believe that you are such an incorrigible criminal. I prefer to delay matters by sending a report to the Audiencia in Lima and keep you in custody while awaiting instructions.'

Beside him, his nephew shifted uncomfortably. 'Perhaps Señor Lynch will give his parole.'

The Governor brightened. Addressing Hector, he said, 'If you promise that neither you nor your colleague will try to escape, there will be no need to lock you up.'

Hector looked across at Jezreel, still standing by the window. 'The Governor asks for our parole,' he said.

'It makes sense,' said the ex-prizefighter with a shrug.

Don Alonso beamed. 'It is decided then. You will remain here as my guests while we wait to hear back from the Audiencia.'

His nephew seemed relieved. 'Hector, you've made the right choice. Escape from Valdivia is impossible. By sea you'd need to get a boat and get past the batteries. An attempt by land would be suicidal. The Mapuche would take you and kill you.'

But Hector had no thought of escape. His ill-judged plan to locate Maria was now in ruins. He had been naive and foolish.

✳

HIS DISMAY deepened some days later. In the main plaza he encountered Don Alonso surrounded by several of his great hairy hounds. The dogs were milling about, clearly excited.

'I'm on my way to inspect the silver mine. Would you care to join me?' asked the Governor cheerfully. 'The workings were abandoned several years ago as unprofitable, but it is my duty to carry out an occasional check to make sure there is no illegal activity.' He bent down and fondled the ears of one of the hounds. 'We'll go on horseback. My dogs will relish the exercise.'

One of the hounds stretched up its muzzle and licked his master affectionately. Something stirred in Hector's memory.

'Are your dogs a special Peruvian breed?'

Don Alonso smiled indulgently. 'My family came to the Americas with the first conquistadors and they brought the ancestors of these dogs with them. Trained to attack, they terrified the Indians.' He leaned across to pat another of the hounds. 'Mind you, this fellow's too fat and lazy to terrify anyone.'

'I've seen a dog very like him, though a different colour, a brindle.'

'Where was that?' Don Alonso asked. He was making polite conversation.

'On a ship, though the unfortunate creature was dead, perfectly preserved.'

The Governor looked up sharply. Hector had his full attention now. 'On a ship, you say?'

'Yes. The vessel was stranded in the ice, off the Cape.'

All of a sudden Don Alonso had gone very still. His eyes were fixed on Hector's face.

'Tell me about it,' he said very softly.

'It was on the way around the Cape, after we'd been driven far to the south. We came across a vessel abandoned on an ice island. She was badly damaged.'

'You know the name of the vessel?'

'No. I went aboard with Jezreel to investigate. I found the man who I suppose was her captain. He was lying dead in his bunk. A dog like this was on the floor close to him.'

The Governor stood stock-still, scarcely breathing. It was the first time Hector had seen him look so serious and solemn.

'What did you do?'

'Our ship couldn't delay. I only had time to cover the captain's face with a blanket. He wore a medallion on a gold chain around his neck. One side of the medallion was worn smooth, the other had a crest on it, the figure of a bird. It was too dark to see clearly.'

'Did you keep the medallion?' The Governor's voice was very low, almost menacing.

Hector shook his head. 'I felt it would be robbing the dead.'

The Governor let out a slow breath. 'Our visit to the silver mine can wait for another day. I want you to come inside and repeat your story to Luis.'

'Why?'

'That poor man was his father and my brother. He always wore that medallion as a keepsake. It belonged to his wife's family. She died giving birth to Luis.'

Don Alonso led Hector back indoors and, as they waited for the ensign, the Governor told Hector more. 'Two years ago Luis' father set out from Valdivia on a small vessel. He was attempting a passage around the Cape, hoping to open a supply route. He took his dog with him. But nothing more was ever heard from him or the crew.'

'Did no one report back? It appeared that the rest of the crew had taken the boats and abandoned the ship.'

The Governor shook his head. 'We heard not a single word. We accepted he had died. But for these past two years Luis and I have long wondered whether he was drowned or killed by the Indians, or dead of fever.'

Hector was about to say how sorry he was to bring such sad news when the Governor gave him a long, sober look and said in a contrite voice, 'Señor Lynch, you cannot imagine how great a service you have done me and my nephew. Now, at least, we know the truth. It makes me ashamed that I have withheld from you what I know of the whereabouts of the Alcalde, Don Fernando.'

For the first time since arriving in Valdivia, Hector felt a brief surge of hope, though it was mingled with a sense of foreboding. The Governor was already speaking again. 'But I think it would be better if you began by telling me exactly why you are seeking the Alcalde.'

Somehow Hector was sure the Governor was a person in whom he could confide.

'Don Alonso, the Alcalde's wife has a companion, a young woman by the name of Maria. The sole reason I returned to Peru is to try to find Maria again. That is why I need to find the Alcalde.'

The Governor nodded a little sadly. 'I didn't think you were a gold-hungry pirate. I feared you bore a grudge against the Alcalde, and were seeking to hunt him down. I thought it better you shouldn't know where to reach him.' He paused to consider for a brief moment, then added, 'What I have to tell you is not what you want to hear.'

'I need to know, in any case.'

The Governor gazed up at one of the portraits on the wall. Clearly he was searching for the right words. 'The affair of the kidnap of the Alcalde's wife by pirates, the flight of the culprits, all that is common knowledge. So too is the outcome of the case brought by the Spanish Crown against the villains in their own jurisdiction, in London.'

Hector's mood darkened. 'Maria was the witness against me at the trial, but she refused to testify. Afterwards she wrote to tell me she was returning to Peru, and that the Alcalde was being promoted to the Audiencia.'

The Governor sighed heavily. 'There was no promotion. When the result of the case was heard – it collapsed and the culprits went free – the Viceroy felt humiliated. There had been great expense and much effort invested in the prosecution. Don Fernando de Costana became a figure of embarrassment. He was sent away, given a new post, as far out of sight as possible.'

Hector felt a chill in his belly. 'Where was he sent?'

'To the Ladrone Islands, as acting Governor.'

For a moment Hector was at a loss. He tried to think where

the Ladrone Islands were. Then he recalled seeing them marked on a chart of the Pacific. 'But they are thousands of miles away, closer to China than to Peru.'

The Governor nodded. 'Yet they are administered by the viceroyalty of New Spain.'

Hector was too stunned to say anything. The Governor was still speaking, his voice sorrowful.

'Fully a year ago Don Fernando left Peru to take up his post in the Ladrones. His wife accompanied him. Doubtless your friend Maria went also. I'm sorry.'

As the Governor's words sank in, Hector felt numb. Despite his present status as a prisoner in Chile, he had still cherished a faint hope that there would be a happy outcome to his quest for Maria. He had even allowed himself to speculate that she might hear of him in gaol, if he was sent to Lima for trial. She might come to find him, and though he did not expect her to save him a second time, she might persuade the judges to spare him from the garrotte and give him a prison sentence instead. The news that Maria was on the far side of the world shattered that fantasy. She would never be aware he'd come to Chile to find her, nor would she ever know what happened to him. For a black moment he despaired as he pictured the vast distance that lay between them.

Then, from somewhere within him, came an obstinate and defiant response: he would not be deterred. He would not waste the long, harsh weeks at sea, or the cruel passage around the Horn. They had brought him a good part of the way to her and if, by some miracle, he was ever free to do so, he would continue his journey to reach her. Unbidden, an image of Maria appeared as he had last seen her at his trial. He remembered how self-assured and beautiful she had been, answering the prosecution's questions with outright lies. He could hear her low, firm voice and picture the set of her jaw and the way she looked straight at him as if he was a stranger and swore that she'd never seen him before. Now he would show similar courage and determination, whatever the consequences. He would not abandon hope of reaching her, though his detention in Valdivia would be harder to bear now that he knew Maria was still so far away.

SIX

It was the time of year when Valdivia braced itself for the winter rains. The weeks that followed Jezreel's capture and Hector's detention saw life in the town become increasingly dank and comfortless. Heavy showers merged into prolonged downpours and, as the season advanced and winter settled over the town, flurries of hail or sleet swept down from the cordillera. Lingering fogs and a fear of marauding pirates deterred shipping and trade, which in summer linked Valdivia with the outside world. Isolated and waterlogged, its people settled into dreary resignation, matching Hector's gloom.

While Jezreel passed the time playing cards with their gaolers and teaching them how to use backsword and singlestick weapons, at which he had excelled since his fairground days, Hector took long, solitary walks. Often he found himself at the waterfront and stood on the dockside. There he would watch the raindrops speckle the dirty brown surface of the river, and think of Maria and of what had happened to Jacques and whether Dan had recovered his eyesight. Then, with Maria's letter still tucked away safe and dry inside his shirt, he would retrace his steps to the Governor's residence, where he and Jezreel remained as Don Alonso's guests.

One afternoon towards the middle of September, when the

rains were at last showing signs of abating and there was a promise of spring in the air, Hector returned to find Don Alonso in his office with a map of the Spanish colonial possessions spread out on a table.

'While the coastal traffic has been at a standstill,' the Governor said, 'there has been no word from the Audiencia about what I should do with you and Jezreel. But the Niebla fortress has just sent word that an aviso, an advice boat, has been sighted off the entrance to the gulf. I expect tomorrow the captain of the vessel will arrive here, bringing my instructions.'

He gestured towards the map.

'Forgive me if I am intruding on your private concerns, Hector, but doubtless Maria has been on your mind these past months, and I wondered if you've considered trying to contact her?' Crossing to the table, he placed a finger on the map, far out in the Pacific. 'This little cluster of islands here,' he said, 'they are the Ladrones. The "islands of thieves" as Magellan, their discoverer, called them. The inhabitants stole everything they could lay their hands on.' He smiled thinly. 'This is where the Alcalde, Don Fernando, now governs by the authority granted to him by the Viceroy of New Spain. Every year the Viceroy sends him an official despatch containing his orders for the coming year.' The finger slid eastwards across to the coast of Mexico. 'The despatch is carried by a galleon that sails from here, from Acapulco. If you'd care to write a letter to your Maria, I will arrange for it to be taken under my seal to Acapulco and given to the captain of that vessel to deliver to her.'

The Governor raised his eyes from the map and studied Hector for a brief moment.

'Of course, it's up to you to decide whether you want to write to her.'

The past four months of anxiety had taken their toll on Hector. He felt dispirited and subdued.

'Don Alonso, you are kind to make such an offer. But I

think it better if Maria no longer even thinks of me. A letter from me now would only raise false hopes.'

The look the Governor gave him was full of compassion. 'My friend, Maria may be suffering the same feelings of uncertainty and sorrow that I endured, not knowing my brother's fate. Sometimes it's better to know a difficult truth than to be left in doubt.'

Later that evening in his room Hector began – and then tore up – half a dozen letters to Maria. He had still not composed a fair copy by the time Luis came early next morning to take him to a meeting with the Governor in his office.

'You're quite a catch, it seems,' said Don Alonso with a mirthless grimace. The map still lay spread on the side table. 'The Audiencia wants you delivered to the capital, to Lima itself, for interrogation. Afterwards you will be tried for piracy.' He lowered his voice. 'Have you written that letter for Maria?'

Hector shook his head.

The Governor gave up. 'Then all I can do is to wish sincerely that you and Jezreel receive a fair trial. Luis will escort you to the dock, where your ship is waiting. When you go aboard, your parole to me is at an end. From then on, you are the responsibility of her captain. He is keen to set off at once.'

As Hector left the room, he glanced back. Don Alonso was rolling up the map and there was a sombre expression on his face. He had the look of a man who had completed a very distasteful task.

'PRAISE BE we're let out of our hutch from time to time,' said Jezreel, standing up to his full six and a half feet and stretching. 'Or I'd have a permanent stoop by now.'

The aviso was a small, lightly built sloop. Since leaving Valdivia, the two friends had been permitted to exercise on her quarterdeck for two hours every afternoon. For the remainder of each day they were confined to a small, windowless cabin, which Hector surmised was normally used as a storeroom. It smelled of old sacks and damp, and the ceiling was so low that the big man was obliged to crouch double or go on all fours whenever he moved about.

'How far do you think we've come?' asked Jezreel. He swung his arms from side to side to loosen his shoulder muscles. His wounds had long since healed, and he looked gaunt, but fit.

'Impossible to say,' answered Hector. He stared out at the mainland coast, some ten miles away to starboard. He could see nothing that might give him a clue as to how the sloop had progressed along her route. The view had altered little in the past three weeks of sailing. There was the same sequence of coastal ranges and the same blue-grey haze where the land rose steeply to the mountain chain that ran parallel to the coast. The only difference was that the mountain crests no longer carried any snow.

'Can't say I'll be sorry when this voyage is over, even if we have to face interrogators at the end of it,' said Jezreel.

'My guess is we'll reach our destination in the next day or two,' said Hector.

The lookout called down that a sail was in sight to the north-west.

The aviso's captain, a stocky and phlegmatic Basque named Garza, growled at the helmsman to hold his course.

'Seems I guessed right,' said Hector. 'We're probably close enough to our destination for our captain to think he can outrun the stranger and get safely into harbour.'

Half a dozen sailors led by the boatswain hurried about the deck. Here and there they made minor adjustments to sheets and braces, though Hector could discern little increase in the vessel's speed. The sloop was already carrying full sail.

Another shout from the masthead, this time confirming that the stranger was definitely on course to intercept.

The steersman watched the captain nervously, as Garza ran

stubby fingers through his beard, made his way to the ratlines and climbed up to join the lookout. A short time later the Basque was back down on deck. 'Friends of yours, I think,' he growled to Hector as he stepped past him.

Jezreel leaped eagerly on to the ship's rail. Grabbing the shrouds to steady himself, he raised one hand to shade his eyes against the sunlight reflecting off the sea and stared at the approaching vessel.

'She's a two-master. I think she's the *Bachelor's Delight*,' he exclaimed gleefully.

The Basque captain overheard. 'Tell your big friend not to get his hopes up,' he called out to Hector. 'That ship will never catch us.' He turned to the helmsman, and Hector caught the words 'inner channel . . . as close as you dare'.

'What's he doing?' asked Jezreel. He jumped down on deck. The sloop was abruptly changing course.

'Our captain has decided to run for the shallows, where the *Delight* won't be able to follow us,' answered Hector. 'The aviso draws less water, and I expect the steersman knows every back-channel and bolthole through which to escape.'

Over the next two hours Captain Garza's tactics were borne out. The colour of the sea changed from dark blue to opaque grey-green as the sloop fled into shoal depths, running fast and keeping well ahead of the pursuit. Hector saw they were steering directly for a narrow channel between a small island and the shore.

'The *Delight* can't follow us through there without the risk of running aground,' he commented to Jezreel. 'She'll be forced to turn back.'

'Maybe Cook, if he's still captain, will catch us as we come out from behind the island at the far end of the channel,' said Jezreel hopefully.

'More likely the aviso will drop anchor in shallow water behind the island, and wait. We're in plain view of the coast, and messengers will already be on their way to alert a Spanish warship to come to the rescue. The *Delight* can't afford to linger like a cat in front of a mousehole.'

Abruptly Captain Garza blurted out what was clearly a Basque profanity. His attention was fixed on the channel ahead.

Looking in the same direction, Hector saw the masts of a ship beyond the island, and the flash of canvas as she spread her topsails. Soon afterwards the vessel herself came in view, sailing down the channel towards them. An instant later he recognized the *Cygnet*.

Behind him Jezreel let loose a great whoop of pleasure. 'Who'd have thought it? Our high-principled Captain Swan has turned pirate. Ha-ha! He's working with the *Delight*.'

The ambush became clearer by the minute. The aviso was now too close to the coast to double-back and flee, and if she continued on her course, she was sure to run into the *Cygnet*'s guns. Captains Swan and Cook, if they were still in command, had executed a neat pincer movement. Their prey was caught.

Certainly the sloop's Basque captain thought so. With a snarl of disgust, Garza cupped his hands around his mouth and called out to his crew to stand by to drop sail. Then he stepped across to the helm and, taking the tiller in his hand, brought the little ship's head to wind. The aviso carried no cannon and had relied on her speed. She was at the mercy of her captors.

The *Cygnet* maintained her confident approach. Smaller than her consort, her shallow draught allowed her to come within hailing distance of the sloop. Hector could see his former shipmates lining the rail as they examined their latest prize appraisingly.

'There's Jacques,' called out Jezreel. The ex-prizefighter swung himself back on the rail and let out a great roar. 'Hey, Jacques. Have you learned to make a decent pudding yet?'

A ragged cheer went up from the *Cygnet*'s crew as, one by one, they recognized Jezreel by his size. They waved their hats, there was a confusion of catcalls and yells of greeting. Someone fired his musket in the air to celebrate. A boarding party scrambled into the longboat and was on its way to take possession of the sloop. Jacques stood in the bows, grinning broadly.

'Mes amis! So they did not waste string to garrotte you,' exclaimed the Frenchman as he scrambled up the aviso's side and gave Jezreel a delighted thump on the back. Jacques beamed with delight as he turned to Hector. 'None of us thought we would ever see you again.'

Hector was more restrained. He couldn't see Dan among the men aboard the *Cygnet* and was worried about his friend. 'Where's Dan? And how are his eyes?' he asked.

'Don't worry about him,' said Jacques cheerfully. 'He is on the *Delight* and his eyesight is as good as it ever was. In fact he's the chosen lookout whenever we set up this little ambush. This is the third vessel we have snared these past few days.'

The rest of the boarding party were busy searching the sloop for plunder, but found little. Their only loot consisted of a few coins and trinkets robbed from the sloop's crew, and several kegs of quince marmalade marked for delivery to a merchant house in Lima. Under Jacques' approving gaze, the barrels were hoisted up on deck and ferried across to the *Cygnet*. Then the boarders attacked the base of the aviso's mast with axes and a saw. In a few moments they'd cut down the mast and sent it toppling over the side.

'That will slow them down,' said the Frenchman approvingly. 'We don't take any prisoners. We have no room to hold them.' He hustled Jezreel and Hector into the waiting longboat. 'You are doubly lucky. Our ambush is getting too well known, so this evening we head off to careen and recuperate.'

'Where to?' Hector asked.

'We have a camp on the Encantadas. They are far enough away for the Spaniards to leave us alone.'

'Does John Cook still command the *Delight*?' enquired Hector. He was unsure of his welcome.

'Cook, he died of ship fever last July. The men elected the quartermaster, Edward Davis, to succeed him. The vote was unanimous.'

The longboat pushed off, and in a few moments they were alongside the *Cygnet*. More cheers and shouts of welcome greeted Jezreel as he climbed aboard. Several men came up to shake his hand and thank him for fighting a rearguard action on the beach at Niebla. 'But for you, I'd have more than this scar from that day,' said one battered-looking veteran, touching the mark on his cheek where a musket bullet had grazed his face.

'The men are glad to have your big friend back aboard,' said a familiar voice behind Hector. He turned and looked into a face that for a moment did not match the voice. Then he recognized Captain Swan. The man was vastly changed. Gone was the plump, fastidious merchant captain, easy-going and genial. Standing before him was a grim-faced individual dressed in a stained shirt and wearing a battered low-crowned hat, and he had a hard glint in his eyes. Swan now looked like a seasoned brigand.

✳

'WHAT MADE Swan turn pirate?' Hector asked Jacques a fortnight later as the *Cygnet* followed the *Bachelor's Delight*. The two vessels were threading their way through the cluster of islands where the raiders had set up their base.

'After Valdivia he tried several more times to open a legitimate trade. But each port turned him away,' answered the Frenchman. 'His crew became more and more restless. Then we met again with the *Delight* cruising for prey, and half the men threatened to desert to the other ship. They said that plundering the Spanish was the only way of making any money.'

'So he had no choice?'

Jacques grinned sardonically. 'Captain Swan has taken to piracy like a duck to water. A good joke, no?'

Hector could only smile weakly. He thought back to the

letter Swan had asked him to deliver to the Governor of Valdivia. In it Swan hadn't hesitated for a moment to betray his fellow countrymen by warning that an English pirate ship was prowling off the Peruvian coast. He wondered if Swan now regretted rescuing the messenger who might know its treacherous contents. The thought left him very uneasy.

A few feet away from him the *Cygnet*'s helmsman cursed softly. An awkward eddy was pushing the vessel off-course. The helmsman – as seasoned a mariner as one could expect to find – complained darkly that the currents among the islands reversed direction whenever the moon was full, and flowed against the wind, and that was against nature. They were the Devil's work, he muttered. To Hector the islands did seem abnormal and strange; there was something otherworldly about the way they rose abruptly from the surface of the ocean so far from any land mass. The archipelago, 165 leagues from Peru, was so remote that the number of its islands was in doubt, and no one had yet charted them properly. The more credulous said the task was futile, for the islands floated from one location to another. That was why the Spaniards called them the Encantadas, the 'Enchanted Ones'.

'I'm surprised you managed to find fresh water on such harsh-looking shores,' Hector commented to Jacques. The slopes of the nearest island appeared to be nothing but cliff and collapsed scree of dark-brown crumbling rock.

'We searched and found only one place where we could bring our casks.' The Frenchman pointed up ahead. 'There, on the island just coming into view and a little beyond where the *Delight* is about to drop anchor. It has a spring at the east end of the beach.'

Hector saw that another ship was already at the same location. She was canted over to one side as if she had run aground.

'That will be Captain Eaton with the twenty-six-gun *Nicholas*,' Jacques explained. 'He too is harassing les Espagnois.'

Hector noted a thin haze of smoke rising from the stranded vessel. What he had at first taken to be a shipwreck was in fact a small brig being breamed. Men moved about her hull, knee deep in the sea, as they burned off the layers of weed and fouling that had accumulated on the vessel's hull and would slow her down when chasing her prey. At high tide they would float her off again.

'Eaton is energetic and drives his men hard, but he has very little luck,' explained Jacques. 'He is fanatic about keeping the *Nicholas* clean. But in nearly a year of cruising against les Espagnois he's taken not a single rich prize.'

'So this place is a real nest of robbers,' observed Hector. He was depressed at the very thought of being caught up once again in the lives of men who made their living by theft and violence.

Jacques failed to notice. 'I have a feeling the *Nicholas* may not be with us for much longer. When I last spoke with any of her crew, they were on the verge of mutiny. They talked of abandoning the South Sea and sailing home. Or turning Eaton out and electing someone with more luck to command them.'

He was interrupted by the shrill of the boatswain's whistle. The *Cygnet* was on her anchoring ground, and the idlers who had been lining the rail and gazing at the beach were being summoned to their work. Hector joined them in brailing up the sails and securing the deck gear, and once the ship was safely moored, he hurried ashore, intent on meeting Dan for the first time since the events at Valdivia.

He found his friend already disembarked from the *Delight* and waiting for him on the white sand of the beach. The Miskito's face, usually impassive, lit up with a grin of delight.

'Hector. How glad I am that you are safe and free.'

Anxiously, Hector searched his friend's eyes, trying to detect any signs of injury. 'How are you, Dan? Jacques tells me you've recovered your eyesight.'

'It has never been better. Now I can see just as well as

before.' The Miskito threw an arm across Hector's shoulders and began to walk with him up the slope of the beach. 'Let's talk privately. How was it in Valdivia as a prisoner?'

'Shouldn't you be heading off to catch some fish or spear turtles for our food?' Hector asked. Jacques and several other cooks had arrived on-shore and were heaping up piles of brushwood as they prepared a cooking fire. The newly arrived crews would be looking forward to eating fresh food after so many days at sea.

'No need to trouble myself with that,' Dan answered. 'I'll tell you as we go.'

The two of them made their way inland through a tangle of shrubs about ten or twelve feet high. They kept to a narrow footpath, for the branches were as thick as a man's leg and armed with rows of sharp prickles.

'You would not think this place could provide anything worth eating,' said Dan. 'See, these bushes do not bear any fruit, and there is almost no soil. But you would be wrong.'

They emerged from the thickets and found themselves on rough open ground strewn with rocks and small boulders. Here the only vegetation was low straggly brush, weed and moss. About a mile away there was a scatter of hillocks covered with some sort of stunted forest, and Hector expected Dan to head in that direction. But Dan veered left, following a path that was clearly familiar to him and which took them parallel to the coastline.

'It was some time before I got used to this place,' said the Miskito. 'When I first came here, I was bewildered. Take the turtles, for example. They are the same as those I hunted on the Miskito coast. The same in size and colour. Back home they wait until dark before they come out of the sea to lay their eggs on the beach, and that is when you search the strand for them. But here they come out in daylight. So you just stroll along until you almost trip over them as they lie waiting to be turned over on their backs.'

'There can't be many turtles left with so many hungry crews about,' observed Hector.

'True. There aren't as many as before.'

A small flock of doves, perhaps a dozen birds, fed on some low bushes ahead of them. They ignored the two men until they were almost within touching distance, then flew up, circled and slanted down again to land no more than a couple of yards away.

'Look at that,' said the Miskito. 'They are half tame. The birds never saw humans before we came, so they would even perch on our hats. That was before our men took to shooting them with their muskets for sport. Now the creatures are a little more wary, though you can still knock them down with a stick when you're hungry.'

They walked on until they came to the edge of a small glen. Here was more ground cover, mostly weeds and small shrubs, and three or four stunted trees spread their branches to provide some shade. Dan turned aside, and Hector thought it was to stop and rest, for it was now midday under a clear sky and, despite the breeze from the sea, he felt the heat of the tropical sun.

Dan pointed to several large, brownish-grey boulders in the shadow of the trees. As Hector approached, the nearest boulder slowly began to lift itself from the ground, using four scaly grey legs.

Astonished, Hector watched a long, serpent-like neck extrude from a cavity. The head that turned to face him was extraordinarily ugly. It reminded him of a very old, toothless, bald man with small holes for nostrils.

He stepped back in alarm before realizing that he was confronted by a giant tortoise.

Dan gave an amused chuckle. 'That is why I don't have to go striking turtle,' he said. 'This island is full of these creatures. Their flesh tastes like chicken.'

The tortoise advanced with agonizing slowness, clearly annoyed. It opened its slit of a mouth and gave a loud, angry hiss.

'Does it bite?' Hector asked.

'It is harmless. The creature feeds on leaves and grass, and its jaws are only useful for nipping,' said the Miskito. He stepped forward, threw a leg over the creature's back and rode the animal as it inched forward, still making a sound like escaping steam.

'There are not many this big left,' he said. 'The men carry them back to the ships as food. It can take four men at a time to lift one. Aboard ship the creatures keep alive and well. Jacques would get a good twenty pounds of fine oil off this one. He likes to flavour our breakfast dumplings with it.'

He dismounted from the back of the tortoise. 'A child could locate and capture these creatures. But there is something else I want to show you.'

Another half-hour's tramping brought them to the end of the island. Here they crunched across loose plates of rock that shifted and clattered under their feet, before they arrived at a small rocky promontory, which sloped down to a reef where the sea was breaking in regular bursts of spray.

Dan found a convenient outcrop on which to sit. 'This is where I come when I need some peace,' he said.

Hector sat down beside his friend. 'I know what you mean. When I was a captive in Valdivia, I used to go down to the harbour to get away by myself.'

'You have not told me what it was like to be a prisoner of the Spanish.'

Hector paused for a moment before replying. 'It's made me see things differently. I was well treated. The Governor of Valdivia was a decent man, and I can't say I relish the thought of plundering Spaniards once again.'

'Maybe that is because your mother was from that country,'

said Dan. 'It would be the same among the Miskito. When someone has a parent from another tribe, it is difficult to go fighting them.'

The two men sat silently for a while, watching a frigate bird as it wheeled and swooped, harrying a pair of gulls, bullying them to disgorge the fish they had caught.

Eventually Dan broke the silence. 'What about Maria?' he asked. 'Have you found out anything about her?'

Hector felt the familiar hopelessness creep over him. 'Maria is no longer in Peru. I brought you and the others on a futile quest.'

'Where is she?'

Hector nodded towards the horizon. 'Somewhere out there. Her employer was transferred to a post in the Ladrones.' His voice was dull and flat.

'I never heard of them. I thought the Encantadas were as far out in the ocean as you can go.'

'The Ladrones are much, much farther, nearly all the way to Asia.'

Dan seemed unconcerned. 'And do you still want to find her?'

Hector shrugged. 'There's no point. Maria is out of reach.'

Dan was persistent. 'These Ladrones, how many days would it take to sail there?'

'I don't know. Maybe six or seven weeks in a well-found ship.'

'The *Nicholas* is a well-found ship, and with a nice clean hull.'

Hector looked at his friend, astonished. 'What on earth are you talking about? Why would Captain Eaton want to go sailing off across the Pacific?'

'Captain Eaton might not want to, but his crew could be persuaded.' Dan picked up a loose piece of rock and threw it, waiting for the splash as it hit the sea. 'Remember how Cook and his men took the *Carlsborg* on the Guinea coast? You and I, Jezreel and Jacques had little choice but to go along.'

'Of course.'

'Well, we could do the same and take the *Nicholas*.'

'That's preposterous. The four of us could never handle such a ship.'

'I don't mean to steal her. Just to use her for what we want. I think that can be arranged.'

Suddenly the Miskito pointed downwards to where the foam was frothing on the rocks. 'See there. That is another thing that bewilders me on these islands.'

It took Hector several seconds to pick out what Dan had spotted. Crawling up the nearly vertical weed-covered rocks were three or four lizard-like creatures nearly as long as his arm and shining wet. They had just emerged from the water.

'They're iguanas, aren't they? Like the ones we used to catch and eat back on the Main.'

'Yes, but we never saw iguanas swimming in the sea. Here they behave like seals.' The Miskito got to his feet. 'Come, Hector. There will be plenty of time to tell me more of Valdivia once we are aboard the *Nicholas* and she is heading across the Pacific. Right now we must get back to camp so that I can speak with Jacques and Jezreel. I need to put matters in hand before everyone at Jacques' barbecue is too drunk and the food has all been eaten.'

Hector was confused and continued to sit looking out to sea. 'It's no good, Dan. Whatever your plan is, I don't want to go back to a life of piracy, sailing with men who think of nothing but plunder and prize.'

Dan touched him on the shoulder and pointed into the air. 'Hector, look at those frigate birds up there. See how they behave, robbers in the sky. That is their nature. Just as man's nature is to thieve when he can. You cannot change that. Just turn it to your advantage.'

SEVEN

NEXT MORNING Hector was awakened by a foot nudging him in the ribs. He was lying face down on sand, head cradled in the crook of his elbow, and a voice above him said insistently, 'I wish to speak with you, mynheer.' He turned his head sideways and blearily opened his eyes. In the half-darkness he could make out the glow of a camp fire and thought briefly it was the same fire that he and Dan had found when they returned to the beach the previous evening. Jacques and the other cooks had served up a feast, and the men from the *Cygnet* and the *Delight* had gathered round, eating and drinking. Hector had joined them and, after filling his belly, had stretched out on the sand, still mystified by Dan's intentions.

The foot nudged his ribs again, more firmly this time. 'Wake up, Gods vloek,' the voice said with some sort of foreign accent. Hector realized the fire couldn't be the one Jacques had used to grill strips of tortoise meat last night. It was too close to where the *Nicholas* was careened. He rolled over and looked up at the man who had roused him. He couldn't distinguish his features against the sky, for the sun had not yet risen. But in the half-light Hector could see he was barrel-chested and powerful. He wore no hat and had shaved his head. Hector had also identified the accent. The man spoke with the unmistakable guttural vowels of a Hollander.

'What do you want?' Hector asked peevishly. It was his first night ashore, and he did not appreciate being woken so early.

'They say you can navigate,' said the Hollander.

'Maybe I can, but what's that to you?'

'Come. Your friends say you might help us,' responded the Dutchman. Thankfully, he had stopped prodding with his foot.

Carefully Hector stood upright. He had drunk only a single glass of wine the previous night. It had been poor-quality vinegary stuff looted from some Peruvian ship. Several empty jars lay nearby, as well as at least a dozen sailors sprawled motionless on the ground. They looked little better than discarded bundles of rags. Clearly not everyone had been abstemious.

'My name is Piet Arianz. I'm quartermaster of the *Nicholas*. We have something to discuss with you.'

'So early?' asked Hector.

'We must tar and tallow before high water.'

Hector accompanied the Hollander along the beach to a score of men gathered around a fire of blazing driftwood. They watched over a large iron cauldron in which lumps of pitch were melting. Looking at the men, Hector guessed they formed the majority of the crew of the *Nicholas*. He recognized none of them individually, but they seemed to be of several different nationalities. A half-dozen olive-skinned men with thin faces and dark hair looked to be either Corsicans or Greeks, while a big blond-headed ruffian with pale china-blue eyes was probably a countryman of Piet's. That was not unusual. The men from the Low Countries were often exceptionally competent seamen and could be found on many buccaneer ships. To Hector's surprise, Jezreel also stood at the fire, and Dan.

There was an air of guarded curiosity among the waiting group. At once the quartermaster made it clear that he acted as spokesman for the rest. 'Would you be able to bring the *Nicholas* safely across the ocean to Manila or the Spice Islands?' he asked loudly enough to be heard by the entire group.

From the other side of the fire, Jezreel quickly added, 'Hector, I told them you've been the navigator on several long-distance voyages.'

The crew of the *Nicholas* looked at Hector, awaiting his answer. He realized from Jezreel's remark what might be expected of him, but he wasn't sure he wanted to go along with whatever scheme might next be proposed. So he replied cautiously, 'I can navigate. But I have no charts or instruments or almanacs, and have never sailed in those waters.'

'Instruments can be found,' said Arianz in his throaty accent. It sounded like a statement of fact.

'How many weeks to reach Manila?' demanded an older man. The daylight was getting stronger and Hector could see that his questioner had a fringe of grey hair around a bald pate tanned the colour of toffee.

'Without a chart to calculate, I can't say. But given fair conditions, I would guess it would take at least fifty days.'

'And is this the right season to make such a long crossing?' The older man sounded dubious.

Again Jezreel intervened. 'The ocean is called what it is because the weather is so calm.'

'Maybe too calm,' the old man whined. 'We could have no wind, and drift until we ran out of water, or the scurvy took us down. Calling it "the Pacific" means nothing.' He had the querulous tone of someone who always found fault.

Arianz brushed aside the objection. 'The French cook says there will be no problem taking aboard enough supplies to last the journey.'

It was becoming increasingly clear to Hector what sort of scheme Dan had hatched with Jacques and Jezreel. His three friends intended to take him to the Ladrones and Maria. They must have talked with the crew of the *Nicholas* during the previous evening's feasting, and planted in their minds the idea of a surprise raid on the Spanish colony in Manila on the far side of the Pacific. He had to admit that adding the lure of the Spice Islands was a nice touch. That would particularly appeal to Piet Arianz and his straw-haired countryman. The Dutch East India Company jealously guarded their lucrative trade with the Spice Islands and shut out all outsiders, including their own countrymen. Hector wondered if Arianz and his colleague had some reason to settle old scores with the Verenigde Oostindische Compagnie.

'It's another way for us to get home,' the quartermaster was saying to his shipmates. 'The Pacific crossing will be easier than sailing around the Cape and risking the storms, and less dangerous than going overland at Panama. None of us want to stay here any longer. We've made too little reward in Peru.'

There was a low mutter of assent from the gathering.

The Hollander turned to Hector. 'Supposing you had the right charts, would you agree to navigate such a voyage for us? You would have a full share, plus a quarter, in any plunder it brings us.'

Hector hesitated. He didn't want to disappoint Jacques, Dan and Jezreel. But they hadn't consulted him, and he was loath to go back to the life of a sea robber. There was no guarantee the *Nicholas* would touch at the Ladrones, though he remembered from the map he had seen in Valdivia that the islands lay on the direct route towards Manila.

'Surely your captain could take care of the navigation,' he answered lamely.

Arianz was blunt. 'Captain Eaton has no part in this. What we do and where we go is our vote. That is the custom. If he does not wish to accompany us, he can stay behind and rot here.' From his tone it seemed he had little affection for his captain.

The quartermaster looked around the circle of his colleagues. 'We put it to the vote. How many of you say that we try for Manila?'

There was a general murmur of agreement.

'And what about you two? You're his friends.' Arianz was staring boldly at Dan and Jezreel. Both men nodded.

Hector made one last attempt to delay what he feared was an ill-considered scheme. 'If Jezreel and Dan are keen to join you, then of course I will come with them. So too will Jacques, I expect. But without charts there can be no voyage.'

'Then we look into that straight away,' grunted the quarter-master. 'The rest of you get on with the job. I'll go and speak with the captain.'

The sailors turned back to the cauldron. The pitch had fully melted, giving off an acrid, tangy smell. The cauldron was lifted off the fire, and a man whom Hector guessed was the *Nicholas'* boatswain began pouring dollops of the black liquid into small turtle shells that served as pails. His assistant handed out crude brushes made from coconut husks.

'Come with me,' growled Arianz. He led Hector up the slope of the beach to where a threadbare sail had been suspended between two posts stuck in the sand and made a simple tent. Standing in front of the tent and deep in conversation were two men. One was Captain Swan. The other reminded Hector of a bare-knuckle fighter. He was leaning slightly forward, balancing on the balls of his feet, and his shoulders were hunched as if he was ready either to dodge a punch or launch a counter-blow. He looked like someone who had difficulty in controlling his natural impatience.

'Ah, Lynch. My friend here claims that these islands are sometimes known as the Galápagos. Have you seen that name on maps?' Swan asked.

'Galápagos in Spanish means "turtles", so that makes sense, though the animals we ate last night were large tortoises, according to William Dampier,' Hector replied. His attention was fixed on the man he presumed was Captain Eaton. The commander of the *Nicholas* had turned to look at him, and Hector was taken aback by the intensity of the scrutiny. John

Eaton was muscular and fit-looking, a man in his early forties. Of average height, he was clean-shaven and tied his dark hair back club-fashion. He was wearing a freshly washed white cotton shirt and pantaloons, with a dark-red sash around his waist. His most striking feature was the colour of his eyes. They were a pale green, and slanted upwards at the outer corners. The effect was to make him look uncommonly like a wolf.

'Have you charts for the Pacific?' Arianz interrupted. He addressed the question directly at Eaton, ignoring Swan.

The *Nicholas'* captain scowled. Hector could feel the animosity simmering between the two men. 'What need have I of such charts?' Eaton replied sharply. 'Panama is where we cruise next.'

'The men don't think so.'

'What?' asked Swan, surprised. 'We are agreed that our two ships, together with the *Delight*, will sail in company as soon as we have rested and repaired.'

Arianz turned to face Swan. 'Mynheer, the company of the *Nicholas* have voted to sail for Manila. We have had enough of the South Sea.'

'But . . .' began Swan.

Eaton cut across him. 'Tell the men I have no charts of the Pacific,' he snapped. 'And even if I did, I wouldn't use them. If you want to go on a madcap voyage, you'd better find yourselves another navigator.'

'We have,' said the quartermaster, jerking his head towards Hector.

Eaton turned his wolf's eyes on Hector. 'Then good luck to him. Let his guesswork steer you to your deaths.'

'Just one moment,' said Swan soothingly. Hector sensed the captain of the *Cygnet* had rapidly reassessed the situation. 'Tell me more of this scheme.'

'The crew of the *Nicholas* have voted to return home by way of Manila, where they have a chance of plunder,' said Arianz.

'There's no chance they'll change their minds?'

'None.'

Swan thought for a moment. 'Captain Eaton, naturally I'd prefer if the *Nicholas* stayed in company with the *Cygnet* and *Delight*. We'd be a more powerful force. But if your crew can't be relied on . . .' His voice tailed off and he gave a shrug.

Eaton looked furious. 'I'll deal with my crew in my own way,' he snapped.

Swan held up his hand in a calming gesture. 'I don't doubt it. But there are other concerns.'

'So what do you propose?' Eaton almost bit off the words.

When Swan next spoke, it was almost apologetically. 'Your crew have placed me in a difficult position, Captain Eaton. I worry that their ambitions for a trip to Manila will infect my crew and those who serve on the *Delight*. You know how easily such people are swayed.'

Eaton gave a snort. 'Every last one is a simpleton.'

Swan sighed. 'To be honest, I'd prefer to be rid of any discontents.'

'So would I.'

'As it happens,' continued Swan smoothly, 'I am able to supply charts of the Pacific.'

He addressed his next remark to Hector. 'Lynch, you'll recall I informed the Governor of Valdivia I was en route to the Indies and had diverted my ship to his port in hopes of trade.'

Hector remembered the episode clearly. Swan's claim that the vessel was bound for the Indies had seemed so flimsy. He waited to hear what his former captain would say next. He was all too aware of how devious and self-serving the *Cygnet*'s captain could be, and at this moment the man wore a sly expression.

'Naturally,' Swan continued, 'I carried Pacific charts and was ready to produce them as proof of my intentions. I still have those charts and will be pleased to lend them to Mr Lynch if he wants to make copies.'

As he spoke these words, Swan avoided looking directly at Hector. But the young man had already understood the real reason why the captain of the *Cygnet* was so ready to assist the crew of the *Nicholas* to sail off on their Pacific venture. It meant he would be rid of Hector and his dangerous knowledge that the gallant Captain Swan had once attempted to betray the crew of the *Bachelor's Delight* to the Spaniards.

Arianz brought the discussion to an abrupt end with a satisfied grunt. 'Good, let us go straight to your ship, Captain Swan, and collect the charts. As soon as the *Nicholas* is ready for sea, we depart.'

✳

IT HAD BEEN altogether too easy, Hector thought. He had chosen a shady spot on the *Nicholas'* quarterdeck, out of the glare of the equatorial sun so that he did not have to squint. He marked the vessel's estimated position on the draft with a tiny cross. Picking up a pair of dividers, he paused for a moment to admire his own and Dan's handiwork. The chart was even better than the original. Among his artist's materials, the Miskito had all the inks and pens needed for making fair copies. Also Dan had produced sheets of first-quality paper that he had looted from a Spanish ship whose cargo included stationer's supplies for the bureaucrats in Lima. Together, he and Dan had copied the necessary maps in less time than it had taken Arianz and his shipmates to finish careening their ship, float her off and set up her rigging. Meanwhile Jacques had seen to the loading of food stores, including several jars of quince marmalade, which he claimed as his share of the prize from the aviso. Even Eaton, initially disgruntled with the project for Manila, had participated energetically in the preparations for the Pacific crossing. Now, after four weeks at sea, Hector was still undecided whether the captain was genuine in his support for the voyage or had assisted because he was fearful of being left behind on the Encantadas.

In return, the crew had agreed to keep Eaton on as captain, though they obliged him to hand over all his navigational instruments and almanacs to Hector.

Spreading the points of the dividers, the young man measured the remaining distance to Manila. If his calculations were correct, there were less than 200 leagues to run. He readjusted the dividers and checked the distance to the Ladrones, where Maria would have moved to live with her employer. The islands lay perhaps two or three days ahead, almost on the direct route. Hector had begun to allow himself a faint hope. Despite his earlier misgivings, maybe his friends had been right all along. If he brought the *Nicholas* within sight of the Ladrones, the crew would insist on stopping there. They would be keen to get ashore, to find fresh water and replenish their supplies.

The last of the Encantada tortoises had been eaten more than a fortnight ago. It was the largest, weighing nearly a quarter-ton, and had needed four men to hoist it aboard. Hector had been sorry to see it slaughtered. The ungainly, slow-paced creatures were not as dull and insensitive as they first appeared. If you put down a handful of green stuff at a distance, the beasts would detect the meal and lumber across the deck towards it. Inevitably the men had taken to organizing tortoise races and laid bets on the results. At first the animals had nudged and collided with one another as they crawled towards their prize. Then, with the ingenuity born of men with too much time on their hands, the sailors had discovered that each animal could be trained to move in a straight line. If the tortoises were prodded and whipped, they soon learned to crawl forward, each on its own separate track.

Now there were no more tortoises left to race, and the men were slack and apathetic. The *Nicholas* was fast and well found, and she covered the sea miles with little incident. Since leaving the Encantadas, the Pacific had lived up to its benign reputation. Apart from one brief squall, which hit them in the dark, the wind had been steady. The sun had shone day after day from a gloriously blue sky. Puffy white clouds sped along in the same direction as the *Nicholas* forged ahead, a fair breeze on her quarter and a clear wake behind. Apart from basic maintenance to the ship, there was nothing for the crew to do except idle away the hours. The ocean offered them no distraction. There were no birds, no whales, and the only fish were the occasional clusters of flying fish. They burst out from the waves, skimmed ahead of the vessel and then, with a barely discernible splash, vanished as suddenly as they appeared.

'Wasting your time again?' Eaton had strolled up behind Hector and, as usual, was mocking his chartwork. 'No one knows the true size of this ocean. And you only guess where we are.'

It was true. With cross-staff and almanac, Hector was able to establish the *Nicholas*' position north or south to less than half a degree. But he had no accurate way of measuring how far west the ship had come. He was relying on nothing more than the total of each day's progress, as recorded by the men on watch. The numbers they provided him with were often suspect, and took no account of ocean currents. Even if he had the *Nicholas*' position right, there was every chance the map itself was distorted. The Ladrones, the China coast, Japan – everything he and Dan had copied down so carefully – might be drawn wrongly on the original map.

Eaton smirked. He had voiced his criticism loudly and clearly so that anyone on the quarterdeck could hear what he said. Hector knew why. The captain resented the fact that Hector was in charge of navigation, and looked for every chance to undermine the crew's confidence in his ability. But that was typical of the *Nicholas*' captain. Eaton was one of those manipulative commanders who maintained his authority by sowing doubt and discord in the minds of his crew. He was at pains to discredit anyone who became too popular or respected. This did not make for a cheerful or steady crew, and Hector often wondered why they suffered such a fault-finding commander.

'It's a pity your French friend failed to check the water stowage for himself,' said Eaton. There was malice in that remark too. During the preparations for departure, Jacques had asked the *Nicholas*' cooper to oversee the filling of the ship's water containers. Unfortunately the man was lazy and incompetent and hadn't ensured the casks and jars of water were packed securely in the vessel's hold. When the squall had struck just two days into the voyage, the *Nicholas* had heeled suddenly. Many of the heavy earthenware jars had shifted and smashed, their contents wasted. From that day forward, the crew had been on a strict water ration. It was another source of discontent.

Hector rolled up the chart, slid it carefully into its wooden tube and stepped across to the side rail to clear the deck space. The men were gathering in twos and threes. Some of them affected looks of indifference. Others had uneasy expressions and glanced frequently out to sea to avoid looking at one another directly. Arianz the quartermaster appeared, tight-lipped and grave. He took up his position by the capstan head and waited until the entire crew was present. In his hand was the wooden dipper that was brought out three times a day so that each man could ladle his single ration from the tub of drinking water that stood beside the mast.

Now Arianz rapped the dipper on the capstan to draw everyone's attention.

'We decide the case of Giovanni Domine. He is accused of water theft,' he announced to the assembly. His eyes flicked towards a small, surly-looking man standing in the front rank. Domine was one of the men who Hector had earlier guessed were from Mediterranean ports.

'Who says he's been stealing water?' shouted the sailor next to Domine. He had the same olive skin, stocky build and dark, heavy eyebrows. It was evident they were cronies.

'Joris Stolck reports that Domine was missing during his watch. He was found in the hold, drinking from one of the casks in the lower tier.'

'Impossible. Those casks are too heavy for one man to handle. And they are buried deep.'

'He was using a musket barrel to suck up water through the bunghole. I saw it,' said a new voice.

Hector craned his neck to see who'd made the accusation. It was Arianz's countryman, the other Hollander. Hector supposed there was bad feeling between the northerners and the men from the Mediterranean. Giovanni Domine sounded like a name from Genoa or Naples.

Eaton added his voice. 'I checked Stolck's accusation. Domine's musket was dismantled. The inside of the barrel was wet.'

The quartermaster looked around the assembled men. 'None of us want to be standing out here in the sun while we argue. You all know our articles, we decide these matters by a general vote. Those who believe Giovanni Domine to be guilty, raise your hands.'

Hector watched as more than half the crew found a guilty verdict. He noted that not one of the Mediterranean group agreed.

The quartermaster finished counting the show of hands and rapped again on the capstan head with the dipper. 'What is his punishment to be?'

His demand was met with silence. In the general hush Hector could hear only the soft sound of the breeze in the rigging, the murmur of the waves against the vessel's hull. There was tension in the air. Someone in the assembled crowd coughed nervously. No one was willing to decide the form of punishment.

From his place beside the quartermaster, Eaton intervened again, pressing the matter forward. 'We all know the rules: anyone found guilty of theft is to forfeit his share of the prize. That's the custom. But we have no prize to divide. I propose we decide a general sanction in which we all share.'

'Thrash him,' called a voice suddenly. 'That's what we did

in the service.' It was the peevish old man who had previously questioned the purpose of the voyage.

'You're not in the Navy now,' shouted an objector.

'Flog him according to our custom,' retorted the old man. 'Each man gives three blows with a two-inch-and-a-half rope, and on a bare back.' He looked around triumphantly.

'So be it,' said Eaton quickly. There was a look of satisfaction on his face. 'Domine, remove your shirt and stand by the mast.' He beckoned to the sailmaker. 'Cut a length of two-inch-and-a-half, and whip the end.'

When the knout was ready, Eaton handed it to the big Hollander, Joris Stolck, who had first made the accusation. 'Yours are the first blows,' he said.

Stolck hefted the rope in his hand, stepped across to where Domine was standing and lashed the rope's end hard across his back. The victim let out a low grunt.

'Two more,' called Eaton. He'd taken charge now. The Hollander lashed out twice more, then handed the rope to his countryman. Arianz ran the rope through his hands and dealt the Genoese three more sharp strokes. His victim flinched with each blow.

So it went on. One by one, the crew took it in turns to flog the culprit. Some blows were heavy and viciously struck. Others, those from his Mediterranean friends, scarcely landed. Domine bore up stoically under the beating, though his back was soon striped with a criss-cross of welts. Here and there the skin broke and blood oozed from the cuts. Unable to watch, Hector looked down at the deck beneath his feet. Out of the corner of his eye he noticed Eaton's hands. They hung loosely by his side. Each time the rope struck Domine's back, the captain clenched his fist. It seemed he was enjoying the spectacle.

When it came to Hector's turn he hesitated. 'You take your turn, just like the rest,' snapped Eaton. Hector took the rope. It felt slick and sweaty in his hands where others had already gripped it. Half-heartedly he raised his arm and struck, aiming to avoid those areas where Domine's back was already bruised and cut. The first blow was accurate, but the second too clumsy and must have hit a tender spot, for the Genoese sucked in his breath in a gasp of pain. Ashamed and hoping to soften the third blow, Hector swung the rope, then pulled his arm back just before it struck. The rope's end flicked like a whip, and to his chagrin the blow split the skin. Behind him he heard Eaton give a low murmur of approval.

After every man had taken his turn, Domine was led away by his friends. They sat him down by the rail. Someone dipped up a bucket of sea water and they began to sponge his back.

The onlookers shuffled away. 'That should put an end to thievery,' observed Eaton to no one in particular. For him the matter was closed. But Hector noted Domine's cronies deliberately turning their backs on the two Hollanders as they walked past. He could only hazard a guess as to how long a common hunger for gold would hold this crew together.

THAT EVENING, if Dan hadn't been at the ship's lee rail, the sinking shallop might never have been detected. The Miskito was helping Jacques, dumping ashes from the galley overboard. He emptied the pan and paused to contemplate the fiery orange glow left by the setting sun. Something on the horizon caught his eye. It was shaped like the horns of a crescent, but so small that at first Dan thought it was nothing more than an unusual double wave crest. But when the mark reappeared, lifted on the next swell, he walked aft and drew the helmsman's attention to what he had just seen. Normally the helmsman wouldn't have troubled himself to adjust course to investigate. But the object lay almost directly on the ship's track and he was bored. So he moved the rudder very slightly.

Night had fallen by the time the *Nicholas* came level with the distant object. It was difficult to see anything more than a patch of deeper shadow. Certainly no one had expected to come across some sort of boat. Yet there it was, barely afloat, the sea washing over its mid-section with each passing swell.

'What do you make of it?' Hector asked Dan. The two men stared into the darkness. Beside them half a dozen of the *Nicholas*' crew lined the lee rail. Quartermaster Arianz had ordered the sheets slackened and the yards braced round, so as to take all way off the ship.

'I have never seen anything like it,' answered the Miskito. The half-submerged vessel was an unusual shape. Some thirty feet long, it was broad and shallow, and each end curved up prominently. It was impossible to say which was bow and which was stern.

'Could have been abandoned or broken free of a mooring,' ventured Jezreel as he joined his friends.

'But from where?' asked Hector. 'We're too far from land.'

'That's not a deep-sea boat,' observed Dan. 'It is too small and too lightly built. And there is no shelter for the crew.' The only structure on the low, wide deck was a hooped cabin of wickerwork, much like a kennel.

'Why are we halted?' asked Eaton sourly. The captain had come on deck and not yet noticed the hulk.

'Some sort of shallop, awash and abandoned,' said Arianz, gesturing over the side.

Eaton walked to the rail and glanced down. 'Floating rubbish. It needn't delay us.' He turned to Hector. 'So much for your navigation. Maybe we're not as distant from land as you'd have us believe.' He laughed contemptuously.

'Maybe there's something worth salvaging?' suggested the quartermaster.

'It's a waste of time,' snapped Eaton.

The quartermaster ignored him. 'I'll send someone to check.'

Dan volunteered for the task. He clambered down the side of the *Nicholas*, lowered himself into the sea and swam across to the abandoned boat. He pulled himself aboard and Hector saw him bend down to peer into the cabin. A moment later,

Dan straightened up and, cupping his hands around his mouth, called out, 'Throw me a line. There's someone inside.'

Quickly the derelict shallop was hauled alongside the *Nicholas*, and the limp figure of a thin, black-haired man, clad only in a loincloth, was hoisted on to the larger vessel. Hector, reaching to help lift the man over the rail, was shocked at how light he was. The stranger weighed no more than a small child. As he was laid on the deck, they could see he was but a living skeleton. His skin had shrunk so that every rib showed starkly. His arms and legs were like sticks, and his body was all hollows and cavities. It was difficult to believe he was still alive. Yet when Hector put his ear against the victim's chest, he could hear the heart beating.

Someone produced a rag soaked in fresh water, and a dribble was squeezed into the man's mouth. His eyes stayed closed. He seemed past reviving.

Dan climbed back over the rail, and dropped lightly down on deck. 'There is nothing else aboard, except for an empty water jar and a straw hat.'

'Back to your posts, everyone,' ordered Eaton curtly. 'We've squandered enough time as it is. Cast off the wreck and make sail.' He turned away and stalked back to his cabin.

'How long do you think he's survived?' asked Jezreel, looking at the wasted figure.

'Weeks or even months,' said Hector. 'Maybe we'll never find out. I doubt he'll last the night.'

But when the sun rose next day the castaway, as they now thought of him, was still alive. He lay on the deck, a blanket wrapped around his emaciated body. Only his head was visible. Once or twice his eyelids flickered. His breathing had become noticeably stronger.

'Where is he from, do you think?' asked Jacques. He'd prepared a broth to give the patient as soon as he was able to swallow.

'He's some sort of Easterner, that's for sure,' replied Hector.

The man's skin was yellow-brown, and he had coarse, straight black hair. 'A Chinaman maybe?'

'Don't think so,' said Jezreel. 'When I did exhibition fights in London, a few Chinamen worked with the shows. They all had round heads and smooth, chubby faces. This fellow's jaw is too long, and his face too narrow.'

'Maybe he can tell us when he comes round,' said Jacques.

The speed of the castaway's recovery took everyone by surprise. The very next day he could sit up and was taking an interest in his surroundings. But his expression gave no clue as to what he was thinking. The crew tried talking to him in every language they could muster. When that failed, they used gestures, hoping to learn where he came from. But he didn't respond and remained silent, impassively observing everything going on aboard the *Nicholas*. Some of the crew believed he was a mute by birth, others that his terrible ordeal had destroyed his power of speech.

'I wonder what he is thinking?' said Jacques two mornings later. The castaway had not moved from his spot, and sat on his blanket with a bowl of soup in his hand. He accepted it from the Frenchman without a smile or nod of thanks. From time to time he raised the bowl to his lips and sipped, but continued to stare at his surroundings.

'He can speak. I'm sure of that,' Hector said quietly.

There was something disquieting about the stranger's behaviour, Hector felt. He scarcely moved his head, but the brown eyes, so dark they were almost black and sunk deep in their sockets, were never still. His gaze darted from one place to the next, observing the crew at work, looking up at the sky and sails, following whatever was going on aboard ship. It was as if he was trying to make sense of his situation with a guarded intelligence, yet hiding the reason why.

A shadow fell across the deck. Hector looked round to find Eaton staring down at the castaway. With him was the quartermaster. 'When can that fellow be put to work?' the captain asked bluntly. 'He's a waste of food and water.'

Arianz squatted down in front of the castaway and peered into his face, no more than a couple of feet away. Hector was struck by the contrast between the big, blond quartermaster with his pale-blue eyes and the gaunt, yellow-skinned unknown, who looked back at him with a flat incurious gaze.

'Seems to have got back his appetite,' said Arianz. He'd seen the soup bowl, now empty.

'He's still very weak,' Hector volunteered.

The words were scarcely out of his mouth when the stranger's arm suddenly shot out and his hand seized the quartermaster's right ear.

Arianz jerked back in shock and pain. 'Laat gaan, you little bastard.'

But the castaway held firm.

'Laat gaan. Let go.'

Now the stranger raised his other arm. For a moment Hector thought the castaway was about to deliver a blow to the Hollander's face. But instead he pointed forward towards the bows.

'What the hell does he want?' shouted Arianz. The stranger had released him, and he was on his feet, stepping back out of reach.

Now the stranger got shakily to his feet. It was the first time he'd stood since his rescue. Clinging to a shroud above him and swaying slightly, he pointed to the horizon, slightly to the north of the *Nicholas'* course. Then he turned around and touched the lobe of his own ear.

The others looked at one another in astonishment. 'What does that mean?' said the quartermaster, still recovering from his surprise.

The stranger repeatedly touched his ear and pointed towards the horizon. All the while he stared intently at his audience.

'He's lost his senses,' said Eaton.

'He's trying to tell us something,' Hector corrected him. He'd guessed the stranger's meaning. 'Jacques, stretch out your right hand a moment. Hold it in front of the castaway.'

The Frenchman glanced at Hector, puzzled, but did as he was asked. Immediately the stranger reached out, tapped Jacques on the finger and again pointed urgently to the horizon. This time he nodded to emphasize his message, and patted himself on the chest.

'It's your ring, Jacques,' explained Hector. 'The gold ring you wear. And it was Arianz's gold earring. The castaway is trying to tell us there is gold over there, in the direction he is pointing, the place he comes from.'

'Is he, by God!' exclaimed Eaton. The sudden pitch of excitement in his voice made several of the crew look round.

'How far away?' Arianz asked stupidly, for the castaway could not understand the question. The stranger kept nodding and pointing.

The quartermaster looked across at Hector. 'Where does he mean?'

Hector was slow to answer. Something wasn't right about the stranger's certainty. 'I've no idea,' he replied. 'The chart shows no land in that direction, not until you reach Japan or the China coast.'

'Only goes to prove the chart is wrong, as I warned you,' said Eaton smugly.

'Saving a man from the sea brings good luck to the rescuers. This proves it,' announced Stolck loudly. He'd come across to join them.

As the news was shared among the crew, excitement spread. Men hurried to the quarterdeck and formed a circle around the stranger, moving closer as they waited anxiously to learn more. Hector was reminded of his schooldays and the carp pond at the friary where he used to toss chunks of hard, stale bread to the fish. They used to swim up from the depths and congregate in a teeming mass, taking it in turns to mouth the floating crust until it was soft. As more and more of the crew appeared, coming up from their berths below deck or hurrying back from whatever work they'd been doing, they clustered around the castaway, relishing his information, discussing it among themselves. The word 'gold' was repeated again and again. Someone produced a silver coin, a Spanish half-real, and held it up to the stranger. He pushed it aside and shook his head. Then he stepped across to Domine, who wore a small gold medallion on a leather thong around his neck. Touching the medallion, the stranger nodded vigorously.

As usual, Arianz was practical. 'How far to this gold place?' the quartermaster asked again, speaking slowly this time. He pointed first to the horizon, then up to the sky and mimed the passage of the sun overhead.

The stranger held up eight fingers.

'Eight days,' exclaimed Stolck. Hector thought it odd that the castaway, who'd been so uncommunicative, should now understand his questioners. But there was no point raising doubts. It was clear the crew of the *Nicholas* was ready to be convinced. They were agog to be persuaded that they had stumbled on a source of easy riches. Hector thought of the carp pond once more. The greedy fish used to cluster just as eagerly around a lump of wood as a piece of bread.

The quartermaster sensed the mood of the company. 'Everyone to assemble at the capstan,' he announced.

The castaway slid back down on deck, laid his head against the bulwarks and closed his eyes. The last few stragglers appeared on deck, and Hector found himself standing beside Eaton in the waist of the ship as Arianz addressed the entire crew.

'The castaway claims he comes from a place where there's gold to be had. It's eight days away, if we sail nor'nor'west. Does the company wish to act on that information, or do we keep to our original design for Manila?'

'How do we know he's telling the truth?' Unsurprisingly the

question came from the old man with the bald pate, the long-time sceptic.

'We'll never know unless we go and find out,' shouted someone in the crowd. Hector sensed a gathering surge of eagerness among the onlookers.

'What does the navigator think?' asked a voice. Expectant faces turned towards Hector. He racked his brains for an answer that might retrieve the situation, but he was caught in a snare of his own making. Only Jezreel, Dan and Jacques knew that he hoped to call at the Ladrones. Most of the crew weren't even aware the islands existed. If he told them now, they'd feel deceived.

Before he could reply, another voice – one of the Mediter-ranean men, by the accent – called out, 'We do not need a navigator. We have our own pilot now. The castaway will show us our course.'

But Hector wasn't spared so easily. 'What about that chart he and the striker copied out? Does that show anything?' The question came from Joris Stolck, the big Hollander.

Hector looked across the crowd, caught Dan's eye and saw the Miskito give a slight shrug.

'I don't have enough to go on,' Hector answered. 'Are we looking for an island or a large country? There's nothing on the chart. Only Japan and China are shown in that direction.'

'Maybe the castaway comes from Golden Cipangu.' This time Hector couldn't see who the speaker was. But the rumour of Golden Cipangu was familiar to every seafarer. It was a legend dating back to Marco Polo's time, telling of a distant island where bullion was mined in such vast amounts that the people valued gold no more than iron or copper. Cipangu had never been found, but it was still a myth that dazzled the credulous.

Now, at least, Hector felt he could give an honest answer. 'Golden Cipangu is Japan itself. The Portuguese and Dutch trade there, but not for bullion.'

Once again, Arianz was down to earth. 'How many days to Manila on this course?'

'A week, maybe more,' answered Hector.

'Then it's little farther if we search out the mystery place. Even if it proves not to be golden, we can stop and fill our water casks.' Raising his voice, he called, 'How do you vote? Those in favour of searching out this Cipangu, or whatever it might be, raise your right hand.'

Looking across the assembled men, Hector saw a forest of hands. The men were animated, bright-eyed with enthusiasm, turning to one another in agreement.

'It's decided then,' announced the quartermaster.

Hector glanced over to where the castaway sat slumped against the bulwark. Now the man's eyes were open and he was watching the assembly. His expression was unreadable.

✳

THE STRANGER knew his way across the ocean – that became increasingly clear as the days passed.

'He pays no attention to the compass. Yet, according to my calculations, he's maintained a steady course for the past week,' Hector said to Dan, who was busy with paper and charcoal. It was soon after dawn on what was promising to be another warm, balmy day, and the two men were by the windward rail. Dan was sketching a portrait of the stranger, whose mattress had been shifted to the quarterdeck, so that he was close to the helm.

'He probably does not know what a compass is,' said Dan without looking up from his work. 'Our Miskito fishermen sometimes get blown off-shore in a gale. They find their way back home by looking at the sea signs – the flow of the current, the direction of the wind, patches of weed and the flight of birds. That is enough.'

Hector glanced across at the castaway, who had made a remarkable recovery from his ordeal. He was still gaunt and hollow-cheeked, but now he was on his feet, quick and alert.

Instead of his previous exhausted sleep, he took catnaps, no more than an hour at a time. For the rest of the day and night he directed the helmsmen of each watch. One thing, however, had not changed: the stranger's attitude was aloof and guarded. He made no effort to communicate with the crew, refused their offers of clothing, and took his meals alone. Hector found this disquieting.

'Well, there aren't many birds around here for him to follow their pathways,' said Jezreel, who had joined them. 'I just hope he knows what he's doing. I'd kill for a drink of fresh water that hasn't got worms wriggling in it.'

'Be grateful none of us are showing signs of scurvy,' said Hector. It was true. With all the fresh food gone, the first signs of the sickness were appearing. Several men had begun to complain of pains in their joints, shortness of breath, sore gums and loose teeth. As yet, Hector and his friends were unaffected.

'Jacques says it's that quince marmalade he's been feeding us,' said Jezreel. 'But that'll soon run out.' He dropped his voice. 'I'm sorry our plan for the Thief Islands didn't work, Hector. Maybe there'll be a second chance if it turns out our castaway friend is leading us a dance.'

Hector shrugged. 'At first I thought he was taking us to Japan. But that's farther north. I'm sure of our longitude, though there's nothing shown on the chart for this region.'

Jezreel leaned over to look at Dan's drawing. 'Not a bad likeness,' he said.

'It would help if he kept still until I have finished the drawing,' muttered the Miskito.

Unusually, the stranger had left the quarterdeck and was making his way forward to the bows.

'Perhaps he's spotted something,' said Jezreel. Just then the lookout at the masthead cried out, 'Land ahead.' Immediately there was a stampede of men to find a vantage point, some in the rigging, others scrambling up on the rails. 'Not even eight days,' someone shouted jubilantly.

The landfall was no more than a thin, dark line on the horizon. But the *Nicholas* was closing rapidly, and by noon it was clear the ship was approaching an island that had a distinctive cone-shaped hill at one end and was covered with dense vegetation. Beyond it, to the north and east, were at least two more islands in the far distance.

'What do you make of it, Hector?' Jacques asked his friend, who was puzzling over the chart.

'Some sort of archipelago. Why it's not marked I don't know. Perhaps it lies too far off the usual shipping routes.'

'Or someone does not want it known about, mon ami,' said the Frenchman. 'Maybe a secret worth keeping.'

'Sounds like you've started to believe in Cipangu,' said Hector with a wry smile.

'I will be so glad to get ashore and stretch my legs. But our pilot friend does not seem very excited.'

It was true. Since sighting land, the stranger had taken up position permanently on the foredeck, close to the bows. He stood gazing forward, completely calm while the rest of the ship's crew jabbered and chatted excitedly.

As usual, Eaton didn't waste the chance to belittle Hector's navigational skills. 'Seems you could take lessons from our friend with the yellow skin. A perfect landfall,' he called out from where he was standing close to the helm.

In the bows the stranger indicated to larboard. 'He wants us to steer close around the island,' said the helmsman tersely, as he looked to the west, worried. 'It'll be dark in another two hours. Could be dangerous to work our way into an unknown anchorage.'

'If he's brought us safely this far, we can trust him the last few miles,' Eaton reassured him. 'I doubt the crew will allow for any delay. Just follow his signals.'

The final approach proved even more perilous than the helmsman had feared. A broad ledge of coral encircled the island, and in the gathering twilight they skirted reefs that stretched for a mile or more out to sea. Here the swells broke in long, ugly-looking slicks of foam, and the helmsman voiced his dismay at the risk they were taking by sailing so close. But he was ignored. The shipmates lined the ship's rail and strained to catch a glimpse of human occupation. But they saw no boats, no sign of settlement on the densely wooded shore, and as the light faded, the island became no more than a dark shape. So it was by moonlight that the stranger finally indicated they should turn in towards the land.

'Hard to starboard. There's a channel through the reef,' came back an excited yelp. By now their enigmatic pilot was no more than an indistinct figure up in the bow, his signals relayed by voice along the deck. Almost immediately followed another cry of 'Brail up. Brail up.'

The *Nicholas* turned sweetly, losing speed as her sails were doused, and she entered the concealed gap. Only the steady stream of muttered oaths from the frightened helmsman broke the tense silence. Moments later the sound of the swell breaking on the coral on both sides of the ship was very, very close. The vessel was lifted upwards on the back of a swell, was carried forward and in less than a cable's length was gliding across a calm surface.

'Anchor now. He's making signs we must anchor,' came the urgent cry.

'As he says,' Eaton shouted back.

A moment later there was the splash of the anchor hitting the water. The cable ran out for a few yards and the vessel slowed to a halt. All was calm. 'Thank Christ that's over,' muttered Jezreel under his breath. 'We could've ripped out her bottom on the coral. That was a mad thing to do.'

In the silence and darkness that followed, there came the sound of a second splash.

'What's that?' called out Arianz in alarm.

'The castaway dived overboard,' came back a shout. 'He's swum away.'

EIGHT

A BRIGHT, WINDLESS DAWN revealed that the *Nicholas* lay safely moored in a shallow lagoon. The water was the colour of pale sapphire and so transparent that her anchor could clearly be seen dug into the sand less than a fathom beneath her keel. To seaward, the narrow entrance passage she had threaded in the darkness now showed as a gap among the breakers, which steadily flecked across the coral shelf. A cable's length away on the landward side, a beach of white sand faintly tinged with pink sloped gently towards a line of small thatched huts, the outskirts of what appeared to be a village of fishermen. Their boats, some two dozen of them, lay drawn up on the strand. Most were dugout canoes, but the larger ones were identical in their crescent design to the waterlogged shallop from which the crew of the *Nicholas* had plucked the mysterious stranger. Of him there was no sign. Indeed, there was no movement whatsoever in the village itself. It appeared to be utterly deserted. Puzzled, the crew gaped at the empty beach and the silent houses. Other than the murmur of the distant surf, the only sounds they could hear were strange bird calls from the village's shade trees covered with orange and white blossom, which echoed round the lagoon.

'Where is everyone?' muttered Jacques.

'I expect they're too frightened to show themselves,' said Hector. He'd glimpsed a furtive movement within the open door of one of the huts.

'Then why did our castaway bring us here?' asked Jacques.

'To save his skin,' muttered Jezreel.

Without waiting for orders, the crew hoisted out the ship's jolly boat from the main deck, where it had been stowed during the ocean crossing, and lowered it into the water.

'Lynch, as you had no idea this place even existed, I suggest you venture ashore and learn something about it.' The sarcastic invitation came from Eaton, who had appeared with a brace of pistols stuck in his sash.

Men clutching muskets climbed down into the jolly boat, and Hector was rowed to the beach with the captain and the half-dozen men of the landing party.

'You might have thought our castaway would have the courtesy to be on hand to greet us,' observed Eaton gruffly, as the jolly boat's keel slid into the soft sand with a low, chafing hiss. He climbed out of the boat and led the way towards the huts. Hector splashed ankle-deep into the warm water and followed him. The armed men fanned out on either side, their guns held ready. As they drew nearer to the little settlement, they could see that the place was neat and well kept. Somewhere a rooster crowed.

'There,' grunted one of the sailors. 'Third hut from the left, someone's coming out.'

As Hector watched, a nervous-looking man stepped out timidly from the shadows. He was small – scarcely five foot high – and dressed in a shabby, loose brown gown with very wide sleeves. The garment reached down to his knees and was fastened at the waist with a simple cord belt. His feet and legs were bare, and his hair, which was long and jet-black, was tied in a knot on the crown of his head. His features were very like those of the rescued castaway. He had the same yellow-brown complexion and deep-sunk eyes, though he was older by perhaps twenty years. Trembling, he came to within ten paces of the strangers, then bowed deeply and continued to advance in a curious stooping shuffle, placing his feet down cautiously as if the sand was hot. He kept his eyes on the ground and in his right hand held out a small branch. Its green leaves shivered in his nervous grasp.

'A sign of peace,' volunteered Hector quietly. He feared Eaton or one of the sailors would use their guns.

'I can see that for myself,' snapped Eaton crossly. He strode forward towards the old man.

'We will do you no harm. We only wish to take on water and buy food,' he announced loudly.

The old man responded by crouching even lower. He sank his head further, and bent his knees until he was kneeling submissively on the sand. At the same time he thrust out the leafy branch to the full extent of his scrawny arm. Now that he was closer, Hector could see the old man's topknot was fashioned by sweeping up the hair on all sides and tying it together in a bundle. Two metal pins, four or five inches long, were thrust from front to back through the hair to hold the topknot in place. The ends of the pins were delicately moulded into the shape of flowers, and their petals appeared to be made of gold. One of the sailors muttered something out of the side of his mouth, and Hector caught the word 'Cipangu'.

Eaton ignored the out-thrust branch and repeated his request. The old man only cringed even more abjectly.

'Try him in Spanish, Lynch,' barked the captain.

The outcome was no different. The old man kept on bowing and thrusting out the branch without a word. Finally Hector stepped up to him and gently laid a hand on his shoulder. It was like touching a dog that had suffered years of beatings and abuse. Hector felt the man flinch.

'We come in peace,' he said. The old man straightened a little and, still avoiding direct eye contact, answered him. Staring down at the ground, he spoke diffidently in a language that had a low, musical quality, but was completely incomprehensible.

'Well, at least he's not a mute like the other one,' Eaton said crossly. He stepped around the old man and began walking briskly towards the line of huts. Immediately the elderly villager uttered a low, anxious cry and scuttled around in front of him, extending both arms, making it clear that his visitors were not to enter the settlement.

Eaton brushed him aside and continued to stride forward. The old man kept pace, still making unhappy pleading noises and gesturing that the captain should turn back.

'Can't imagine what he has to hide,' Eaton said, and in a few more paces the landing party was in the village itself.

The place was as humble and unassuming as it had appeared from the ship. A web of narrow sandy footpaths meandered between flimsy huts. Their walls were made of closely interwoven cane and the roofs were thatched with straw. Wickerwork fences divided off small vegetable plots or chicken runs. Peering into one of the huts, Hector saw the interior was clean and neat and arranged as a single room. There was a raised hearth at one end, reed mats on the floor, and there were one or two shelves against a wall, from which hung some simple wooden agricultural tools and fishing gear. Apart from a couple of bed rolls, there was no furniture. It was clear to Hector that the huts had been hastily vacated, and very recently. A curl of smoke rose from the embers of the hearth. Abandoned utensils lay in a corner. The sides of the heavy clay jars used for holding water were damp and covered with condensation, and someone had scattered fresh scraps of food for a trio of piglets snuffling in a makeshift sty.

Disappointed, the landing party returned towards the beach. The old man was still visibly distraught as he accompanied them.

'Why's the old boy so upset?' one of the sailors wondered out loud.

'There must be a spring or well somewhere close by,' Eaton

told him. 'Get back to the ship and tell the others to start bringing the empty water barrels, and that it's safe to set up camp on the beach.'

The sight of the *Nicholas'* sea-weary crew eagerly coming ashore minutes later seemed to convince the old man there was nothing he could do to prevent the intrusion. Still clutching his branch of peace, he retreated into the village, and a short while later reappeared at the head of a party of about forty men. Doubtless they were villagers who had been hiding in the bamboo groves, for all wore the same drab workaday gowns and dressed their hair in an identical style. To the pleasure and astonishment of the men of the *Nicholas*, the new arrivals came down the beach and, after bobbing and bowing nervously, began to assist in carrying the sailors' belongings on to the land.

'Amazingly friendly people, are they not?' said Jacques soon after he'd come ashore. Two of the villagers had insisted on taking a heavy cauldron from him and staggered off with it along the beach. There they set the pot down above the high-water mark, and within minutes several of their comrades had begun heaping up a stack of firewood, ready for use.

'There's a reason for what they are doing,' Hector answered. He'd been watching closely. 'They're making sure we set up camp well clear of their village.'

'Probably they are afraid we will interfere with their women,' said Jacques. He looked around. 'Mind you, I have not yet seen a woman, or even a child.'

'There's something else I don't see,' said Hector.

'What's that?'

'Not one of these people is carrying a weapon. Not even a knife.'

'They could have hidden any weapons in the forest before they came out into the open.'

'I didn't see any swords or spears when I was in the village. Only a couple of fish tridents, which Dan would find very puny.'

'Well, I've never seen any people so obliging,' Jacques said contentedly. There was a holiday atmosphere to the day. The entire crew of the *Nicholas* had come ashore, leaving their muskets and cutlasses behind. They were whooping and cheering, running up and down the beach, glad to stretch their legs. A few of them cast curious glances towards the village, but as yet no one ventured in that direction. It was sufficient to enjoy the sensation of being on dry land and away from the confines of the ship.

'Jacques, you're wanted over here. There's been a vegetable delivery,' called Jezreel. He was near the cooking gear on the beach. Several more villagers had arrived with baskets on their heads and were looking around for instructions.

As Jacques hurried off, Hector became aware that the old man who had first greeted them was standing meekly just a few paces away, waiting to be noticed.

'What is it?' asked Hector gently. He was quietly gratified that he'd won the confidence of the village elder.

The old man bowed submissively once more and, turning, beckoned to a figure lurking half-hidden among the bamboo thickets at the back of the beach.

In most respects the person who came forward resembled the other villagers. He wore the same coarse cotton gown and, like them, he was barefoot and had narrow eyes and a yellowish skin. But his long grey hair – instead of being in a topknot – hung loose around his shoulders, and he had a straggly beard that reached to the middle of his chest. Thin-faced and spare, his weather-beaten features made it difficult to judge his age, but he must have been in his late sixties or maybe older. He lacked the diffidence of his comrade, and his dark-brown eyes were full of confident curiosity. Up close, there was something else that Hector had not observed on any of the other villagers: a faint blue mark about two inches long in the centre of his forehead. It was in the shape of a hollow, elongated lozenge and had been inked into the skin.

The village elder gave a low, apologetic cough and in his soft, tuneful language murmured something to the newcomer. Looking at Hector directly, he said slowly and carefully, 'My name is Panu. I help. I translate.'

The accent was very strong, and Hector was so startled it took a moment for him to realize he'd been addressed in Spanish.

'We have come here for water and rest,' he replied.

'Are you captain?' Panu asked.

'No. That is the captain over there.' Hector pointed out Eaton standing at the campsite, talking with Arianz, the quartermaster.

'Jeema asks you please go soon.'

Hector presumed Jeema was the village elder. 'We will stay only a few days,' he assured the translator.

'Anything you need, tell Jeema. The village will try to give.'

Intrigued, Hector asked, 'Where did you learn to speak Spanish?'

'Know Holland more.'

For an instant Hector was baffled. Then he realized that Panu preferred to speak in Dutch. Seeing Stolck not far away, Hector called him over and, with the Hollander's help, began to piece together Panu's story.

He came from a small island some distance to the southwest, where once there had been a Spanish trading fort. As a child he'd learned a little Spanish from his father, who had worked as a warehouse foreman for the white foreigners. The Spaniards had suddenly abandoned the fort when Panu was in his early teens, and, a few years later, the Dutch had arrived to occupy it. They had confirmed Panu's father in his former job, and took on Panu as his assistant.

'What was the name of this Dutch fort?' asked Stolck. From the Hollander's quickened interest as he translated, Hector surmised once more that Stolck had worked for the Dutch East India Company at some time in the past.

'Fort Keelung.'

Stolck frowned. 'I don't remember hearing of such a place.'

'Perhaps it was too small. My father retired and I had taken his place as foreman when the Chinamen took over.'

Stolck's brow cleared. 'Now I remember. The Company had a small fort on one of the little islands to the north of Formosa. One year it ceased to exist, and I never heard what happened to it.'

'The Chinamen drove out the Dutch.'

'What happened to you?' asked Hector through Stolck.

Panu seemed to retreat into himself as if shrinking from a painful memory. 'I tried to cling on to my job. My father was already an old man and he was killed in the fighting. Later I lost my family and my home when the town was burned to the ground.'

'And what brought you here?'

Panu made a grimace of resignation. 'I was useful to the Chinese because I spoke the languages of commerce. Sometimes they needed me to go on their junks that traded with Japan.'

'That's impossible,' said Stolck to Hector, and then translated for Panu. 'The Japanese forbid any trade with China.'

Panu gave him a weary look. 'There is always smuggling. The Chinese junks did not sail to Japan itself. They came here, to these islands, and dealt with the Japanese merchants through intermediaries. It was very profitable for both sides.'

'So you can speak some Japanese as well?' Hector asked. He was impressed by the man's calm competence, though there was an undercurrent of real sadness.

A look of caution crossed Panu's face. 'The villagers took me in when I chose to desert the China merchants. I have been able to make myself useful.'

Hector turned to Stolck. 'That settles where we are. This island lies somewhere between Japan and Formosa. It's not marked on my chart, but, equally, it's not Cipangu.'

Stolck refused to let his hopes be dashed so easily. 'Tell me,' he said, speaking directly to Panu, 'where do the villagers obtain the gold on their hair pins?'

The interpreter relayed his question to the village elder, who had stood there patiently, and all of a sudden Jeema looked more frightened than ever. He shook his head and muttered a short, unhappy-sounding answer.

'He says this is not a fit question. The Ta-yin decides who can wear a golden sign and he distributes the emblem.'

A spark of suspicion lit up Stolck's eyes. 'He is dodging the question,' he grunted. 'Who is this Ta-yin?'

Panu looked at him steadily. 'In the language of these people it means "the great man". He gives out the pins, and decides who shall receive them. A gold pin is a symbol of authority. Jeema here is the leader of the village council.'

'And where is this Ta-yin now?'

Panu did not consult the village elder before answering. 'No one ever knows when the Ta-yin will arrive, or how long he will stay. He is the master.'

Jeema edged away, looking increasingly ill at ease, as if he did not wish to hear any more of this discussion. Now he bowed once more, then scurried off down the beach at a half-run. A string of empty water barrels had been towed ashore from the *Nicholas*, and he joined his fellow villagers in helping to roll them up the sand.

Hector strolled over to Jacques, who was still sorting through the food baskets delivered by the villagers. For the most part the fruits and vegetables were familiar. He recognized onion, sugar cane, coconut and papaya, though the sweet potatoes had an unusual purple colour. The Frenchman held up a long, green vegetable the shape of a cucumber, but with a spiky skin.

'What do you think this is?' he said, cutting off a slice and offering it.

Hector nibbled the sample cautiously. 'Tastes like melon.'

Jacques surveyed the array of baskets with a gleam in his eye. 'I'm going to enjoy cooking with all this,' he gloated. He picked out an ugly, rough, knobbly object like a misshapen potato with a pale-brown skin, and broke it in half. The flesh inside was a vivid orange-yellow. He sniffed the exposed end and gave a sigh of satisfaction.

'I have never had a chance to cook with this before.' He held out the root for Hector to smell. There was a scent of orange and ginger, and a hint of mustard.

'Turmeric,' the Frenchman announced happily. 'It will give a peppery, earthy taste to my fricassées, and change the colour of the food. But I will not warn the crew in advance. I will enjoy seeing their faces when I serve them yellow gravy.'

He continued to rummage through the baskets and uncovered a cluster of round, green fruits, which looked as though they might be some sort of lemon. He bit into one, made a face and spat out the juice and skin. 'Ugh! That's sour enough to pucker an angel's lips.' Then he grinned. 'But I know something that will take away the after-taste.' He turned to an array of earthen jars standing upright in the sand. Each jar was wrapped in straw, its neck sealed with a cloth plug. Picking up one of the containers, Jacques pulled out the stopper and tipped a dribble of clear liquid into his mouth. He swilled the drink around before swallowing, and gave a contented smile.

'I thought they had brought me jugs of water,' he said, rolling his eyes theatrically. 'But they kept on pointing at them and crying out something like "Awamori. Awamori" until I tried some. It is delicious. My guess is that it is some sort of alcohol made from rice. I have no idea how much you need to drink before you fall down, but doubtless the crew will soon find out.'

Stolck must have reported on his conversation with Panu to Eaton and Arianz, for the three men now came over to where Hector and Jacques stood.

'Look's as though we won't starve on this island,' Eaton said as he surveyed the villagers' offerings.

Hector wondered to himself just how long the humble villagers could be so generous.

'This could be all the extra food the villagers have in reserve,' he said.

Eaton shrugged unconcernedly. 'If we run short, we'll find ways of extracting more. They're a servile lot.'

Arianz rubbed his chin thoughtfully. 'We could put them to work for us.'

Eaton looked at him questioningly.

'They're fishermen, aren't they?' said the quartermaster.

'They don't seem to be doing much fishing at the moment,' grunted Eaton.

'Quite so. If they are idle, why don't we have them make new sails for us? Stolck says their headman offered to provide anything we needed. We should ask him to supply some cloth, and then we can set his people to cutting and stitching.'

Eaton allowed himself a bleak grin. 'The men will like that. It'll take a few days to sort out our sails, and that should give us plenty of time to discover if there's any gold to be found in this place.'

Hector felt he had to speak up. 'But the headman asked us to depart as soon as possible. That's why he and his people are being so helpful.'

'No need for us to dance to his tune,' Eaton retorted callously. 'We'll leave when we want to.'

✱

HECTOR WAS disheartened to see how accurately Eaton had judged the temper of his crew. After they had eaten the meal prepared by Jacques, they voted unanimously to spend at least a week on the island. With full stomachs they sat around in the sunshine, swilling the rice wine and luxuriating in the easy life on offer. Stolck was not alone in refusing to abandon the belief that the island would prove to be rich in bullion. Many of the men were still in the grip of gold fever, and there was much discussion about golden hair pins and the mysterious Ta-yin. The general conclusion was that the 'chief man' controlled the supply. The handful of gold trinkets worn by the villagers was only a hint of what could be obtained if they got their hands on the Ta-yin. All the world knew how Francisco Pizarro had succeeded in Peru by holding the Inca ruler to ransom until his people had filled an entire room with gold. The windbags and braggarts among the crew of the *Nicholas* grew increasingly tipsy on awamori and boasted that when the mysterious 'big man' showed up with his retinue, they would take him prisoner and not release him until they were paid a fortune in gold to go away.

Weary of such bombast, Hector wandered up the beach to get away from their grandiose talk. He found Panu, the interpreter, and Jeema seated unobtrusively in the shade of the bamboo thickets. They were watching over the campsite, and, from the troubled expressions on their faces, Hector guessed neither man was much impressed by the visitors.

'Panu, can you ask Jeema why the villagers are not out fishing on such a calm day?' he asked.

'The Ta-yin stop us to launch our boats,' answered the old man in his stilted Spanish.

'But surely fishing is the village's livelihood?'

'Ta-yin punish us because we allow Ookooma go.'

'Who's Ookooma?'

There was an awkward pause. Then the old man answered, 'The man you bring back from the sea.'

Hector had forgotten about their vanished castaway. No one had seen him since their arrival at the island.

'Maybe it is better he die,' added Panu softly.

Hector looked at the interpreter in astonishment. 'But didn't he have a family, a wife and children to feed and look after?'

'His family feel same.'

'I don't understand,' said Hector. He was perplexed by the stolid resignation in Panu's tone.

'For long time, the villagers not allowed to leave island.'

'But Ookooma was near death when we picked him up. It looked as though he was adrift by accident.'

'Yes, Ookooma was fishing. He good fisherman. That day he go too far and the sea take him away and boat broken. The sea takes him far away.'

'So it wasn't his fault.'

'No matter,' said Panu. 'Ookooma not come home.'

'But why should that result in a ban on the villagers using their boats?'

Panu gave a sigh. 'The Ta-yin say whole village must pay Ookooma's disappearance.'

Jeema must have guessed what was being discussed, for he said something and waited for Panu to translate.

'Jeema say we must obey the Ta-yin and make sure others same.'

Hector shook his head in disbelief. 'Where's Ookooma now?' he asked.

The old man merely stared at the ground, and would not answer.

NINE

THE DAYS PASSED, and Hector could see why Eaton and his men chose to ignore Jeema's requests – repeated over and over again – that they leave the island. The anchorage was the ideal haven, where the crew of the *Nicholas* could recuperate after weeks at sea. Night and day the temperature scarcely varied, and the air was warm enough for the men to sleep on the beach in the open. Rain showers were rare and mostly fell in mid-afternoon. They lasted no more than ten minutes, and the men had no need to take shelter, knowing that the sun would soon reappear and dry out their clothes. By the end of the third day on the island the ship was entirely deserted and lay to double anchors, swinging gently to the regular variation of land and sea breezes. Her crew loafed about on land.

There was little for them to do and nowhere to go. In both directions the beach ended in tumbled masses of coral rock, so broken and jagged and overgrown as to be impassable. Behind the village Jeema showed Hector the terraces carved into the flank of a hill. They were for growing rice, while the middle slopes were planted with fruiting trees. Apart from the faint trace of a footpath leading through the orchards and then up into a thick pine forest that extended to the crest of the hill, the place seemed totally cut off from the outside world.

The visit to the rice fields revealed the whereabouts of the women and children of the village. They were working on the terraces. When Hector appeared – even though he was escorted by the village headman – they fled like startled deer, running until they reached the edge of the woods. There, at a safe distance, they paused as a group and looked back at the visitor. As far as Hector could tell in that distant glimpse, the women wore much the same humble gowns as their menfolk, and Jeema gave him to understand through sign language that at nightfall many of them crept back to occupy their huts with their families, then made sure they were gone by first light in case the strangers entered the village.

'They must feel we are like locusts,' said Jacques ruefully when Hector told him what he'd seen. 'The men still deliver baskets of food to me to cook. But the quantity is smaller day by day. Yesterday there was no pork, and today no more eggs. I think the villagers go hungry.'

Hector looked across to where the village's fishing boats still lay unused on the beach. It was mid-morning and yet there was no sign anyone was preparing to put to sea. 'They would rather starve than disobey their "great man" and go out fishing,' he said.

'Without Dan and his striking iron we would also go hungry,' remarked Jacques.

Each dawn the Miskito borrowed the handiest of the village dugout canoes and paddled out to the reef with his harpoon. There he took quantities of fish, many of them bright with vivid patterns of orange, purple and yellow. Spearing them was easy in the crystal-clear water.

'It's fear of their Ta-yin that makes them so obedient,' said Jezreel. He had sauntered across to join them, his backsword in hand. He was finding the inactivity tiresome and had spent half an hour going through a complicated routine of cuts and slashes, steps and turns, whirling the weapon in all directions until he had worked up a good sweat.

'While you were playing the dancing master, waving that blade, they kept their heads down like they were embarrassed to see it,' observed Jacques with a nod to where a score of villagers sat cross-legged on the *Nicholas*' sails spread on the sand. They were sewing patches where the canvas had torn, restitching weak seams and splicing in bolt ropes that had worked loose. The ship's sailmaker and his assistant sat over to one side, occasionally getting to their feet and strolling among the labourers to give instructions or check the quality of the repairs. Neither man troubled himself to wield needle and thread.

'Eh bien, what is that troublemaker up to?' said Jacques. The sailor named Domine, the man found guilty of stealing water, had left a group of his friends lounging on the sand and watching the sail repairers. He walked across the spread-out canvas towards one of the villagers who sat, head down, concentrating on his work. Reaching the villager, Domine leaned down and whipped out one of the hair pins that held the man's topknot in place. Without pausing, Domine turned and strutted back towards his cronies. He held up his trophy in triumph while his shipmates gave an encouraging cheer. His victim looked up in shocked surprise, dismay and consternation on his face. Slowly, almost hesitantly, he rose to his feet and followed Domine up the beach, holding out his hand for the return of the six-inch pin.

Domine reached his grinning friends and stood before them, holding out the pin to display its golden finial. The villager touched him on the arm. Domine swung round angrily. Putting a hand on the man's chest, he shoved him roughly, sending the villager staggering backwards. 'Basta,' he shouted.

He was showing the pin again to his comrades when, stubbornly, the pin's owner approached a second time. Politely and firmly he tried to take the pin from Domine's grasp. Domine's friends jeered at the sight of the villager, a small wizened man, tackling the sailor. Stung by their mocking,

Domine lost his temper. He swung an arm and struck the man across the ear, knocking him to the ground.

Undeterred, the villager got up and came forward again. Exasperated, Domine transferred the pin to his left hand. Reaching inside his shirt with his right hand, he pulled out the knife that hung in its sheath from a leather thong around his neck. The weapon was not a sailor's working blade, but a slender, lethal stiletto. With a warning scowl Domine held up the weapon and waved it menacingly in front of his tormentor. His shipmates crowed in delight. Sensing the approval of his friends, Domine held up the pin tauntingly with his left hand. Then, as the villager approached, the sailor thrust the stiletto forward, obliging the villager to jump back. More chuckles from his audience, and Domine began to show off. He skipped from side to side, grinning and alternately holding the pin out to the villager, then pulling it back out of reach as he darted the dagger towards his victim.

Still the villager wouldn't give up. He came forward and retreated again and again. Little by little the spectators began to lose interest in the horseplay. 'Prick him where it hurts,' shouted one of them. 'Don't damage his stitching hand,' added another, to a guffaw of laughter. The look on Domine's face changed from mockery to deadly intent. He stopped skipping and settled into an assassin's stance. He held up the pin one last time and dropped the hand with the stiletto lower, level with his thigh.

Watching from a distance, Hector knew what was coming, but was too far away to intervene. The next time the villager advanced, Domine's dagger would come thrusting upwards, puncture the victim's belly low down and leave a wound that was almost impossible to staunch. Desperately Hector looked round for Eaton, hoping the captain would intervene and put a stop to the fatal game. But Eaton stood off to one side, his eyes fixed on the action and, judging by his rapt attention, he had no intention of ending the charade.

The villager came at Domine once again, more cautiously this time, for the sailor's vile mood was evident. Domine's lips tightened as he judged his distance. He held up the pin, and in the same moment stepped forward with his left foot and struck with his stiletto.

What followed was difficult to understand. As the blade travelled upwards, the villager twisted to one side, reached out with both hands and seized Domine's arm in a painfully firm grip. As Domine continued his lunge, his arm was pulled forward and down, throwing him off-balance, and a moment later he was cartwheeling through the air.

The sailor landed sprawling on the sand, flat on his back, with an impact that knocked the breath out of him. There was an interval of astonished silence from the onlookers. Humiliated, Domine scrambled to his feet. He still had his dagger in his hand. Now he ran at his opponent, the stiletto weaving back and forth to confuse his victim. The villager stepped nimbly to one side and avoided the charge. Domine ran past him, and the old man delivered a smashing left-footed kick into the lower part of Domine's back. The sailor felt an agonizing flash of pain in his kidneys, tripped and went face downward.

'How in God's name did he do that?' blurted Hector. Panu had appeared beside him some moments earlier, and the young man turned to him enquiringly. But Panu was no longer there. Looking down, Hector saw that he was doubled up and on his knees. For a moment Hector feared Panu had suddenly been taken ill, and then he became aware that all the villagers who'd been working on the sails were now in the same posture, crouching down, their faces pressed to the ground. Their bodies all pointed up the beach.

Turning to look, Hector saw a figure standing in front of the green wall of bamboos – a man dressed in a type of scaly armour. Layers of metals discs were laced together to make an apron-like surcoat to protect his body. Flaps of the same material covered his shoulders, arms and thighs, and he wore shin guards. His legs were encased in long white socks and thrust into thick-soled straw sandals. Around his waist a broad sash held a three-foot-long sword and a shorter dagger. But it wasn't the weapons and the military style of dress, or the glitter of the lacquered iron platelets, which held Hector's attention. In his right hand the man grasped a nine-foot staff with a banner. The shape of this guidon was rectangular, much taller than it was broad. It hung from a short wooden spreader so that the emblem on the flag was visible even when there was no breeze.

For a strange, unnerving moment Hector was transported back to his childhood. He had seen that same emblem many, many times during his schooldays. It had been scratched on rocks and stones, leaded into windows, embroidered on clothing, drawn and painted on parchment. The friars who taught him had revered it as the symbol of their faith. It was a cross within a circle.

But the villagers, crouched on their knees, were not venerating the flag's mark. Their rigid backs and utter stillness were signs of abject terror.

The curiously armoured man came forward. He walked with a formal, stiff-legged gait, a curious strut, the staff and banner held up before him. He halted and bawled out an order in a strange language.

Instantly all the villagers jumped to their feet and ran like chicks to their mother hen, forming a tightly packed group behind their headman. Then they scuttled forward in formation and, some twenty paces in front of the mysterious man-at-arms, they dropped down and knelt submissively. Not a word was said.

More men emerged from the thicket of bamboos. Many wore the same layered coats of scaled armour. At least a dozen of them carried heavy matchlocks of an antique design. Others had long pikes, their metal tips decorated with red and white bunting. All had long swords thrust through their sashes.

Close behind came a straggle of porters dressed in the same drab garments as the villagers and stooped under heavy packs and bundles. Two of them trotted between the shafts of a sedan chair with dark-green side curtains.

Hector felt a sharp tap on his ankle. 'The Ta-yin. Get down,' murmured Panu. 'And your friends too, or they will die.'

The bearers had placed the sedan chair beside the man with the banner. The curtains were drawn aside and out stepped the Ta-yin.

A short, bulky man, he was comfortably dressed in flowing black trousers and a loose white shirt tied at the wrists. It was difficult to guess his age. His bland, flat face with its dark, almost black eyes was unwrinkled and smooth. He had a small rat-trap mouth, a short neat nose that was slightly hooked, and his jet-black hair had been tightly tied in a queue. He had shaved his hairline back by several inches. It was impossible to know the natural colour of his complexion for his exposed scalp and all his face were covered in a thick coating of white powder.

The Ta-yin completely ignored the men of the *Nicholas*, who stood stock-still, gaping. He walked across and said something to the village headman, who cringed, then rose to his feet and disappeared into the village.

There followed a long, uncomfortable pause. Belatedly the crew of the *Nicholas* realized that they had been taken off-guard. All their weapons were aboard the ship and they were defenceless. Arianz, Stolck and a handful of the crew began to edge quietly towards the cockboat drawn up at the water's edge.

One of the men-at-arms – their officer, to judge by the brilliant lacquer and gilt detailing on his chest armour – barked an order. A dozen of the matchlock men immediately ran down the beach and formed a cordon, preventing Arianz and his men from advancing farther. When Stolck tried to push past, one of the musketeers swung and hit him hard with the stock of his gun.

Hector, still on his feet despite Panu's whispered pleas, saw the village headman scuttle back from his errand. He rejoined his people, bobbed humbly to the Ta-yin and dropped back on his knees.

A movement beside the nearest hut caught Hector's eye. It was Ookooma, the fisherman they'd rescued. He'd not been seen since their arrival in the lagoon. Now Ookooma was on hands and knees, crawling forward. He moved close to the ground like a beaten dog, until he crouched at the feet of the banner man.

The Ta-yin spoke. His voice was angry. Each sentence was short and brusque.

'What's he saying?' Hector whispered to Panu.

'Ookooma has disgraced village by leaving, but worse crime to return with strangers.'

'Christ, he had little choice,' muttered Hector.

The Ta-yin nodded to the man-at-arms in the gilded armour. He marched forward until he was an arm's length from the cowering fisherman.

'Who's that?' Hector asked Panu.

'A bushi. He lead Ta-yin's personal escort.'

The Ta-yin was speaking again, haranguing the group of motionless villagers who kneeled on the ground.

When the Ta-yin finished speaking, the bushi reached down and seized Ookooma by his topknot, hauling him up on his knees. The soldier twisted the topknot cruelly, forcing Ookooma to look towards the open sea. Then he twisted again so that the fisherman faced the crew of the *Nicholas*, who still stood open-mouthed at the spectacle. The fisherman's eyes were tightly closed. The man-at-arms growled an order, and Ookooma opened his eyes. Hector tried to make out some expression on the gaunt face, but Ookooma seemed to be in a trance. There was no trace whatever of the alert, calculating castaway rescued from the sea.

The bushi released the topknot, and at once the fisherman's

eyelids dropped shut again. The man-at-arms stepped back half a pace with his left foot, placed his right hand on the hilt of his longer sword, then uttered a low, sharp grunt. Ookooma's eyes popped open. In one smooth movement the bushi drew the sword, and the long, glinting blade swept through the air. The fisherman's head leaped off his shoulders and his headless corpse fell forward. Blood gushed from the severed neck and seeped into the sand. The head rolled once and lay still.

Hector's stomach heaved. He clenched his hands and swallowed hard. The bushi calmly produced a pad of snow-white cotton and delicately wiped down his blade. Then he carefully slid the sword into its scabbard and strutted back to take up his position at the head of his soldiers.

The 'great man' had shown no interest in the execution. Even before Ookooma fell, the Ta-yin was on his way towards a line of tents and pavilions, which the porters and attendants were busily erecting at the rear of the beach.

'Should I go to speak with him?' Eaton asked Panu. The captain had gone pale under his tan. The crew of the *Nicholas* were slinking away, forming small, anxious groups and murmuring amongst themselves as they cast worried glances towards the armoured troops. Four villagers carried away Ookooma's corpse.

As Stolck translated Eaton's question, Panu blanched. 'On no account approach the Ta-yin without a summons from him,' advised the interpreter hastily. 'He will take it as an affront. You and your men must stay where they are, until he wishes to speak with you.'

✳

THAT EVENING the crew of the *Nicholas* ate only leftovers and scraps. The villagers shunned their camp and could be seen carrying their panniers and baskets to the Ta-yin's tents. None of Eaton's men complained of their meagre meal. When dusk fell they were still debating what they should do next.

'If we fought our way back to the ship, we could turn her cannon against those bastards,' suggested Stolck.

'Fight them with what?' came an immediate objection. The speaker was the elderly, bald curmudgeon who was almost relishing their predicament.

'Knives and cudgels. Jezreel could lead us. We know how good he is in a scrap, and he has his backsword with him.'

'That'll never be enough. You just saw what one of their blades can do.'

Stolck was not to be put off. 'We rush the cordon. A few of us take the jolly boat out to the ship and grab our guns.'

This time Eaton objected. 'Their muskets look antique. But the men in the boat wouldn't stand a chance. They'd be shot to pieces before they got halfway to the *Nicholas*.'

There was a silence, and then Arianz spoke. 'Maybe we should try stealth. Swim out to the ship in the darkness, up anchor and slip quietly away.'

'On wings?' called a voice from the darkness. 'All our sails are still on the beach, and we'd need a pilot to bring us through the channel, as well as a fair wind.'

The discussion dragged on until the small hours. Nothing was decided except that it would be better to stay out of the Ta-yin's way.

They awoke to the unwelcome sight of a work party of villagers at the water's edge. Under the direction of the bushi, they were manhandling three of their larger fishing craft down the beach. Soon a squad of men-at-arms was being rowed out to the ship, and the onlookers could see them clambering aboard.

'The swine are plundering the ship,' said Arianz in disgust. Men were moving about the deck, and a short while later it was evident they were lowering various packages and a number of kegs down into the fishing boats that headed for the shore.

'They're stealing all our gunpowder, the bastards,' added the quartermaster. 'I hope it's too strong for those matchlocks and they blow up in their faces.'

'I've been trying to recall where I saw their emblem before. Now I remember,' Stolck said unexpectedly. Those closest to him fell silent.

'It was when I was working in the VOC's factory in Ke-cho. We received an occasional shipment from Japan. Some boxes had seals with that cross in the circle. The same mark was painted into the glaze of those big jars they used for packing high-value goods. Am I right?'

He looked across at Panu. The interpreter had earlier arrived from the direction of the Ta-yin's encampment.

'The cross in circle is the mon, the emblem of the Shimazu clan,' said Panu softly through Arianz. 'They are overlords of this island and many more, all the way to their homeland in the north, Satsuma.'

At last Hector understood. The *Nicholas* had blundered on to an island lying somewhere between Japan and Formosa. The area was notorious for reefs and shoals and was generally avoided. It was unlikely to be on any chart.

'How far away is Satsuma?' he asked.

'At least a week's sailing with a good wind. The Shimazu forbid outsiders to come to their islands. The people here are their bond servants.'

'Slaves, more like,' grunted Jezreel.

'The Ta-yin follows his own people's code,' said the interpreter carefully. 'He knows no other way. He is bound by honour and a sense of duty.'

'Enough talk of honour,' snapped Eaton. 'I don't care whether that cold-blooded savage wishes to talk to me or not. Let's go find out what he intends to do with us.'

✳

THE TA-YIN's own pavilion was easily identified. Two men-at-arms stood guard in front of it with long pikes. They wore bowl-shaped metal helmets in addition to the now familiar scale armour. Each helmet had a small visor jutting out to protect the eyes, and a long, thickly padded flap hanging down the back of the neck.

Panu had warned the men from the *Nicholas* to stay well back. Led by Eaton and Arianz, they came to a ragged halt some fifteen paces away from the guards.

'My dad brought home a lobster hat like that after his time in Cromwell's cavalry,' remarked one of the sailors. His companion nudged him to be silent. The front of the tent had been pulled aside, and the Ta-yin emerged.

He was wearing the same loose black silk trousers as the day before, and a sleeveless jacket of dark-brown silk. The shoulders of the jacket were so exaggerated they extended well beyond the body. Silver thread picked out the circular mon of the Shimazu on his breast. The Ta-yin's face was again powdered white, but this time his queue of jet-black hair had been oiled, twisted tight and brought up over the crown of his head, then doubled back again. This cockscomb was topped by a round cap of black gauze held in place by a white tape under his chin. He was unarmed, and the handle of a fan protruded from his sash.

An attendant ran forward with a folding stool even as Panu dropped into a humble crouch. The Ta-yin sat, placed his hands on his spread knees, straightened his back and threw out his chest so that, without lifting his chin, his gaze took in the assembled crew. They stood, curious and apprehensive and uncertain what to do. For a full minute the Ta-yin said nothing. His eyes glittered with disdain. When he spoke, his voice came from deep within his chest.

'The Ta-yin says . . .' translated Panu. He shifted his crouching position so that his voice could be heard more clearly by Stolck, who relayed his words into English so that all could hear. 'The Ta-yin says that if he had his way, he would behead all of you forthwith. But he is obliged to consult his superiors and await their instructions.'

'We came here in good faith . . .' began Eaton. The Ta-yin turned on him a look of such ferocity that the captain's voice trailed away.

The Ta-yin was speaking again, and Panu and Stolck were gabbling as they tried to keep up with his words. 'In the Ta-yin's opinion, you are like mongrel dogs who trespass, then lift their legs and piss to mark their territory.'

Eaton coloured with annoyance. 'Tell him we came here by chance, and wish to leave quietly and without trouble.'

Panu muttered his translation, and the Ta-yin's response was curt. 'What is the true intention of your voyage?'

'We are merchants seeking new markets.' The captain was glib with the falsehood.

'You lie. My men have searched your ship and found no trade goods. Only weapons.' The Ta-yin gestured towards various items lying at the feet of his guard commander. The bushi picked up a musket and brought it forward. It was a flintlock from the *Nicholas*.

'Such guns as these are much sought after,' explained Eaton. If he hoped to placate the Ta-yin with an offer to sell him arms, he was promptly disappointed.

'We have no need of guns.'

'They are of modern design, very efficient.' Eaton had adopted a huckster's wheedling tone.

From close to the ground, Panu hissed, 'The Shimazu manufacture their own guns, copies from long ago. Please don't insult them.'

The bushi brought forward a canvas bag and a wooden tube. Uneasily Hector recognized the knapsack in which he kept his navigator's equipment. The Shimazu had ransacked his berth. The bushi opened the tube, slid out the precious chart and unrolled it for the Ta-yin's inspection.

'This is forbidden.'

The bushi meticulously ripped the chart to shreds.

Next, he produced from the knapsack Hector's backstaff.

He turned it over in his hand, uncertain which way up to hold it. Hector felt he should intervene.

Stepping forward, he took the backstaff and then walked a couple of paces towards the stony-faced Ta-yin. Immediately the two men-at-arms lowered the points of their pikes to aim at his chest. Hector came to an abrupt halt.

'This instrument is used for reading the sky,' he began, then slid the vanes back and forth to demonstrate their action.

The Ta-yin's angry interruption cut across his explanation.

'Please step back,' Panu begged, still crouching on the ground. 'The great man says you stink.'

Hector was aware how unwashed and filthy he was compared to the immaculate grandee in front of him. Awkwardly he retreated. The bushi retrieved the instrument and, without waiting for instruction from his master, proceeded to smash the backstaff to splinters.

Next from the knapsack came the almanac. Hector felt a twinge of anxiety. He could make himself a replacement backstaff. But without the almanac and its tables, he would be reduced to using the North Star to establish his vessel's latitude. The Ta-yin had opened the almanac and was idly turning the pages.

'My Lord,' he said loudly, 'that book helps in divination. It foresees the positions of the celestial bodies.'

The Ta-yin lost interest in it and handed the undamaged book back to the bushi, who next offered him a folder of papers. At last the 'great man' showed a flicker of interest. He leafed through the folder, pausing from time to time. Then he returned the portfolio with a single grunted comment.

'What did he say?' whispered Hector.

'Simple and untutored,' Panu translated. The bushi tore up the contents of the folder. Scraps of coloured paper fluttered to the ground. They were the drawings Dan had made on the Encantadas.

Panu swallowed nervously before he relayed the Ta-yin's

next announcement. 'The Shimazu have forbidden on pain of death the ownership or use of weapons of any sort. Yet this morning a bond servant was robbed, then threatened with a knife. Both are capital crimes.'

Several of Eaton's men glanced nervously towards Domine, who was standing in the front rank and close enough to hear the interpreter. A few of them edged away, leaving clear space around him. To his credit, the dark-haired sailor stood his ground. Staring straight at the Ta-yin, he casually spat on the sand.

A shiver of apprehension ran through the crowd of onlookers. At a word from his master, the bushi moved forward, hand on the hilt of his sword. Hector expected to see the blade flash out and cut down the insolent sailor. Instead the man-at-arms carefully disengaged the long sword, still in its scabbard, from his sash. Nodding to an attendant, the bushi handed him the weapon. Then he gestured for Domine to step forward.

Cautiously the sailor moved out into the open. The bushi reached to his sash and withdrew his second sword from its sheath. The blade was short, no more than ten inches long, and clearly designed for close-range hand-to-hand fighting.

Domine understood what was expected. A hint of a smile appeared on his swarthy face. He made a tiny click of approval with his tongue and suddenly the stiletto was in his hand. He edged forward to give himself more room, shifted on his feet to find his balance, and narrowed his eyes as he watched the armoured bushi moving towards him. While the man-at-arms was still several yards away, Domine cocked his arm and threw the stiletto. The attack was delivered with perfect timing and total surprise. The dagger flew towards its target, the bushi's face. An instant later the man-at-arms flicked his blade up. There was a sharp impact of metal on metal, and the stiletto fell harmlessly to the sand.

Domine spun round and ran for his life towards the water's edge and the cockboat.

The Ta-yin gave a single, sharp grunt of disgust. The bushi

didn't bother to chase his adversary, but slid his short sword back into his sheath. A moment later there was a yelp of pain as Domine ran headlong into the cordon of musketeers. He was tripped and then clubbed as he lay on the ground.

Hector held his breath, waiting for what would come next. The men behind him stirred uneasily, overawed and subdued. Someone was quietly muttering a string of profanities. The bushi faced his attendant and accepted back his long sword, bowing and receiving it with both hands in a formal gesture. Carefully he returned the weapon to his belt.

The Ta-yin stayed very still, his gaze unwavering as he inspected the men clustered before him. Slowly and deliberately he drew the fan from his sash and, without opening it, used it to point at someone in the crowd. Hector turned his head to see who it was. A head taller than all those around him, Jezreel was easy to pick out.

The Ta-yin was making some sort of pronouncement. 'That man is also to be punished,' translated Panu. It flashed into Hector's mind that his friend was being made some sort of example because of his huge size. Then Panu added, 'He is guilty of wearing a weapon.'

Projecting over Jezreel's right shoulder was the hilt of the backsword he carried slung on his back.

Understanding that he had been singled out, Jezreel came to the front of the crowd. When Panu repeated what the Ta-yin had said, the former prizefighter spoke calmly to the interpreter. 'Tell him I have earned my right to wear a sword, just as much as that man there.' He nodded towards the bushi.

There was a long interval before the Ta-yin replied.

'The barbarian boasts because he is very big and strong. My captain will teach him that great size is of no consequence in swordsmanship.'

He spoke a few words and an attendant fetched one of the bowl-shaped helmets and handed it to the man-at-arms, who settled it on his head.

Jezreel had already unslung his backsword and was unwrapping the greased rags that kept the blade from rusting. He rolled the rags into a ball, which he tossed to Jacques. The crowd of sailors shuffled back, allowing space for the big man to take a few practice swings with the heavy blade. But Jezreel merely kicked off his shoes and, wearing only a shirt and breeches, stood with sword in hand hanging loosely by his side.

The man-at-arms hesitated and, looking down at the ground, spoke humbly to his master. 'The bushi does not wish to draw his sword,' translated Panu. 'He says it would dishonour his blade to use it against another coward, someone who is preparing to run away.'

The Ta-yin turned his white-powdered face towards the crew of the *Nicholas* and spoke scornfully. 'He says,' continued Panu, 'that, to encourage the big man to stand and fight, he will allow him and his comrades to leave in their ship if he is the victor.'

Apparently reassured, the bushi bowed and placed his right hand on the handle of his longer sword. In a single, graceful movement he withdrew it from its scabbard, raised it over his head and made a sideways movement with his right foot. He brought up his left hand to take a double grip. The blade came slicing down through the air. He stiffened his wrists and the tip of the shining blade came to a stop, pointing straight at his opponent. It was an elegant and controlled display from a lifetime of rehearsal.

Hector looked from one man to the other, desperately trying to imagine how his friend could possibly win the contest. Jezreel towered over his opponent and had a longer reach by at least six inches. But the bushi was armoured from his helmet to his shin guards while, by contrast, the ex-prizefighter was vulnerable to the slightest touch of the Shimazu blade. Hector recalled the lightning speed of the blow that had sliced off Ookooma's head, and the reaction that was quick enough to deflect Domine's stiletto in mid-air. He feared Jezreel would be outpaced. Nor were their two weapons anything like evenly matched. Jezreel's backsword was a utility tool, dull and sturdy, a blade two inches wide and nearly straight, a simple cross-piece and two plain hoops to protect the hand. The bushi obviously held a masterpiece of the swordsmith's art. The blade was designed for both cut and thrust, a glistening strip of polished steel with a gentle curve towards an angled tip, a razor-sharp edge. Hector had a glimpse of the hilt before the bushi drew the sword from his sash. The handle was cross-laced with thongs to provide a perfect grip.

The two combatants faced one another, some ten paces apart in the bright sunlight. There was very little breeze. The Shimazu warrior was tensed and ready, his sword absolutely still, his eyes under the helmet's visor fixed on his opponent. Jezreel still had not lifted his backsword. He seemed distracted, thinking of something else. From time to time he shrugged his massive shoulders, easing the muscles.

Time passed, and Hector was aware of a growing impatience and confusion among the men from the *Nicholas*. He supposed they were wondering if Jezreel had lost his nerve or was regretting that he'd provoked the fight. Hector knew his friend too well to think the same, yet as the minutes dragged by, he was puzzled by Jezreel's inaction.

Across the sandy fighting ground the Ta-yin sat on his folding stool, unmoving and impassive, his face expressionless.

The bushi made a slight move. He brought his left hand up and touched his helmet. For a moment Hector thought he was making some sort of salute or challenge. Then it was clear the man-at-arms was adjusting the position of the visor, the better to shade his eyes.

With a brief stir of hope, Hector wondered if Jezreel was calculating on the benefit of having the sun's glare behind him. He checked where the bushi's shadow fell. But it was barely past midday, and there was very little advantage, if any.

Without warning, Jezreel let out a great bellow. At the same moment he launched himself forward. In huge strides, he covered the ground faster than seemed possible, even for a man of his height and bulk. Still roaring, he charged straight at his opponent's sword. Raising his backsword high above his head, he delivered a massive downward cut at the bushi's helmet. The speed and directness of the onslaught took everyone by surprise, including the Shimazu man-at-arms. For an eye-blink the bushi stood still, as if locked in his rigid pose. Then his training took over. Two-handed, he swung up his sword high enough to protect his head and held it parallel to the ground. It was the correct, classic blocking move. Jezreel's backsword smashed down on the Shimazu blade with a tremendous ringing clang. Under their protective shoulder pads, the bushi's arms flexed like springs to absorb the impact. Then the man-at-arms took a quarter-pace backwards. It was the proper response, to make space for a counter-strike. But Jezreel's backsword was already descending again. The speed of raw violence was shocking. The big man pressed forward, looming over his armoured rival, raining down blows in such quick succession that the clashing steel made a continuous clangour. The bushi was a consummate swordsman. Without losing control he carefully edged backwards, fending off the attack, safe within his armour. He was ready to turn Jezreel's overwhelming strength against the giant. Instead of blocking the backsword, the man-at-arms offered up his own blade at an angle, so that Jezreel's weapon would slide aside and leave the big man open to attack. But Jezreel was not to be deflected. He turned his wrist just before his backsword made contact, so that every blow struck square and with terrific force.

The method was brutal, ugly and graceless. The flurry of blows owed nothing to the finer techniques of fencing. By sheer strength the former prizefighter was battering down his opponent's defence. Gradually the bushi's blocking moves became less effective. His defence began to sag. Too proud, or untrained, to turn and seek a safer distance, he started to weaken. The descending backsword came hacking closer and closer to its target. Finally it connected with the bowl-shaped helmet. Two or three more blows, each more shattering than the last, and the bushi's knees buckled. Like a blacksmith beating metal, Jezreel unleashed one final strike, this time with the hilt of his backsword. He smashed it down on the centre of the bowl-shaped helmet, and the stunned man-at-arms fell face down.

There was a murmur of amazed shock from the watching crowd. The display of rampant physical strength had been stupefying. Several of the Shimazu musketeers were fingering their guns and looking towards their master, waiting for instructions. Hector feared they'd be ordered to shoot Jezreel where he stood, or to fire into the crowd. Backsword still in hand, his shirt soaked with sweat, Jezreel took a moment to catch his breath. Then he addressed Stolck and Panu without even looking at the Ta-yin, 'Tell the "great man" that his honour is now at stake.'

Panu appeared unable to look the Ta-yin directly in the face. The interpreter had risen to his feet during the fight and was about to translate Jezreel's words when the Ta-yin's sour voice broke in. The tone was scathing, the words clipped, spoken in short bursts, this time allowing for translation.

'Barbaric and brutish . . . Only a savage would fight like that . . . but I honour my word. Anyone who is still here this time tomorrow will be killed.'

The men from the *Nicholas* looked at one another with a mixture of relief and urgency. Those in the rear began to hurry back to their camp. Eaton was bold enough to request that the goods stolen from the ship be returned.

The Ta-yin gave him a baleful look. 'No, I promised to let the men go free. Not the goods. Besides, without gunpowder for your guns, you will be obliged to begin learning the true way of fighting with the blade.'

TEN

'HOW DID YOU know what to do?' asked Hector. It was the following day and he and Jezreel were on the main deck of the *Nicholas*, tidying up loose ropes as the vessel carefully eased along the channel through the reef.

'The deft way he beheaded Ookooma.'

Hector winced. He could still picture the single slashing sword stroke, the head jumping off the fisherman's shoulders. 'That would have deterred me,' he confessed.

Jezreel paused to adjust a coil more neatly over a belaying pin. 'When that fellow mentioned that his dad owned an old lobster helmet, it put me in mind of how they did away with King Charles. The headsman used a heavy axe against a chopping block.'

'How did that persuade you to rush on your opponent like a man possessed?' asked Hector.

'King Charles lost his head to a single axe stroke. Everyone knows a headsman sometimes needs three, even four, blows to finish the cut. So imagine what sort of sword you need to do the same job so cleanly.'

'It hadn't ever occurred to me,' said Hector drily.

'Something with an edge so finely honed, and yet so strong and slender, it whips through sinew and bone as you or I might lop a twig from a tree.'

Hector recalled the design of the Shimazu sword. It had a slight curve towards the tip, a longish handle and – if he had seen it correctly – the blade was ridged in the centre.

'And how light it was,' Jezreel continued. 'I watched that warrior wielding it. The sword was like an extension to his arm, beautifully balanced and easy to swing. It wasn't the weight of the sword that carried it through the castaway's neck. It was the quality, shape and flexibility of it, as sweet a blade as you could imagine.'

Jezreel was enjoying his subject. Edged weapons and their use had been part of his livelihood as a prizefighter. 'That warrior had good reason to treat that blade like something very precious.'

'I still don't see the connection between his regard for the sword and the way you attacked him,' said Hector. He recalled how carefully the man-at-arms had handed his sword to the attendant before he went forward to face Domine and his stiletto.

Jezreel was working on a rope's end that had become kinked. His big, scarred hands untwisted the strands until they lay snugly together again. 'I guessed he'd do anything to protect that blade. The cutting edge would easily chip if it hit hard against something really solid. And to knock out even a tiny sliver of metal would be sacrilege, as far as he was concerned.'

'So you rushed at him to threaten the blade, rather than the man himself?'

'Precisely. His first instinct was to defend himself with a blocking blow, using the blunt edge of his sword. Once I'd tricked him into raising his sword, reverse side up, I was going to pin him down, keep him in place and batter him into submission.'

'You picked up his sword after the fight.'

'Yes. I just wanted to check I'd been right. The leading edge was as sharp and fine as a razor, and it had what a cutler calls a grind ridge down the centre of the blade. That left the back edge blunt and gave the blade its strength.'

'But didn't you think of the risk when you hurled yourself forward so blatantly?'

'I worried that my backsword would shatter against such wonderfully wrought steel. But in the end it did the job for me.' He looked across to Dan as he approached them. 'Here's our pilot now. Looks like he got his job done as well.'

The Miskito had spent the last half-hour perched out on the bowsprit, peering down into the water. He had been conning the ship along the channel, giving hand signals to the men at the helm. As usual, he looked very self-composed.

'Safely clear?' asked Jezreel.

'No more coral heads I could see, and after three days of going out to strike fish on the reef, I know the channel well enough to say that we are finished with it.'

Jezreel turned to Hector. 'So it's up to you now. You're still our navigator, even though the fancy topknot made trash of your charts and backstaff. Where do you think we should go?'

'We still have our compasses, so we can retrace the same course that brought us here,' Hector answered without hesitation. He had been mulling over the problem from the moment the *Nicholas* had weighed anchor.

'You mean we head back towards the Thief Islands?'

'With Dan to help me, it'll take only a couple of days to make a replacement backstaff and I've still got the almanac. So I'll soon be able to fix our latitude.'

Jezreel gave Hector a shrewd look. 'Have you come round to our way of thinking that we might find Maria?'

Hector felt uncomfortable and bewildered. He knew he owed a debt to his friends. Their scheming had brought his search for the woman he loved much farther forward. Yet as the possibility of reaching the Ladrones grew stronger, he had begun to have doubts. He secretly dreaded what he'd find in the islands. Maybe Don Alonso in Valdivia had been wrong, and Maria's employer had never taken her to the islands and she was still in Peru. Or Maria had moved on and was no longer there. Worse, some misfortune might have befallen her. There were so many hazards in Spain's far-flung colonies – fevers, unknown diseases, sudden contagions – and few places could be more remote than the Ladrones. If Maria fell sick in such a place, there'd be no doctors, only local remedies, and her death would have been unremarkable. Except to him.

And even if he did find Maria, how would she respond to him after all this time? Maybe she'd changed her mind or had forgotten him for another man. Everything was so uncertain. The more he tried to understand his feelings about her, the more confused he became and the less inclined to share his misgivings.

'Maybe Maria won't even recognize me if we do ever find her,' he mumbled.

Eaton called for him from the quarterdeck, and Hector was grateful to break off the conversation and make his way to where the captain was in conference with the quartermaster.

'Lynch, the quartermaster thinks we should return on the same course that brought us here.'

'I agree. In a couple of days I'll have a replacement backstaff. Dan can help me. He's clever with his hands. And I have the almanac.'

'Do you remember anything from that chart that was destroyed? Any details that might help?'

Hector shook his head. 'No. But I do know the right latitude for the Ladrones. Our safest course is to sail south until we reach that parallel, then turn west until we strike the islands. They should lie across our track.'

'Let's hope we don't overrun them,' said Eaton. 'We've only enough water for ten days, even on short allowance.'

The *Nicholas*' abrupt departure under threat from the Ta-yin had been a hectic scramble. There had only been enough time to carry the half-repaired sails back aboard and load two dozen barrels of fresh water. There had been no point in asking the villagers for supplies. They were cowed into submission by their overlords.

'There'll be no more lolling about on-shore or easy times,' said Eaton grimly. 'When we reach the Ladrones, we keep our weapons and our wits about us, and make it clear that anyone who troubles us suffers.'

*

HECTOR WAS feeling pleased with himself. As he had predicted, land had been sighted after eight days at sea. The lookout at the masthead had reported two islands side by side. But as the *Nicholas* drew closer, the dark double hump on the horizon was revealed as a single large island with a high summit at each end and a saddle of land between.

'Any idea what that place might be, Lynch?' asked Eaton. Like the rest of the crew, Hector was on the foredeck, trying to distinguish the main features of the shoreline. Behind the usual fringe of coral with its breaking waves was a quiet lagoon maybe a hundred yards across. From its beach a coastal plain extended to a line of reddish-grey bluffs, which marked the boundary of a plateau. Farther on, the ground climbed steeply to rugged highlands. Everywhere was solid green – the feathery tops of coconut palms on the lowland, dense jungle on the bluffs and lower slopes of the mountain, open grassland on the summit.

'One of the Thief Islands,' Hector answered. 'But I have no idea which one.'

'This time we won't poke our heads in a noose. We work our way round to the south until we get into a lee. Then we'll either heave to or drop anchor.' Eaton walked briskly back to the quarterdeck. A short while later the *Nicholas* turned and began to follow the coast.

Hector continued gazing at the shore. His eye was caught by a pale triangle among the breakers crashing on the reef.

154

Moments later he saw several more of these triangles, rising and falling to the rhythm of the waves, keeping pace with the ship. It took several minutes for him to realize they were sails. The boats beneath them were either too small or too low in the water to be visible at that distance.

'Frisky little beggars,' observed a sailor standing beside him. 'You'd have thought they'd capsize in that surf.'

The sailing boats quickly worked clear of the surf and set a slanting course to intercept the *Nicholas*. Hector squinted in surprise. Something was strange. He'd grown accustomed to the pace of movement at sea: the initial glimpse of a distant sail, the long, slow approach as the other vessel drew closer and closer, and the sudden haste in the final moments. But this was different. The cluster of triangular sails, at least a dozen of them, was approaching at the pace of a troop of horsemen moving at a brisk trot. They were catching the *Nicholas* as if the larger ship was dawdling, instead of pressing forward under full sail.

Hector took another look at the oncoming boats.

They reminded him of a school of hurrying dolphin. They surged across the surface of the sea, spray flying, thrusting the water aside, often showing the full length of their hulls, which were painted a rusty red with white trim.

The sailor beside him let out an admiring whistle. 'They must be doing twelve knots, maybe more,' he said. 'You wonder they don't thrash themselves to bits.'

Soon the boats were very much nearer. Hector could see their general resemblance to the dugout canoes on the coast of West Africa. Yet these craft were altogether lighter and more finely shaped. Projecting out from the side of each of them was a structure that he had never seen before. A frame of poles supported a second, much smaller hull some six or seven feet away. This second hull acted as a long, narrow float and balanced the vessel so that it skimmed over the tops of the waves instead of ploughing through them.

Several of the *Nicholas'* crew had gone below to fetch their muskets. They were back on deck, loading powder and shot and checking the flints were dry.

'Don't shoot unless you have to. We must conserve our powder,' shouted Arianz from the quarterdeck. Everyone knew his meaning. The Ta-yin's men had carried off the kegs that contained the vessel's reserve stock of gunpowder. All the men had left was whatever they had previously transferred to their powder flasks.

'They do not look warlike,' observed Dan. He had joined Hector on the foredeck and was watching the approaching canoes. The Miskito's dark eyes lit up with approval. 'Now there is something I would like to try out at home,' he said. 'Those side floats are ingenious. They make their craft sit higher, and able to carry more sail, than we would among my people.'

The leading canoe had drawn level with the *Nicholas*. The canoe's crew were skilfully spilling wind from the sails to slow down their craft and keep pace with the lumbering visitor. Hector saw Eaton glance farther aft. The remaining canoes were also closing the gap. Soon the *Nicholas* would be surrounded by a squadron of the strangers.

'Don't let any of them come aboard,' the captain ordered harshly. 'Make them keep their distance.'

The lead canoe carried four or five men, who stood and shouted.

'What is it they are calling?' Jacques asked.

Hector strained to hear. 'I think they're calling out "Hierro, hierro", Spanish for iron.'

'Well, at least they have a few words of a language we can understand,' grunted the Frenchman.

One of the canoe men picked up a basket from the bottom of his craft and held it up on show.

'He wants to trade iron for whatever he has in that basket,' said Hector.

As usual Dan had the keenest eyesight. 'They've brought out coconuts and other fruit.'

'Mon Dieu, thank God for that,' exclaimed Jacques. 'I'm sick of the men complaining about mouldy salt fish and the maggots in the bread.'

Several of the *Nicholas*' men had begun waving at the other canoes to come closer, but a bellow from Eaton stopped them. 'Wait until we have found shelter. Then we'll trade.'

For the next half-hour the *Nicholas* ran on, the strange spidery canoes keeping pace with ease. The vessel cleared the southern point of the mainland and an obvious anchorage came into view, where a small island offered shelter from the north-east breeze. Slowing, the *Nicholas* headed for a patch of smooth water. The leadsman cried out that there were twenty fathoms of water, and her helmsman put her sails aback. Even before the anchor was let go, her escort of canoes came clustering forward.

'Remember, allow no one aboard,' repeated Arianz.

'Hierro, hierro,' the natives shouted.

'I'll give them hierro,' growled a suspicious sailor. 'Bunch of arse-naked savages.'

Not one of the islanders wore a stitch of clothing. Big, strapping men, their skins were a dark tawny colour with a very slight hint of yellow. They were taller than many on the *Nicholas*, and had large, square, fleshy faces. Most wore their long, black hair loose, though a few had shaven skulls and top-knots. They appeared self-confident and friendly.

'Have we any spare iron to trade with them?' asked Jacques.

'Only odds and ends,' said Jezreel.

One of Eaton's men was holding up a couple of broken links of anchor chain for the canoe men. They shook their heads and began making a circular motion with their arms.

'What are they trying to tell us?' asked Hector.

Dan clicked his fingers as he worked out the answer. 'They want iron barrel hoops – most ships would carry them.'

The cooper was sent for, and he reluctantly agreed to dispose of three damaged hoops from his stores. These were waved in the air, and immediately two of the canoes shot closer.

A barter followed. Stolck leaned over the gunwale, acting as negotiator. Eventually, after much sign language and haggling, it was agreed to exchange two iron hoops for five baskets filled with fruit. Then a native on the second canoe pointed to some large gourds lying at his feet, and held up one finger.

'What is that one trying to sell?' asked Jacques.

'Coconut oil, I guess,' said Dan. The islander mimed wiping the contents of the gourds on his skin and using it to dress his hair.

'Fresh coconut oil,' said Jacques eagerly. 'Let me have that. I will mash up the last of our stale bread and make fried doughboys.'

'Make sure they don't cheat us,' Dan warned Stolck. 'Get the fruit and oil on board before we part with the iron hoops.'

The two canoes sidled alongside, ropes were lowered and baskets and gourds attached. Only when these were lifted into the ship were the iron hoops relinquished. The crews of the canoes appeared to be very pleased with their trade. Their sheet-handlers tightened their lines. The men in the stern twisted their paddles to act as rudders and the canoes veered away, rapidly gaining speed as they headed back to the distant shore.

Stolck brought the first basket of fruit across to Jacques and laid it on the deck. 'There you are, Cook. There should be plenty to go round.' He began to lift out the coconuts. Then he swore. Underneath the top layer of fruit the basket had been filled with rubbish and gravel.

Jacques dipped a spoon into the coconut oil and licked it. 'Delicious,' he announced. Then he looked down at the surface of the gourd and frowned. He dipped the spoon again, tasted and spat. 'Putain!' he exclaimed. 'We have been cheated. The coconut oil is only floating on the surface. The rest is sea water.'

Jezreel threw back his head and gave a huge roar of laughter. 'Well, now we know for sure that we're at the Thief Islands.'

*

IT WAS A disgruntled boat crew who pulled ashore to the small island next morning in the jolly boat. Three men with loaded muskets stood guard on the beach while the rest of the shore party set about climbing the nearest coconut trees and throwing down the fruit. No natives were to be seen, though everyone had the uncomfortable feeling they were being watched. A rivulet spilled out on the beach close to the landing place, and the men dug a cistern trench so that the casks and big earthenware jars could be filled. But the supply of fresh water was little more than a trickle, and it was clear that the *Nicholas* would be staying several days.

For safety, most of the men stayed on board while the laborious task of watering slowly went forward. They could see many triangular sails of the native craft in the distance. But it was not until the third morning that one of the vessels was seen heading for the anchorage. It came directly to the *Nicholas*. This time the natives on board were not nude, but wore long, sack-like shirts made of palmetto leaves sewn crudely together. Their leader – a tall, brawny man with an impressive mop of hair – offered up a leather pouch, which was brought to Eaton. Opening it, he pulled out four sheets of paper. After a quick glance he beckoned to Hector.

'Lynch, come over here. You can make better sense of them.'

Hector took the pages and read through them slowly. 'All four are the same,' he said, looking up at Eaton. 'It's just that they're written in Latin, Spanish, Dutch and French.'

'What do they say?' asked Eaton.

Hector selected the Spanish version and read out, 'To the commander of the unknown vessel now lying off Cocos Island.

We would know your purpose in coming here. If you are Christians, you will find safe shelter at our port of Aganah. Our messenger will guide you here. Trust him, but not the Chamorro.'

'Who are the Chamorro?'

'They must be natives, the indios as the Spanish would call them.'

'And who sent this letter?'

Hector pretended to check the signature again. But he had no need to. It had been the first thing he had looked at, wondering if the letter came from the Governor of the Ladrones, Don Fernando de Costana. He should have been in office for at least a year now, with his wife, Maria's employer. But Hector hadn't recognized the name.

He made a conscious effort to hide his disappointment. 'It's signed by Sarjento Mayor Damian de Esplana. He describes himself as Maestre de Campo at the Presidio of Guahan.'

'Well, at least we know exactly where we are,' Arianz broke in. 'Guahan is the largest of the Thief Islands, and Aganah is the provincial capital.'

Eaton rubbed his chin thoughtfully. 'Why should this Esplana offer us shelter in his harbour? Sounds like a trap.'

'I think not,' said Arianz. 'He hopes we are either Spanish or French, or even Dutch, and therefore friendly.'

'And what about the Latin?'

'He's guessing that we would know the language if we were Catholics.'

'Or because Latin is a common language between nations,' pointed out Hector.

The quartermaster ignored him. 'Aganah is the most isolated place in the entire Spanish empire. This Esplana probably doesn't see more than one ship or two in a year. He'll be keen to enlist our help.'

Eaton frowned. 'What makes you say that?'

'Because he said not to trust the Chamorro. If they are the native people, then he's obviously on bad terms with them.'

'The men who brought the message are natives.'

'Tame ones. Not like the mother-naked lot we saw first.'

Eaton was no longer listening. He thrust the French version of the letter towards Jacques.

'Here, tell me whether it's written by a Frenchman.'

Jacques read through the letter, then shook his head. 'Definitely not.'

'Can you pass yourself off as a French officer?'

The Frenchman gave a sarcastic laugh. 'This brand on my face will not help.' He rubbed the galérien's G on his cheek, the brand faintly noticeable beneath his deep tan.

Eaton turned to Hector. 'What about you? He's your friend. Will you support him?'

Hector was wary. He and Dan both spoke reasonable French. They had first teamed up with Jacques when all three had served in King Louis' galley fleet. 'It depends what you want me to do.'

'I want you to go to meet with this Esplana.'

'So you won't take the *Nicholas* into his harbour?'

Eaton shook his head. 'Too dangerous. He'd soon work out we're not to his liking.'

Hector thought long and hard before answering. He was being offered the perfect chance to investigate whether Maria was on the island. Yet if he came face to face with Don Fernando, everything would be ruined.

'I can't do it,' he said finally. 'The Governor might recognize me.'

'You know the Governor?' Eaton's pale-green wolf's eyes suddenly filled with suspicion.

'When he was a high official in Peru, I negotiated with him for the ransom of his wife. I was told that he'd moved here when I was held prisoner in Valdivia,' Hector confessed.

Eaton's voice took on a menacing rasp. 'That's the first I heard of it, Lynch. I thought you were slippery when you hoodwinked my crew back on the Encantadas. Now I know for sure. Is this where you wanted to come all along?'

Hector refused to be cowed. 'I've had no hand in what has happened these past few weeks. The crew made their own decisions.'

Eaton glared angrily at the young man. Then he swung round to face Jacques. 'Lynch is too craven to meet the Spaniards, so you'll have to manage on your own. I want you to scout this place of refuge we are being offered. Find out if its defences are weak enough that we can seize and loot it. Say that we are a royal ship sent by King Louis to search for new lands for trade and plantation.'

Jacques shrugged casually. 'Bien. If this Esplana asks about my face, I will say I was released from the galleys because I am a skilled mariner and volunteered for this exploring mission.'

'The question may never arise,' said Eaton.

'We can't attack Guahan,' said Arianz. 'We don't have enough powder for our guns.'

Eaton's expression grew more cunning. 'I've thought of that. If Esplana wants our help against the indios, then we'll say we'd be happy to assist. We'll claim that our stock of powder got ruined by the sea air, and ask him to send us a few barrels.' He gave a nasty smile. 'Then we'll use it to attack him.'

*

JACQUES BOURDON, former Parisian pickpocket, burglar and ex-galérien, enjoyed masquerading as a seasoned mariner. Wearing a set of Eaton's better clothing, he perched on the centre thwart of the native sailing canoe as it headed north along the coast of Guahan. Normally Jacques disliked small boats. He found them slow, wet and unsteady, and they made him seasick. But this vessel was different. The side float made it much more stable, almost comfortable, and the stiff breeze pushed the vessel along at a fine pace. This would not be a long trip.

Jacques shifted position slightly so that he could see past the sail of palm-leaf matting. The canoe – he had managed to learn from the crew that they called it a 'galaide layak' – was running into a sheltered bay. There was no sign of any coral reef. Deep water extended all the way to a short wooden pier, where a collection of thatched roofs lay along the lower part of an attractive valley. The grasslands on the slopes above the settlement were washed a pale lime-green by the morning sunshine.

'Aganah?' he asked, pointing forward. Close to the jetty rose the solid square shape of a small fort. It had to be the Spaniards' Presidio.

The boatman with the extravagant bush of hair nodded.

Ten minutes later Jacques had clambered up on to the pier and was walking by himself towards the settlement. The houses with their weathered grey thatch were nothing more than overgrown cabins, too humble for the Governor of the Ladrones. His residence would be inside the fort itself, safe behind its fifteen-foot walls of coral blocks. Two small towers served as cannon platforms, and an open space had been left clear to provide a field of fire. But there was no sign of a sentry on the parapet, and the double gates of the entrance were closed.

Jacques picked up a stone and banged on one of the gates. The thick timber gave back a muffled thud. After an interval a voice demanded to know their business.

'Visiteur,' Jacques shouted, emphasizing his French accent.

The heavy gate eased just enough to enable him to step inside. Immediately he was through, it was dragged shut behind him. Jacques looked around. The area within the walls was considerably larger than he had expected. There was space for a little chapel, a barracks block and several storehouses. They were all modest, single-storey buildings with tile roofs and mud-brick walls. Small windows had unpainted shutters against the sun, and one or two were barred. The only substantial two-storey building had a balcony and porch and overlooked the parade ground. Judging by the flagstaff in front of it, this was where the Governor and his senior staff had their offices and accommodation.

Jacques presumed the four men whose combined strength had been required to shift the heavy gate were members of the garrison. They were uncommonly slovenly and, judging by their expressions, they resented being disturbed.

'The Governor?' Jacques asked in Spanish. Before he received an answer, he became aware of a man in a faded blue jacket of military cut, who emerged from the larger building and was striding across the parade ground.

'You must be from the foreign ship,' announced the new-comer. A short, brisk man in his mid-forties, everything about him spoke of a regimental background: close-cropped iron-grey hair, straight back and square shoulders, crisp manner of speech, the frank appraising stare he gave the visitor.

'My name is Louis Brodart. I am sailing master of the *Gaillon*,' Jacques said in French. Inwardly he was gleeful. It was unlikely anyone but a Parisian would know that the Gaillon district of the city was renowned for its open sewer. Or that he had borrowed the surname of the most corrupt government official in France, the Intendant of the Royal Galleys.

'Sarjento Mayor Damian de Esplana, at your service,' answered the officer. He spoke halting but competent French. 'Welcome to the Presidio of Guahan.'

Jacques decided he should get straight to the point. 'My captain asked me to deliver his compliments to the Governor.'

'Don Fernando de Costana is absent. I am the commanding officer of the garrison.'

'Will the Governor be returning soon?'

'He has gone to another island to deal with the indios. I do not expect him back for at least a month.' If the Sarjento

Mayor had noticed the galérien's brand, he was too polite to mention it.

'A pity. My captain's instructions are to present our credentials solely to the Governor. The Secretary of the Navy, the Marquis de Seignelay, was most particular in this regard.'

Esplana brightened. 'Then, by all means, your captain can take his vessel to Saipan, the island where Don Fernando has gone. But first let me offer you some refreshment. I would appreciate hearing news from the outside world. We see few ships.'

He escorted his visitor towards the building with the porch. On the way they passed a sizeable vegetable patch dug in a corner of the parade ground. The Sarjento Mayor gestured apologetically.

'Not a very military sight. My men are better gardeners than soldiers. But under the circumstances, it is sensible to grow some of our own food.'

Esplana's office was entered through a side door. The room was spartan, with whitewashed walls, a plain desk with a black iron candlestick, four chairs, an army chest and no decoration except for a small wooden cross, a mirror of polished steel and a sword and baldric hanging from a peg. A servant appeared with a tray of glasses. Jacques picked up his drink and tasted. It was mildly fizzy, with a pleasant, alcoholic tang. Esplana noted his appreciation. 'The natives call it "tuba". Fermented from the sap of the coconut palm.'

When the servant had withdrawn, Esplana gestured for the Frenchman to take a seat. Going to his desk, Esplana adopted a more serious expression. 'Thank you for coming here so promptly in answer to my message.'

'My captain regrets he is unable to bring his vessel directly to your port. He's instructed to seek out new lands for trade and plantation. Our visit to the Ladrones—'

'Las Marianas,' Esplana corrected him. 'They were renamed some years ago during the regency of the late King's widow.'

Jacques wondered if his slip had aroused the Spaniard's suspicion. A French government mission would be expected to know the archipelago's official new name, though ordinary mariners still spoke of the Thief Islands. He ploughed on. 'We called at the Marianas only to take on water. Very shortly we continue on our way.'

Esplana placed both hands on his desk and leaned forward, his eyes grave, almost pleading. 'Before you depart, I hope your captain will find time to prove the friendship that exists between our two countries.'

'My captain has authorized me to decide what is in the best interest of our mission,' said Jacques neutrally. He waited for the Spaniard to explain.

'You have seen the indios, the naked natives, I'm sure,' said Esplana. 'The Governor is charged with their reducción, as we say – their conversion to the faith, their civilization. But they resist fiercely.'

'The few we have met seemed friendly enough, though in need of clothing.'

'Don't be fooled. The Chamorro are vicious, brave and stubborn. They cling to their old ways. Governor Costana has taken the best of the men and sailed north to Saipan to put down an uprising there. The Chamorro murdered a missionary priest.' The Spaniard gestured towards the door. 'You've seen the sort of men I've been left to work with. Idlers, drunks, former gaolbirds sent here from New Spain.'

That explained the absence of a lookout at the fort and the closed gates, Jacques thought. The Sarjento Mayor had decided to stay bottled up within the Presidio. 'The town did seem to be very quiet,' he ventured.

'The situation is very tense,' Esplana went on. His eyes flicked towards the open window. 'We hold hostages, a couple of the Chamorro chiefs, but . . .'

'The message boat you sent was manned by indios, as you call them.'

'They belong to a clan that favours us. Fortunately the Chamorro spend more time fighting among themselves than trying to defeat us. Without the rivalry between the clans we would be lost.'

'Are they well armed?'

'Thank God, no. They have no firearms. They use slings and spears tipped with human bone.' The Spaniard gave a sour smile. 'They say they prefer killing the taller strangers because their longer shinbones make better spear points.'

'Dangerous foes,' Jacques agreed.

Esplana was blunt. 'Your men and the firepower of the *Gaillon*'s cannon would make a great difference.'

Jacques seized the opening. 'Unfortunately we must conserve our gunpowder. Much of what we took aboard in Brest when we sailed was useless. The rest got wet on the voyage and is spoiled.'

'I can remedy that,' said Esplana promptly. 'I can send you twenty, maybe thirty kegs, from our own reserves.'

'Won't that leave you short?' asked Jacques.

'I still have enough to repel an assault on the Presidio. I am expecting resupply quite soon. The Acapulco Galleon should pass through the straits within the month.'

'The Acapulco Galleon?' Jacques was momentarily at a loss.

'You would know it better as the Manila Galleon.'

Jacques must have continued to look puzzled because the Sarjento Mayor went on, 'I speak of the galleon on its westward trip, to the Philippines. The vessel carries travellers on their way from New Spain to Manila and the silver needed there to pay for the China trade. Either it makes a stop in Guahan to unload mail and passengers. Or, if the voyage is behind schedule, the ship waits in the straits north of here, and our friendly natives go out to take off the supplies.'

So that's why the Chamorro came out to huckster with us, Jacques thought. They greet any passing ship in this fashion.

Esplana continued to press his case. 'And even if the

Acapulco Galleon cannot spare the munitions, a patache is also due from New Spain. Indeed, she may get here sooner than the galleon. The patache carries stores specifically destined for us, including gunpowder. Afterwards she continues on to Manila. If your vessel could sail to Saipan to assist the Governor, we could breathe easily. Don Costana will teach the indios a lesson, with the help of your cannon.'

'Very well,' said Jacques. 'On behalf of my captain, I assure you that the *Gaillon* will go to the assistance of your Governor. We can save a few days if you send us the gunpowder we require and a native who can pilot us to Saipan.'

They toasted their agreement and drained their glasses. As the officer poured him another drink, Jacques gave him what he hoped was a friendly look. 'It must be a lonely life here.'

'For most of us it is,' confessed the Spaniard. 'My troops, if you can call them that, form attachments with local women. For myself, I have devoted my life to the service of my country.'

'How about Governor Costana? Does he feel the same?' asked Jacques offhandedly. He intended to lead the conversation around to the Governor and his domestic arrangements. That way he would be able to tell Hector whether Maria was living in the fort.

'He was posted here from Peru. The result of some scandal, I believe. He brought his wife with him, Doña Juana. A fine woman. She too has a sense of duty.'

From the parade ground came the sound of the chapel bell striking noon. To Jacques' disappointment, Esplana got to his feet. 'I would ask you to join us for our midday meal. But frankly our cook is useless, and the sooner you carry my message back to your vessel, the happier I will be.'

As Jacques accompanied the Spaniard outside, he thought quickly.

'Commandant, I have a small favour to ask.'

'What is it?'

'That vegetable garden . . .'

'It varies an otherwise monotonous diet.'

'Would it be possible for me to carry back some of the produce to the ship? I see there are some carrots and celery. My captain would greatly appreciate some green stuff on his table.'

'Of course. I'll have a man select what you need.'

'And we are also short of spices. I understand this island produces excellent ginger.'

Esplana smiled. 'You live up to your nation's reputation. Our mess cook is so incompetent he thinks salt is an exotic spice. But maybe the Governor's kitchen has some ginger to spare. If you will accompany me, I will make enquiries.'

They walked across to the main entrance of the administration building. Esplana knocked. The door was opened by a maidservant in her teens. She wore a shawl worked with Peruvian patterns, and Jacques guessed she'd been brought from South America with the Governor's entourage. She curtsied politely.

'Ask your mistress if we may speak with her cook,' Esplana said.

The girl held the door open for them to step inside and disappeared into an inner room to consult her mistress.

A moment later a door opened, and a young, handsome, dark-haired woman dressed in a plain brown skirt and grey bodice stepped out.

'Sarjento Mayor,' she said, 'I'm afraid our cook is not here. He accompanied the Governor.' Her glance took in Jacques and for a heartbeat she seemed to falter.

'May I introduce Monsieur Brodart of the French ship *Gaillon*,' said Esplana. He turned to Jacques. 'I have the pleasure of introducing Señorita Maria da Silva.'

Jacques bowed. 'Delighted to meet you, Señorita.'

Maria looked at him strangely.

Esplana was in a hurry. 'I apologize for disturbing you, Señorita. We had a small question for the cook, but we can discuss it another time. Monsieur Brodart is on his way back to his ship.' He ushered Jacques out of the house. Jacques only had time to bow once more. As he did so, he deliberately held her gaze and willed her to recognize him.

✳

HECTOR HAD waited anxiously for Jacques' return. The moment the messenger boat came alongside the *Nicholas*, he climbed down to help his friend lift a basket of vegetables from the bilge. 'Did you see Maria?' he whispered.

The Frenchman nodded.

'How is she?' Hector's voice was hoarse with tension.

'She is fine.'

'Did you manage to speak to her?'

'No. I had to get away. The Governor's wife might have shown up. If Doña Juana had recognized me, that would have been a disaster.'

An impatient shout from Eaton put an end to their hurried conversation.

'I will tell you more later, Hector,' Jacques muttered as he scrambled up the ship's side.

Eaton and Arianz listened carefully to what Jacques had to say about his visit to the Presidio. 'Sounds like we could storm the fort,' said Arianz.

'And for very little reward,' Eaton retorted sharply. 'I have a better idea. Call the men together.'

With the crew of the *Nicholas* assembled in the waist of the ship, Eaton asked Jacques to repeat to them what he had witnessed in Guahan. 'Don't leave anything out, including your conversation with the Sarjento Mayor.'

When Jacques had finished speaking – omitting only his encounter with Maria – Eaton raised his voice.

'I propose we wait here at anchor until we receive our gift of gunpowder.'

There was a general mutter of agreement. Even those most

eager to continue the homeward voyage preferred to sail in a ship that could use her cannon.

Eaton paused for effect. Then he announced, 'Immediately afterwards, we sail north.'

There was a puzzled silence. 'What for?' someone shouted. 'We'd be better leaving this shithole.'

'Because we would be turning our backs on the biggest prize of all if we didn't,' called Eaton.

'What's that?' He had their full attention now.

'The Acapulco Galleon. You heard the Frenchman. The vessel carries the silver from New Spain to pay for a year's worth of silks and valuables that have accumulated in Manila.'

'We can never take a galleon. She'll be too big, too well armed, too many men aboard.' As Eaton had expected, the objection came from the elderly, balding deckhand who always found fault.

'The Acapulco Galleon will have been eleven weeks at sea,' Eaton countered. 'Her crew will be on short rations, tired and slack. It's the moment to attack.'

'But there will still be one or two hundred men aboard. Even if they're famished, that is more than we can handle.'

'We won't be alone.' There was a triumphant, calculating look on Eaton's face.

'What do you mean?' called another voice.

'I propose that we enlist the help of the indios.'

There was a surprised but thoughtful silence from the assembled crew.

'And how could they help us?' Eaton saw that the speaker was the Dutchman, Stolck.

'We take the Acapulco Galleon by surprise.' Eaton was relishing the chance to display his cunning. 'When the vessel enters the strait, our Chamorro allies will go out in their canoes to meet the ship, as is their custom. No one on board the galleon will suspect anything.' He paused to look out over the expectant faces of his men. 'As usual the Chamorro will offer to barter.

Hidden among them will be some of us with our muskets. At the right moment we spring our ambush, shoot down the helmsmen, board the ship. We can rely on the indios to deal with the rest.'

There was an interval while his audience digested the audacity of the plan.

'I wouldn't trust those heathens,' shouted the old man. 'They'd slit our throats.'

But his shipmates were looking at one another, considering the captain's proposal. Some were doubtful. They didn't like the idea of working with the natives, and said so. Others were more excited. There was a babble of comment, nearly all of it favourable. Suddenly the loot from a rich Spanish galleon seemed within their grasp.

Arianz stepped up to the rail. 'We put it to the vote. Those in favour of attempting to seize the Acapulco Galleon, raise your hands.'

The quartermaster counted the vote.

'Those who would continue on for home.'

Fewer hands rose.

'Then it's decided.'

Standing among the men, Hector's mind was in turmoil. He was giddy with excitement that he had located Maria. She was alive and apparently well, and he longed to see her. For a mad moment he toyed with the idea of deserting the *Nicholas*, swimming ashore, finding his way to the Presidio and locating Maria. But he knew that was utterly impractical. It would mean abandoning his friends, which he couldn't do, and it was reckless. Governor Costana, when he came back from campaign, would be merciless. In his eyes Hector was still a murderous sea robber. Maria, who had once seemed so far away, was very much closer. But in another sense she was still as distant as she had ever been.

ELEVEN

MAESTRE DE CAMPO DAMIAN DE ESPLANA proved to be as efficient as his manner had suggested. The evening after Jacques got back to the ship, a galaide layak delivered a dozen kegs of gunpowder to the *Nicholas*, and with them a Chamorro pilot. A gaunt, taciturn man with a heavily pockmarked face, he was dressed in cast-off European clothing and had a small crucifix on a cord around his neck. In halting Spanish he said that his name was Faasi, and he had a paper to deliver to the captain.

'Let's have a look at it,' said Eaton. It was a crude sketch map of the Ladrones. The fifteen islands, varying in size, stretched away in a chain running northwards. Guahan was marked by name, as were half a dozen of the others. The rest were anonymous.

'Is that where we find the Governor?' said Eaton, placing his finger where Esplana had drawn an arrow on the map against one of the farther islands.

The Chamorro stared at the map, but looked blank when Hector translated the question.

'I don't think he understands maps,' said Hector. 'He probably hasn't seen one before.'

'Maug – the island is called Maug, according to what's written here,' snapped Eaton.

At the mention of the name, Faasi's face cleared. He nodded. 'Yes, Governor at Maug,' he said.

'How long to sail there?' enquired Eaton.

'Two days, no more,' answered the Chamorro.

Eaton frowned. It was impossible to judge the scale of the sketch map. But clearly Esplana had made an attempt to draw the islands to their relative sizes.

'Looks like more than two days' sail to me,' he said, 'unless the ship grows wings.'

'Best to get started right away, now that we've got our powder,' suggested Arianz.

Eaton treated the Chamorro to a thoughtful glance. Hector guessed the captain was trying to judge whether Faasi was capable of recognizing that the ship wasn't French.

The quartermaster must have been thinking along the same lines. Laying a hand on the captain's arm, he drew him to one side and Hector overheard him ask quietly, 'Do we really need a pilot now that we've got a map? We should toss him overboard as soon as we're off-shore.'

Eaton shook his head. 'The map's too vague, and we still need the man to tell us exactly where we lie in wait for the galleon and where we can recruit our new allies.'

Arianz tugged at his earlobe doubtfully. 'You seem very sure that the natives will fall in with our plan.'

'That is where the pilot can be even more helpful, though he does not know it yet,' the captain assured him.

Eaton wasted little time. He weighed anchor at first light, and by early evening the *Nicholas* was abreast of the northern end of Guahan. Here the Chamorro pilot pointed out the place where the Acapulco Galleon normally paused to transfer her cargo.

'Ask our pilot if he knows a safe anchorage on the next island along the chain,' the captain demanded. He had the sketch map in his hand. 'It's name is written here as Rota.'

When Hector relayed the question, Faasi's eyes widened in alarm.

'He says the people that live there are his enemies. It's not the place where he was told to bring us.'

Eaton allowed himself a mirthless smile. 'Then that's precisely where we pay our next call.' He ordered the helmsman to maintain course and the crew to shorten sail. Throughout the night the *Nicholas* crept forward until the rising sun showed Rota's hills some five miles ahead. The masthead lookout called down to say that he saw no sign of a barrier reef. 'Make a slow, leisurely approach,' Eaton ordered the helmsman. 'The slower, the better. We want our arrival known. Lynch,' the captain went on, 'I'm sending you ashore to contact the locals. Our pilot here will go with you.'

'I doubt he'll want to.'

Faasi was fingering his little wooden cross nervously and casting worried glances around the ship. Clearly the sight of Rota so close up had rattled him badly.

'He'll have no choice,' said Eaton. He nodded to Stolck and Arianz. The unfortunate pilot was seized and his arms pinioned. He was so shocked that he offered no resistance as his wrists were lashed behind his back.

'We'll offer him to our future allies,' Eaton smirked. 'When they see you land with him trussed up like a chicken and recognize him as an enemy, they'll listen to what you have to propose.'

'And what am I meant to tell them?'

Eaton grinned, a flash of white teeth in his tanned face. 'Explain that we come as foes of the Spanish and wish to loot the Acapulco Galleon. Say that we'll supply four musketeers for every sailing craft they can provide for an ambush.'

Hector's mind raced. Here was an opportunity to get off the *Nicholas* – and maybe his friends as well. Once ashore, they might be able to take control of their lives.

'I want my friends with me – Jezreel, Dan and Jacques,' he said.

'By all means,' Eaton was expansive. 'The striker looks enough of an indio himself. That should reassure the locals.' He paused. 'But I wouldn't want you getting any ideas as soon as you are out of sight. So I'm sending Stolck with you to keep an eye on you.'

❊

OVER THE NEXT few hours, Hector watched the coast of Rota take shape. Low cliffs made a landing difficult. The swells heaved and broke against them, churning into froth. Here and there great lumps of reddish-brown rock had broken off and tumbled into the sea. Beyond the cliff wall the ground swept upwards to the rim of what must be an interior plateau, its edge sharply defined against the puffy white clouds and a blue sky. The cliff tops and hill slopes were smothered with dense green vegetation. Despite the lushness of the landscape and the gentle, summery feel of the air, the place looked inaccessible and mysterious, as if it was guarding secrets. Apart from the flittering swoops of two fairy terns in their brilliant white plumage, there was no sign of life.

The ship hove-to a cable's length off the first suitable spot to get ashore, a small cove backed by a low cliff. Watched by the crew, Hector and his friends climbed down into the jolly boat. Jezreel had his backsword slung over his shoulder, and Dan chose to bring along his satchel of artist's materials. Hector and Jacques had nothing more than their sailors' knives. Only Stolck carried a musket. Arianz had claimed that if the landing party showed too many weapons, they'd scare off the natives, and Hector wondered if the quartermaster was conniving with Eaton to put them deliberately in harm's way. But Stolck's presence reassured him. The big Hollander was a close friend of Arianz, and Hector doubted that his countryman would allow him to be abandoned.

The luckless Faasi was passed down like a bundle, his hands still bound. The boat crew bent to their oars and Hector watched the sides of the *Nicholas* recede. The ship looked weary and sea-worn. Her hull planks were pale grey, bleached by months of sun and salt spray. The tracery of rigging was marred with knots and splices, the ropes whiskery with use. But she was still remarkably seaworthy, a testimony to the ship skills of her crew. She rolled gently, showing the beard of weeds that coated the tar applied so long ago in the Encantadas. Someone had hoisted a home-made French ensign at the mizzen. Hector doubted that the colours of France rippling in the slight breeze meant any-thing to those on Rota who were watching.

The keel of the little boat crunched on the shingle, and a moment later he climbed over the gunwale, feeling smooth pebbles slither beneath his bare feet. Behind him he heard Jezreel grunt as he lifted the Chamorro pilot out of the boat and set him upright.

The boat crew backed water, Dan gave the prow of the boat a shove to help it on its way, and the jolly boat began its return journey to the waiting ship. Hector paused at the water's edge and gazed up at the wall of broken cliff behind the little cove. Now that he was closer, he could see the faint trace of a footpath. It led upwards, picking its way back and forth between scree and boulders, a sign that someone occasionally came here. Beside him, Faasi was petrified and shivering with fright.

Hector asked Jezreel for the loan of his backsword and walked over to the wretched pilot, intending to cut his bonds.

'I wouldn't do that,' growled Stolck. He pointed his musket at Hector. 'You heard what the captain said. This savage is our calling card.'

Hector ignored the warning. He cut through the ropes that bound Faasi's wrists. The instant he was free, the Chamorro took to his heels. With a clatter of shingle, he ran back down the narrow beach and plunged into the water. Stolck raised his musket to shoot the runaway, but then thought better of it and lowered the gun. Soon only Faasi's head could be seen as he swam out. He headed beyond the line of breaking swells and turned southwards and, still swimming strongly, kept parallel to the coast until he was out of sight.

'Well, there goes our interpreter,' said Jacques, picking up a pebble and skimming it across the water. 'Let us hope our reception party shows up soon.'

The five men settled down to wait. The narrow beach was less than forty paces long. Cliffs closed it off at each end. The only access was by the little track Hector had noticed earlier. Out to sea the *Nicholas* hovered, still hove-to. An occasional glint of light indicated that someone on her aft deck, either Eaton or Arianz, was watching them through a spyglass. Dan, as unconcerned and calm as always, took pen and ink and a sheet of paper from his satchel and began to sketch the distant vessel. Jezreel took off his backsword, laid it on the ground, lay down beside it, closed his eyes and began to doze. After some minutes of fidgeting, Jacques copied him. Stolck was in a grumpy mood after Faasi's escape. He moved away from the others and sat by himself, his musket across his knees. Only Hector continued to watch the lip of the cliffs above, waiting for some activity.

An hour passed. The shadow cast by the cliff gradually shortened as the sun rose higher. The only sound was the low grumble of the swells on the pebbles. The two fairy terns Hector had noticed earlier were joined by another pair, which circled for some time, then all four birds abruptly flew off. Behind the salt tang of the sea he caught the faint, musty smell of tropical vegetation.

Jacques suddenly sat up. 'I ought to tell you a story that I heard from the Maestre de Campo.'

Jezreel opened his eyes. 'As long as it helps pass the time.'

'He was escorting me back to the Presidio gate. Before he said goodbye, he wanted to emphasize why he was so committed to the programme of reducción – converting the natives.'

'What did he tell you?' asked Hector.

'That the missionary who was murdered recently was not the first priest to be killed by the Chamorro. Some years back they assassinated the chief apostle to these islands, a man named Vitores. They ran him through with a spear, then slashed his head open with a cutlass.'

'Charming,' muttered Jezreel.

'The murderers tried to dispose of the corpse at sea. They took it out on one of their canoes and threw it overboard. But twice the dead man came floating back to the surface and reached out and grasped the outrigger. He only sank when the Chamorro smashed in the skull with a paddle.'

'You could have told us that story earlier,' said Jezreel. 'We might have thought twice about being dumped on this beach.'

'Oddly enough,' Jacques went on, 'Esplana was rather proud of what had happened. He said that every new-found country needs a martyr.'

'I hope we won't add to that number,' said Hector softly. 'There's someone coming down the cliff path now, and he certainly doesn't look like a Christian.'

The newcomer was well over six feet tall. A muscular, heavy-set but athletic-looking man, his chocolate-brown skin was smeared with oil so that it glistened. His long, dark hair had also been oiled and was tied up in a double knot and piled on the crown of his head. His easy, confident stride as he came down the path gave Hector the impression that here was someone of importance. The stranger was empty-handed, and there was no question that he had any concealed weapons. Apart from a belt of coconut rope, he was completely naked.

Stolck scrambled to his feet and levelled his musket at the stranger. 'Stop where you are,' he shouted.

The newcomer gave him a puzzled glance, ignored him and turned to face Hector. Everything about the stranger was large: a barrel-shaped torso, heavily muscled arms and legs, powerful hands, and big feet set firmly on the shingle. His deep-set brown eyes under prominent brows regarded Hector coolly. Then he smiled and Hector's stomach lurched. The stranger's lips parted to reveal teeth sharpened to points so that they resembled a row of fangs. Appallingly, the gums and teeth were stained blood-red. Visions of cannibals and human sacrifice flashed into Hector's mind. Then he realized the stranger had been eating some sort of highly coloured food.

Tearing his gaze away from that hideous mouth, Hector said in slow, careful Spanish, 'We are friends. We wish to speak with your headman.'

There was no response. The brown eyes continued to observe him, placid and uncomprehending.

Hector repeated himself, first in Spanish, then again in all the languages he knew – English, French, the lingua franca of the Barbary slave barracks, even the Irish he had learned as a child. There was still was no reaction. He might as well have been speaking to a graven image, except for that bloody smile.

Finally, when Hector had fallen silent, the man spoke. His voice was deep and powerful, the words musical and clear. They made no sense whatsoever.

The big man turned his head deliberately and looked at Dan, Jacques and the others for several moments. Moving quietly across to Dan, he leaned over to examine the sketch of the *Nicholas*. Then he looked out at the ship and back at the drawing. His face was full of wonder. 'Maulek, maulek,' he said and made an admiring, chuckling noise. Next he walked across to Jezreel, and pinched the giant on his upper arm and nodded approvingly. Before Jezreel could stop him, the man bent down and picked up the backsword from the ground, slid it half out of the sheath and gave a low snort of admiration. 'Maulek, maulek,' he said again. He turned his head aside and spat – evidently a sign of approval – and a blood-red blob of spittle splattered on the stones.

'That's betel nut he's been chewing. I saw it in my time in

the Indies,' said Stolck, who had regained his composure. It was evident that the big stranger was peaceable.

The naked man was showing an interest in the Hollander's musket. He reached out and stroked it and frowned, then shook his head wonderingly.

'He has no idea what it is,' said Stolck. 'He must have come right from the hills.'

'He is certainly more curious than fearful of us,' observed Jacques.

'I'll show him that we are not to be trifled with,' said Stolck. He raised the gun. 'Here, you,' he called out. 'Watch this. Magic.'

Turning on his heel, Stolck took aim at the cliff face at the far end of the beach where a landslip had exposed bare soil studded with small stones. He pulled the trigger. The bang of the musket and the cloud of smoke were instantly followed by a shower of earth and gravel as the musket bullet struck home.

If Stolck had expected the savage to be impressed, he was badly mistaken. The report of the gun was still echoing back from the cliffs when the big native let out a loud, shrill whistle. In the same instant he sprang forward and scooped up Jezreel's backsword. Jezreel lunged, trying to retrieve the weapon. The two men grappled, struggling for possession. They fell, rolled over on the ground and began to fight, gouging and punching.

Stunned by the sudden turn of events, Hector was groping for the knife from his belt, ready to go to Jezreel's rescue, when he felt a violent stab of pain as something struck his left shoulder. The force of the blow spun him half around, and for a moment he was disoriented. A yard away Jacques had mysteriously been knocked to the ground. Dan was still on his feet, but acting strangely. He was ducking and weaving from side to side as though fighting off an unseen attacker. He had his canvas satchel wrapped around his right arm and was holding it up as a shield. Something smacked on to the pebbles at

Hector's feet and skittered off. It was a disc-shaped stone about the size of a hen's egg. Looking in the direction from where it had come, Hector saw a line of naked men standing on the lip of the cliff. They were whirling slings and discharging a hail of missiles at the beach.

Stolck was cursing steadily as he tried to reload his empty musket. He tugged a cartridge from his bandolier, ripped open the paper with his teeth and tipped the powder down the barrel. He screwed up the empty paper and dropped it after the gunpowder. He was about to follow with a musket ball from the bag hanging at his waist, when a sling stone struck him on the head. His knees gave way and he pitched backwards, stunned.

Hector ran to pick up the musket. Dan was shouting and pointing at the cliff face. A file of islanders was scrambling downwards. Six or seven naked men armed with spears came bounding from rock to rock, as agile as goats. Before Hector could reach the gun, the first of them had leaped down, landed on the pebbles and dashed forward, his spear aimed at Dan.

Hector dithered. He did not know whether to help Jezreel, still locked in his fierce struggle with the big stranger, or to go to Dan, who had turned to face his attacker.

He heard running feet behind him, and a moment later Hector felt someone leap upon his back. He lost his footing and toppled forward, tried to twist free, but the arms that had clamped themselves around him were locked tight. He hit the ground with a thump. As a hand roughly pushed his face into the pebbles, he could smell the reek of coconut oil and feel the bite of rough cord as someone tied his wrists behind him. He lay still, winded and helpless.

The sounds of fighting continued. He raised his head and saw that Jacques had also been tied up. Stolck lay on the ground, guarded by another of the natives. Three spearmen had cornered Dan against the foot of the cliff. One of the attackers was bleeding from a shoulder wound, and Dan had somehow found himself a knife. He stood with his back against the rock, the blade in his hand. Jezreel was still locked in combat. He'd risen to one knee and had pinned down his assailant, and was trying to throttle him, though his hands were slipping on the oily skin. Even as Hector watched, three more of the natives, all big strong men, flung themselves on Jezreel and pulled him off his victim. There was a warning shout in their unknown language, and the point of a spear was held to Jezreel's throat. He stopped struggling and glared at his attackers.

Jezreel's adversary, the first of the natives to appear, rose to his feet. His right eye was puffed up where Jezreel must have butted him, and he nursed his throat where Jezreel had got a grip. Otherwise the stranger seemed remarkably composed. He looked across to where his companions had cornered Dan and spoke sharply. The three men stepped back a pace, though they did not lower their spears. He was clearly their commander.

He turned towards Hector, who had been allowed to stand. 'Tell your friend to drop his knife,' he said.

Hector gaped. The stark-naked warrior had addressed him in flawless, slightly accented Spanish.

'Dan, put down the knife,' Hector called.

Dan did as he was asked, and the leader of the war party issued what seemed like a stream of orders as his followers began to herd their captives together.

'We were tricked,' complained Jacques, shaking his head. 'That whoreson knew exactly what a musket was.'

'There was no need to attack us,' Hector said to the big man. 'We came in friendship.'

'No white person is our friend,' retorted the Chamorro crisply.

'You're wrong,' Hector insisted. 'You see that ship out there? It has come to attack the Spanish, and the captain and crew need your help.'

'They seem to have changed their minds,' said the Chamorro. The sarcasm in his tone made Hector turn around and look out to sea. The *Nicholas* was making sail. As he watched, the fore and main topsails unfolded from their yards. He could just make out the figures on deck as the crew sheeted home the canvas. Gradually the *Nicholas* began to turn and take the wind on her quarter. Someone was lowering the blue and white French ensign from the mizzen peak. It was clear that Eaton had changed his mind. He must have witnessed the scuffle on the beach, seen the capture of the landing party and decided to abandon his scheme.

The *Nicholas* sailed off, leaving the landing party to their fate.

Stolck gazed after the departing ship. Still groggy from the blow on his head, his blue eyes bulged with rage and disappointment. 'God vervloekte bastaarden,' he mumbled under his breath.

The big Chamorro looked around the group of prisoners. 'Which of you is the chief man?'

'I can speak for them,' said Hector.

'We go to my village. There the council will decide what is to be done with you.'

'Who are you?' asked Hector.

'My name is Ma'pang and I am a Chamorro.'

'I thought you were all Chamorro.'

The big man gave a sardonic grunt. 'That shows how little the guirragos – the white men – understand us. The Chamorro are a class, the chiefs, the people who rule.' He examined Hector quizzically. He did not appear particularly hostile. 'If you are an enemy of the Spanish, how is it that you speak the language so well?'

Hector felt bold enough to say, 'I might ask you the same question.'

'The missionaries taught me, until I decided to run away and come back to live among my own people.'

'My mother was Spanish, but my father came from another nation,' explained Hector.

Ma'pang looked surprised. 'If we marry outside the clan, we only do so with a clan that is an ally.'

There was something about the big man that encouraged Hector to be frank. 'I did not come here to fight the Spaniards, but to find one of their women.'

'You would marry her?'

'If she would agree.'

Ma'pang shook his head in astonishment. 'That is even more remarkable.'

IT TOOK TWO HOURS of hard marching to reach the Chamorro village. Their captors loosened the bonds to make it easier to climb up the cliff path, and they eventually removed the ropes altogether, once Ma'pang had pointed out that escape was useless as there was nowhere to go. In hot sunshine they followed narrow, dusty footpaths across ridges covered with sawgrass and small bushes, and by mid-afternoon they descended into a thickly wooded ravine. Faintly, in the distance, Hector heard the shouts of children playing, and after another few hundred yards the travellers emerged into what was evidently the main thoroughfare of the settlement. It was a peaceful domestic scene of dogs dozing in the sun, chickens scratching in the dirt, and children running excitedly to call their friends to see the strangers. There were about thirty houses neatly built of bamboo and wooden poles, their steeply pitched roofs thatched with palm leaves. Before each dwelling stood a large, flat-topped boulder with a hollow scooped into the surface. At one of them a robust woman was husking rice with a pestle, a toddler beside her. She laid down the pestle and stood to watch them pass. Jacques sucked in his breath in appreciation. Apart from a tiny strip of bark cloth between her legs, the woman was naked. Broad shoulders, deep full breasts and swelling hips made her statuesquely beautiful. Even more striking was her mane of luxuriant, thick hair, which reached to her thighs.

Ma'pang chuckled at the Frenchman's reaction. 'We think that the guirragos look stupid and ridiculous dressed in their clothes.'

'But what about her hair?' asked Hector, trying not to stare. The woman's hair was near-blonde.

'Even if they don't wear clothes, our women still want to be attractive,' Ma'pang replied. 'Those who wish to, colour their hair with lime.'

Followed by a swarm of gawking, giggling children, they arrived before a massive, barn-like building. It was raised ten feet off the ground on mushroom-shaped stone pillars.

'This is the uritao, the house for the unmarried men. You will stay here until the council decides what is to be done with you,' said Ma'pang.

They climbed a bamboo ladder and found themselves in a long, cool, high-ceilinged shed smelling pleasantly of palm thatch. Neatly fashioned windows gave light and air. The floor was of massive timber planks lashed in place with coir, the surface worn smooth by feet. The place was spotlessly clean. Mattresses of palm matting stuffed with dried coconut fibre had been laid against one wall. 'The council likes to discuss matters at length before it reaches a decision,' explained Ma'pang. 'So you should make yourselves comfortable.'

Jacques sank down on one of the mattresses with a sigh. 'Hector, this is better than being on a ship,' he announced. 'All I need now is for one of the village girls to bring me a glass of wine.'

✳

OVER THE NEXT WEEK they found it increasingly difficult to remember they were prisoners. Hector presumed that Ma'pang had persuaded his clan that their captives were enemies of the Spanish, for the five men were permitted to wander freely about the village by day. Naturally the children followed them everywhere, pulling faces and pretending to be scared, but their parents got on with the routine of their daily lives. In the cool of the morning the women walked to the nearby plantations and gardens. There they tended small plots of taro and yam, weeded sugar cane, cleared the ground around their banana trees and gathered breadfruit, until it was time to come back and prepare the afternoon meal. The men and older boys set out in the opposite direction. They took the footpath leading down the valley to the beach. Dan asked if he might go with them and discovered that it was less than ten minutes to the spot where they kept their fishing canoes.

'There are some things that even the Miskito could learn from them,' he said when he returned at dusk, carrying a string of flying fish for supper. 'They make miniature canoes for the young ones. Some of the boys are only six or seven years old. Yet they go out fishing on their own. They keep inshore, of course, under the eye of the older men. But the boys bring back a share of the catch.'

'Did you show them how to strike fish?' asked Jezreel.

'They do not have the right equipment for it,' answered the Miskito. 'Their tridents are tipped with bone or sharp wood. I think iron is too precious to risk losing at sea. Besides, they do very well with these . . .' He held up a beautifully crafted fish hook made from carved shell. 'One of the older men gave me this. I think he thought I brought him luck. He came back with a tuna that must weigh at least twenty pounds.'

He was interrupted by the arrival of Ma'pang. The big islander came each evening to the uritao to report on the long-drawn-out deliberations of the village council. His broad, dark face was solemn as he squatted down beside the five foreigners.

'The council talk and talk, but reach no conclusion,' he said.

'What would you have them do?' asked Hector.

'Have the courage to make the Spaniards leave us alone, so that we can continue with our own ways and customs.' Ma'pang was chewing betel. He shifted the wad from one cheek to the other.

'Is that why you took us alive, when you could have killed us?'

Ma'pang gave the young man a sharp glance. 'You know what I had in mind?'

'You wanted us as hostages.'

Ma'pang nodded. 'The Spanish keep some of our chief men locked up in their fort as a guarantee for our good behaviour. I hoped to have the prisoners released in exchange for your return.'

'And what does the council say, now they know we're valueless?' Hector could see fierce determination in Ma'pang's eyes.

'I've suggested that we gather other clans, storm the fort and free the prisoners while the Governor is away.'

For one brief moment Hector imagined a horde of naked, yelling warriors swarming into the Presidio and ransacking it, while he searched for Maria in the confusion, and then the two of them escaping together. 'What did the council say?'

Ma'pang's reply crushed his hopes. 'They reminded me that five years ago four hundred warriors, more than we could hope to assemble nowadays, tried to take the fort. They were driven off, with heavy loss, by the same Spanish commander who is in charge now. A brave man.'

Dan had been following the conversation, and now he asked quietly, 'Could we not get into the fort secretly and release the prisoners? Jacques says the garrison guards are very slack.'

The Chamorro smiled wryly, his blood-red gums showing. 'Even if we succeeded in climbing the walls, we would never manage to enter the cells. They are locked, and the prisoners are shackled. We have no experience of dealing with such things.'

It was true, Hector thought to himself. There were no doors to the houses in the Chamorro village and therefore no locks or fastenings. Nothing was ever hidden or guarded; everything was left lying about in the open and was treated as common property.

If someone needed an item, he or she simply picked it up and used it.

'Ma'pang,' he said earnestly. 'If you can arrange to get myself and Jacques and Dan into the fort, we can deal with the locks and chains. Jacques knows all about padlocks and how to open them. But in return you must help me contact the young woman I told you about.'

'The one you would marry?'

'She lives in the Governor's quarters. I need to find her and talk to her, and if she agrees, I want her to come away with me.'

Ma'pang's heavy eyebrows shot up in surprise. 'You think she would agree?'

'I'll not know until I ask. Do you think the council will consent to such a plan?'

'They don't have to,' Ma'pang answered without a moment's hesitation. 'There are six or seven men who would help me. The same ones who captured you on the beach that day.'

'And how will we get to Aganah?'

Ma'pang rose to his feet. 'Two galaide layak can sail across the straits under cover of darkness, and land us a few miles to the north of the town, without being seen. From there we march overland.'

TWELVE

INCH BY INCH Dan raised his head. He was crouched in the sawgrass on the hillside above Aganah. Below him lay the untidy sprawl of the native town and, beyond that, the rectangular block of the Spanish Presidio. He faced down into the valley, held his breath and opened his mouth. He kept totally still, for that was how his father had taught him to listen when scouting. It had been part of his training for slaving raids on the inland villages where the Miskito kidnapped their servants and concubines. Dan could still remember the excitement of his first raid: the cautious river journey by canoe, a landing well short of the target village, the silent march through the jungle, the lone scout sent ahead to examine the best line of attack.

Now he assessed Aganah in the same way. He'd been at his vantage point since first light, watching the houses, counting the number of people moving about, noting where they were going and how soon they returned, gauging the best route to reach the walls of the Presidio without raising the alarm. Tonight there was no moon, and if the sentries were as incompetent as Jacques had reported, it was unlikely they'd spot the raiders approaching the wall. The real risk of discovery would come sooner, while crossing the town itself. If the local residents were disturbed, the raid would be a disaster. That was why he listened so carefully, ignoring the background whisper of the breeze through the tall grass around him and the buzz and scratchy chirps of insects in the warm early afternoon. He picked up snatches of voices from below, indistinct and very faint, the thumping sound of someone chopping or pounding, the cry of a baby. For a moment he was startled by a long, hollow moan. Then he recalled hearing that the Spaniards had brought water buffalo from the Philippines as draught animals and for milk. But it wasn't the water buffalo that concerned Dan, or the handful of imported horses, which had so terrified the Chamorro, who thought of them as outlandish monsters. Dan was listening for dogs.

They were the real guardians of the settlement, and as yet Dan hadn't seen any. A single cur, awoken during the night and barking loudly, would wreck the entire plan.

Dan resumed breathing. At the back of his throat was the faint taste of wood smoke from the cooking fires in the houses below. He eased himself down into the grass, and crawled to where Hector and the others were waiting.

As he slithered through the long grass, Dan thought of Ma'pang and his clan. He feared they would suffer the same fate as the native peoples of Peru and New Spain, when the confident pale-skinned strangers had insisted they worship a different god and adopt new and alien ways. Unless the Chamorro followed the example of his own people, the Miskito, they would lose both their lands and their identity. They needed to arm themselves with the white man's weapons, and draw so much blood they would always be left alone.

Once the Chamorro had their hands on enough firearms, Dan knew they'd quickly learn to look after them, as well as use them. For the raid, Jacques had drawn sketches of a set of pick-locks that he required if he was to open the door to the prison where the hostages were kept. Within half a day the Chamorro fishermen had fashioned a dozen hooked and curved tools of different thicknesses, lengths and shapes. They had made them from bone and shell and sticks of close-grained hardwood. When Jacques had decided the tools were strong enough for the prison doors, but might snap in the heavy fetter padlocks, Ma'pang had produced the bronze cross he'd been given by the missionaries. A Chamorro craftsman had reshaped it into exactly the stout pick-lock the Frenchman specified.

Dan smiled to himself, amused at the thought that the symbol of the foreigners would be used to free their captives.

He reached the clearing where Hector and the others waited. There were just five of them altogether: Jacques, Jezreel, Ma'pang, Hector and himself. Stolck had stayed aboard the galaide layak that had delivered them under cover of darkness to a sheltered bay on the northern side of the island, and would return the following evening to collect them.

'The north wall of the fort is the best place to climb in,' Dan said. 'It is farthest from the watchtower where the night sentry might be. There are also huts on that side of the town, which seem to be storehouses rather than homes. They should give us some cover.'

'What about the wall? How high is it?' asked Jezreel.

'Maybe twenty feet. Easy to scale,' Dan answered.

Jacques had earlier explained the layout of the fort's interior. Now he looked at Hector with a worried expression. 'If we climb over the north wall, we will have to divide. I believe the Chamorro hostages are kept in the long, low building that looks like stables. The windows there have bars. Maria is in the Governor's quarters, and they are in the opposite direction.'

'We stick to the plan we discussed,' Hector insisted. 'You, Dan and Ma'pang go in search of the hostages. Jezreel stays with the ladder to secure our line of retreat. I'll go on my own to find Maria.'

To Hector's surprise, Dan shook his head. 'No, I will go with you. Jacques and Ma'pang are enough to free the hostages.'

Hector saw the stubborn expression on Dan's face. He looked at the others to see if anyone objected.

'If that's the way you want it, we'd better get going.'

*

THREE HOURS LATER Hector stood with his back pressed against the inner face of the Presidio wall. He could feel the rough coral blocks through his thin cotton shirt. Everything had gone exactly to plan. Dan's assessment had been faultless. An hour before midnight, when the town's folk were asleep, the intruders had stealthily made their way through a skein of back alleys without being noticed. They had then scuttled across the open ground around the fort that provided the Spaniards' field of fire. Ma'pang had carried a makeshift scaling ladder made by driving cross-bars through a length of stout bamboo. He had set it against the wall, scrambled up and waited on the wooden walkway that ran along the inside of the top of the wall. Here the others had joined him. Then the ladder had been used again to descend into the fort itself. Now it was time for the group to split up.

There was sufficient starlight for Hector to get his bearings. He could make out the shape of the little chapel, the darker shadows of the barracks, even the patch of the garrison's vegetable garden. Everything was as Jacques had described. To his left Ma'pang and Jacques were already creeping away. They would follow the line of the wall until it brought them to the outbuilding with the barred windows. Jezreel was to wait at the spot where they had entered the fort, staying well within the shadow of the overhang of the walkway in case a sentry should chance to make his rounds. His task was to guard the ladder until the others returned.

Hector felt a touch on his shoulder. Dan pointed in the direction of a large square building, pale white in the starlight, which faced the central parade ground. It had to be the Governor's quarters. Quietly the two men began to move to their right, circling to position themselves where the bulk of the building would shield them from the watchtower.

Hector noticed how easily and confidently Dan covered the ground. The Miskito seemed to glide along. Now and then he paused to listen and check the shadows, alert to every noise or movement. Hector felt clumsy and awkward by comparison. Anxiously he tried to follow directly in Dan's path, stopping whenever he stopped, placing his feet gently. Yet he feared he might blunder and make a noise at any moment.

Several minutes of this furtive progress brought them to the rear of the Governor's quarters. Hector relaxed a little. They were no longer in the sentry's line of sight, and even if he left his watchtower, Dan and he could hide in a lean-to shed built against the back wall of the Governor's quarters. From the smell, it was obviously used by the kitchen staff as a place to pluck chickens, gut fish and put out the slops.

Treading lightly, Hector approached the back door to the house. Gently he lifted the latch. It was as he'd feared: the door was locked and barred from the inside.

He stepped back and looked up at the rear face of the building.

Above and a little to one side of the lean-to shed, a window was ajar. Hector thought back to Jacques' description of his brief visit to the Governor's residence. The front door opened into an entrance hall. From there a stairway led to the upper floor, and it was safe to assume that the best rooms – those that overlooked the parade ground – were used by the Governor and his lady, probably as their bedroom and a drawing room. Maria and any other members of staff who slept in the house would have rooms at the rear of the building.

Hector counted the number of upper windows. There were five. He guessed that the central one gave on to the stairwell and those on each side were for bedrooms. The half-open window was one of them.

He slipped off his shoes and gestured to Dan to hoist him

on to the roof of the shed. The tiles of the lean-to shifted and grated alarmingly as he scrambled for purchase. Despite his care, there was a slight clatter as a section of broken tile slid away and fell to the ground. He froze and flattened himself to the roof. With no reaction from the house, and after a few moments, he rose on all fours and slowly began to crawl forward. At the rear wall, he gingerly stood upright and stretched for the open window. But he'd misjudged. The window ledge was too far away for him to reach. He cursed under his breath and shuffled backwards, afraid to turn round for fear of dislodging another tile. As he reached the edge of the roof, where Dan should have been ready to help him back to the ground, he looked down and saw that the Miskito had gone.

He thought Dan must have ducked under the roof. He waited, but the Miskito was nowhere to be seen. Very cautiously, Hector lay forward on his stomach, eased his legs over the edge of the roof, slid himself backwards and dropped to the ground with a slight thud. Once more he held his breath, fearful that he'd woken someone in the house. Still there was no sign of Dan.

As he groped for his shoes, he saw a shadow coming towards him. He realized it was his friend, and he carried the bamboo ladder that Jezreel had been guarding.

The Miskito put his mouth close to Hector's ear. 'You need this,' he whispered.

Hector was alarmed. 'What about the others? If anything goes wrong, without the ladder they'll be trapped,' he hissed.

Dan gave a dismissive grunt. 'Jezreel said you need the ladder more than they do. Now don't waste any more time.'

Together they put the ladder into position against the rear wall and Hector clambered upwards. He eased the window fully open, his heart in his mouth. He was well aware of the extravagant risk he was taking. There was no way of knowing whose bedroom he was entering. It could be some stranger's, or where the Governor's children slept. Even if it was Maria's room, she might be sharing it with another member of the Governor's staff.

With excruciating care he eased himself into the darkened room and stood by the window waiting for his vision to adjust to the gloom. It was a bedroom – that was clear. Close beside him, where the light from the window was strongest, stood a small chair. Some garments lay across it. The farthest corners of the room were deep in shadow, so it was impossible to see what was in them. The middle of the room was dominated by a large, ghostly white shape reaching to the ceiling. It took Hector several moments to realize it was a net canopy to keep out insects. Whoever used the room was asleep inside. He could hear nothing, not even breathing.

For a long while the young man stood still, undecided. He didn't know whether to tiptoe to the door, leave and attempt to find some clue as to which was Maria's room, or just try and check who was sleeping under the canopy, without waking them.

He stood there, gripped with uncertainty, when a voice spoke softly and clearly from within the canopy.

'Is that you, Hector?'

He felt as if the ground had dropped from beneath his feet and he was in mid-air. The air was sucked from his lungs. His throat went dry and, unable to speak, he went to her. The canopy was drawn aside and a woman's shape sat up, dark hair loose and falling around her shoulders. Then Hector was on his knees, his arms around Maria.

For what seemed an age, neither of them spoke. He was dizzy with emotion. Then, very gently, she put her mouth close to his ear and whispered, 'I knew you would come.'

Reluctantly, slowly, he eased his embrace. 'I want you to leave with me,' he murmured. It was a simple, brief statement. There was no time to say more.

She didn't answer, but laid her hand on his arm and freed

herself from his embrace. She swung her legs over the side of the bed and rose to her feet, and the canopy fell back in place as she walked swiftly to the other side of the room. Dimly Hector saw the lid of a chest lift, and then Maria was back beside him with a bundle in her arms and a dark hood tied around her hair. Only then did he realize that she'd been sleeping fully dressed.

'Jacques and the others are waiting outside,' he began, but Maria merely laid a finger on his lips to silence him, kissed him quickly on the cheek and was already on her way towards the open window.

In a daze, Hector followed her as she climbed over the windowsill and, without a moment's hesitation, began to descend the ladder to where Dan was waiting.

Hector's feet had scarcely touched the ground when Dan was already leading the way back to the outer wall, moving at a quick walk, the ladder balanced over one shoulder. With every step Hector expected to hear a shout behind him or the sound of a musket shot. But the entire Presidio was still quietly asleep. Everything was happening so fast that his mind could only concentrate on what was immediately in front of him. All that mattered now was to stay as close as possible to Maria, not to let her out of his sight. He took a deep breath and caught a faint waft of her perfume. He felt weak at the knees.

They reached the outer wall and turned to the right. Another couple of minutes of rapid walking and Hector saw ahead of him the unmistakable bulk of Jezreel lurking in the shadow of the walkway. Beside him were three more men. At the last moment Hector realized he hadn't warned Maria about Ma'pang. It would be a shock for her to come face to face in the darkness with a huge, naked islander with sharpened teeth.

He needn't have worried. As they joined the waiting men, the young woman nodded politely to the nude savage, then gave Jacques a quick embrace.

'Good to see you again, Maria,' whispered the Frenchman.

'Hello, Jezreel,' she said softly, laying a hand on the big man's arm. 'I'm glad to see you're here as well.'

Something was wrong, Hector realized belatedly. There should have been at least three or four escaped hostages waiting to escape up the ladder. But there was only one additional figure. In the darkness it was difficult to make out his features, but he appeared to be an older man, small for a Chamorro and dressed in a smock. 'Where are the others?' he asked Ma'pang quietly.

'We couldn't find any others,' the Chamorro replied. 'Maybe the Spaniards took them north. Only Kepuha here.'

Hector felt a twinge of disappointment. He had found Maria, but the mission was only partly successful.

'Did you search elsewhere?' he asked.

Ma'pang shook his head. 'Already we have stayed long enough. We must leave now.'

'There is no one else held in that building,' Jacques added from the shadows. 'The other rooms are used as the armoury. That is why the windows are barred.'

'Did you get inside?' Dan enquired.

'Of course,' Jacques gave a quick grin. 'I thought it might be the strongroom where the pay chest is kept. Tant pis, no such luck.'

'Hector,' said Dan, 'I need another few minutes. You and Maria get out now. Ma'pang and his friend can go with you. I will need Jacques and Jezreel to stay behind with me. There is still something useful we can do.'

With Maria beside him, Hector did not feel like arguing. What mattered most to him at that moment was to make sure the woman he loved was clear of the fort. 'Don't be too long, Dan. Our luck can't hold forever.'

He held the ladder steady with Jezreel, as Maria followed Ma'pang and the Chamorro hostage up its stubby rungs. Behind him he heard Dan say, 'Jacques, show me the way to that armoury.' When Hector next looked round, the two men had melted away into the darkness.

*

THE FIRST GLOW of dawn was seeping into the sky, turning the shadows from black to grey, as the raiders scrambled up the slope and regained the comparative safety of the hill above Aganah. They had succeeded in making their way back through the town undetected and were moving at a brisk pace, walking and jogging by intervals. Ma'pang was in the lead, with Kepuha, the rescued hostage, close behind him. As they reached the first bushes the old man paused long enough to strip off his smock of plaited palm leaf and hide it in the undergrowth. Now he was as naked as his fellow clansman. Hector, looking past Maria who was directly in front of him, could see Kepuha's thin shanks and buttocks and bony shoulders moving steadily as he kept up the stride, his head of white hair bobbing at each step. Farther back in their little column Dan and Jacques each carried two Spanish muskets they had taken from the armoury, and Jezreel was draped with half a dozen bandoliers. The sack over the big man's shoulder contained bullet moulds, half a pig of lead and several large cartridges of gunpowder, which had been intended for the fort's cannon.

To Hector, Maria looked more graceful and shapely with each passing minute. She was wearing a maid's working skirt, and she had pulled up her petticoat and tucked it into a sash to allow her legs free movement. On her feet were plain flat shoes, and her dark-brown bodice with its long sleeves matched the skirt. Hector wondered if she'd selected the colours to be less conspicuous. They hadn't exchanged a single word during the quick dash over the wall and the furtive scurry through the native township. Now, as the little party paused for breath, he just had time to say, 'So you did recognize Jacques when he came to the Governor's house.'

Maria turned towards him. There was a mischievous twinkle

in her eye. 'How could I forget a man with a convict's brand on his cheek?' Hector hardly heard her words. It was the first time he'd seen her face properly in nearly three years, and he was drinking in the sight. Here was the image he'd tried so hard to retain in his memory. Now, in the strengthening light, he saw that she had indeed changed. There was a maturity that hadn't been there before. It enabled him to see more clearly the harmony of her features, the wide-set brown eyes, the neat, straight nose and the generous, soft mouth. Her eyebrows were thicker and more pronounced, accentuating her level, confident gaze. Her complexion seemed to be slightly darker than he remembered. She had obviously been much exposed to the tropical sun, but she'd also lost the fresh bloom of earlier years. Now her skin had taken on the colour of newly peeled hazelnuts. There was still the scattering of light freckles. He wanted to reach out and stroke her cheek.

'Here, let me carry that,' he said, and took the small bundle she had brought from her room. It was very light in his grasp. He guessed it contained just a few clothes.

She glanced at him gratefully, when Dan called out that they should move on. He worried that a party from the fort was in pursuit.

They marched on at the same blistering pace. The day soon turned very warm, but Ma'pang was unrelenting. No one spoke, preferring to save their breath for the effort of travel over the broken ground. Occasionally they had to force their way through the undergrowth, and there were places where the path dipped down into awkward gullies or traversed patches of bare hillside and the footing became treacherous with loose soil and gravel. As the hours passed, Hector worried that Maria might not be able to continue. Great sweat stains began to soak her bodice, and there were moments when she stumbled and nearly fell. Yet she made no complaint, and from the determined set of her shoulders Hector knew she would reject any offer of help. Grimly he pushed himself forward, turning over in his mind what he would say to her when, at last, they had a chance to be on their own. He was overawed that she'd been ready to run away with him with no need of persuasion.

The sun was well past its zenith by the time they finally reached the spur of high land that overlooked the bay where the galaide layak would come to collect them. Here at last they stopped. Dan returned along their path to watch for any signs of pursuit, and the others made a small clearing in the long grass and went to ground. Silently Hector took Maria by the hand. 'Let's sit by ourselves,' he suggested. The two of them quietly made their way to a patch of shade by a large boulder.

Maria sat down, her back to the rock, pulled off the headscarf and shook out her hair. Then she leaned her head forward to rest on her knees. Clearly she was exhausted.

Hector sat down beside her, and for several minutes there was a silence. Finally he asked softly, 'Maria, how did you know it was me?'

She didn't raise her head. 'Because I'd waited,' she replied. Her voice was muffled and Hector had to strain to hear. He heard a hint of sadness in her tone and was overwhelmed with confusion. He didn't know what to say.

The silence between them lengthened and Hector began to sense that something between them was slipping away. He felt wretched, fearful of saying the wrong thing. Finally he said, 'Do you remember the letter you wrote me after the trial in London?'

'Every word . . .' Again the muffled response.

'I read it every day.' The words sounded lame and pointless even as he spoke them.

This time there was no reply.

His bewilderment growing, Hector tried again. 'You haven't asked where we are going.'

Again the flat reply, the curtain of hair hiding her face. 'It doesn't matter.'

There was a finality in her voice that shook Hector. He looked down at an ant crawling slowly between the crushed stalks of grass, as it clutched a green leaf. The leaf was several times larger than the ant, and the insect faltered under the strain. He and Maria had each been carrying their own burden, he thought, a burden of hope. For a grim moment he wondered if he'd been deluding himself, if he was about to lose Maria.

As he watched the ant struggle onwards, a small dark spot suddenly appeared on the dry earth. Then, as it faded, another appeared close beside it. With a lurch, he knew they were tear drops. Maria was crying silently.

Bereft, he reached out and took her hand and squeezed it comfortingly. To his utter relief he felt her squeeze back, certainly and strongly. He allowed himself to feel reassured, to think all would be well. But he knew, in that same instant, it would be better to wait. The two of them could talk later about all that had happened while they had been apart, and what each hoped of the other.

THIRTEEN

THE GALAIDE LAYAK slipped into the cove soon after dark to collect the little group, and next morning delivered them safely back to Rota. Ma'pang's villagers were far from disappointed that only a single hostage had been rescued, and came splashing out into the shallows with whoops of welcome. Their women gazed with open fascination at Maria, the first guirrago female they had ever seen, then whisked her away to the village. Hector and his companions followed, escorted by a chattering crowd and heralded by four Chamorro warriors jubilantly waving the muskets that had been stolen from the fort. The group had hardly arrived at the bachelor house before a celebration feast was under way. Hector, Jacques and the others were assigned places of honour, seated on the ground before a cooking trench filled with glowing coals. Heaps of fish and plantains were grilled and handed around, and several large jars of palm wine were set out, with coconut shells as cups. Trying to locate Maria, Hector spotted her standing beside Ma'pang's wife on the fringes of the watching crowd.

'They do love the sound of their own voices. He has been shouting for a good half-hour,' Jacques said, as he turned to watch a Chamorro warrior striding up and down, haranguing the assembled villagers in a lather of enthusiasm.

'What's he saying, Ma'pang?' Hector asked. He couldn't understand a word, but clearly the orator was repeating himself.

'That Kepuha is a great makhana. Now he is back among us, he will intercede with the spirits of the otherworld, and they will rise up and protect the village from the guirragos.'

'What's a makhana?'

'The missionaries have a word for such people – a shaman.'

Dan spoke Spanish well enough to have followed the conversation and gave Hector a meaningful glance. 'Hector, you have to tell him the truth,' he said.

Hector paused, unwilling to offend his host. Then, keeping his tone as neutral as he could, he said, 'Ma'pang, you will need more than the help of the spirits if you are to defend yourselves and your families.'

Ma'pang set aside the fish head he had been sucking, and wiped his fingers on the ground. 'You are going to tell me that we must become like Dan here.'

Hector couldn't help but admire the way the naked warrior often seemed one step ahead of what he was about to say.

'That's right.'

'And that is why he stole those muskets when we were in the fort?'

'Yes, with enough powder and shot and those muskets, your people—' he began.

'A handful of muskets is not enough. The guirragos have many guns and cannon.' Ma'pang broke off a fishbone and began to use it to pick at his sharpened teeth.

Hector ploughed on. 'Even half a dozen muskets have their uses. Your people must first learn how to use guns. Dan and Jezreel can show them how to load and aim, how to fit new flints and keep such weapons in good repair.'

'And after that?'

'You obtain more muskets, distribute them to all your warriors and to any Chamorro clans who are your allies.'

'And where do we find these extra guns?' Ma'pang was

watching Hector narrowly, a gleam of real interest in the deep-set brown eyes.

Hector drew a deep breath. This was something he and Dan had discussed during the journey back from Aganah. It was their chance to leave the islands.

'Do you remember what I said to you on the day you captured us on the beach?'

'That you had been set ashore to make an alliance with us. With our help you would seize the big ship that comes here yearly to supply the guirragos.'

'Exactly. The muskets we already have are sufficient to carry out that attack ourselves, using exactly the same plan.'

'Go on.' Ma'pang flicked the fishbone into the embers of the cooking fire.

'Your people paddle out to the ship, pretending to want to trade. Dan, Jezreel, Jacques and I will lie hidden in the canoes. Stolck can bring his musket. After the initial shock of our gunfire, your warriors can climb aboard and seize the ship.'

Ma'pang belched softly. 'Five of you will not be enough. The ship is too big, too many men on board.'

'But we don't ambush the big galleon. Instead we seize the much smaller one, which, according to Jacques, is due very soon. She carries enough weapons to arm everyone in your village.'

The Chamorro warrior lifted his chin as he stared down at Hector. 'And what would you want from us in exchange?'

'Every guirrago ship brings a smaller boat that we call a launch. It is either stowed on deck or towed behind her. We ask that the Chamorro give us that boat and enough water and food to last three weeks, and allow us to leave Rota.'

'And where would you go?'

'Towards the setting sun, because that is downwind. Eventually we will reach a place where we can contact our own people.'

Ma'pang's red lips gleamed wetly as he spat out a shred of food. 'I will explain your plan to the council of the old men. It is up to them to decide. But I warn you. If the plan succeeds, you will have a long, long voyage. We call our islands tano' tasi — "land of the sea" — because we are so far from any other country.'

✳

SEVERAL DRUNKEN Chamorro were snoring on the ground by the time the feast ended some hours later, and Hector had lost sight of Maria. He supposed she'd gone back to Ma'pang's hut with his wife and, as it was getting dark, he decided it would be more appropriate if he spent the night in the uritao. But he got little rest. He lay awake, turning over and over in his mind what he should say to Maria.

Shortly after dawn the next day he climbed down from the bachelor house and succeeded in making a pack of bright-eyed, giggling Chamorro children understand that he wanted to find the guirrago woman. They led him to one of the larger huts at the far end of the village. As he arrived, Maria had just emerged. She'd washed and changed, and combed out her hair so that it hung loose around her shoulders. Barefoot, she wore the same plain brown skirt as the previous day and had put on a fresh, dark-blue bodice that she must have carried in her bundle of clothes. Hector thought she looked strained, and was not entirely recovered from the hectic events of the previous two days.

'Let's walk down to the beach,' he proposed. He felt self-conscious and awkward. 'The village fishing fleet makes quite a sight.'

She treated him to a guarded smile. 'I'd like that. All the time I was in the fort, I never saw how the local people really lived.'

In silence they strolled along the track to the beach. The path wound its way through a ravine where ferns and creepers grew among tangled roots of wild banyan. They startled a bird, a native dove with an iridescent green body and a rose-coloured head, which had been feeding on fallen seeds. It flew up with a sudden clatter of wings and they stopped and watched it weave its way among the branches. Hector stepped aside and broke off a bright-yellow blossom from a small, shrubby tree.

'Dan tells me the Chamorro use the fibres from this tree to make their fishing lines and nets,' he explained, as he held out the flower to Maria.

She took the blossom from him and looked at it for a moment. 'The same flowers grew around the fort in Aganah. I love their bright colours, but there's something sad about them. Each flower lasts no more than a day. By night the petals have faded and begun to fall.'

They emerged on to the open beach. The day was hot and sunny, but a few clouds were building up on the far horizon. The Chamorro fishing fleet had been at sea since dawn and was spread across the glittering surface of the bay. For some minutes they stood and watched the youngsters fishing with hook and line from their miniature dugout canoes. Farther out, the larger boats were tacking back and forth under sail.

'Let's find somewhere to sit down,' suggested Hector, and together they walked to where a fishing canoe lay drawn up on the sand, covered with palm fronds to protect it from the sun. Hector watched Maria reach out and run a finger along the red and white lines that decorated the hull. He knew she was waiting for him to begin. Yet, in his uncertainty, he did not know how to start.

'It must feel strange for you to be among these people,' he ventured.

'Not really,' she replied. 'It's similar to the village where I grew up. We had the same concerns – tending the crops, providing for our families, teaching the children. The people here are more fortunate in one way. They don't fear the winter cold.'

'Have you heard from your family?' he asked. He knew she came from a village in Andalusia and that her parents were plain, unpretentious people. They'd encouraged their only daughter to take up a position as companion to the wife of Don Fernando at a time when he was an up-and-coming government official in Peru with a bright future ahead of him.

Her poise weakened a little. 'I haven't had a letter in all the time I've been here. In her last letter my mother wrote to say my father was in poor health. His chest was weak and he had difficulty in breathing. I don't know if he still lives.'

As if making up her mind about something, she turned to look at him directly.

'Hector,' she said firmly, 'I know you're worried about me, and my decision to come away with you. Does it help if I tell you I had already resolved to leave Aganah?'

'Even if I hadn't come?'

She nodded. 'My life here has not been good.'

Hector sensed she was holding something back. 'Because of me?'

'Not in the way you're thinking. Of course, I was longing and hoping to see you again.'

'Can you tell me what happened?'

Maria gazed out across the sunlit bay, unseeing. 'After I refused to testify at your trial for piracy, everything changed.'

'Were you accused of lying?'

'Not openly. But I was ignored, almost shunned. The same Spanish officials who had brought me from Peru to London, to give evidence at your trial, treated me as though I had betrayed my country.'

Hector felt guilt rise slowly within him. 'I'm so sorry,' he said. 'You made that sacrifice for me. Without you I'd have been condemned to hang.'

She looked directly into his eyes. 'I'd do it again,' she said. 'But the days and months that followed passed so slowly, and I had no idea what would happen.'

'It was the same for me,' he said. 'But now it will be different.'

'From the bottom of my heart, I hope so,' she answered. 'Two days ago I wept, not because I was sorry to abandon Aganah and come away with you, but from relief that finally my wait was over.'

Hector felt humbled. 'Was your life here so difficult?'

She nodded, and he noticed that her eyes were moist with tears once again. 'When I first arrived in these islands, I told myself I'd wait two years, no more. If after that time you hadn't come, I'd force myself to forget you. I'd make a new beginning.'

'What did you plan to do?'

'Ask Doña Juana to release me from service. I'm sure she would have agreed. At heart she's a kind woman. She'd have persuaded her husband to find me passage to Manila on the next ship.'

'Was it Don Fernando who was difficult?'

Maria bit her lips. 'The Governor blamed me for his own troubles. He never said anything outright. But from the moment I returned to Peru, he was against me. Weeks would pass without him speaking to me directly, and I could sense his anger seething within him. And in all truth I was partly responsible for his disgrace.'

Hector allowed a long moment to pass before he touched on a subject that he knew would be a delicate one.

'Maria,' he said at last, 'to leave these islands, we must have a suitable boat. The only way we can do that is to seize it from your compatriots. There will be bloodshed and—'

'Perhaps it's better if you don't tell me any more,' she interrupted.

Hector shook his head. 'No. There mustn't be secrets between us. Dan, Jezreel and the others will join me in an ambush. We intend to capture the patache that brings supplies to Aganah. The Chamorro will loot the vessel for weapons. We are to be given her launch for our voyage westwards.'

Maria looked at him in consternation. 'Then we won't leave the islands for many months,' she said.

'Why not?'

'The patache has already been and gone.'

Hector thought he'd misheard. 'But the Maestre de Campo told Jacques he was expecting more supplies, that a patache would be here at any time.'

Maria was struggling to keep her voice calm. 'The patache did arrive, late last week. She dropped anchor off Aganah and stayed only long enough to unload, and then sailed onwards for Manila. The following day you and the others climbed in over the wall.'

Hector's spirits sank. He'd built up his hopes, and had begun to believe he would really be sailing west with Maria. Now it was all in ruins. 'I'll have to tell the others. Maybe one of them will have another idea,' he said lamely.

Just then they heard the sound of a distant musket shot. Alarmed for a moment, Hector thought the village was being attacked. Then he realized that Dan and Jezreel must already have started to train the Chamorro.

'WE'RE TOO LATE. We've missed the Spanish vessel,' he told Ma'pang bitterly as soon as he and Maria arrived back in the village. The Chamorro was standing outside his hut, deep in conversation with Kepuha. A little farther off, Dan was demonstrating to a group of Chamorro men how to knap a gun flint and install it in the doghead of the lock.

'Did your woman tell you this?' asked Ma'pang. He glanced at Maria, already surrounded by a cluster of children fascinated with her clothes.

'She did. We must abandon our plan for an ambush.'

Ma'pang took the shaman by the arm and led him to one side and there was a long, animated exchange between the two men. Finally Ma'pang returned to Hector and said, 'The council has already made its decision that we should attack the Spanish vessel. Kepuha believes it is not too late.'

Hector was taken aback. 'But the ship left for Manila three days ago. We'd never catch her.'

Ma'pang seemed unconcerned. 'Tell me how long you think it will take this vessel to reach Manila?'

Hector made a quick calculation from what he remembered of the charts aboard the *Nicholas*. 'She's a patache, and probably sails faster than a galleon. Maybe ten days,' he said.

'Are you and your friends still willing to attack with muskets, if we meet up with her?'

Hector recalled a sea fight off Panama, three years earlier. On that occasion a flotilla of musketeers in canoes – including Dan, Jezreel and himself – had tackled a trio of small sailing ships armed with light cannon. The musketeers had won.

'We are,' he said flatly.

'Then come with me,' said Ma'pang. He called out to the men under Dan's instruction, and immediately several of them ran off in the direction of the beach. Ma'pang, Hector and Kepuha followed.

They passed the place where the little fishing canoes lay drawn up on the strand, then veered to the right and a short distance farther on came to a grove of coconut palms. Set back among the trees was a barn-like building. Its palm-thatch roof was supported on stone columns similar to those that held up the uritao. It was a great cavern of a place, even larger than the bachelor house. The Chamorro stripped away the palms fronds that covered whatever was stored inside and gradually the shape of a boat emerged, similar to the fishing canoes, but much, much larger. At nearly sixty feet long, it was a substantial vessel. Like its smaller cousins, it had a long float attached to the side of the main hull by three curved, slender wooden struts. The float had been hollowed from a single large tree trunk. That was impressive enough, but Hector found it difficult to imagine what sort of giant tree had been used to provide the main hull. It stood taller than a man and was carefully shaped, with one side swelling in an elegant curve, while the other was nearly flat.

Ma'pang stood back, looking proudly at the giant canoe. 'That is our village's sakman,' he said.

Hector noticed a massive pole slung from the rafter of the boat shed. 'Is that her mast?'

Ma'pang nodded. 'And that long bundle next to it, her sail.'

Hector stepped across to the huge canoe, and squinted down the length of the narrow blade of the hull. 'I can see why the village takes such good care of her,' he said wonderingly. 'She must skim across the surface of the sea.'

Ma'pang caught the note of admiration in his remark. 'Only a few sakman remain. The Spaniards take care to burn them if they find them. Only a handful of old men still know how to construct them. Even if we can find trees large enough.'

'And the village council is willing to allow you to use the sakman to pursue the Spanish ship?' Hector asked.

Ma'pang reached out and, almost lovingly, touched the sharp prow of the great boat. 'The council agreed it would do honour to our proudest possession.'

A worrying thought struck Hector. 'Ma'pang, what happens if we manage to overhaul the patache and take her far out to sea? How will you find your way back to Rota? I expect we'll find charts and navigation instruments on the patache. But they will be of little use to you and, while I am willing to guide you back to Rota, I'd prefer to head on directly westwards.'

To Hector's astonishment, Ma'pang threw back his head and began to laugh so hard he started to cough and splutter. When he finally caught his breath and had wiped away a runnel of red saliva from his chin he said, 'Now you speak like a true guirrago. You think that you know everything, and that we, the Chamorro, are stupid.'

He translated Hector's questions to Kepuha, and the old man's face crinkled into a knowing smile. He beckoned to the young man to follow him.

'Go with the makhana,' said Ma'pang. 'He'll reassure you

that we won't get ourselves lost on the ocean. But hurry. We leave before nightfall, and there is much to do.'

Mystified, Hector accompanied the shaman at a fast walk back towards the village. Halfway along the track they turned to their right and plunged into the undergrowth. Pushing their way through the dense vegetation, they arrived at the foot of a low cliff draped with lianas and climbing plants. Kepuha pulled aside the vines. A section of the cliff face had been painted over with a light wash of lime. Here and there someone had made black marks with soot. Other mysterious symbols were drawn in red ochre.

Still holding back the vines, Kepuha looked back at Hector and waited expectantly.

Hector scrutinized the marks, trying to guess their meaning. When he failed to decipher them, the makhana stepped up to the wall and tapped on a symbol. It was larger than most, the size of the palm of his hand, and showed a hollow circle with four short curved lines radiating from it. He pointed up into the sky and made a sweeping movement from horizon to horizon. Next, he touched three or four of the black marks and again pointed to the sky, but this time in different directions.

Hector began to understand. 'The sun? Stars?' he enquired.

The makhana nodded. He carefully snapped off several twigs from a nearby bush and laid them on top of one another on the ground to make an open framework. Walking in a circle around the twigs, he stopped at various points to look up into the sky, then turned on his heel to face the opposite direction and again made a sweeping motion with his arm above his head. All the while he crooned what sounded like verses of poetry in his own language. He intoned with such reverence that Hector was reminded of the monks who'd taught him scripture during his childhood in Ireland. He understood that the makhana was trying to tell him something to do with the stars and sun, and that it had to do with the coming voyage. So he nodded and smiled politely and pretended to understand what the shaman was saying. Then, as soon as Kepuha finished, he hurried back in search of Maria to tell her of the new developments.

He found her in the village, talking with Jacques.

'What's going on, Hector? Everyone seems in a great hurry,' she asked. There was indeed a general bustle as Chamorro men and women busily filled baskets with dried fish and fruit and carried them off towards the beach.

'Stores for a long voyage, Maria,' Hector said. 'Ma'pang is sticking with the plan to loot guns from the patache. He seems to think he can catch up with her at sea.'

'Surely it's far too late. The patache will soon be halfway to Manila.'

Hector shrugged. 'He seems very confident. They've got a giant ocean-going canoe.'

'Will you, Dan, and the others be going with them?' she asked.

'The Chamorro don't yet know how to use guns correctly. They need us as musketeers if there's a fight.'

'Of course there'll be a fight,' she said a little grimly. She had another of the yellow flowers and twirled the blossom in her hand.

'Maria, it would make more sense if you came with us,' Hector said seriously. 'I don't want to leave you alone here on Rota. There's no point in sailing all that way, then bringing the boat back to fetch you.'

Maria began to pull the flower to pieces, petal by petal. Clearly she was unhappy. 'Of course I'll go with you,' she said in a small voice. 'But I didn't expect this to happen so soon.'

Hector frowned. 'What do you mean?'

She grimaced. 'I always knew my whole life would change once I went with you. But this is piracy. And if I'm with you, that makes me a pirate too.'

'But the Chamorro are at war. They're not pirates.'

'I don't think my countrymen understand the difference.'

'There need be very little bloodshed.'

She looked up at him, doubt in her eyes.

'We'll take the patache by surprise,' Hector went on, trying to sound more confident than he felt. 'Board her quickly. The Chamorro want guns, not a fight.'

'And what will the Chamorro do with the patache's crew?'

Hector forced a smile that he hoped she'd find reassuring. 'A living Spaniard is more valuable as a hostage to the Chamorro than a dead one,' he explained.

Even as he spoke the words, Hector had misgivings. He knew of only one prisoner taken by the Chamorro – the interpreter who had run away from the beach when they first landed from the *Nicholas*. Ma'pang had told him the wretched man had been caught farther along the coast. Regarding him as a traitor and turncoat, the Chamorro left his body on the shore with a spear driven through his mouth.

FOURTEEN

IT REQUIRED TWO TEAMS of Chamorro, forty men in all, to haul the sakman from her boathouse. They chanted as they heaved on the heavy coir ropes, and the vessel emerged into the evening light looking, Hector thought, like a crouching sea beast reluctantly dragged from its lair. The Chamorro threw heavy logs down on the sand as skids, and carefully manoeuvred the boat to the water's edge and pushed her afloat. Clay jars and bamboo tubes filled with water and the last of the stores were loaded. Hector, Maria and the other guirragos were told to climb aboard with their muskets and stay out of the way. Ma'pang was to be the captain, but the greater respect was paid to old Kepuha. He came down the beach, tenderly holding a framework of wooden sticks like the one he had shown to Hector. But this contrivance was brittle with age, its flimsy joints tied together with thin strips of coconut fibre. Here and there seashells had been attached like random barnacles.

Kepuha laid the contraption carefully inside the thatched hut that formed the only accommodation on the sakman. Then the vessel was pushed out farther into the sea until the helpers were chest-deep in the water. For a few minutes they held the sakman in position while Ma'pang shouted orders, and his crew of eight Chamorro fishermen raised the mast and fitted its heel in a central step. Heavy rope stays were led fore and aft, and secured. More rigging was taken out sideways to the float and fastened in place. As soon as the mast was held firm, the bulky cocoon of the single sail was attached to a halyard and unrolled. The fabric of the sail was woven from strips of palm leaf and was so fine that at a distance it could have been mistaken for canvas. Even before the sail was fully hoisted, the sakman began to sidle and shift, answering to the breeze.

The wading men were pulled off their feet and let go their grasp. Instantly the sakman began to gather way, moving so smoothly and quickly that Hector was scarcely aware the voyage had begun. One moment he was within a stone's throw of the watching crowd of villagers on the beach, close enough to make out their expressions of mingled pride and anticipation, and the next time he looked back, they were far away and indistinguishable. All he could see was the swaying of green palm fronds waved in farewell.

He turned again to look forward over the bows. The sakman had already crossed the width of the bay. He had to restrain himself from shouting out in alarm. The vessel was heading straight towards the barrier reef. In less than a minute she would smash into the jagged coral. Ma'pang, who held the steering paddle in the stern, let out a warning cry. To Hector's utter astonishment, it seemed that the sakman's captain had panicked. He threw the steering paddle into the water. In the same instant two of his men loosed the sheets that controlled the sail. Two others seized the forward end and ran with it aft to where Ma'pang was standing. The sakman slowed, hesitated and then began to move backwards. The abandoned steering paddle, Hector now saw, was attached to a cord. It floated past the opposite end of the hull, where another member of the crew retrieved it, placed it in a notch in the gunwale and began to steer. Now everything was back to front. The vessel's bow had become its stern, and the sakman was accelerating in the opposite direction, heading for the gap in the reef. Ma'pang treated

Hector to a jagged-toothed grin. 'Something else the guirragos have to learn,' he laughed.

As the sakman cleared the bay, she began to feel the full force of a steady breeze from the north. What had appeared a fast pace earlier now became a swooping rush. The boat seemed to lift, then surge across the surface of the sea, swaying lightly from side to side, barely heeling to the pressure of the wind as it filled the great scoop of the sail. The water bubbled and swirled in her wake. The Chamorro crew hurried from one part of the vessel to another, tightening knots, checking lashings, ensuring the structure of the vessel was snug.

Dan, standing beside Hector at the foot of the mast, watched with undisguised admiration. 'I would not have believed it possible,' he said. 'How fast do you think she is moving?'

'Quicker than I've ever sailed before,' Hector answered. 'If we continue at this pace, maybe Ma'pang was right. We'll catch the patache with ease.'

He ducked as a burst of spray swept across the gunwale and wetted his face. A Chamorro crewman crouched in the bottom of the hull was beckoning to Dan and holding up a wooden scoop. Dan moved away to join him, calling out over his shoulder, 'She is taking water fast. But as the timber swells, the leaks will slow, and the lighter we keep the boat, the quicker she will move.'

'Cold food from now on, I suppose. No one could possibly cook under these conditions,' said Jacques morosely. He was half-sitting, half-standing, his feet braced against one side of the hull, his shoulders pressed to the opposite gunwale.

Hector looked for Maria. She peeked out from the little deckhouse where she'd taken shelter. He smiled at her encouragingly. Beside her he caught a glimpse of Stolck looking glum. Ever since he had been stranded ashore by his countrymen, the Hollander had been downcast and listless.

Holding on to the mast's mainstay to keep his balance, Hector cautiously edged across to the deckhouse.

'Are you all right, Maria?' he asked, kneeling down and peering in. Inside the little shelter there was only room to sit or lie down, and the place smelled strongly of coconut oil. He saw that all their muskets had been laid out carefully, side by side, and someone had wrapped them in strips of oil-soaked cloth. The rags were the same colour as the dress that Maria had been wearing on the day they had fled the Presidio.

She caught his glance and shrugged. 'Jezreel said the muskets would be ruined if they were exposed to the salt air.'

'It'll be dark very soon,' he said. 'Try to make yourself comfortable for the night.'

'I'd prefer to be out in the open air,' she replied. Hector looked back to see what Ma'pang and his crew were doing. Clearly their work was complete. Most of the men were lounging wherever they could find space within the main hull. Ma'pang and one other man squatted in what was now the stern of the sakman. But there was no sign of a steering paddle. They were controlling the direction of the vessel by the set of her sail.

'Everything seems to have settled down,' he said. 'Let's go up into the bow.'

Together they clambered forward. A Chamorro crew member tactfully moved aside so that they could stand side by side just behind the sharp beak of the prow, the vast open expanse of the ocean stretching before them. The setting sun was very close to the horizon, and the sakman was running directly along the gleaming red-gold path of its reflection. In the far distance a line of fair-weather clouds hung motionless, their undersides tinged with pink. The sakman now had the wind on her beam, and Hector felt something flicker lightly across his cheek. It was a strand of Maria's hair lifted by the breeze. She put up her hand to tuck it back in place.

'Let's hope this wind holds through the night,' he said.

Maria didn't reply. He sensed that she was absorbed by the immensity of what lay before them. Very quietly, she laid her head on his shoulder. He feared to move a muscle and stood, barely breathing, and felt the tender weight of her. Gently he put his arm around her shoulder. They stood in quiet, contemplative silence while beneath them the sakman raced onwards, its hull rising and falling to the rhythm of the waves with an urgent, rushing sound.

✳

THE NEXT MORNING dawned clear and bright. The wind had shifted and now blew from slightly ahead of their track. If anything the sakman was moving even faster, racing across the sea, leaving a well-defined wake. By unspoken agreement with Ma'pang, the tiny cabin had been given over to Maria. Dan, Jacques and the others had copied the Chamorro, who curled up wherever they could find a resting place among the baskets and other clutter. Hector had spent the night sleeping by the foot of the mast. Several times in the hours of darkness he'd woken to the sound of someone scooping water from the bilge and tossing it overboard. Each time he'd looked aft and seen the dark shape of Kepuha sitting cross-legged by the stern, a palm-frond cloak around his skinny shoulders. The old man took no part in handling the vessel. He merely sat and watched from his vantage point. He was there now.

Hector rose and made his way aft. Ma'pang held out half a coconut shell filled with water, and he accepted the drink gratefully.

'How does Kepuha decide which way we steer?'

'I thought he had explained that to you,' answered the Chamorro.

'Not in a way I could understand,' admitted Hector.

'You saw the star wall. That is used to instruct learners how to read the skies.'

'He showed me, but I couldn't make sense of the twigs he laid out on the ground.'

Ma'pang searched for the right word. 'It's what you call a

map,' he said. Seeing that Hector was still puzzled, he went on, 'All the ocean around tano' tasi is shown on that map.'

Hector had a flash of understanding. 'Those shells on the stick framework, they represent the islands?' he asked.

'Yes.'

Hector stole a sideways glance at the shaman. He couldn't see the twig device. Instead Kepuha was holding in his lap a human skull, desiccated and yellow with age.

Ma'pang dropped his voice to a respectful tone. 'Kepuha knows the star paths by memory. He does not need to consult the map of sticks. He brought it on this voyage out of respect to the ancestors.'

Kepuha's lips were moving. He was singing some sort of chant in a low, quavering voice, the phrases long drawn out, and the sound rising and falling. Hector was reminded of how the old shaman had sung before the star wall, but these chants were different.

'He sings to the sea gods to bring us good weather,' said Ma'pang.

Elsewhere on the sakman various crew members woke and stretched, beginning the new day. Every few moments Hector glanced towards the little cabin, waiting for Maria to appear.

A shout from one of the Chamorro and an outstretched arm made Hector look to stern. Half a dozen dolphins were surging back and forth about twenty paces astern of the vessel. Their backs glistened as they came thrusting half out of the water, twisted and dived and reappeared in a churning froth of activity. He could hear their explosive grunts as they emptied and filled their lungs. They were in a hunting frenzy. Hector was pushed aside by the sudden rush of a Chamorro crew member running to the stern. He had a coil of fishing line in his hand, and with a quick flash the bone hook hit the water and the man paid out the line. Almost immediately there was a tug and the fisherman hauled in a fish, silver and yellow and a foot long. Another cast of the line, and another fish came tumbling in over the gunwale, flapping and leaping as it thrashed across the bilge, leaving a track of silver scales. The first Chamorro fisherman was joined by another, and in minutes they had caught a dozen fish. Without warning, the hunting dolphin abruptly disappeared, and the fishing ceased.

'It seems we won't go hungry,' observed Jacques, bleary-eyed and scratching his close-cropped head. He must have slept badly.

A whiff of burning surprised Hector. At the foot of the mainmast, deep down in the hull and sheltered from the breeze, one of the Chamorro had struck a flint and set alight a twist of dried coconut husk. He waited until the flame was steady, then touched it to a little pile of charcoal heaped on a flat stone. He crouched over the tiny fire, blowing gently, nursing the flame until the charcoal was glowing. The newly caught fish were gutted and cleaned by his companions, then grilled one by one and distributed.

Hector returned to sit by Ma'pang and discuss the prospects for the voyage. He learned that the sakman carried enough water for ten days at sea. When that reserve was halfway exhausted, the vessel would have to turn back. He found it difficult to concentrate. His attention strayed constantly towards the little cabin. When Maria did emerge soon afterwards, she looked more relaxed than he had yet seen her. Her hair was tied back with a ribbon and she was dressed in a simple petticoat, with her arms and feet bare. Watching her as she made her way to the base of the mast and accepted a serving of the cooked fish, Hector felt thwarted and impatient. She was so close physically and yet, with everyone's eyes upon them, he had to keep a distance.

So the day wore on. The sakman maintained its remarkable pace. The Chamorro crew took turns to steer, very occasionally adjusting the slant of the sail in response to a murmur from

Kepuha. The old man sat unmoving for hour after hour, seemingly impervious to the sun and wind.

The midday meal was a ration of breadfruit washed down with a few mouthfuls of water. The breadfruit came as a mash scooped from a basket, half-fermented. Heated on the stone cooking slab, it had a slightly sour taste. By then Hector was hungry and found it delicious. Then, an hour before dusk, the wind finally failed them completely. It had been easing in strength all afternoon, and the sakman had been travelling slower and slower. Now the vessel moved at less than walking pace. The great sail hung slack, filled and then went slack again. The sakman rose and fell as a long, slow swell passed under her. Ma'pang balanced his way along one of the struts holding the outrigger and lowered himself into the sea. He stayed in the water for a good ten minutes, hanging on to the float, motionless. When he climbed back on the boat, he went immediately to Kepuha and spoke quietly to the old man.

'What's happening?' Hector asked.

'The makhana must be kept informed.'

'Informed of what?' asked Hector, puzzled.

'Of the current.'

Hector looked at the big native in open disbelief. The water had not yet dried after Ma'pang's swim. His dark skin glistened, and a few beads of water gleamed in his bushy hair.

'You can tell what the current is doing by immersing yourself?'

'Of course,' Ma'pang replied as if speaking to a simpleton. 'If you keep still, you can feel the current. The direction it goes and how strongly.'

Hector suppressed his doubts. Anything that would help Kepuha in his navigation was valuable.

'How long do you think the calm will last?'

Ma'pang shrugged. 'Kepuha says that the wind will come again tomorrow in mid-morning. After the full moon.'

'And what about the patache? Does Kepuha know whether it too is delayed?'

Ma'pang shook his head. 'We can only hope that the patache is caught in the same calm as us.'

As the sun dipped below the horizon, the sakman was completely motionless on a glassy sea. The meagre supper of leftover fish scraps and another gulp or two of water were consumed in silence. An air of patient resignation settled over the company. Everyone knew there was nothing they could do but wait for the wind to return. Even Kepuha ceased his prayers and chants. After the brief tropical dusk, a full moon rose, shining hard and bright. Hector joined Maria as she sat on an outrigger strut beside the shelter, suspended above the calm sea. Neither of them spoke. The moonbeams were so strong they penetrated several feet into the water. Looking down from their perch, Hector could see three or four fish, each as long as his arm, cruising slowly back and forth beneath the shadow of the vessel. He recognized their blade-shaped bodies and high, blunt heads. They were the same voracious creatures that hunted flying fish by day. Now they seemed relaxed and sociable, spreading their fins so that they appeared to be balancing on underwater wings of blue. The only sound was the gentle swash of water against the hull as the sakman rocked a few inches at a time.

'Do you think we will overtake the patache?' Maria asked softly.

'It all depends on the wind,' Hector answered. 'Kepuha forecasts a good breeze tomorrow.'

'The crew seem to respect him.'

'Ma'pang says that Kepuha is one of the greatest navigators the Chamorro have ever known.' He looked up at the sky. Beyond the halo of the moon he could faintly detect the pinpoints of the distant stars. 'The Chamorro believe that at the beginning of time their god-like ancestors made voyages through the heavens. They marked their passage with stars.

Kepuha knows their paths and follows them. Above every island the gods left certain stars to mark their location.'

'Does that make sense to you?'

'It's a different way of looking at the heavens. I measure the stars and sun to decide where I am, then use a chart and compass to plot a course to my destination. Kepuha's system is more direct. For him, the stars are signposts in the sky.'

They sat together in companionable silence for several minutes. Then she said softly, 'If only we had signposts.'

Hector took a deep breath. 'To show us where to direct our lives?'

'Yes.'

'And if you had to select a way, where would you wish to go?'

'Somewhere safe and calm, a place where our differences and backgrounds are of no concern to others.'

'If such a place exists, then we'll search for it and find it,' he said, though he was conscious that his reply sounded a little boastful.

She seemed to accept his answer. 'Hector, I'm so happy that we are together. I know you love me, and I have the same feeling for you.' She hesitated before continuing. 'But until we find that place, something will be left unfinished. I hope you can understand that.'

Hector struggled to put his thoughts into words. He knew that Maria was setting the boundaries for their relationship in the days or weeks to come. 'I do understand, Maria, and I will be content for us to cherish one another. We'll wait to find that place where we can be safe together.'

She turned and kissed him lightly on the mouth. 'Hector,' she said, 'sometimes when I'm with you, I feel just like this, floating on a quiet expanse of calm.' Then she moved to one side and disappeared into the little cabin.

✳

AS KEPUHA PREDICTED, the wind came next morning. It arrived in dramatic fashion, bringing a torrential rainstorm that swept down from the north and enveloped the sakman. Visibility was reduced to a few yards, and within moments everything on the vessel was soaked. The sakman leaped forward, her water-logged sail filling with an alarming creaking of the mast and stays. Ma'pang eased the mainsheet to reduce the pressure of the wind, and the Chamorro crew scrambled to place clay jars where they would catch the runnels of fresh water cascading off the sail. Then the vessel ran blindly through the murk.

When the rainstorm passed on, it left behind a dull, overcast sky and a sullen, lumpy sea, no longer deep blue but a dingy slate-grey. The air was still warm, but damp and clammy. Nothing dried. Hector watched to see if Kepuha would manage to set a course now that he no longer had the sun to guide him. The makhana appeared unruffled. He sat at the stern as if nothing had changed.

'How does he know which way to steer?' Hector asked Ma'pang quietly as they ate a meal of raw fish. The charcoal for the cooking fire had been saturated.

'The wind and waves tell him,' answered the Chamorro. 'Kepuha will not lose his way. You need not worry.'

But Hector did continue to fret. All that day and the next a veil of heavy cloud obscured the sky, and he became increasingly doubtful that the makhana could succeed in tracking down the patache. The more he thought about their mission, the worse seemed the odds against success. Quietly he resigned himself to the moment when Ma'pang would announce that they must turn back for Rota before their supplies ran out, and he wondered how his companions would react to the failure. Maria, he was relieved to observe, had come to terms with the tedium and the cramped conditions of the voyage. She would sit in the door of the little shelter, watching the pattern of the waves. Occasionally her watchfulness was rewarded with a brief sighting of sea life

— the leap of a dolphin or, once, a pod of whales so close to the sakman that the fishy smell of their exhalation swept across the boat. By contrast, Jezreel with his massive frame accumulated bruises and scrapes as he moved around the crowded vessel. Jacques showed an almost limitless capacity to doze away the time, and Dan was happy to pass hour after hour with a fishing line. Stolck, however, was a cause for concern. A rash of salt-water sores, raw and oozing, had developed on his wrists and ankles where his clothes rubbed, and he appeared to be sinking into a profound depression.

The fifth day of their voyage began under the same lowering grey sky. The sakman had run smoothly all through the night with a steady breeze on the beam, and Hector calculated that she was covering ten miles every hour on the long swell rolling across their track. He had just finished eating his breakfast — a fist-sized lump of the sour breadfruit mash — when he noticed that Kepuha had risen to his feet and was staring intently downwind. The young man turned to look in the same direction, but could see nothing except the rounded backs of the waves as they travelled towards the horizon. Nevertheless, Kepuha stood there for several minutes. He seemed alert, yet puzzled. After an interval he spoke to one of the Chamorro crewmen, who made his way to the foot of the mainstay and began to haul himself aloft. From there the lookout called down to the deck.

'What's he say?' Hector asked Ma'pang.

'There's a guirrago ship in the distance. About ten miles away.'

Kepuha was beckoning. 'You better come with me,' said Ma'pang to Hector. 'This is a surprise and may change our plans.'

Ma'pang and the makhana conferred briefly. Then Ma'pang turned to Hector and said, 'Kepuha is certain the ship to the south of us cannot be the patache. It is in the wrong place.'

Hector refrained from asking how the shaman was so sure about the distant vessel. He feared the question would offend the old man. Instead he said, 'Perhaps we should investigate.'

There was a rapid exchange between the two Chamorro, and then Ma'pang nodded. 'Kepuha says that if we change course now, we'll lose time and may not catch up with the patache.' His deep-set brown eyes searched Hector's face. 'I leave the choice to you.'

Hector was in a quandary. The sakman had shown that she was fast enough to overtake her prey, but even if both vessels had shared the same weather conditions – and that was by no means certain – the Chamorro might already have overhauled the Spaniards and sailed right past them in the darkness or in poor visibility. On the other hand, the unknown vessel could be well armed and powerful enough to beat off an attack by Chamorro pirates. Then he remembered Maria's fears that they'd kill her countrymen. The unknown vessel might not be Spanish and yet might carry weapons the Chamorro could plunder.

'I say we try our luck with that stranger,' he said.

At a shout from Ma'pang, two of his crew began to ease out the mainsheet. Two others brought the forward corner of the sail aft until it was level with the mast, and a third eased on the halyard. The great sail ballooned out across the vessel, almost flying free. The sakman turned and began to sail downwind, the bow dipping and rising as the ocean swells overtook her.

✳

'WHAT SORT OF ship do you think she is?' Hector asked Dan half an hour later. The two men, loaded muskets in hand, were in the bow of the sakman, trying to make sense of what they saw less than half a mile away.

The unknown vessel appeared to be a small merchantman of about a hundred tons. She had an unusual, very old-fashioned appearance. Two small aft decks rose one on the other to give a high, narrow stern, and there was a long run amidships to a low, shortened forecastle, so that she looked as though at any moment she would topple forward and bury her nose in the sea. She was rigged with three masts, but had only her foresail set, barely enough to propel her forward. She sat unnaturally low in the water, and was wallowing and pitching aimlessly. The sail flapped and slatted, and there were regular glimpses of a rich green coating of weed and growth clinging to her hull. Her rigging was slack and slovenly, and even at that distance an unhappy groaning could be heard as her masts worked in their steps. Most puzzling of all, she showed no signs of having seen the sakman bearing down on her.

'There,' exclaimed Dan. 'Did you see it? Someone on her quarterdeck.'

Hector looked closely, but could see nothing. The vessel's rudder was banging back and forth, swinging loosely from side to side. It appeared there was no one at the helm.

'It could be a trap,' said Stolck, who had come up behind them. He looked more animated now that there was something unusual happening, and he too carried a loaded musket.

'Dan thought he saw a movement,' said Hector.

Stolck gave a grunt and crouched down. He rested the barrel of his musket on the edge of the canoe's hull and aimed at the merchantman. 'If anything moves again, I'll deal with it.'

The sakman was closing the gap very rapidly. Hector had advised Ma'pang to approach from directly astern, the point at which the strange vessel would be unable to use her broadside, if she had one. Now he worried that the sakman was moving so quickly she'd overshoot her victim.

'Where is everyone on that ship?' asked Jacques.

It was puzzling. Aboard the merchantman there was no one in the rigging or on deck. Several ropes trailed over her side, dragging through the water.

Stolck was muttering under his breath. He sounded irritable

and impatient. 'They're waiting until we are alongside. Then they run out their guns and we'll be blasted to pieces. I'll give them something to think about.'

Without warning he pulled the trigger of his musket. The sound of the gunshot echoed across the water, and Hector saw splinters fly up from a stanchion under the poop rail. But once again there was no reaction.

Hector glanced back over his shoulder. Ma'pang was in the stern at the steering paddle, and three of his crew had made their way to the outrigger struts. They crouched behind the little cabin, hidden from anyone on the merchantman. With a knot in his stomach, Hector realized the cabin was the obvious target for any gunfire from the strange vessel. Maria had decided to stay out of sight inside, and its flimsy thatch would provide no shelter from a musket ball. She'd be far safer crouched in the bottom of the sakman's main hull. But it was too late to do anything about that now.

The sakman was very close, less than a stone's throw from the high stern of the vessel. Hector looked up, trying to distinguish the flag. But the cloth was tangled around its staff. He could only make out part of a white stripe on a blue background and a small red blotch.

The sakman suddenly swerved as Ma'pang twisted hard on the steering paddle, and the boat swept under the stranger's overhanging stern. There was a brisk flurry of action as the palm-leaf sail was dropped, and at the same moment the three crouching crew members raced out along the struts and put their full weight on the outrigger. The float dipped into the water, caught and held, and the sakman slowed abruptly to a halt, almost as if she had dropped anchor in mid-ocean.

'Ho there! Anyone aboard?' Hector shouted up at the silent ship. There was no answer. He put down his musket and grabbed for one of the trailing ropes. He hauled himself upwards hand over hand, his feet scrabbling for purchase on the stained side of the ship. Beside him he was aware of Ma'pang armed with a spear and moving even faster, and of Jezreel with his backsword hanging from a lanyard around his wrist.

Hector reached the ship's rail and clambered over. He found himself standing in the waist of the vessel, on the deserted main deck. To his right a short ladder led to the foredeck, and to his left a similar companionway gave access to the half-deck and the quarterdeck above it. All around him was the usual clutter of ship's gear – blocks, ropes, a wooden bucket, several chests lashed to the rail, a small skiff lashed upside down over the central grating. He counted six cannon ranged along each side. None of them was prepared for action, their gun carriages were still lashed to ring bolts in the deck. He heard someone's tread on the deck behind him and turned hastily, heart pounding. It was Stolck. The Hollander was breathing heavily, his shaven head shiny with sweat. He had his reloaded musket in his hand.

'What's going on?' he asked.

'There's no one aboard,' answered Hector.

Just then he caught a whiff of something burning. Stolck let out an oath, ran across the deck and began to stamp frantically on a thin rope. Hector saw a wisp of smoke beneath his feet.

At that moment a musket shot rang out, and a musket ball whirred past his head. Shocked, he spun round on his heel and was just in time to get a glimpse of a musket barrel being withdrawn through a small hatch in the bulkhead under the foredeck. A cloud of gun smoke hung in the air.

Hector dived for cover behind the skiff. Now he knew. The crew of the merchantman had retreated to close quarters. They had barricaded themselves into the forecastle, from where they would shoot down any boarders at point-blank range.

He lay flat on the deck, his eyes searching out the objects around him. A crew in close quarters usually left explosive devices on deck. They filled chests and glass bottles with gunpowder and scraps of metal and fitted fuses that could be lit from within their refuge. When the boarders arrived on deck, the home-made bombs and grenades were exploded, with devastating results. Stolck must have stamped on one such fuse. Perhaps there were others.

Ma'pang appeared from behind the mainmast, sprinting towards the forecastle. Another musket shot, and it must have missed, for the naked Chamorro vaulted up on to the foredeck in one huge leap. Now he was out of the line of fire.

Hector watched as Ma'pang poked and prised with his spear point, searching uselessly for a way to break into the stronghold from above.

Someone inside the forecastle began coughing loudly. The black powder must have blown back into the loophole. Then came a shout, and Hector caught words that sounded like 'swart bastert'.

The accent sounded familiar, and Hector was trying to identify it when Stolck's voice came from less than an arm's length away, from the other side of the launch, where the Hollander had also taken cover. Stolck bellowed, 'Halt ofsjitte, du idioat.'

There was a sudden silence.

'Hwa bisto?' called the voice from inside.

'Stolck ut Friesland.'

Another long silence. Hector could hear the creaking of the ship. He wondered what was happening on the sakman, still lashed alongside the merchantman and out of sight.

There was another shout from within the forecastle.

'What's he saying?' Hector hissed.

For the first time in several weeks the Dutchman gave a smile. 'He asks what the hell I am doing in the company of naked savages.'

'Tell him we're trying to get a lift,' Hector said. When Stolck relayed the answer, there was a pause. Then a heavy wooden door in the forecastle slowly opened and a strange figure emerged shakily. It was a heavily bearded man, coughing and stooped, dressed in worn sea-going clothing, his greasy, matted hair hanging down to his shoulders. He was nervously fingering a musket. He gave a great start as Ma'pang dropped down on the deck from behind him and wrenched the gun from his hands.

'Don't be afraid,' called Hector, rising to his feet. 'He's a friend.'

Now that the man was closer, Hector could see he had the pasty skin and rheumy eyes of an invalid. 'Are you in charge of these sea robbers?' the sick man wheezed, speaking English now and in a very evident, deep guttural accent.

'Ma'pang here is our leader. Who are you?'

'Hendrik Vlucht, captain and part-owner of this shitten, luckless *Westflinge*.'

A slight movement in the open doorway behind Vlucht caught Hector's attention. Another man emerged. He hung on to the door jamb to keep from falling. He too was coughing, his skeletal frame racked with spasms.

As the newcomer tottered forward, Hector noticed Ma'pang backing away, keeping his distance. There was an expression on his face that Hector hadn't seen before: a look of alarm.

Hendrik Vlucht spoke again. 'Thought our luck couldn't get any worse, and then we saw your vessel coming towards us. No one fit to man the ship, let alone fight her guns.'

'Where's the rest of your crew?' Hector asked.

'Haven't had time to check recently,' answered the Dutchman sourly. 'Started out with twenty-three, and dropped a dozen of them overboard before we lost the strength to do so.' He doubled up and retched. When he straightened up, his knees sagged and he had to reach out to hold on to the launch for support. He nodded vaguely towards the poop deck. 'Piet and I are strong enough to pull a trigger. But the others are too weak to move.'

'What about the surgeon? Couldn't he help?'

The Dutchman gave a cadaverous grin. 'Never shipped a surgeon. Couldn't afford one and there were no volunteers.'

'But I thought every Company ship had to carry a surgeon.'

It was a piece of information that Hector had picked up from Stolck. Every ship of the Dutch East India Company carried a medicine chest and some sort of doctor. He presumed that the *Westflinge* belonged to the Verenigde Oostindische Compagnie, which held Holland's monopoly of the East India trade.

'Who says we're a Company vessel?' retorted Vlucht with a twist of his mouth. Hector recalled the colours of the ensign on the stern. They were not the red, white and blue of the Company.

Ma'pang broke into their conversation. The Chamorro warrior was still standing several paces away. 'Hector, we must get off the ship at once. They have the shivering sickness.'

'No, Ma'pang. I think they are suffering from sea fever.'

He could see that the big Chamorro did not believe him. Ma'pang's voice was thick with fear and disgust. 'If my people become ill like this, they die.'

He was already moving away across the deck, returning to the sakman.

'Believe me, Ma'pang. I have some knowledge of this illness. I was once an assistant to a doctor,' Hector called out to him.

Ma'pang shook his head vehemently. 'Even the most skilful makhana cannot drive out the evil spirits that cause this sickness.' He had reached the rail now.

'At least take some guns with you,' Hector said. 'That's what you came for.'

'I know that the sickness travels. I do not want to bring it back to Rota with me. You and your people can do what you want.'

'Then ask Dan, Maria and Jacques to join me,' said Hector. He turned to face Vlucht. 'There are four healthy men with me, all experienced seamen.' He was speaking hurriedly, trying to make his point before Ma'pang left with the sakman. 'There's also a woman, and she can nurse your invalids. If you supply these natives with muskets and powder, we will stay aboard and help bring your vessel to safe harbour.'

The Dutch captain allowed himself a cynical laugh. 'And if I refuse, then these savages will take our guns anyway. Of course I accept your offer.'

'Wait, Ma'pang, wait just a few minutes,' Hector called out. He turned back towards Vlucht. 'Quick, where's the arms chest?'

The Dutchman pointed towards a door under the overhang of the quarterdeck. Hector beckoned to Jezreel and together they ran to find the *Westflinge*'s store of guns. Moments later they had dragged the arms chest to the ship's rail. Jezreel smashed open the lid and they began handing its contents down to the Chamorro, who nervously accepted the weapons while keeping as safe a distance as possible.

Maria and the others had scarcely set foot on the deck of the Dutch vessel before the Chamorro were casting off the lines holding the sakman alongside. They were in near-panic, handling the ropes as though fearful to touch them. They wouldn't even reach out and fend off against the side of the merchant ship. Instead they waited for the rise and fall of the swell to drift the sakman clear. Nor was there a backward glance as the spidery shape of their vessel turned and headed back to the Thief Islands.

FIFTEEN

THE REGULAR THUMP and shudder as the *Westflinge*'s steering gear slammed from side to side with each roll of the ship was grating on Hector's nerves. 'Do you mind if I deal with that?' he asked the Dutch captain. Vlucht was racked with another fit of coughing and weakly waved a hand, indicating that, as far as he was concerned, Hector and his comrades could do as they liked.

Leaving Maria and the others, Hector went with Dan and Stolck to the half-deck. The helm was an old-fashioned, heavy whipstaff and it was banging back and forth. Dan picked up a short length of rope, took a turn around the tiller bar and secured it. The slamming stopped. Hector climbed on up to the quarter-deck with Stolck and walked aft to inspect the flag tangled around its staff. He unwound the cloth and let it flap in the breeze.

He had never seen the design before: three diagonal silver stripes on a dark-blue field. Stitched on the stripes were red heart-shaped symbols. He counted seven of them.

'Whose flag is that?' he asked Stolck.

'Frisia — the place I come from,' answered the Hollander. 'Those red hearts represent the seven islands of our region. Some say there should be nine of them; others insist that they aren't hearts, but pompeblêdden, leaves of water lilies.'

'And why would Vlucht choose to fly such a flag?'

Stolck snorted. 'Because we Frisians are pig-headed and stubborn. We like to show our independence.'

'So Vlucht doesn't see himself as a Hollander?'

'Not unless it suits him. I'd say this ship is an interloper.'

Hector had come across interlopers before, in the Caribbees. Smugglers in all but name, they made surreptitious voyages to places where they had no right to be and trespassed on trading monopolies belonging to larger companies.

Stolck spat over the rail. 'If the holy and sainted Dutch East India Company caught Vlucht in this area, the *Westflinge* and her cargo would be confiscated and he'd be given a stiff gaol sentence, whatever flag he was flying.'

'Then surely there's little advantage in sailing under false colours?'

'It helps in foreign ports. If Captain Vlucht goes into Canton, for example, and claims he's a Frisian ship – not Dutch – then the local merchants can do business with him directly, instead of going through the Company's local agent and paying a commission.'

Hector looked at Stolck thoughtfully. The Hollander seemed to be remarkably well informed about interlopers and the China trade.

They made their way back to the main deck. Maria had just emerged from the forecastle, where Vlucht and his crew had been holed up. 'Hector, we need to attend to the sick quickly,' she said firmly. 'You should see for yourself how ill they are.'

Hector followed her through the open door to the crew accommodation. As he stepped inside the gloomy, unlit cabin, the rancid stench of damp, sweat and vomit caught him by the throat. With its low ceiling, the forecastle was so dark that it was difficult to make out any details. There was a rough table and two benches in the centre of the room, all of them fixed to the floor. Crude bunks like stable mangers extended along the bulkheads, and sick men lay in them all. On the floor were several shapeless bundles. One of them moved slightly, and Hector realized it was a man struggling to sit up.

'There are very sick men in here,' Maria said. 'They must be cared for.'

Hector made no reply. He'd recognized one reason for the smell. It was the rotting stink of scurvy, mixed with a sweetish fetid odour that he knew was the smell of dead flesh.

'It started with Batavia fever,' said Vlucht. He'd come into the doorway behind them, blocking out most of the already feeble light. 'A few of the men began to complain of head-aches and bone pains when we were only a couple of weeks into the voyage. That's normal enough in these waters. Nothing to worry about.'

The invalid on the floor held out a tin cup. His arm was shaking. Hector saw that the man's mouth was deformed by some sort of soft growth bulging from his gums. Maria took the cup and went to find water.

'The fever did the rounds, as we expected, and soon we were accustomed to it. But the Chinese customs people used it as an excuse to send us on our way,' Vlucht continued. 'Quarantined the ship for a month before obliging us to leave.' He laughed savagely. 'Of course that was after they had impounded our cargo.'

Maria returned carrying the water and knelt down by the sick man, holding the cup to his ghastly mouth so that he could drink. Even from a yard away, Hector could smell the foul stink of his breath.

Maria rose to her feet. 'Hector, we must get these men on-shore or they'll not live.' He didn't answer, but took her by the elbow and gently led her outside. Speaking softly so that no one else could hear, he said, 'Maria, I'll do what I can. But this ship is a near-wreck, and I have no idea how far it is to the nearest port.'

She pulled her arm from his grasp. 'Then find out. That Dutch captain has little care for his men.'

'I'll check if there are any medical stores aboard,' he assured her. 'Jezreel can help move the sick men out on deck so that the forecastle can be cleaned up. We might even be able to fumigate it, or spread some vinegar if it's available. But don't expect too much. Most of the invalids are likely to die.'

She glared at him. 'Two of the men back in there are dead already.'

'Captain,' Hector called out. 'What's the *Westflinge*'s current position?'

'I may be sick, but I can still navigate,' said the Frisian sourly and set off at a slow shuffle towards his cabin. Hector followed him and helped spread out the chart that lay on the captain's unmade bed.

'This was our position yesterday at noon,' said Vlucht, laying a grimy finger on the map. Hector took in the situation at a glance. The *Westflinge* lay a little south of the direct route from the Thief Islands to Manila, less than a hundred miles from the Philippines. The makhana had been a remarkable navigator. The sakman had followed the patache's track like a bloodhound.

'And where are you headed?' Hector asked.

The Frisian's finger hesitated and then slid across the map, south and west. It came to rest on a cluster of islands. 'Tidore is our destination.'

Hector looked up at Vlucht in surprise. 'But that's in the Moluccas, the Spice Islands.'

'Indeed it is,' said the Frisian. A crafty look crept into his eyes. 'Young man, I do not take you for a fool, and doubtless you have guessed already that I would seek to avoid anything to do with the Company. But I have had dealings with the Sultan of Tidore, and we have an understanding.'

Hector looked back down at the chart. It was all laid out before him. A series of small crosses and pin pricks marked the *Westflinge*'s outward track. The ship had sailed from the Spice Islands, visited the port of Hoksieu in China and then begun to retrace her route.

Vlucht guessed his thoughts. 'The Chinese turned us away at the instigation of the Company's agent of course, and because they saw a chance to get something for nothing. The contagion spread because my crew were denied a chance to go ashore and recuperate, or even to have a change of diet, because the port authorities also refused to let us take on fresh supplies. For the past month we've been limping south, with scarcely enough men to manage the ship.'

'But you will find an agent of the Company in Tidore as well.'

Vlucht's voice had a contemptuous edge. 'The Company isn't as all-powerful as it likes to make out. The Sultan of Tidore pretends to heed what their local agent says, and even allows the Company to keep a few soldiers on his island. But he has plenty of back-door dealings with the likes of me.'

'Do you think the *Westflinge* in her present condition can make it as far as Tidore?'

'We could always divert to Manila. That's closer.' A sly look passed across Vlucht's face as he made the suggestion.

Hector thought about what might happen to Maria if they sailed into a Spanish-controlled port. She would be arrested as a runaway and a traitor. He felt the Dutchman's eyes on him, watching for a reaction.

'I believe my friends would be willing to help get the ship to Tidore,' he said.

'I thought you might prefer that course,' said Vlucht meaningfully. 'When I heard you and the young lady speaking Spanish together, and I took account of the strange circumstances of your arrival, it occurred to me that your own situation is similar to my own – there are certain places we would wish to avoid.' He sat down heavily on his bed, beads of sweat breaking out on his grey face. 'I'm in no condition to bring my ship to Tidore, so I would welcome your help. I suggest you check the hold. You'll see there's no time to be lost.'

Hector left the Frisian in his cabin, and went to find Dan.

As he made his way across the main deck he noticed that Jezreel and Stolck had already carried several of the invalids out on deck, and that Jacques was stoking up a fire in the galley. Dan had filled a bucket with a mixture of wood chips, rags and tar, ready to fumigate the forecastle.

'Dan, leave that to Jezreel. I think the two of us should take a look below,' he said. Together they removed a hatch cover and descended into the darkness of the cargo hold. If anything, it was gloomier than the forecastle and it too had a strong smell. Hector pinched his nose.

'Cloves. It's lucky the ship was carrying a cargo of spice to China. This hold hasn't been cleaned for years, and someone's been using it as a latrine,' he said. The distinctive fragrance of cloves was still discernible, overlying the stench of human waste.

Dan went forward, stooping low under the deck beams as he explored. 'Nothing much here,' he called back. 'Just a few odds and ends. A couple of boxes. The ship is virtually empty.' He paused. 'Do you hear that noise? Let's check the bilges.' They could hear the slop and gurgle of water surging back and forth beneath their feet. Dan hooked his fingers underneath a deck board and prised it up. They peered down into the dark gap. A shaft of light from the open hatch above them glinted off a black, gleaming surface less than a foot below.

'No wonder she rides so sluggishly,' Hector exclaimed. 'There must be at least four feet of water in the bilge.'

They stared in dismay at the gently swirling water.

'The crew did not have the strength to pump her out,' said Dan. 'Let's hope the leaks are not too bad.'

They hurried back up to question Vlucht, who told them that the vessel hadn't been pumped for a week. He'd intended to dry her out and recaulk her hull in China, but that was another thing the Chinese had refused to allow. He suspected the *Westflinge*'s seams were seeping badly.

Hector called a hasty conference with his companions. The

five of them were enough to set and manage the sails, handle the ship, keep watch and steer. But whether they could keep the ship afloat long enough to reach Tidore was another matter.

'We'll have to take it in turns to man the pump and see if we can lighten the ship. If she continues this waterlogged, she'll barely crawl.'

'We can start by dumping her cannon overboard,' suggested Jezreel. 'There're several tons of useless metal there.'

Hector was more cautious. 'Let's keep one gun each side. Just in case we have to defend the ship. There are enough of us to make a single gun crew.'

Jezreel went off to find an axe and a maul, and soon he and Dan had hacked a hole in each bulwark wide enough for the guns. They found long hand-spikes and, one by one, levered the cannon into the gaps and shoved them overboard. They made a satisfyingly deep plumping sound as they struck the water and vanished into the opaque depths. Then the team moved to the halyards and sheets and set more sail. There was a steady breeze out of the north-east, and with an adjustment to her mizzen sail, they found they could make a course for the Spice Islands without the help of the rudder, so they left the whipstaff lashed in place.

'Time to try the pump,' said Jezreel. He and Stolck went to the aft side of the mainmast, where the T-shaped handle of the pump protruded from the deck. Like her steering gear, the *Westflinge*'s bilge pump was an old-fashioned affair. A wooden tube made from a hollowed-out tree trunk led to a foot valve in the bilge, and a long shaft worked up and down to provide suction. They gave the pump handle a tentative pull and, after a couple of strokes, the water began to trickle out on to the deck and run to the scuppers.

'Twenty minutes each,' grunted Jezreel as he began to send a steady jet of water across the deck.

Hector took an oar from the skiff and went back below to plumb the bilge. As he had feared, there was close on four feet of water. With his knife he scratched a mark on the oar handle as a reference. Turning to leave, his eye fell on a line drawn with chalk on one of the frames. Above it someone had scrawled a crude cross in broad strokes. He guessed it marked the level at which someone had calculated the ship would founder and drown her crew. The line was less than a foot above the water.

Twenty minutes at a time, the men took it in turns to pump. Jacques rummaged through the cook's stores and found some dried peas, half a cask of rancid butter and a box of biscuit. The last was mostly dust and weevils, so he cooked up a thin gruel, which Maria fed the invalids, though several of them had mouths too damaged to accept the food.

In mid-afternoon, after three hours of continuous pumping, it was time to check the water in the bilge once more. To Hector's disappointment, the level had dropped barely an inch. Dispirited, he returned to Vlucht's cabin and asked to borrow the chart and a pair of dividers. The Frisian captain was lying huddled in his bunk, his eyes bright with fever.

'Will we make it?' he whispered after watching Hector make his calculations.

Hector put down the compasses. 'If the wind holds fair, it could take seven or eight days to reach Tidore. I doubt we can last that long. Sooner or later the water will gain on us.'

'Then we should abandon ship before she sinks. Head for land in the skiff, once we are close enough to the Spice Islands,' the captain murmured.

'But there isn't room for all of us in the skiff,' Hector objected.

'Leave the worst of the invalids behind,' wheezed Vlucht. 'You and I both know they'll die anyhow.'

Hector left the cabin without answering and made his way back to the main deck. What Vlucht had said about the invalids was true. With men so far advanced in the grip of scurvy, their chances of survival were slim. Yet Maria would never agree to leave the ship and abandon her patients. For that reason, if no other, Hector had made up his mind that as long as the *Westflinge* was afloat, he would keep her on course for Tidore.

✳

OVER THE NEXT few days progress was achingly slow. The ship advanced at less than walking pace, heaving and wallowing sluggishly on a sea that seemed determined to hold back their progress. They kept at the pump until muscles and backs were aching, hands blistered. From time to time they formed pairs and hauled buckets up through the hatches and dumped the bilge water overboard. Jezreel spent one entire morning lugging up ballast stones and dropping them into the sea. But it made little difference. On the second day they only managed to hold their own, and during the morning of the third day the water was gaining on them perceptibly. Dan stripped off and pulled up boards at various places up and down the length of the hold and wriggled in through the gaps. He held his breath, ducked down and groped in the noxious water, feeling between the frames and among the remaining ballast, trying to locate the source of the leak. But he found nothing – no eddy or current that indicated an obvious weakness in the hull. The water appeared to be seeping in all along the seams.

It was after the last of these fruitless dives that he reappeared on deck carrying in his arms one of the wooden boxes that had been left in the hold.

'I could do with some more kindling for the galley,' Jacques remarked. He was scraping green mould from a piece of salt fish he'd discovered in a locker.

'First, let's see what's inside,' said Dan. Scratches and gouges showed that the box had been opened and loosely nailed back down. The Miskito took a marlin spike and levered open the lid.

'This will make you happy, Jacques,' he said, peering in. 'There is a fine fat chicken nesting here in straw.'

'All that pumping has turned your brain to soup, lourdaud,' retorted the Frenchman.

Dan reached into the box and took out several handfuls of packing straw. He lifted out a large, rusty metal cube. On top of the cube stood an eight-inch-tall model of a hen, with four chicks at her feet. They too were covered in rust.

'What have you there?' Jacques demanded.

'Some sort of clock,' said Dan. He brushed off stray wisps of the packing material and turned the cube to show Jacques that one side was inscribed with a clock face. He felt again inside the wooden box and found the hour and minute hands, which had become detached.

'Pity we cannot get that hen to lay. Fresh eggs would be useful,' Jacques commented, turning back to his work, his nose wrinkled in disgust at the rank smell of the putrid fish.

Dan was examining the hen more closely. 'The wings are hinged at the base, and the chicks are fixed to some sort of disc,' he said. He put the clock down on the deck. 'I wonder what it is supposed to do.'

'Sweeten the Governor of Hoksieu and his chief of customs,' said Vlucht. The Frisian had shuffled out of his cabin. 'Give a Chinaman a fancy clock, and the happier he will be. They're mad for those things. I purchased that hen-and-chickens in Batavia, and several other plain timepieces. Cost a fortune, but nearly got me flogged for insolence.'

'What happened?' Jacques was intrigued.

'The device worked well enough when I bought it off a thieving Zeelander. Must have got damaged during the voyage. When I presented the clock to the Governor at a formal reception, he asked for a demonstration. Nothing happened except that it made a nasty sound like a slow fart. He took it as an insult. Did more harm than good.'

Dan opened the flap in the back of the clock and inspected the mechanism. 'Looks as though a mainspring was dislodged.'

'So you think you know something about clocks?' said Vlucht scornfully.

'Looks much the same as an old-fashioned wind-up musket lock,' said the Miskito. 'Do you mind if I try to make it work?'

'You can throw it overboard for all I care,' grumbled the Frisian and stumped away.

Tinkering with the insides of the clock was a diversion from the chore of pumping. Dan took most of a day to clean and replace the cogs and wheels, and to work out how they should mesh and turn. Jacques used his knowledge of locks and metal springs to advise, and provided dabs of rancid butter to grease the mechanism. Finally, when they were satisfied with their efforts, they invited everyone who was fit enough to climb to the poop deck at five minutes before noon, there to witness a grand inauguration of their handiwork. When their audience had gathered, Jacques held up the cleaned and polished clock to show it off. Dan wound the mechanism with a key, closed the flap and carefully positioned the two hands to show just before noon. Then Jacques placed the device on top of the helmsman's compass box, stood back and waited.

Hector entered into the spirit of the occasion. He stepped forward with his backstaff to take his usual noonday sight. When the sun reached the zenith he called out the time. Everyone turned round and watched the clock expectantly. There was a long pause while nothing happened. Then the minute hand jerked to the vertical with an audible click. Cogs and wheels whirred internally. The four chicks began to move around in a circle at the hen's feet. The mother hen tilted forward and half-raised her wings, only for something to go wrong. Instead of flapping, the wings stuck halfway and vibrated with a grinding noise. Then, to a general burst of laughter, the automaton let out a false, rusty cockerel's crow. 'Even if the device had worked in front of the Governor of Hoksieu, I doubt he'd have been very impressed,' commented

Hector to Vlucht with a smile. 'Surely even in China, hens don't crow.'

∗

LATER THAT SAME afternoon the weather turned against them. The wind, which had been steadily in their favour, backed into the south-west and then rose to a half-gale with driving rain. The *Westflinge* lurched and shuddered on the increasingly boisterous waves. Vlucht shambled off to his bunk, leaving Hector in charge. Hector helped his comrades to hand the sails, then went with Dan to check the hold once again.

'The vessel is working badly,' Dan commented. Little jets of bilge water were now spurting up between the planks in the floor of the hold as the vessel rolled.

They returned to the half-deck and Hector tried moving the whipstaff. He felt the ship barely respond under his hand. With each passing hour she was becoming more of a floating hulk. 'I don't know how much longer she'll stay afloat,' he confessed.

'How much farther to Tidore?'

'Another hundred leagues, maybe more.'

Dan gazed downwind. A large grey seabird, an albatross, cruised back and forth, unconcerned by the gale, the tips of its immense wings skimming the surface of the sea.

'The vessel will never make it,' the Miskito said in a matter-of-fact tone.

Hector thought back to the calculations he'd made, estimating and re-estimating the distance to the nearest land. He wasn't confident the ocean currents had not affected their course, and he doubted the accuracy of the chart that Vlucht had on board. He marvelled once more at the way the Chamorro makhana had been able to navigate. 'Our best chance is to try to beach the ship as soon as we sight land,' he said at last.

He was aware of Maria approaching up the companionway. She was bare-headed, and her bodice and working skirt were rumpled and stained. She'd found a man's large shirt, which she wore loose as a gown, and the sleeves were rolled up to her elbows. The expression on her face was infinitely weary, resigned. Since coming aboard the *Westflinge*, Maria had spent all her time with the sick in the forecastle.

'There are two corpses to be dealt with,' she said simply.

'We must put them overboard without delay,' he said, knowing he sounded heartless.

'Then please do so,' she said, turning away.

He heard the catch in her voice and answered, raising his voice so that, without meaning to, he sounded harsh. 'Maria, every hour we keep the bodies on the ship, we risk spreading the sickness. And depressing the surviving invalids.'

She wheeled around. There were tears in her eyes. 'This voyage began so well. When we set sail with the Chamorro, I was so excited and full of hope. But the last few days have been a nightmare. Everything we do seems so pointless.'

A sense of helplessness swept over Hector. He dreaded telling her the full extent of their difficulties – that the ship was likely to founder. 'Maria, we all have to be patient . . . as you were at Aganah. Things will change, I promise.' He sounded so feeble, he thought. He was stating the obvious.

She put a hand to her cheek. Hector couldn't tell if it was to wipe away a tear or raindrops. He was aware that Dan had moved away to a tactful distance.

'In Aganah it was different,' she said. 'I got used to waiting and had set myself a deadline. I knew it would all come to an end, one way or another. But now, I've allowed myself to hope, and that makes the disappointment and setbacks harder to bear.'

'Maria, you've done all you could to save those two men. They were mortally sick when first we came on board. I promise you we'll head for the first land we see. If you can keep your patients alive until then, they should survive.'

'And how long will that be?'

'One or two days at most.'

'I pray you're telling me the truth,' she answered. She turned and made her way to the far rail and stood facing out to sea, her hands gripping the wet rail, her knuckles white.

Hector nodded to Dan and together the two men descended quietly to the main deck and entered the cabin. It still reeked of sickness and damp, but it was much more orderly and cleaner than before. The invalids in their cots and on the floor rested quietly on mattresses. Hector looked around, wondering where to find the dead men. One of the invalids in a bunk struggled up on an elbow, watching him silently. He moved his eyes deliberately, looking across and down. Two long shapes lay on the floor, covered with blankets. Without a word, Hector took one end of the nearest bundle while the Miskito picked up the other. Together they carried the corpse out on deck. It was a few steps to the gap in the rail they had cut when they dumped the cannon overboard. The burden between them was very light. 'Wait a moment,' said Dan as they reached the gap. They laid the dead man gently on the deck.

Jacques was nowhere to be seen, but Stolck had noticed what they were doing, and walked across and stood looking down at the corpse.

'Would you care to say a prayer over him?' Hector asked Stolck.

'I'm no pastor,' answered the Frisian in a defensive tone. 'But I'll help you carry out his companion.'

With Stolck's assistance, Hector brought the second corpse out from the forecastle.

Dan had disappeared down into the hold and now he reappeared with several fathoms of cord and two of the remaining ballast stones. 'We won't be needing these,' he said as he knotted a web of cord around each rock, then fastened the weights securely to the dead men's feet.

As soon as he was done, they slid the dead men overboard without ceremony. The whole business had taken no more than fifteen minutes. When Hector looked up, he saw Maria still standing at the rail, her back to the ship. She was drenched, her clothes plastered against her body, and she still gripped the rail with both hands.

✳

THANKFULLY THE RAIN eased early on the following day and the visibility improved. It revealed a dark smudge on the horizon to starboard. At first it was so indistinct it could have been a low bank of cloud, but as the hours passed it gradually became evident that land lay in that direction.

'What do you make of it?' Jacques asked Hector as they stood on the quarterdeck, gazing at the faint shadow. The sea had calmed, but this only served to emphasize that the *Westflinge* was almost dead in the water.

'Difficult to tell. But my guess is that it's one of the Spice Islands, possibly the north end of Gilolo.' Hector turned his attention to a small, yellow-brown clump of floating seaweed. It was nuzzling against the side of the ship. 'If I'm right, we've drifted farther south than I'd hoped and we have no hope of reaching Tidore, not with the ship in this condition.'

The clump of seaweed had barely moved an arm's length along the hull. The *Westflinge* was virtually stationary.

'Is there a harbour on Gilolo?' Jacques asked.

'Not on this side, according to Vlucht's chart. The east coast of the island is very little known. Nevertheless, I propose we run the ship aground there. At least we have a chance of getting everyone ashore, including the sick.'

'And if we come upon a coast full of rocks and reefs?'

Hector shrugged. 'We have no choice.'

Slowly, desperately slowly, the *Westflinge* edged closer to the land. The wind fell slack, barely filling the sails, and now only the current carried her along. The coast crept by, low and featureless and covered with dense jungle. There was no sign of a barrier reef, fortunately. The ship was so low in the water that she did not answer to the helm at all. Those on board could only watch and wait.

By dusk less than a mile separated the ship from the shore and she drifted onwards through the darkness. A heavy overcast obscured any light from the moon. It was pitch-black though close to dawn when they finally heard the low, grinding sound as the *Westflinge*'s keel touched. There came a series of shuddering, scraping noises as she slid gently on to her final resting place. A last muffled groan of timber, and all forward motion ceased. The only sound was an occasional low thump and tremor as a slight swell lifted and dropped the vessel, still upright, farther on the seabed.

They all waited on deck to see what daylight would reveal.

The *Westflinge* had gone aground a quarter of a mile from land. The water around her was clear enough to see the wavering outlines of grey and brown coral heads on which she was stranded. Directly ahead was a long, straight shoreline where a solid mass of vegetation came right to the water's edge, the branches of the larger trees overhanging the sea. The same dense green wilderness extended inland across broken country, and without a break as far as the eye could see. Except for the slow drift of pale-grey shreds of morning mist curling up from the jungle canopy, everything was silent and still.

Hector pointed a little to the north. There seemed to be a slight break in the wall of trees.

'That looks like a place where we could try to come ashore.'

'And what then?' demanded Stolck bluntly. 'This is a wasteland.'

'At least it's dry land,' Jezreel reminded him. 'Let's get off the ship while the weather's calm. The ship's so rotten she'll fall to pieces the moment there are waves of any size.'

They manhandled the skiff overboard, and Dan and Jezreel rowed off to investigate. They returned in less than half an hour to confirm they'd found that a small river emptied through a narrow creek and there was enough depth for the skiff to enter and unload.

All that morning they laboured, making several trips with the skiff. Dan selected a level spot on the river bank suitable for a campsite and they cut back the undergrowth, leaving small trees between which they ran ropes and draped sails as makeshift tents. They worked fast because thunderclouds were building up, towering over the interior and, as the first raindrops fell, they ran for shelter in the newly erected camp. Water drummed on the canvas, the rivulets carving runnels in the soft black soil. The unaccustomed smell of wet earth filled the air, and when the tropical downpour ended as quickly as it had begun, they heard the dripping and splashing from myriad leaves and branches as they shed the last of the deluge. While the others ferried the invalids ashore, Dan pushed his way through the wet thickets to investigate their surroundings. He came back to report that the river quickly dwindled into a stream and ran through rocky shallows, where he was sure they would be able to catch fresh-water prawns. He also brought back handfuls of small yellowish fruit the size of crab apples. They were full of seeds and had a sour, astringent taste, but Jacques thought he could use them in a stew that would help cure the sick.

'Not a bad place to be cast away. Reminds me of my days cutting logwood on the Campeachy coast,' observed Jezreel, slapping away an insect as he dug a small channel to drain away future downpours from the campsite.

Hector watched Maria carry a pitcher of water to the tent designated as a sick bay. She appeared to have regained her composure.

'Tomorrow we'll take off anything else from the ship that will be useful,' he said to no one in particular. Now that they'd abandoned the *Westflinge*, there seemed to be a general acceptance that Captain Vlucht had no further authority.

'How long do you think we will have to stay here?' asked Stolck.

Hector looked out to the wreck on the coral shelf. The merchant ship lay slightly canted over on one side, her three masts still standing.

'Not long,' he answered encouragingly. 'Anyone sailing along this coast will see the ship and come ashore to investigate.'

'And what if no one passes this way?'

'We'll have to think about sending a scouting party inland or along the coast in the skiff. See if they can fetch back some help.'

As usual Stolck chose to be pessimistic. 'And what about the invalids?'

'If they're not well enough to travel, you might have to volunteer to stay behind to look after them,' Hector snapped. He was becoming irritated by the morose Hollander.

That night few of them slept well. The sensation of being on solid land was unsettling and strange. All around them in the darkness they could hear the sounds of the jungle – the snap of a branch breaking, the slower and more ponderous crash of a dead tree falling, unidentifiable noises as wild creatures moved through the undergrowth.

※

SHORTLY BEFORE DAWN, an ugly cacophony of cawing and squawking woke them. The sound was so strange that Dan left his tent to see what was causing the commotion.

'Come and take a look. They're the strangest birds I have ever seen,' he said when he came back some minutes later. He led his friends along the river bank towards a clump of small trees. The noise got louder and louder as they approached, and they saw the branches were covered with a flock of jungle birds, several hundred strong. The birds fluttered, jostled and flitted incessantly from branch to branch, maintaining their raucous chatter.

'Reminds me of magpies back at home,' Hector whispered to Jezreel.

'No need to lower your voice,' said Dan. 'They will ignore you. Probably have not seen humans before.'

One of the birds was still for a moment, and Hector blinked, thinking he'd seen double. The creature appeared to possess two pairs of wings. He looked again, and saw that he was mistaken. The forward set of wings was a remarkably long, pointed ruff of striking iridescent green, which the creature could extend at will. Then, as he watched, the bird suddenly raised four long, feathery white plumes from its back so that they stood straight up in the air, like a peacock spreading its tail.

'What's the creature so excited about?' muttered Jezreel.

'What do you think, mon ami?' observed Jacques. The bird pranced up and down excitedly on the branch, fluttering his white plumes in a blur and calling out harshly. 'He is trying to impress that little dark bird opposite him. This is cock and hen.'

Abruptly the male bird stopped his frantic fluttering, gripped the branch with bright-red claws and squatted down. Then he extended his glistening green ruff and held his position, quivering with desire. Jezreel guffawed. 'There you are, Jacques. That's just like your iron chicken, stuck halfway and vibrating.'

OVER THE next week Dan made several exploring trips. He cast in a wide circle around the camp and tramped for hours over the soggy leaf mould at the foot of huge trees eighty and ninety feet tall. But he found no trace of any humans. The others continued to take the skiff out to the wreck of the *Westflinge* daily. They stripped the ship of anything that might be remotely useful. Vlucht retrieved his charts, almanacs, hourglasses and navigation instruments. Jezreel and Stolck collected muskets, powder and shot, and Jacques, besides salvaging two copper kettles and a gridiron, brought back the hen-and-chicks time-piece, though he endured some mockery from Jezreel. Mean-while the diet of wild fruit that the Frenchman prepared each day was proving effective. The five survivors from the *West-*

flinge's original crew began to regain their health. Their stiff joints eased and their swollen gums shrank, although the invalids were left toothless. Soon they were sitting outside their tent in the sunshine and even taking some exercise.

'She's finally bulged,' Captain Vlucht commented to Hector.

It was mid-morning on the tenth day since they had run aground, and the two men had strolled down to the mouth of the creek to look out at the wreck of the *Westflinge*. The ship lay heeled at a greater angle than before, and they could see a gaping hole in her side where the hull had split open. Her main topmast had collapsed, giving her an increasingly bedraggled appearance.

'In another few days we can start building something bigger than the skiff. One of my men is a carpenter,' Vlucht added. 'He'll be able to put together a launch big enough for the entire company. There's plenty of timber out there.' He nodded towards the *Westflinge*. 'Then we can sail coastwise until we reach Tidore.'

Hector was about to say that it would have saved him a lot of worry if he'd known earlier about the carpenter. Instead his attention was caught by a new sound – a steady rhythmic chant, very faint. He listened again. He heard the lapping of water on the beach, the thin piping calls of a seabird standing on a tiny coral outcrop, and then on a waft of the breeze he heard the sound again. He recognized a chorus, a single phrase repeated over and over by many men, and behind it the regular thump of a drum maintaining the tempo.

Vlucht heard it too. He blanched and looked anxiously along the coast in both directions, and then out to sea. 'Hongitochten,' he blurted out, shocked.

Hector was still baffled. The sound grew louder, but he still couldn't see where it came from. Then suddenly, from behind the wreck of the *Westflinge*, something emerged that looked like a giant insect, rippling forward on a double row of short legs, its head and tail raised in anger. It was a long, snake-like native vessel, and the moving legs were row upon row of paddles, flashing up and down. Two ranks of paddlers sat on the edge of the main hull, but at least sixty more were perched on boards attached to the outriggers, which projected from each side of the hull. All of them – close on a hundred men – were churning up the sea vigorously with their blades. They chanted together as a drummer on deck thumped out the rhythm. Occasionally a cymbal clashed. Out on the prow, like a living figurehead, stood a man in a long, flowing white gown. He had a hand cupped around his mouth and called out encouragement in a high, wailing voice.

'Kora kora,' said Vlucht anxiously. 'Native war canoe. The Company sends them on punitive sweeps, called hongi-tochten, to impose their control on the islands by brute force.'

'But I don't see any white men aboard,' said Hector. He could make out a cluster of men standing on the main deck, just in front of a small cabin of thatch, all of them gazing intently towards the mouth of the creek. None was dressed in European clothes. They wore long shirts and loose pantaloons and coloured turbans.

'Each Sultan maintains his own fleet of kora koras. They use them for personal transport and wars against their neighbours,' said the Dutchman.

The kora kora raced towards them, much closer now. Hector could see crimson, green and yellow ribbons fluttering from short staffs on the prow and stern. A chance gust of wind caught the huge banner flying from the stubby central mast so that it rippled sideways. The flag had an unusual shape, two triangles, one above the other. Its background was a deep distinctive violet, and the symbol on it was a golden python, coiled, tongue flickering and about to lunge.

SIXTEEN

THE KORA KORA headed directly towards them. Clearly the commander of the vessel knew exactly where to find the river mouth, and he'd seen the two castaways on the shore. Hector judged it wiser to stand his ground. Beside him Vlucht shifted nervously. 'Vicious bastards,' he warned. 'Treat them respect-fully. They take offence easily and would lop off your head if they thought you lacked respect.'

Within minutes the war canoe was close enough for a shouted command and a final thump of the drum. The paddlers relaxed, and the vessel glided into the little creek and nuzzled gently into the muddy bank.

With the chance to examine the crew more closely, Hector decided they weren't as fearsome as their reputation. Many of the paddlers were scrawny old men with stick-like arms and there was a sprinkling of youngsters who were little more than boys. They were half-naked, wearing only faded blue loincloths and head shawls, and their skins ranged from coffee-brown to a rich, dark mahogany. With short, fuzzy hair and broad, flattish noses, they were distinct from any of the people Hector had encountered on his travels. None of them looked particularly fierce or frightening as they rested on their paddles and cast curious glances at the two Europeans. In contrast to the huge, shimmering silk banner of violet and gold, the rest of the vessel was grey and shabby. There were several discoloured areas where the hull had been patched, and the thatch on the small hut that served as a cabin was frayed and tatty. Nor was the group of men clustered on the kora kora's deck very imposing. One or two were smartly turned out in long white gowns, but most of them were dressed in scraps of old uniforms, mismatched jackets and skirt-like sarongs, and they clutched matchlock muskets that were poorly maintained. The only weapons that appeared to be in good order were their long daggers with broad, slightly curved blades and a number of well-honed spears. There was no sign of any deck armament, and Hector doubted that the kora kora was sturdy enough to carry cannon.

Hector and Vlucht hurried forward to greet the landing party. It was led by the tall, thin man in the white gown. He had a narrow, scholarly face and shrewd brown eyes beneath a plain white turban. He appeared to be wary, rather than hostile, as he sprang ashore.

Unexpectedly he greeted them in heavily accented, but clearly understandable Spanish. 'From which country do you come?' he asked.

Hector nodded towards the wreck of the *Westflinge*. 'The ship is from the Netherlands, so too are her crew, and her captain here.'

The tall man was quick to note the omission. 'And yourself?'

'I come from Ireland.'

The tall man looked vaguely disappointed. 'Yet you speak Spanish?' he asked.

'I learned it from my mother. I had not expected to hear the language spoken so far from her homeland.'

'The Spaniards first came here during the reign of my Sultan's great-grandfather. They sought trade and we established good relations with them,' the tall man explained. He watched Hector and Vlucht closely, trying to decide what sort of people they were. 'I am Ciliati Mansur, and my family has provided court chamberlains over many generations. I was taught to speak the foreign tongue. But in the time of the present Sultan, the Spaniards have not returned.'

'Forgive me if I seem ignorant or impolite,' said Hector, 'but our vessel was leaking badly and we had no choice but to run her ashore. We do not wish to trespass, nor do we know on whose territory we have landed.'

The court chamberlain drew himself up to his full height and said with grave formality, 'You are on the lands of His Majesty Said Muhammed Jihad Saifuddin Syah ab Ullah, Sultan of Omoro. I have the privilege of presenting you to his son, His Highness Prince Jainalabidin.'

During the exchange a small, slight figure had emerged from the cabin on the kora kora and made his way to the bow. Hector saw that it was a child. One of the half-naked paddlers had left his place and gone to stand on the muddy bank, immediately beneath the upturned prow. He bent forward, hands on knees. The child stepped down on to the shoulders of his attendant, who carried him up the slippery bank and set him on his feet beside the chamberlain. Hector found himself looking down into the solemn yet haughty expression of a boy who could not have been more than seven years old. He was dressed in a dazzling white sarong, over which he wore an elegantly cut miniature jacket of cloth of gold with red facings. A turban of the same material was wound around his head, and his small feet were encased in white silk slippers. The lad's complexion was noticeably fairer than that of his attendants.

The boy spoke in a light, clear voice. There was no mistaking that he was giving orders to the chamberlain.

'His Highness,' Mansur translated, 'says that you are to come immediately to the palace. There you are to stand before the Sultan and explain your presence to him.'

Hector bowed diplomatically as Vlucht beside him muttered under his breath, 'Do whatever the puppy asks.'

The chamberlain turned to the kora-kora crew and waved.

A score of the Omoro left the war canoe and began to move off towards the camp.

'If Your Highness will excuse me, I must attend to my companions,' Hector apologized and hurried off to catch up with them.

The Sultan's men wasted no time in dismantling the camp. They took down the makeshift tents, rolled up the canvas and retrieved the ropes and cordage. They collected all the items that had been brought ashore from the *Westflinge* – the boxes, blankets, guns, tools, Vlucht's navigation instruments and Jacques' cooking gear. Everything was carried back on to the kora kora and stowed. Nothing was left behind, and soon the campsite was nothing more than a bare patch of ground. Jacques, Jezreel, Stolck and the invalids could only look on until the moment they were ushered firmly but politely on to the kora kora. The skiff, which had been moored to the bank, was untied and attached by a towline to the stern of the war canoe. Maria was nowhere to be seen.

'Where's Maria?' Hector asked Dan, catching him by the arm.

'She went off for a walk in the jungle,' the Miskito answered. 'She cannot have gone far.'

Hector turned to the Omoro chamberlain. 'One of our party is missing,' he said.

'We cannot delay,' Ciliati Mansur answered. 'The Sultan expects our return in time for maghrib, the sunset prayer.'

'Please allow me a few moments,' Hector begged.

Fortunately it took him no more than a few minutes to locate Maria. She had only gone as far as the tree, hoping to catch another glimpse of the remarkable birds. When Hector returned with her, the chamberlain was taken aback.

'You did not say that your travelling companion was a woman,' Mansur said in surprise.

'She is my betrothed,' Hector answered.

'But you are not yet married?'

'No.'

'And her family permits her to travel without female companions?'

'That is our custom,' Hector answered.

The chamberlain sucked in his breath softly. Hector guessed Maria was the first European woman he'd ever seen, and he didn't approve of her lax foreign ways. 'Then she must remain in the cabin until we arrive home,' he said firmly.

※

THE JOURNEY to the Sultan's capital proved to be a short one. The kora kora's crew looked to be frail, but they kept up a brisk pace. Four hours of steady paddling along the coast brought them to their destination, and Hector used the time to question Ciliati Mansur about what to expect. The Sultan of Omoro, the chamberlain informed him, had ruled for nearly forty years over a small coastal kingdom that was once rich and powerful, but now increasingly impoverished. Mansur blamed this decline on the shadow of the Sultans of Ternate and Tidore. They had intercepted the only trade that brought much money to Omoro – the sale of exotic bird skins.

'We call them manuk dewata, "God's Birds",' explained the chamberlain. 'In truth, Allah put the creatures in our jungle so that we can have something to offer in exchange for the items we lack – guns, powder, and so forth. Traders come from as far afield as Malacca to buy our bird skins.'

'Are the feathers really that precious?' asked Hector.

A slight smile twitched the corners of Mansur's mouth. 'Yes, thanks to the vanity of man. We pretend the birds are enormously difficult to catch. We claim they have no legs and so they can never alight on land, but soar up into the sunbeams and catch and fix the colours of the rainbow in their plumage.'

'I've seen the creatures settle and squabble on the branches of a tree, and they were noisy and very down to earth,' said Hector.

'Then you are one of the very few outsiders to have witnessed such things,' said the chamberlain. 'In reality the birds are not so difficult to take. The hunters spread a sticky gum on the branches where the birds gather, and the creatures are trapped. The bird catchers wring their necks, strip off the skins with the feathers attached and bring them to the Sultan's agent. He alone has the right to sell them on to the Malay traders. That tale of the legless birds started because the hunters cut off the birds' legs while they are skinning them.'

Hector glanced across to the young prince seated on a cushion by the door of the cabin into which Maria had gone. 'Does the Sultan have other sons?' he asked quietly.

'Prince Jainalabidin is the Sultan's only male child. Allah withheld that blessing for many years. Our Sultan is old enough to be Prince Jainalabidin's grandfather.'

Hector remained silent. When both he and Dan had been prisoners of the Barbary Turks, he had observed how greatly the Muslim rulers valued having a male heir.

'When will I be allowed to speak with my betrothed? I have to reassure her that all is well,' he said. Everything had happened so quickly that he hadn't had a chance to exchange more than a few words with Maria, and she'd been confined to the cabin since coming on board.

'That will be for the Sultan to decide,' the chamberlain answered blandly. He paused, as if considering what to say next. Then he added in a cautionary tone, 'When you meet His Highness, please remember that he is full of years, and that old men are given to strange fantasies. Their decisions sometimes seem erratic.'

Hector was left wondering uneasily whether his fate, and that of his companions, would now depend on the whims of a capricious dotard who ruled a bankrupt kingdom.

✳

THE KORA KORA turned into a narrow, steep-sided river mouth on which the Sultan's capital was situated. The place, Pehko, was a ramshackle settlement of bamboo and thatch houses. The nearest were little more than shacks poised on stilts over the grey-green surface of the fetid backwater. As the kora kora glided into harbour, Hector could see women and children standing on the rickety platforms, their arms held up to shade their eyes as they gazed at the return of their menfolk. A strong odour of drying fish and rotting debris mingled with the scent of wood smoke from the cooking fires and drifted across the water. Chickens and ducks foraged along the foreshore, where dozens of small dugout canoes were drawn up, and festoons of nets hung to dry on posts driven into the mud. He glimpsed more thatched dwellings farther up the slope, half-hidden among groves of tall trees, their foliage a deep, luxuriant green with glimpses of red and yellow fruit. There were only two buildings of any size. One was the mosque, for he could hear the call to prayer from its roof. The other was an untidy sprawling structure situated on high ground behind the town, where a curve of hillside gave a view directly down into the estuary. Even at a distance he could see the extravagant profusion of flags and banners sprouting from every corner and angle of the building, along the ridge of the roof and from triple flagstaffs in front of the grandiose portico.

'Kedatun sultan, the palace of the Sultan,' murmured the chamberlain as the kora kora came to rest against the wooden pilings of a jetty on the right bank. On the dockside six Omoro warriors were waiting. They were armed with spears and shields trimmed with horsehair. Behind them stood a bizarre-looking vehicle. The two rear wheels were almost the height of a man, their spokes and felloes painted in blue and green patterns, now faded and peeling. The two front wheels were one-third of the size and similarly decorated. Slung between them by leather straps hung a gilded sedan chair, its door panels showing pictures of leaves and flowers. But instead of horses between the shafts, the contraption was to be pulled by four servants, barefoot and wearing loincloths. On their heads, in imitation of horse decoration, they wore long, nodding plumes, orange and black, thrust into their turbans. As he watched, the young prince disembarked from the kora kora and stalked across to the carriage. The door was held open by a kneeling servant. The small prince stepped inside, and a moment later the team of humans were trotting away, dragging the carriage up towards the Sultan's palace on the hillside.

A discreet nudge from Dan brought Hector's attention back to his immediate surroundings. The chamberlain was indicating that it was time for him and his party to disembark and follow him. Hector turned to look for Maria, but it was too late. A cordon of armed Omoro already blocked his view and they were hustling Vlucht and the other Hollanders on to the jetty. Hector had a feeling that while he and his friends were not exactly prisoners, neither were they free to do as they pleased. He tried to push through the cordon back to the cabin, but his path was barred. Thwarted, he ran to catch up with Mansur, to ask again if he could speak with Maria. But Mansur was already at the entrance to a long, low building erected on pilings over the water.

'Please make yourselves comfortable in here until the Sultan sends for you,' he said suavely, standing aside so that Hector and the others could enter. 'Food will be brought to you very soon.' There was an awkward pause, and then he added, 'The baru baru will be on hand to make sure that you are not disturbed.' Then without another word he turned away, and an armed guard took up his position at the door. It was clear that the baru baru were the Sultan's soldiers.

Hector and his companions found themselves in what was evidently some sort of warehouse. To judge by the mouldy smell, it had not been used for a very considerable time. Jezreel pushed open a wickerwork shutter to let in the light.

The window looked out over the anchorage, and to their right they could see the kora kora still tied to the jetty. As a group of natives unhitched the towrope of the skiff, the goods that had been taken from the camp already lay in a heap on the waterfront.

'We could break our way out of here at any time we wanted to,' said Jezreel, tapping on the wall. It was flimsily made of leaves woven into frames of bamboo.

'First, I've got to get Maria back,' said Hector.

Jacques had been exploring the warehouse, which was partitioned into a number of large rooms. He came back with an armful of empty sacks that could serve as bedding. 'Might as well make ourselves comfortable,' he said cheerfully, throwing them on the floor.

Without warning, the door to the warehouse swung open and a file of a dozen women came in. They wore narrow dark-blue skirts that reached down to their bare feet, short cotton blouses and their hair was covered in headcloths of blue and white cotton. They were carrying covered earthenware bowls and several baskets whose contents were hidden beneath large leaves, and two large pitchers. These they set down on the floor and one of the women unwrapped a cloth bundle, which contained some wooden ladles and bowls. Then they withdrew. Not a word had been said, and it was noticeable that they had avoided looking directly at the strangers.

'Now what have we got here?' said Jacques with happy anticipation. He lifted the lid to one on the bowls and sniffed. 'Fish stew, and a good one. And what are these?' He peeled back the covering to one of the baskets and picked out what looked like a bun and bit into it. 'Not bad. Reminds me of wheaten bread, but a little bland.'

'Sago cake,' said Vlucht. 'Cheap food for the locals. Made from the pith of the sago palm. It grows wild in these parts.'

'Cheap or not, it is a welcome change from rice,' said Jacques appreciatively. He selected a ladle and stirred the fish soup vigorously. The ingredients swirled to the surface and he scooped up the floating morsels. After sucking up the contents of the ladle, he chewed for a few moments, then put his finger into his mouth and extracted a shred of white flesh.

'What is this?' he said, holding it up. 'I thought it was fish stew.'

'Sea slug,' said Vlucht. 'I came across it in China. Considered a great delicacy. Said to help your virility.'

'Could be easier on the teeth,' observed the Frenchman. 'A bit chewy for some of our toothless Dutch friends over there.'

Toothless or not, the *Westflinge*'s survivors joined hungrily in the meal, before the company settled down for the night. Vlucht's crew chose one of the adjoining rooms as their dormitory, and Hector and his friends, after neatly piling up the empty bowls and baskets near the door, spread out their sacks on the wooden floor and prepared to go to sleep. The only sound was the water lapping around the wooden pilings that supported the building.

Hector lay staring at the rafters. He was anxious about Maria. He sensed her captors wouldn't harm her, and he was sure that she was well able to look after herself, but he was depressed by the feeling that somehow he'd failed her. Again and again he went over the events of the day, wondering if he could have done things differently and kept her beside him. But everything had happened so quickly and uncontrollably. He fretted that Maria would change her mind, that she wouldn't want to share a future with someone whose life seemed to lurch from one crisis to the next. Beside him he heard Dan stir, and in the darkness he heard his friend's quiet voice. 'Maria is strong. She waited a long time for you to find her, and she'll know that you will not let her down now. Try to get some rest, for tomorrow we will need to keep our wits about us.'

✳

CILIATI MANSUR came to fetch them soon after dawn. He had changed his immaculate white gown for a similar flowing garment all in black, and his plain turban had been replaced by a strange-looking black velvet cap in the shape of a pyramid.

'My court dress,' he explained. 'As well as being His Majesty's chamberlain, I also hold the rank of jogugu, his prime minister.' He adopted a more formal tone. 'His Majesty commands me to bring before him all those of you who speak Spanish.' Seeing Hector's puzzled look, he added in a more normal voice, 'The Sultan is proud that he knows a few words of Spanish, and likes to demonstrate that knowledge to his courtiers.'

Hector looked around his friends. 'Dan, you should join me, and Jacques too. But Jezreel can stay behind with Stolck. What about the crew of the *Westflinge*?'

The chamberlain shook his head. 'The captain can come. The Sultan may wish to question him. But it is better that the others stay. Often His Majesty is angered by the sight of Hollanders. They remind him that their trading company favours Ternate and Tidore, and this harms his own kingdom. It will be better for everyone if His Majesty remains in a favourable mood.'

'What about my betrothed, Maria? When will I be able to see her?' Hector enquired firmly.

Mansur made a soothing gesture. 'All in good time,' he answered. 'She is well looked after.'

Hector tried not to let his impatience show as the little group left the warehouse. The air was pleasantly cool and fresh as they made their way through a fishermen's market, which had already been set up on the waterfront so that the night's catch could be sold before the heat of the day. The displays of small fish on racks of trays were dazzling – spots and stripes and bands of silver and ultramarine and yellow, bright orange and crimson, deep black. Mongrel dogs with curly tails nosed for scraps beneath the stalls, and an occasional cat shrank back and crouched in alarm at the sight of the strangers passing. Soon Mansur turned into the broad, leafy lane that climbed towards the palace, and ten minutes of walking brought them to a point where the path widened out and gave a clear view of the Sultan's residence just ahead. Unlike the simpler homes of his subjects, the Sultan's palace was built with brick walls and had a roof of dark-red tiles. A broad portico, its roof supported by tall wooden columns, ran the full length of the front of the building. Two small saluting cannon stood on each side of the steps leading to the double entrance doors. The guns pointed out over the harbour, and the strange carriage of the day before was parked prominently close by.

'A gift from the Spanish, long ago,' the chamberlain explained, indicating the carriage. 'They left some horses as well. But the animals soon died. Nevertheless, the Sultans of Omoro still set great store by its use. No other ruler has such a conveyance.'

Several natives who looked like palace guards lounged at the head of the steps. When they saw the chamberlain coming towards them, they scrambled to attention, and one of them hurried inside.

'Those are kabo, the Sultan's gatekeepers, and they have gone ahead to announce our arrival. You must follow our rules of etiquette,' warned Mansur as he led them up the steps and in through the tall double doors. 'Always address the Sultan as "Your Majesty" and do not approach closer than ten feet. It will also be appreciated if you would speak loudly and clearly. He is getting a little deaf.'

They passed through an antechamber where several more kabo were on duty, and then into a large reception hall. Shafts of sunlight streamed in through small windows high in the walls and made pools of such bright light that it was difficult to see into the shadowy outer fringes of the room. There was very little by way of furniture – some carved chests, a few low tables and several silk screens. The floor was covered in coir matting. Various men were standing about, but appeared to be doing nothing more than passing the time in silence. They were dressed like Mansur in long, loose black gowns and the same pyramid-shaped velvet caps, and Hector presumed they were attendants and courtiers. A faintly musty fragrance pervaded the air and reminded Hector of the disused warehouse. There was a general sense of lethargy and inactivity. The chamberlain led his little group into the centre of the room, and a rhythmic swaying movement in the far shadows caught Hector's attention. It was caused by a large feathered fan, its long shaft held by a servant. He was wafting it back and forth. But the action was so slow and lazy that it scarcely disturbed the air.

Hector blinked. Beneath the fan and seated cross-legged on a low divan amid a mass of cushions was a small, very wizened old man. He wore a dishevelled white robe edged with yellow, and his lopsided turban was loosely tied and supported a tall spray of orange-red feathers. Under the bulk of the turban his face had so shrivelled with age that the bones of the skull stood out clearly. There were shadowed hollows at his cheeks and his temples where the flesh had fallen away, and his mouth was a pucker of wrinkles. From this ancient face peered a pair of watery, red-rimmed eyes. Hector guessed the shrunken old man was the ruler of Omoro and at least eighty years old, possibly more.

Mansur performed a low, graceful bow, bringing his hands up to his face in a gesture of obedience. Hector copied him, as did Dan, Jacques and Vlucht.

In a loud, high voice the chamberlain launched into some sort of introduction. When he finished there was a pause while the Sultan squinted several times as if trying to focus his gaze. Then he waved a tiny, claw-like hand towards a small inlaid box on a low table beside him and croaked a few words in a language that Hector found incomprehensible.

'His Majesty asks if you will partake of betel nut with him,'

Mansur translated into Spanish, quickly adding in a low voice, 'You are not expected to accept. This is a formality.'

Hector realized that his companions behind were waiting for him to speak up on their behalf.

'Your Majesty,' he said in Spanish, 'it is a very great honour to be received at your court.'

The Sultan gave a sudden grimace, which Hector took to be a smile. There was a manic air about the old man. It was as if he might suddenly burst into a cackle of laughter or shriek angrily. The old man looked straight at Hector and mumbled a few words, which were clearly meant to be understood without the need for an interpreter. Hector surmised that the Sultan imagined he was speaking Spanish. If so, his meaning was lost.

To cover his confusion and hide his ignorance, Hector bowed again.

Mansur came to his rescue. 'His Majesty thanks you for your presents,' he murmured.

For a moment Hector failed to understand what the chamberlain meant. Then one of the Sultan's attendants emerged from behind a screen. The man was holding a cushion on which lay the *Westflinge*'s main steering compass. He advanced towards the Sultan, knelt and placed the cushion and compass on the ground in front of him. Moments later another attendant appeared with the ship's spare compass, then in quick succession the servants brought in half a dozen of the muskets that had been recovered from the camp and laid them out on the wooden floor.

Behind him the *Westflinge*'s captain gave a derisive snort. 'Another way of robbing us, like those bastards did in China,' he muttered under his breath.

As the array of items increased, the Sultan sat hunched amid his pile of cushions. Occasionally he cracked his knuckles with an unpleasant, squelching sound. The only time he displayed any animation was when the attendant carried in Vlucht's hourglass. The Sultan beckoned and the attendant brought up the object for closer inspection. The Sultan reached out and took the glass, then turned it over so that the sand began to run. He stared at the trickle of grains for half a minute before handing the instrument back to the servant and waving him away. The hourglass joined the pile of items salvaged from the ship.

Vlucht gave an unhappy grunt. Two attendants had appeared, carrying between them the box that contained the hen-and-chickens clock. They set the box on the ground before the Sultan, opened the lid and lifted out the mechanical toy. They placed it on the lid of the box and stood back. The Sultan eyed the model balefully. Then he turned to his chamberlain and spoke.

'His Majesty asks what the purpose of this device is. He says he is offended by the gift of a humble chicken,' said Mansur.

'Please tell him that it is a clock,' said Hector.

There was a rapid exchange between the chamberlain and his master, and then Mansur said, 'His Majesty says you have already given him a timepiece. Why do you give him a second one?'

At that moment Hector realized the Sultan was not as senile as he looked. He had worked out for himself the reason for the sand running through the hourglass.

Hector decided to take a chance. 'The clock with the bird is very special,' he said. 'It is for His Majesty's entertainment. There is no other clock like it.'

Behind him Vlucht sucked in his breath in surprise. 'Christ, lad. Watch what you are doing.'

The Sultan leaned forward unsteadily and spat a feeble jet of red betel juice towards a silver spittoon beside his couch. Most of the liquid splashed on the floor, and a dribble of the juice was left running down his chin. He spoke disdainfully to his chamberlain.

'His Majesty does not believe that a bird and its young ones can tell the passage of time,' said the chamberlain.

'Dan, can you show him how the clock works,' said Hector out of the side of his mouth.

'Dear God, let's pray it performs better than in Hoksieu, or we'll never leave this place alive,' the *Westflinge*'s captain muttered as the Miskito walked forward and wound up the spring to drive the mechanism. He adjusted the hands to a point just before midday and stepped back. Once again everyone waited and watched for the machine to work. Even the courtiers had edged forward to get a better view.

The cogs inside the machine's base began to whirr. The chicks started their circuit around the mother hen's feet. The hen leaned forward and began to raise her wings. Then, as before, something went wrong. There was a muffled twang, and all movement abruptly stopped. The mechanical hen remained at half-tilt, her chicks frozen in place.

There was a nervous silence, which lasted for several moments. No one moved. Hector was aware that beside him the chamberlain had gone tense, as if awaiting an angry outburst from his master.

During this interval Dan calmly stepped forward and opened the metal flap that concealed the clockwork. Ignoring everyone, he felt inside and must have reset the mechanism, for he closed the flap, reset the hands of the clock and took a pace backwards.

Once again the hands of the clock came together and the hen and her chicks began to move. All went well until the moment came for the hen to raise her wings and flap and crow. Instead she had raised them halfway when a cog slipped and then jammed. The mother hen jerked forward. Her wings began to quiver and vibrate madly. The creature let out a harsh metallic cry.

The Sultan clapped his hands with delight. 'Manuk dewata. Manuk dewata,' he cried.

The tension in the room evaporated. The courtiers murmured their astonishment, and the chamberlain allowed himself a smile of relief. 'He believes it mimics one of those birds that we saw in the forest,' whispered Jacques beside Hector.

Abruptly the Sultan clapped his hands again, angrily this time. Immediately all noise stopped as the courtiers waited for the old man's next pronouncement. The Sultan was glaring at his foreign visitors, and with a sudden clench in his guts Hector remembered the chamberlain's warning about the old man's whims.

The Sultan's hand shot out, pointing at Dan as he snapped a question.

'His Majesty wishes to know whether that man can also repair guns,' translated Mansur.

'Please tell His Majesty that Dan has worked in an armoury and knows how to repair muskets. Also, that I and my companions are ready to help him.'

The Sultan was racked by a coughing fit. When it was over, there was a long pause while he struggled for breath before finally speaking to the chamberlain.

'His Majesty the Sultan thanks you for your gifts. He graciously gives permission for you and your companions to stay while you are repairing the guns of his soldiers.'

'What about me and my crew?' asked Vlucht.

'The audience is at an end,' replied the chamberlain brusquely. He was already bowing and getting ready to leave. Clearly he was relieved at the way the meeting had gone and was eager to be gone.

'And what about Maria?' begged Hector, adding his voice. 'Ask His Highness where she is and when I might see her.'

When the chamberlain failed to relay the question, Hector stepped forward and faced directly towards the old man. In clear, loud Spanish he repeated his demand.

A shocked hush fell over the room as everyone waited for the Sultan's reaction. He cocked his head on one side and must have understood, or at least guessed, the meaning of Hector's words, for the wizened old man's expression was full of malice as he answered.

'What did he say?' asked Hector, turning to Mansur.

'His Majesty says he has been told that this woman is betrothed to be your wife. But such an arrangement is not recognized in his kingdom until he has given his royal assent. Instead he is of the opinion that the woman would make a suitable servant and companion to his son, and teach him foreign ways and tongues.'

With that the chamberlain bowed again to his master and took Hector firmly by the elbow and hustled him out of the audience room.

SEVENTEEN

'Get a hold on yourself,' Vlucht hissed under his breath to Hector as Mansur briskly ushered the little group through the guard room. 'That old goat might as easily have decided to add your woman to his own collection of wives.'

'He has no right to decide what happens to Maria,' Hector protested.

'You don't know how these eastern despots behave,' Vlucht raised his voice as they emerged on to the portico. 'They do precisely what they want to do, and you could ruin everything for the rest of us.'

Hector was seething. He wanted to turn around and force his way back into the Sultan's presence. But Mansur was oblivious to Hector's angry mood. 'In keeping with His Majesty's wishes, I will arrange for any special tools that you may need for musket repairs — there is a metalworker in the bazaar who—'

Hector interrupted him rudely. 'Do you know where Maria is being kept?'

The chamberlain was unruffled. 'If she is being considered as — how do you say? — a governess for His Royal Highness Prince Jainalabidin, she will be lodged with the Sultan's women. You should not worry. They live very comfortably.'

'And how long am I supposed to wait until I can see her?' Hector snapped.

'There may come a moment when a discreet meeting can be arranged . . . or perhaps the circumstances will change,' the chamberlain murmured.

'What do you mean?' Hector demanded. He resented the bland way Mansur deflected his questions.

'His Majesty is increasingly forgetful. One day he issues an order, the next day he no longer remembers what he has commanded. Or he contradicts what he has said previously. It is part of my duties to smooth over any inconsistencies.'

'And what if I simply found my way to wherever it is that Maria is being held?'

The chamberlain looked at him in open disbelief. 'Enter the women's quarters? That would not be easy or sensible.' Noting the stubborn expression on Hector's face, he went on, 'His Majesty has only one son, but he has a number of daughters. They too live in the female quarters until the time comes when they are to be married off to neighbouring rulers. That is how Omoro builds its alliances. The virtue of the princesses is of state importance and jealously protected. The guards would deal harshly with an intruder.'

In glum silence they descended the path that led down to the town. Arriving at the warehouse where they were lodged, Hector noted that the number of sentries at the door had been doubled. Inside, the crew of the *Westflinge* were picking over the remains of another meal. They were only interested in knowing when they would be allowed to leave Pehko. It was Jezreel who tried to raise Hector's flagging spirits.

'I'd take the chamberlain's word that no harm will come to Maria,' he said. 'These people don't seem to be nasty. They've looked after us well so far, and the truth is we really have no choice but to do what the Sultan wants. But that won't stop us from trying to get you and Maria together again.'

✳

So another week dragged by. Dan set up a workshop in one of the empty rooms within the warehouse. There, with help from Jacques and Jezreel, he set about repairing the dozens of rusty, damaged weapons that were delivered by the Sultan's men.

Whenever Hector stepped outside the building, he looked up towards the palace on the hill and wondered if the Sultan's women ever spent any time in the open air so that he might catch a glimpse of Maria. Once or twice he tried walking up the footpath to the Kedatun sultan, but was intercepted by the guards and turned back. As he agonized about Maria, Hector also began to fear that he and his companions were sinking into the same slow torpor he'd sensed on the first day they arrived in Pehko. It was obvious that Vlucht and his crew were content to do very little. They loafed around the building, the invalids visibly returning to health, and Stolck preferred to spend much of his time with his countrymen.

Meals were delivered with admirable regularity, though the menu of rice, sago cakes, fish stew and fruit never varied. In fact there was little to distinguish one day from the next. Each cool dawn was followed by a hot and humid morning as thunder clouds swelled inland before advancing on the town, delivering a sudden downpour and then drifting out over the sea. The puddles they left behind steamed in the returning sunshine and disappeared by the time the swift tropical dusk fell, and the inmates of the warehouse lay down to sleep with the certain knowledge that the pattern would be repeated the following day.

The arrival of a foreign ship was the only break in the monotony. On the fifth day after the interview with the Sultan, a vessel came gliding into the creek on the tide and dropped anchor directly in front of the warehouse. According to Vlucht, the newcomer's twin side rudders and boxy shape identified her as a small jong, a merchant ship from Malacca, and that evening Hector met her captain on the jetty as he returned from presenting his compliments at the palace.

Musallam Iskandar was a man of indeterminate age. He was

running to fat, with slightly bulging eyes, greying stubble and a scattering of pockmarks on a face whose features hinted at Arab rather than oriental ancestry. He greeted Hector cheerfully in passably good English.

'Mansur told me that there were foreigners in Pehko,' he said. 'I noticed that little jolly boat of yours tied up in the harbour, but I do not see your vessel.'

'We were forced to run our ship aground farther along the coast,' Hector explained. 'The Omoro found us cast away and brought us here.'

'You were fortunate. The Omoro don't venture far nowadays.'

'That big kora kora came across us,' said Hector, nodding towards the outrigger vessel, which had not stirred since their arrival.

'On their way back from hongi-tochten against the Sugala, I expect,' observed Musallam. 'It's an annual ritual. The Sultan of Omoro quarrels with his neighbour, the Rajah of Sugala, over who owns the forest and the right to harvest the wild birds. Every year Sultan Syabullah sends a war party to menace his rival, but the raid never solves anything. The Sugala know what's coming, and they built a palisade around their capital years ago. So they retreat within their defences, the Omoro fire off a few shots and then come back home.'

'You seem to know a lot about these people,' Hector observed.

The merchant captain shrugged. 'I trade in the bird skins. It's the only item that makes the long voyage here worthwhile, and the forests in this region are the prime sources for God's Birds, whoever controls them. So I alternate. One year I go to Sugala and collect up all the skins they have in stock. The next year I come here and do the same.'

'But I was told that the Ternate Sultan has taken control of the trade.'

The shipmaster gave a dismissive wave. 'My family has been

coming to Omoro for more than three generations. My grand-father and father both did business with the old Sultan, and I'm not about to give up the contact.'

Behind the Malaccan captain, Hector could see cargo being ferried ashore from his ship.

'How long will you stay here?' he asked.

Musallam rolled his eyes. 'As long as it takes. The Sultan gets to meet very few foreigners, and likes to talk with them. They are a diversion for him. So the negotiations will drag on for a month at least. They always do.'

'When you leave, would it be possible that my companions could sail with you? There are about a dozen of them.'

'Only with the Sultan's permission. I need his authority if I am to take any passengers.' The shipmaster gave Hector a shrewd glance. 'What about you? Do you plan to stay on in Pehko?'

'There is a woman without whom I cannot leave.'

'And where is this woman now?'

'She is living at the palace.'

The captain drew a sharp breath. 'Meddling in the Sultan's affairs is ill advised. He may be old, but he resents any inter-ference with his royal prerogatives.'

He turned to watch a dugout approaching the jetty. The canoe was piled with so many bales of cloth that it had taken on an alarming list and looked about to capsize. 'Excuse me,' he said, 'I must attend to the unloading of my vessel. There is much to be done. Doubtless we will meet again. Pehko is a small place.'

*

IT WAS ON the third morning after that encounter that Jezreel woke Hector half an hour after sunrise, shaking him out of a deep sleep.

'Hector,' the big man was saying, 'the Hollanders have gone.'

'What do you mean?' asked Hector. He sat up, struggling

to shake off his drowsiness. Jezreel was squatting down beside him. The dim light filtering through the shuttered window highlighted his friend's look of exasperation.

'Vlucht and the others. They've done a flit.'

Now Hector was wide awake. He scrambled to his feet. 'Show me,' he said.

They went to the room that the *Westflinge*'s crew used as a dormitory. The sacks on which the men had slept lay scattered on the floor, but there was no one there.

'Maybe the guards took them away in the night,' Hector ventured.

'I don't think so. They've cleared off. Look here.' In the flimsy thatch wall facing the harbour someone had ripped a large hole. Hector went across and peered out through the gap. Directly opposite him the Malacca trading jong rode quietly at anchor. There was no one to be seen on her deck. He craned his neck and looked in the opposite direction and noticed at once that something was missing. The *Westflinge*'s skiff, which had been towed into harbour behind the kora kora when they first arrived, was no longer where it was usually moored against some pilings.

'They made off with the jolly boat,' he said. 'Must have taken it during the night and dropped down on the tide.'

'And left us in the shit,' growled Jezreel. 'The Sultan will fly into a rage when he finds out.'

Hector's stomach churned at the thought of how this might affect Maria's situation.

'We've no time to waste. We have to explain to Mansur that we knew nothing about this.' A sudden thought struck him. 'Where's Stolck?'

Together they returned to their own room to find Dan and Jacques both awake. But the corner where Stolck usually slept was empty. He too had left with his countrymen.

✳

'What will happen to Vlucht and his men if they are caught?' Hector asked Mansur an hour later. The chamberlain had hurried to the warehouse in response to a message from Hector. For the first time the courtier was genuinely perturbed, and an expression of distaste crossed his face. 'Traditionally the punishment for defying the authority of the Sultan is death by strangulation. But in this case I fear the culprits are likely to be thrown off a cliff in his presence.'

'Why the difference?' asked Jacques, who was listening.

'That is how the Dutch executed some rebel princes some years ago. The Sultan has said that, given the chance, he is keen to return the compliment.'

'And what happens if the fall isn't fatal?' asked Jacques glumly.

The chamberlain grimaced. 'If the victim survives, he's carried up half-alive and thrown over a second time.' He looked around the little group. 'His Majesty will want to know exactly how many of you are still here. I think that all of you should appear before him.'

As they made their way across the bazaar to reach the footpath to the palace, Hector noticed a change in the reaction of the market traders. Usually they were friendly and curious, but today they avoided his eye and seemed frightened and wary.

The same tension was palpable when Mansur brought them into the audience chamber in the palace. The courtiers hovered at the outer fringes of the room, clearly reluctant to come near to the Sultan, who was in his usual place, seated among the cushions. It was as if everyone was waiting for a storm to break. Hector looked anxiously about him, searching the farthest corners of the hall, still hoping to catch a glimpse of Maria. But there were no women present. The clock with the hen-and-chicks was now displayed prominently on a tall stand. Clearly the gadget had caught the Sultan's fancy.

At the Sultan's right-hand side sat his only son, Prince Jainalabidin. The youngster was dressed even more gorgeously than before, in a dazzling robe of white cotton striped with yellow, embroidered slippers on his feet, and a yellow turban with a small spray of jewels pinned to it. He was staring fixedly in their direction. Hector found it impossible to guess what was going on in the boy's mind, but he had the uncomfortable feeling that, whatever it was, it was tinged with dislike.

Mansur bowed and made the customary introduction, but this time the Sultan did not invite the newcomers to share betel nut. Instead he sat silently for a long interval, blinking his rheumy eyes and staring malevolently at the foreigners. When eventually he spoke, Mansur translated in a low, obsequious voice.

'His Majesty has been informed that your colleagues have stolen away in the night like thieves.'

'We knew nothing of their plans,' Hector answered.

'You must have overheard them plotting this act of disobedience.'

'They are not of our people. When they speak among themselves in their own language, neither I nor any of my companions know what they are saying.'

The Sultan shifted irritably on his cushions, crossing and recrossing his legs. He swayed back and forward slightly as if suffering from stomach cramps, then beckoned to one of his attendants, who came forward with a metal cup of water. The Sultan took a sip. Hector sensed the courtiers in the room behind him were holding their breaths, waiting for an outburst of royal rage. Seconds passed and the atmosphere grew more and more tense. Prince Jainalabidin was totally still, but stared at the visitors, his eyes glittering. Hector was reminded of a small, very poisonous viper about to strike.

Abruptly the Sultan let out a high-pitched cackle. The sound was unsettling, a demented gleeful noise, which ended in a series of watery coughs before the old man delivered his next pronouncement.

'His Majesty says he is delighted that the Hollanders have gone,' Mansur translated. Relief was evident in his tone. 'His Majesty states they were useless mouths, expensive to feed, idlers who did not do any work.'

The Sultan's eyes were streaming, the tears trickling down the grooves in his wrinkled face. An attendant hurried forward with a cloth. When the coughing had subsided and the Sultan had wiped his face, Prince Jainalabidin leaned across and whispered something in his father's ear. The Sultan flapped the cloth towards Jezreel and wheezed a few words.

'His Majesty says the big man is to join his troops. He is a skilful soldier, and Omoro needs good warriors,' Mansur translated.

'My companion has done some sword fighting in the prize ring, but he was never in the army,' Hector answered. He was puzzled at how the Sultan had come to the idea that Jezreel was a professional military man. The Sultan's next remark provided the answer.

'That is not what my son tells me.'

Hector glanced at the young prince. Maria must have told the youngster that Jezreel was a soldier, he thought. She'd probably been trying to impress the lad with the importance of their captives, hoping they'd be better treated. The prince had been staring at them out of curiosity and boyish admiration, not with dislike.

The Sultan spoke again. 'His Highness Prince Jainalabidin has asked to lead another hongi-tochten against Sugala,' translated Mansur. 'He says that our men now have muskets that work properly and the Sugala will not be expecting a second attack this season. He will take them by surprise and teach them not to trespass on our forests.' The old man glanced down at his son indulgently. 'The prince is clever. He knows that the more bird skins we have to sell, the more traders will come to Omoro and the richer we will become. That way our kingdom will regain its former glory.' The Sultan hawked into the cup from which he had been drinking. A lackey hurried forward to remove it from his shaking hand.

Hector thought quickly. A successful campaign against Sugala, with Jezreel taking a leading part, was the obvious chance to obtain the Sultan's favour. He stole another look at the boy sitting beside the Sultan. He could see that Prince Jainalabidin was agog at the idea of leading another attack on Sugala. His eyes were shining with anticipation. It occurred to Hector that the youngster's eagerness might just as quickly turn to disappointment and blame. It was more than likely Jezreel and his colleagues would be made the scapegoats if the new expedition was a failure. He recalled what the Malaccan trader had said: all previous campaigns against the Sugala had achieved nothing. Jezreel's presence would make no difference.

He worded his answer carefully, hoping to discourage the idea of the new expedition, without contradicting what he thought were Maria's claims about Jezreel's prowess.

'Your Majesty, I am sure my friend Jezreel is eager to serve you. I have been told that the Sugala are fearful of the Omoro and hide behind their walls.'

The Sultan reached out and laid a wizened hand fondly on his son's shoulder.

'His Majesty says his son is clever. He has already asked to take with him our lantaka to destroy their defences. Never before have our lantaka left Omoro, but His Majesty has given him permission to use them on this campaign.'

Hector hadn't the slightest idea what the Sultan was talking about.

'His Majesty says you and your companions will prepare the lantaka for the hongi-tochten,' Mansur continued. 'You will also be responsible for their safe return, so that they stand before the palace as proof of the high regard in which His Majesty is held by distant peoples.'

For a moment Hector could think only of the bizarre four-wheeled vehicle parked outside the palace. He failed to see how it could be used against the Sugala. Then he recalled the two bronze cannon on their wooden gun carriages. His heart sank. In his boyish enthusiasm, Prince Jainalabidin had come up with the notion of using these guns to batter down the Sugala defences. His idea was utterly impractical. The two guns were showpieces, presented a generation ago by foreigners seeking to gain favour with the Sultan. The weapons looked impressive, but they were little better than popguns. They might be good for firing a salute, or a shower of small shot that would tear into human flesh. But they had never been meant for serious warfare and certainly not as siege weapons.

He caught the gleam of triumph in the prince's eye. The lad was feeling very pleased with himself, and Hector realized that he'd insult the youngster if he dismissed the ill-judged scheme out of hand. 'An inspired suggestion,' he said, then added what he hoped would be a practical objection. 'We would need gunpowder of very good quality.'

The Sultan positively beamed at this new opportunity to boast of his son's intelligence. 'Prince Jainalabidin has told His Majesty that the jong from Malacca brought a dozen kegs of the best powder to exchange for our bird skins. His Majesty has given him permission to take as much of the gunpowder as he wants to make his attack on Sugala a success.'

Out of the corner of his eye Hector could see Dan looking across at him in astonishment. The Miskito had been following what was being said and knew how unrealistic the new scheme was. Yet Hector could see no tactful way to dampen the prince's enthusiasm or deflect his father's decision. So he bowed. 'With your permission, my colleagues and I will begin to prepare the lantaka without further delay.'

The moment they were outside the portico, Dan hurried over to take a closer look at the lantaka. He stuck a finger into the muzzle of one of the guns. 'Not even a one-inch bore,' he commented wryly. He gave his friend a serious look. 'The ball would bounce off the flimsiest palisade.'

Hector agreed. The lantaka were just three feet long. Their bronze castings had acquired a rich dark-green patina and were embellished with swirling floral patterns and whorls. Each rested on its heavy wooden sledge, made of some dark tropical wood. These gun carriages were exquisitely carved with patterns to mimic the guns' decoration. It was as he'd feared: they were elegant, showy and of little practical use beyond firing salutes or scatter-shot.

Jezreel stooped over one of the lantaka and put his massive arms under the barrel and the knob of the cascabel. He gave a grunt and lifted the weapon clean out of its carriage. 'Well, no difficulty in taking it with us,' he said with a grin.

Dan ignored him. He was looking thoughtful. 'I suggest we clean up these pea-shooters and test-fire them to make sure the Malaccan gunpowder is of good quality.'

Jezreel lowered the gun back into its carriage. 'Even if it turns out that the Malaccan is trading in shoddy goods, I get the impression the Sultan will still indulge his son and send out another expedition under his command.'

The Miskito did not appear to have heard him. He was looking out to sea, over the township and the harbour. 'We could try using one of Captain Vlucht's cannon to knock down the defences of the Sugala, provided they're not stone-built. Let us hope that the *Westflinge* is still hung up on the reef.'

EIGHTEEN

CLEANED AND POLISHED, the lantaka made a brave show lashed securely to the foredeck of the kora kora. The little cannon gleamed in the early morning sunshine as the expedition headed out from Pehko. The Sultan's purple banner was once again hoisted from the vessel's stubby flagstaff, and the crew seated on their outrigger benches had caught the optimistic mood of the departure. They roared their work chant as they chopped at the water with their paddle blades. Through the soles of his feet Hector could feel each sudden surge as the kora kora was thrust forward, and he couldn't help glancing back towards the Kedatun sultan high on the hillside. Mansur had told him that the royal women were required to stay out of sight whenever there were strangers in the palace, but at other times they were free to go about the building as they pleased. He was wondering if Maria was standing on the portico and watching the kora kora head out to sea.

'Good morning. How are you?' The question startled him. Prince Jainalabidin had emerged from the little hut-like cabin behind him and was addressing him in halting Spanish.

Hector overcame his surprise. He guessed the boy had received lessons from Maria. Clearly the youngster had a good ear and a quick intelligence. Here, at last, was a chance to find out how she was.

'Your Highness speaks Spanish well. His teacher will be pleased.'

The lad flashed him a smile. 'You are her man, yes?'

Hector had not expected Maria to have talked about him with her pupil. He felt a thrill of pleasure that she had done so.

'Is Maria well?' he asked.

'My sisters her friends.'

The boy reached into a fold of his robe. 'She say me to give you this,' he said and pressed a scrap of paper into Hector's hand.

Hector felt the blood rush to his head as he scanned the few lines of writing:

Dearest Hector,

I hear that you are well and that Captain Vlucht and the Hollanders have gone, but Dan and our other friends remain. I long to see you. News comes to me at second hand, and I am told that you will soon be leaving on an expedition of war. The prince speaks much about all of you and has agreed to give you this note. He is a good boy. Make sure that you come back safe, and that he does also. Do not worry about me for I am in good health, my days are comfortable and I will be waiting for your return. You have my love.

Maria.

The prince was watching for his reaction. Hector gave him a grateful look. 'Thank you for bringing me this note. It has made me very happy.'

'We come back, we have a . . .' The lad's voice trailed away as he searched for the right word. He beckoned to Mansur and spoke to him in his own language.

'His Highness says that his father the Sultan has promised him a great victory celebration on his return to Pehko,' Mansur translated for him.

'My companions and I will do everything we can to make sure of that victory,' Hector replied. He was not at all sure the expedition would be a success, and it felt very strange to be under the command of a child. He wondered again what the penalty would be if the expedition turned out to be a disaster.

❋

THE WRECK OF the *Westflinge* came in view shortly before midday. The ship still lay crumpled across the reef. Even at a distance, it was clear that her back was now broken. The tall, narrow stern of the vessel had become detached and drifted a short distance from the rest of the hull, which was still impaled on the coral where she'd been abandoned. At the waterline the midships section had bulged, bursting open like a rotten melon. There was no sign of any of the three masts. They must have toppled overboard and been carried away by the current. The gnawing of the tide and the action of waves had searched out the wreck's weaknesses and were prising her apart. There were breaches in her sides through which daylight showed. In places the planks had cracked off short, leaving jagged ends. The remaining timbers were dappled with blotches of black fungus.

The kora kora approached cautiously, a lookout in the bows searching for a clear passage between the coral heads, the paddlers barely dipping their blades into the water. Eventually, a hundred paces from the remains of the *Westflinge*, the lookout called a halt. The kora kora could approach no closer without risking her own fragile hull.

'Hector, let us see if we can get at those guns. Best keep your boots on, or the coral will cut your feet,' Dan advised. He was already pulling off his shirt, and a moment later was clambering down the outrigger struts and lowering himself into the warm, pale-green water. Hector followed him, and together they half-waded, half-swam towards the wreck. As they floundered forward, they could hear the suck and gurgle of the tide washing through the gaping holes in the *Westflinge*'s side, and caught the flicker of small, brightly coloured fish that clustered near the hull, feeding on the growth of weed.

They came close enough to the wreck and circled round so that they could climb in through the open stern. Dan reached up and took hold of a plank's end to pull himself inside. As he tugged, the plank broke off and he slipped back with a splash. He regained his feet and looked down at the fragment of wood still in his grasp. 'Now we know why we couldn't find any leak,' he said. He held out the timber to show to his friend. The three-inch-thick piece of wood was riddled with passageways the thickness of a straw. Dotted amongst the passageways were small, pale shelly grubs smaller than a fingernail. Looking closer, Hector saw they were tiny, burrowing animals, each with a spiral-shaped head like a miniature drill.

'Shipworm,' declared Dan. 'The hull is consumed with them. I am amazed she stayed afloat as long as she did. She must have been leaking in dozens of places.'

He reached out again and snapped off another chunk of wood. It came away in his hand like a section of honeycomb. Grimacing with disgust, he threw it into the sea. 'In another couple of years there'll be nothing left of her on this reef, except a few iron bolts and a pile of ballast stones.'

'Not many of them, either. We dumped most of the ballast overboard,' Hector reminded him.

Together they climbed through the opening and found themselves in the aft section of the hold. The water was up to their knees, and there was a reek of decay in the half-lit belly of the ship. Small, grey crabs scuttled up the curved frames of the hulk and fled into dark cracks in the timber as they waded carefully towards the companionway leading up to the deck. They trod gingerly. The footing was uneven where sections of plank had buckled inwards, and layers of seaweed and slime made the footing treacherous. They climbed the companionway – half the steps were missing – and emerged on the decaying deck. Skirting around the more obviously rotten patches, they made their way to the starboard gunwale. There, still lashed down to ring bolts, was one of the two cannon they'd kept back. Dan tapped the barrel. 'That is lucky. Brass,' he said. 'Old-fashioned, but more durable. If it had been iron, we could have had a problem with the weight.'

Hector was looking at a coat of arms cast into the metal of the barrel. A large letter V impaled the letters O and C. 'The crest of the Dutch East India Company,' he said. 'I wonder how Vlucht got his hands on it.'

'Probably looted it from some luckless Company ship. I reckon he was as much a pirate as he was an interloper.'

The Miskito circled the gun muzzle with his hands, gauging the size. 'Five-pounder, or thereabouts,' he commented. He rubbed away the dirt from the touch-hole. 'Nothing here that some careful attention cannot fix. We'll need the right tools, and some round shot. Let's see if we can find a wormer.'

They searched what remained of the vessel above water. In the forecastle Hector located the gunner's stores. There was a wormer with a threaded head, which Dan would need in order to clean out the barrel after firing, a powder ladle, three heavy spikes to use as levers for moving the gun, and a rammer.

'No sign of a sponge?' asked Dan as Hector brought out these tools and set them down beside the cannon.

'No, but there's a box of wads that should fit.'

'We will need those. We can always wrap some wet cloth around the butt end of the rammer to make a sponge.'

'There was another tool – a rod with a set of springy claws at one end. But I left it behind.'

'That will be a searcher for checking for cracks inside the barrel. No use to us, as we could not mend any flaws even if we found them. We'll have to take a chance that the guns are sound. Did you manage to locate any round shot?'

'No.'

Dan looked serious. 'That's odd. We can load the two little lantaka with musket balls and pebbles, but if we want to use the big cannon against a stockade, we need to have the right-sized shot.'

'Maybe these guns were just for show,' said Hector.

Dan thrust an arm down the barrel. 'I can feel the wad, though it's soggy and damp. Behind it there's the ball. I'd say he was a captain who preferred to leave the guns charged and shotted in case they were needed in a hurry.'

He withdrew his arm and together they crossed the sloping deck and investigated the second cannon. It, too, was ready-loaded. 'Are you sure you've looked everywhere for a shot locker?' Dan asked.

'There's nothing. I guess Vlucht was too mean to keep proper artillery stores,' said Hector.

'No point in salvaging two cannon when we have only two rounds of shot to fire from them. One cannon will have to do,' said Dan.

Hector looked across at the kora kora, still hove-to fifty paces away on the fringe of the reef, unable to come closer. 'How do you propose to do that?' he enquired doubtfully.

'Ask the Omoro to build a raft on-shore, and then come out at high tide and take this gun off.'

They waded their way back to the war canoe where Prince Jainalabidin's face lit up with excitement when Hector explained how Dan wanted to proceed. The boy spoke rapidly to the chamberlain.

'The prince says that we Omoro know all about building rafts,' translated Mansur. 'We use them for fishing in the river. His Highness says that he can order his men to have a raft ready in less than three hours, and they will remove the cannon from the wreck by nightfall.'

Hector hid his doubts that the work could be done so quickly. 'Then, with His Highness' permission, I suggest that Jezreel and Dan go back to the *Westflinge* and get the cannon ready. Jacques and I will stay in case we can be of assistance.'

The kora kora shifted to the same creek where the *West-*

flinge's castaways had earlier set up their camp, and soon Hector had to admit that he'd underestimated the Omoro. Her crew divided into teams and disappeared into the jungle. Within half an hour one squad returned carrying stalks of giant bamboo, six inches in diameter and thirty feet long. They stripped off the leaves, and then used their heavy knives to shave away the hard, shiny outer skin. This, according to Mansur, meant that the lashings of the raft would grip. Meanwhile another team had reappeared with lengths of rattan and split the vines length-wise. When all the materials were ready, the entire workforce set about fastening the bamboos side by side with the rattan strips, then attaching cross-braces to give the raft its shape. By mid-afternoon they had pushed the raft into the water and, with Hector and Mansur aboard, were propelling it towards the wreck of the *Westflinge*.

They found that Dan and Jezreel had used the hand-spikes to manoeuvre the brass gun to the edge of the deck and had unbolted the trunnion caps that held the weapon to its carriage. Jainalabidin's men looped a length of rattan around the gun while their colleagues on the raft rigged spare bamboos to make a simple crane. Taking advantage of a slight uprise on the swell, the cannon was lifted from its carriage, swung across the gap and lowered safely on to the raft. Minutes later, the gun's wooden carriage followed.

'Neatly done,' said Jezreel approvingly. With a round shot in each hand, he stepped across to the raft. Dan and Hector gathered up the rammer and hand-spikes and the box of wads and followed him.

THREE DAYS LATER Hector found himself gazing up at Haar, the chief town of the Sugala and the residence of their Rajah. He could see why the Omoro had failed to subdue their rivals. Haar was perched on a headland jutting from the coast. Cliffs, 200 feet high, protected it on three sides, and the only approach from the sea was by a footpath cut into the steep bluff, which faced over the stony landing beach. The fishermen there had taken to their heels and scampered up the path to the town the moment they'd seen the war canoe approaching.

Hector flinched as a musket bullet splashed into the water close by. The Sugala were firing off occasional warning shots at the kora kora as it cruised slowly past the deserted landing place. But the range was too far for any accuracy.

'Boom, boom!' Prince Jainalabidin made enthusiastic artillery noises and pointed excitedly, first at the lantaka and then at the brass cannon, still on its raft being towed behind the kora kora.

Hector shook his head. With just two rounds of shot in their armoury, it would achieve nothing to lob a cannonball at the town on the crest of the headland. 'We must get closer for our guns to be effective. We have to attack the town from the land,' he explained to the chamberlain.

'That will be dangerous,' Mansur cautioned. 'On the land-ward side Haar is protected by a stout palisade of tree trunks, and the Rajah's people keep the jungle cut back so that their musketeers have a clear shot at any attackers. The ground there is flat and level, with nowhere to hide. Last time we had two men wounded when they got too close.'

'We don't have any choice, if we want to use our cannon,' Hector answered.

The older man looked unconvinced. 'There's no way to get the large gun up there. The hillsides are very steep and covered with thick forest, and the only track to the summit follows the bed of a stream. In many places you are obliged to scramble knee-deep in the water.'

Hector forced himself to sound cheerful. 'Then we must turn that into an advantage. The Sugala will never expect us to bring cannon up that route. So they won't try to intercept us. They'll stay behind their palisade and wait for us to go away. We'll give them an unpleasant surprise.' He turned to Prince Jainalabidin and said in slow, careful Spanish, 'Your Highness, can your men bring the big gun through the jungle and up behind the town?'

The boy bit his lip, and cast an anxious look towards the chamberlain. It was clear that, for the first time, he was being asked to overrule his father's minister in a major decision. Mansur translated Hector's words so that there should be no misunderstanding. After a brief silence the prince said proudly, 'Of course. My men will do what I ask them.'

Hector felt ashamed that he'd taken advantage of the prince's youthful bravado.

'Then I suggest we land the cannon out of sight of the Sugala, so they have no idea what we're doing,' he said.

Mansur seemed to have accepted his prince's decision. 'There's a small bay just around that spit of land over there. We've used it before as a campsite.'

He shouted an order and the paddlers began to turn the kora kora, heading away from Haar. As they retreated, they heard a final flurry of musket shots and a faint jeering from the defenders.

'They've plenty of gunpowder to waste,' commented Jezreel drily.

'Probably got it from that same trader who sold it to the Sultan,' said Hector. He was watching the coast ahead. He could already see the spit of land behind which the kora kora could shelter. 'Jezreel, I think I should go ahead, while you and the others supervise the landing of the cannon. I want to scout that footpath we'll be using. See if it's as bad as Mansur claims, or if there's some way we can get the five-pounder along it.'

✳

LEAVING THE OTHERS on the beach, Hector headed inland. He had gone barely twenty yards when he began to appreciate just how difficult it would be to haul the cannon uphill. Had it not been for his guide, an Omoro warrior who had taken part in the previous expedition against Haar, he would never have guessed there was any sort of footpath through the jungle. He lost all sense of direction as he shouldered his way through thickets where the plants grew head-high, and his guide led him around the tangled roots of fallen trees piled awkwardly across one another. When that was impossible, he had to scramble over their massive rotting trunks, his hands sliding on the greasy coating of damp moss. Everywhere the ground was soggy, each footfall squelching into the thick layer of leaf mould. It was obvious the thick, eight-inch solid wooden wheels of the brass cannon's carriage, designed to roll on a ship's deck, would bog down and be useless in the jungle.

When at last they reached the stream whose course they had to follow, the conditions became even more awkward. It was impossible to stay on the bank. Shrubs and bushes forced Hector to step down into the water. The rocks in the stream bed shifted treacherously when he put his weight on them. Once or twice he tripped and fell forward, saving himself by throwing out his arms and plunging elbow-deep into the water. After twenty minutes of slow, bruising progress he reached the conclusion that Mansur was right. A short distance ahead of him the stream cascaded down a set of rapids, which an agile man might pass by clambering from one rocky shelf to the next, but it would be impossible to haul a heavy cannon up the cataract.

Disheartened, he paused to catch his breath. He felt insignificant within the immensity of the forest. Overhead the canopy of enormous trees blocked out the sunlight and any view of the sky. He was aware only of the constant sound of the rapids, the swirl of water rippling past his ankles, the musty smell of the damp earth, and the myriad itching insect pinpricks on his neck and arms.

The sudden loud, metallic cry of a large bird made him jump. It was a double squawk, very noisy and close at hand. The cry was repeated after a few seconds, then again, echoing through the jungle. From somewhere in the far distance, he heard an answering call. His Omoro guide had stopped abruptly a few yards ahead and held up a warning hand. Hector cautiously peered upwards, trying to see the bird. The nearest trees had straight trunks that soared upwards for at least eighty feet before spreading their mass of branches. They reminded him of the tall columns within a cathedral.

The metallic call came again, even closer. He looked towards his guide, who was making a dancing motion with both hands. 'Manuk dewata,' the man mouthed softly.

God's Birds, Hector thought to himself. This was why he was here: to decide the rights of ownership over this green wilderness and the brilliant coloured plumage of the birds that lived within it. He scanned the jungle canopy, but could see nothing.

The next call was shockingly close by, no more than ten yards away. It came not from the branches high above him, but from the lip of the stream bank just to his right. He looked in that direction and, as he did so, a man stepped into view. He was, at most, five feet tall. Small-boned, with a thick bush of wiry black hair surrounding a head far too large for his body, he was completely naked except for a loincloth. He had a gourd hanging on a cord around his neck, and in his hand was a bamboo hoop to which clung three small, bright red and green parrots.

The extraordinary apparition looked at Hector and his companion for a long, slow interval. Then the grave face broke into a shy smile. Turning away from Hector, he faced into the jungle, lifted his free hand and pinched his nose. He took in a breath through his mouth and let loose a loud, metallic squawk through one nostril.

Somewhere in the distance the call was answered. The forest man was a bird hunter, tracking down his prey.

Cautiously Hector clambered up the bank and approached the stranger, careful not to frighten him. The little man had the manner of a timid forest creature who might suddenly take flight. 'Salaam aleikum,' Hector said gently. The man bobbed his head in a friendly way and stood his ground, but made no reply. The three gaily coloured parrots twittered and scrabbled on their perch, using beaks and claws to maintain their grip. Hector looked back enquiringly at his Omoro guide, who shrugged helplessly. It seemed the Omoro did not speak the newcomer's language. Hector turned back to the bird catcher. 'Is there a way to Haar from here?' he asked in English. Large brown eyes regarded him wonderingly, and Hector thought to himself it was probably the first time the little man had seen someone with a pale skin and grey eyes. Hector raised his left hand, palm upwards, and made a walking motion across it with the fingers of his right hand. Then he pointed uphill and spread his arms wide, indicating a broader track.

The bird catcher considered for a moment, then beckoned Hector to follow. He turned and made his way between the trees, angling across the slope of the hill. Keeping up was difficult. The little man slipped nimbly through the forest, casually dangling his parrot perch. From time to time he paused and waited for Hector and his Omoro escort to catch up. Eventually, after some fifteen minutes, he came to a stop and pointed uphill. They were on the edge of what must have been a landslip some years earlier. A substantial section of the hillside had collapsed from the rim above and slid downslope. The torrent of rock and earth had swept away the taller trees and left a deep scar down the flank of the hill. They were standing at the midway point of the landslide, and, looking downslope to his right, Hector could see where the narrow coastal plain began.

Hector hid his disappointment. The gash in the forest caused by the landslide might once have provided an open track up the steep hill, but the undergrowth had grown back with tropical vigour in the intervening years. The way to the summit was now completely choked with a tangled mass of bushes, shrubs, saplings and ground creepers. It was impossible as a roadway for a heavy cannon.

'Thank you, thank you very much,' he said, nodding and smiling.

The bird catcher gave another of his shy smiles and gestured that he was willing to lead them towards the crest in the direction of Haar. But Hector had seen enough. He was despondent and tired, and it was time to return to the beach to report his findings. He shook his head and retraced his steps to where he had left the stream. The bird catcher darted ahead. Within moments he had outdistanced them and disappeared altogether. Hector slipped and slithered for another few paces until he again heard the metallic bird call. This time it definitely came from the treetops. Looking over to his right, he was astonished to see the bird catcher gazing down at him. The little man was perched forty feet off the ground on the branch of a huge tree, and was tying his parrots to the branches.

Raising a hand, he waved them goodbye.

✳

'ONE OF THE forest people,' said Mansur, when Hector got back to camp and reported what he'd seen. 'They bring their catch, alive or skinned, to the town, sell them and then vanish back into the jungle. They are subject to no one, nor do they believe in Allah.'

They were standing beside the brass cannon, now back on its wooden gun carriage.

'How much do you think the gun weighs?' asked Mansur.

'About half a ton,' said Dan.

'Let me talk to the kora-kora men to see if they can bring it to Haar by the route he showed you,' said the chamberlain. He went to confer with several of the older men from the crew of the big war canoe, and returned to say that they were confident they could haul the gun up the steep incline.

'Did you warn them the slope is overgrown with bushes and small trees?' Hector asked.

'I did, but they aren't worried,' said Mansur soothingly. 'They say they will make a start tomorrow at dawn. All you need to do is bring them to the base of the landslide.'

Hector kept his doubts to himself next morning as he watched the Omoro dismantle the bamboo raft and use the materials to build a sturdy sledge. Within half an hour the cannon was balanced on its new platform and on the move. Thirty men tugged it along by the long rattans they used for ropes. Another team went ahead with heavy knives and slashed a path through the bush. Others placed skids under the runners of the sledge whenever it was checked. At the rear walked those with the jars of gunpowder, bullets and stores. Four men carried each lantaka slung on loops between them. Jezreel insisted on carrying the two precious round shots, one in each hand. When they arrived at the place where the ground began to rise steeply, the column came to a halt. Here, at the base of the landslip, the porters set down their loads and the hauling team paused to rest. With a clatter Jacques dropped the gunner's tools he had been carrying and sat down on the ground beside Hector.

'I wonder what those lads are up to?' said the Frenchman. They watched a group of the younger men clambering up the landslip until they vanished over the crest of the slope.

A few minutes later Mansur came walking towards them. 'The kora-kora men say where you are sitting is dangerous.'

Puzzled, Hector got to his feet, and he and Jacques moved aside. Soon afterwards there was a shrill whistle from above, immediately followed by a crashing noise, which grew in volume and suddenly came closer. A moment later a large tree trunk came slithering and bouncing wildly down the hill, and came to rest at the bottom of the landslide. Almost immediately a second massive log came careering down, following in the track of the previous one. As Hector looked on, a dozen more logs hurtled past, one after another, throwing up sprays of dirt as they ploughed through the ground.

There was another whistle from above, and the bombardment of timber stopped. The hauling team got to their feet. Hector hurried to help them tip the gun from its carriage, then attach their hauling cables to the trunnions. He had seen how the slithering logs had carved out the track up which the men now intended to pull their burden. Two teams of forty men began to heave in unison, gradually sliding the gun up the groove that the logs had gouged in the earth. Every few minutes they stopped to rest. Then the heaving began again. An hour later the cannon was over the lip of the plateau and on level ground. The gun carriage and the sledge followed.

'The Omoro say that Haar is less than half a mile ahead,' said Dan. 'We need to take a look at the town's defences before we go any farther.'

Hector and Jezreel accompanied him through the undergrowth until they came to the edge of the jungle where the undergrowth had been cut back in a straight line. 'No farther,' said the Miskito crouching down. 'We're just within range of their muskets.'

It was as Mansur had warned. The ground between the town and the forest had been cleared of all cover for a distance of a hundred paces. At the far side of this killing ground stood the ten-foot palisade that guarded the landward side of the town. It was made of tree trunks planted vertically in the soil. In the centre was a heavy double gate, also made of timber and now firmly shut. The turbaned heads of the defenders could be seen above the stockade. As Hector watched, there was a puff of smoke as a musket was fired towards them.

'Telling us to keep our distance,' said Dan. 'Jezreel, what next?'

'We bring up the two lantaka. Fire scatter-shot at intervals. That should keep the defence occupied while we organize something more damaging.'

Hector scanned the palisade. 'Where's the weakest point, do you think?'

'The gate. It looks stout enough to stop a musket ball, but not a five-pound shot.'

'Good, let's put the Sultan's lantaka to use,' said Hector and they crawled away.

Ten minutes later he was explaining to Mansur that a dozen Omoro should be assigned to each of the little cannon. They were to bring the guns to the edge of the forest.

'Jacques will go with them,' he said. 'He will show them how to load and aim and fire.'

'It's much like using a musket, but on a larger scale?' asked the chamberlain.

'Yes, but they must be sure to swab the barrels and clean out any embers that might ignite the next charge too early. Warn them that if they cram in too many bullets and stones, the barrel might burst or the range will be too short.'

'What about the big gun?' asked the chamberlain. 'His Highness is most eager to see it in action.' Hector could see the boy's eyes were shining with excitement as he tried to follow their conversation.

'Inform His Highness that Jezreel intends to bring the big gun up to the edge of the forest, directly in front of the town gate. From there he will fire at the palisade.'

Mansur translated Hector's statement, but was met with a sharp retort from the prince. The chamberlain had a worried expression as he turned back to speak to Hector.

'His Highness insists that he will fire the gun himself.'

Hector opened his mouth to say that the old brass gun had never been tested and might have flaws. If the barrel burst, it would kill anyone standing close by.

The prince cut him short with a single brief sentence.

Mansur flinched. 'The prince says that is not a request. It is his command.'

'Very well. We will bring the gun forward on the sledge. But it will be safer if we load it now, where we cannot be seen by the Sugala and we can take our time.'

Jezreel had already taken off his shirt and wrapped it around the head of the reamer. He was using it as a swab to clean out the barrel.

'How much powder do you think she'll need?' he asked Dan.

The Miskito shrugged. 'Half a ladle should be enough.'

Jezreel used his thumb to rub away at the bowl of the powder ladle brought from the wreck of the *Westflinge*. He eyed the faint lines marked on the scoop. 'Let's hope this is the correct ladle for this gun, and not for larger cannon,' he said. He took the stopper out of a powder jar and tipped out a trickle of greyish-black gunpowder until the scoop was filled halfway.

'Wait,' said Dan. He was holding a thin strip of bamboo. He poked it into the cannon's touch-hole and pushed it down as far as it would go. Marking the point where the bamboo strip emerged from the gun, he withdrew it and then held it vertically across the muzzle of the gun.

Behind him, the prince spoke to Mansur. 'His Highness wishes to know what you are doing,' said the chamberlain.

'I'm checking to see if the cannon shoots high or low as you take aim, by looking along the barrel,' Dan answered. He tossed aside the bamboo strip. 'A little high. Hector, can you cut me a wedge of hardwood, say eight inches long and three inches thick across the base?'

Carefully Jezreel inserted the half-full ladle down the barrel, turned his wrist and dumped the gunpowder deep in the chamber. He withdrew the empty ladle, took the rammer and packed tight the charge. Hector handed him a wad, and that too was thrust home.

'You carried it all the way, so you do the honours,' said Dan, handing Jezreel the five-pound round shot. Jezreel placed

.the iron ball into the muzzle of the gun and pushed it down as far as it would go. Dan rammed it hard against the wad, then added a second wad on top so that the shot stayed in place.

'We'll prime it once we have the gun in position,' said Dan. To their right they heard the sudden report of a lantaka firing its scatter-shot towards the Sugala defenders' palisade. 'Let's hope that makes them keep their heads down,' grunted Jezreel. He threw his weight on a hand-spike and levered the sledge forward.

Slowly the gun crept through the undergrowth.

✳

Dan called a halt when the sledge was still within cover, ten yards short of the open ground. 'No point exposing ourselves to enemy fire,' he said. The scrub and bush were sparse enough for them to see the town gate set in the line of the palisade. He crouched behind the gun and squinted down the length of the barrel. 'A little to my left,' he said. Jezreel and Hector used their hand-spikes to line up the gun until the Miskito was satisfied. Next he asked Jezreel to place the tip of his hand-spike beneath the cannon's breech and to lever upwards.

'A fraction more,' the Miskito called as the muzzle of the gun dipped slightly. 'Hold it.' He thrust home the wooden wedge.

Mansur was standing with Prince Jainalabidin several paces to one side and both were watching keenly. 'His Highness wishes to know whether you are aiming at the top or bottom of the gate,' said the chamberlain.

'Neither,' said Dan. 'I'm aiming at the ground twenty paces in front of the gate, in case the gun shoots even higher than I calculate. It won't matter if the shot bounces on the ground before it strikes the target. Might even make the impact more destructive.' He busied himself with a powder flask, pouring a trail of gunpowder into the touch-hole.

From the palisade came a spatter of musketry, almost

immediately followed by the angry snap of a lantaka in retaliation.

'All ready,' said Dan calmly, putting back the stopper in the powder flask.

Stepping to the nearest bush, he broke off a straight, slender branch about two feet long. He stripped off the leaves and prised open a split at one end. He turned to one of the Omoro musketeers and took from him a length of burning match-cord. He wound it around the stick and jammed the lit end into the cleft.

'If Your Highness would like to fire the cannon, but please stay well back,' he said, handing the match-stick to the boy.

Hector had to admire Prince Jainalabidin's composure. Without further prompting, the boy approached the cannon and lowered the glowing end of the cord to the touch-hole.

There was a tremendous explosion and the gun reared back. The force of the recoil lifted the front of the sledge several inches off the ground, and the discharge seemed to jolt the youngster off his feet. Mansur darted forward just in time to catch the boy as he stumbled. Angrily the prince waved him away. The lad's face was streaked with burned gunpowder, his clothes speckled with black marks, but the smile he turned towards his companions was radiant.

Standing clear of the cloud of black smoke that billowed from the muzzle of the gun, Hector watched the flight of the shot. A black dot hurtled across the killing ground. There was a spurt of dust as it hit the ground and bounced. Even as the dust was still rising, a section of the palisade immediately to the left of the gate whirled away in a cloud of splinters.

For several moments Hector was deafened. His ears were ringing with the explosion. When he regained his hearing, he was aware of a shocked silence. There were no musket shots from the palisade ahead of him. Even the two lantaka on either side had ceased firing.

'A little to the right, I think,' Dan announced.

Jezreel had the reamer in his hand and was already at the muzzle of the gun, hooking out the fragments of burned wadding. After several passes with the reamer, he peered into the barrel.

'I'll need my shirt again,' he said. He wrapped the grubby garment once more around the head of the reamer, then rudely turned his back on the prince and his entourage. Their puzzled looks turned to understanding as they realized that the big man was relieving himself copiously on to the cloth.

There was a slight hiss and an acrid smell of scorched urine as he swabbed out the barrel.

It took another ten minutes to reload the cannon to Dan's satisfaction. Then he had Jezreel shift the rear of the sledge a few inches to the left. At last he was ready and held out the match-stick once again to the prince. 'Let's hope this one finishes the task for us, Your Highness.'

The boy's arm was fully extended and his hand trembled slightly as he applied the lighted match to the touch-hole a second time. Again the brass gun leaped on its sledge as the charge exploded and sent the shot hurtling towards Haar.

This time the entire left-hand section of the town gate was demolished. It collapsed backwards, and its partner on the right side sagged on its hinges.

'A perfect shot,' exclaimed Hector, and the boy grinned with delight.

There was a fraught silence as they peered towards the palisade. 'Well, what next?' asked Jezreel. 'That was our last shot, though they don't know it.'

For a long interval nothing happened. Then out from the wreckage of the town gate emerged five men. They were unarmed and one of them was holding up a staff from which hung a red and blue flag. The little group was walking towards the spot from where the brass cannon had fired.

'They must have seen our gun smoke,' said Jacques.

Mansur allowed himself a smile of grim satisfaction. 'That

tall man in the black gown beside the flag. He's the Rajah's chief minister. I've negotiated with him a dozen times in the past. This time there'll be no haggling and humbug, for I will dictate the terms.'

NINETEEN

'CONGRATULATIONS. I hear that you persuaded the Sugala to settle their differences with the Sultan,' said Musallam Iskandar. The Malaccan trader was in the front rank of the excited crowd clustered on the landing stage to greet the expedition's return to Pehko's muddy creek. A few yards away a squad of jubilant citizens was manhandling the brass cannon ashore from its raft, and the two smaller lantaka had already been carried off by teams of porters.

'Have you heard anything about a foreign woman living in the palace?' replied Hector impatiently. He hadn't expected to see Maria among the welcoming crowd, but he scanned the faces of those on the jetty nevertheless.

The Malaccan looked at him sharply. 'The woman you mentioned before? There's a rumour about a foreign woman in the Sultan's household, but I don't know any details. The bazaar gossip is all about the victory celebration the old man has promised his son. It's due to take place tomorrow.' His tone became more sympathetic. 'I have received permission to set sail for home after the ceremony. There's space for you and your companions on board, if the palace agrees.'

'I will only leave Pehko if that woman can come with me,' Hector told him.

The Malaccan shrugged. 'I am not accustomed to female passengers on my ship. But if the Sultan says she may travel with you, then naturally I will follow His Majesty's wishes.'

Hector's elation at the victory over the Sugala had faded during the journey back to Pehko. It had been replaced by a premonition that he would face exactly the same problems he'd left behind. 'Even if Maria is allowed to leave,' he said, 'I don't know where we'd find the money to pay you for our passage.'

Musallam waved the objection aside. 'I expect no fee. I hear the Sugala agreed that the skins from God's Birds will be sold only through Pehko. So in future I need only come to this port to collect the harvest. That puts me in debt to you.'

The crowd was beginning to thin out. They had succeeded in getting the brass cannon up the slipway and were attaching drag ropes to the gun. Clearly they were intending to shift it up to the Kedatun sultan. Mansur had hurried off to the palace immediately after landing, just as Hector was hoping to speak with him about Maria. But the chamberlain hadn't come back. Hector was beginning to feel that he and his companions were being discarded now their usefulness was over.

Musallam Iskandar tried to cheer him up. 'Why don't you and your colleagues stay aboard my vessel tonight? Tomorrow we can go together to the palace to attend the celebrations, and there maybe you will be able to speak to your woman.'

HECTOR PASSED a restless night aboard the jong and was already on deck and waiting to go ashore when a drizzly, grey dawn heralded an overcast day well suited to his sombre mood.

'This rain is a sign the monsoon will soon be here,' commented Musallam, wiping his pockmarked face as he joined Hector. The trader was wearing a fresh white gown and a neat black and white checked turban, which gave him a formal appearance. 'It will bring the wind we need if we are sailing for the Straits.'

The dugout that served as the jong's tender was already alongside. As soon as Jacques, Jezreel and Dan appeared, all five of them were paddled ashore, and together they began to climb the path leading to the palace. Around them the people of Pehko were hurrying up the hill. They were dressed in their best clothes – crisp sarongs and newly laundered shirts, head-cloths in blue and red. By comparison Hector felt he and his friends were pretty shabby in the threadbare shirts and breeches they'd been wearing for the past eighteen months.

By the time they reached the top of the hill, the rain had stopped and the sky had begun to brighten. Hector noted that the two lantaka had already been returned to their customary places in front of the palace. Between them stood the brass five-pounder, its muzzle pointing out over the town and decorated with a garland of orange flowers.

A line of the Sultan's subjects was filing respectfully through the palace doors, which stood open to receive them. Judging by the air of suppressed excitement, invitations to visit the palace were rare.

But when their little group reached the doorway, a door-keeper resplendent in a helmet decorated with plaques of turtle shell stopped them. He waved the Malaccan trader on through, but after a disdainful look directed the others to a side entrance. They found themselves in a cramped vestibule, where palace servants explained with sign language that the visitors could not go farther unless they changed out of their soiled garments. They were offered loose trousers of fine white cotton, long-sleeved shirts in the same material and sashes of violet silk.

'I'm not surprised. This smells of grease and cooking,' said Jacques, wrinkling his nose as he unbuttoned his grubby shirt and pulled on the fresh clothes. 'How do I look now?' He pirouetted in his new get-up. 'I feel that I am about to go on stage in an opera.'

'In the role of a clown,' suggested Jezreel, as he struggled to fasten the buttons of his new shirt, which was too small for him.

Self-conscious in their new costumes, they were ushered through a door that gave directly on to the main reception hall of the palace. Hector blinked with surprise. The gloomy cavernous chamber of his earlier visit had been transformed. Great swags of yellow, pale-blue and rose-pink muslin were suspended from the bamboo poles wedged between the rafters. The shutters along the walls had been thrown open to let in light and air. Fresh matting had been laid on the boards, the wooden pillars that held up the roof were wrapped in bright-green palm fronds, and small spirals of smoke rose from incense burners, which gave off a heady, sweet perfume. A band of a dozen musicians in yellow and grey gowns played a melody on gongs, flutes and drums.

Three or four hundred people were gathered in the room. Most were men, but here and there Hector saw women demurely dressed, some with black veils, others with shawls over their heads. He looked among them hopefully, trying again to find Maria, but was disappointed. The crowd stood in a hollow square facing the Sultan's divan at a respectful distance. The royal couch with its red velvet cushions had been raised on a low plinth covered with brocaded silk. The old man himself was nowhere to be seen, but he was obviously expected because many of the courtiers Hector remembered from his previous audience stood ranged on each side of the divan. Instead of their black pyramid caps, they were wearing towering headdresses made from the feathers of God's Birds.

It took Hector a moment to recognize Mansur among them. The tall, thin chamberlain was standing next to the empty divan, and his headdress was a particularly magnificent arrangement of black and orange-yellow plumes. Hector was considering whether to walk across boldly and ask about Maria when the band stopped playing and there was the clash of a large gong. All the courtiers turned and faced to their left, the plumes of their headdresses bobbing and nodding in a ripple of colour. The muslin curtains had been drawn aside, and the old Sultan came hobbling through the gap. Immediately behind him stalked an attendant holding up a ceremonial parasol of yellow silk. At the old man's right hand a courtier carried the silver betel box, and to his left another attendant held a silver spittoon. Slowly they advanced into the room while the crowd hushed. The old man wore a pure-white sarong over a pair of black trousers, a broad belt of red silk, and a tight, long-sleeved jacket of black velvet slashed with gold and a high stiff collar, which failed to hide his thin neck with its folds of wrinkled skin. On his feet were finely worked purple slippers. Instead of a feathered head-dress he wore a head piece of gold filigree.

He reached his divan and lowered himself stiffly on to the cushions. The attendants placed the betel box and spittoon beside him, bowed and withdrew. The servant with the parasol took up position directly behind his master. The Sultan slowly turned his head, blinking his red-rimmed and rheumy eyes as he surveyed his subjects. He reminded Hector of one of the tortoises he'd seen so long ago on the Encantadas.

The gong sounded again, a gentler stroke, and this time it was Prince Jainalabidin who entered. The boy was dressed in the same costume as his father, but bare-headed. Behind him came an attendant bearing a smaller ceremonial parasol. The boy took his place standing on the step below his father, at his right hand.

A short pause was followed by a tapping of drums and the sound of a stringed instrument that reminded Hector of a viola. The crowd parted to allow a troupe of a dozen women and girls to glide into the open space before the Sultan. They were dressed in matching costumes – sarongs of flowered red silk and short green satin jackets fastened with buttons of shell. On their wrists and ankles they wore an array of gold bangles, and they kept short shawls of green gauze draped over their heads. With their gaze demurely on the ground before them, they performed a slow-paced sinuous dance, gyrating gracefully, moving their hands and arms, and every now and again holding a pose whenever a small gong was struck.

As he watched the show, Hector became aware of furtive movements at the rear of the crowd of onlookers. A number of shadowy figures were emerging from what must have been a hidden door at the far side of the audience hall. He took care not to look at them directly so as not to appear rude, but out of the corner of his eye he estimated some twenty women had joined the onlookers to peer between them and watch the performance.

The dance ended, the performers bowed gracefully to the Sultan and left by the way they had entered. The audience stirred in anticipation, and abruptly the drummers broke into a much faster and more energetic rhythm. Now a team of ten young men came bursting through the audience. They were barefoot and their loose trousers were gaudy with red and white stripes. Billowy white shirts were open at the chest, and their hair was tied back with narrow brow-bands. They bounded into the open space before the Sultan, and began to weave back and forth with short stuttering steps, leaning forward, arms held close and waggling their bodies from side to side. Belatedly Hector realized that they were imitating the mating dance of manuk dewata, when the music changed and the young men were ducking and twisting as they mimicked fighting with sword and dagger, performing great leaps and turns, until the music rose to a crescendo and ended with a tremendous booming crash of the gong.

'Do you think that was the sound of our five-pounder?' whispered Jacques beside him. A nudge from Jezreel silenced the Frenchman. The dancers had left, and the Sultan, still seated, was delivering a speech to his people. The old man's voice was thin and reedy and Hector strained to catch the words. He did not understand the language, but it was clear that the old man was congratulating the boy on the outcome of the expedition against the Sugala. From time to time the Sultan turned proudly towards his son.

Hector kept looking towards the women he had seen at the rear of the audience. They had retreated in a group to a shadowy corner. All of them wore veils, and those he was able to see more clearly kept a fringe of the scarf drawn across their mouths to hide all but their eyes. Try as he might, Hector couldn't tell if Maria was among them, for he was now sure they were the palace women.

He was caught off-guard when Mansur stepped from the line of courtiers and began to walk towards him. Suddenly he was aware the Sultan had stopped speaking and the audience was looking on expectantly.

'His Majesty wishes to reward you for your help,' said the chamberlain.

The crowd shuffled backwards, leaving Hector and his friends standing on their own, exposed.

'Each of you will receive a gift of twenty skins of manuk dewata,' announced Mansur.

Hector gathered his wits. 'His Majesty is very kind. I thank him.'

Mansur had not finished. 'He understands that you wish to return to your own people. He would prefer that you stay in Pehko, but his son has asked that you and your comrades be allowed to sail with the ship of Musallam Iskandar. Permission is granted.'

Hector swallowed. 'I would like to ask His Majesty the Sultan that my betrothed leave with us.'

The old man squinted at Hector as the chamberlain repeated the request, and croaked out his response. He sounded petulant.

The chamberlain turned back to Hector. 'His Majesty says that you have already been told the relationship between yourself and this woman is not recognized.'

Hector felt the anger rising within him. 'Then tell His Majesty—' he began recklessly.

The prince's treble voice cut across him. The boy was saying something to his father; his words were shrill with indignation. The old man didn't answer but, turning his head, wheezed a few words to the attendant who stood by his spittoon. The man hurried from the chamber and a short while later came back, carrying a small tray covered with a white cloth.

Mansur took the tray and brought it across to Hector.

'At the request of his son, His Majesty the Sultan has graciously consented that you be given the opportunity to regularize your position according to our custom.' He held out the tray.

Puzzled, Hector lifted the cloth. Underneath was a silver coin. He recognized it at once by its lumpy, uneven shape. It was a two-real piece. Every year hundreds of thousands of them were roughly punched out from sheets of bullion in New Spain or Peru. Every buccaneer dreamed of laying his hands on them. Hector wondered for a moment if it was to be a symbolic purchase price for Maria. The thought made him uncomfortable.

'What must I do?' he asked.

Mansur was regarding him seriously. 'When a man wishes to marry, he sends to the woman a coin. But first he chooses which side of the coin represents their future together. If she returns the coin correctly – that is, with the proper face showing – then fortune will smile on their union and the Sultan will approve their marriage. If not, the man must wait for another day, or the woman has rejected him.'

'But that leaves everything to chance,' Hector blurted.

'To chance and a woman's intuition,' answered the chamberlain gravely. 'If the woman truly understands her suitor and wants to marry him, she will know which face of the coin to select. If she rejects him, she can always blame it on bad luck, and thus she causes no offence.' He held out the tray. 'Now you must decide your side of the coin.'

Hector picked up the coin and took a closer look. It was older than he had first supposed. One face was stamped with the shield bearing the castles and lions of Spain and had the words 'CAROLVS : ET : IOHANA : REGES' around the rim. He turned the coin over in his fingers. The reverse bore an image of two pillars standing on waves and the legend 'HISPANIARVM : ET : INDIARVM' – 'Spain and the Indies' – around the edge. Written across the centre between the pillars were the letters 'PLVS VLTR'. He guessed there had been no space for the final A.

He hesitated. It seemed nonsense to have to make a choice, but he could see no other way. 'I choose the side with the two pillars on it,' he said.

Without a word Mansur replaced the cloth and went towards the group of veiled women. Silently, the crowd parted to allow him through.

Hector looked on. It was difficult to see exactly what was happening at the far end of the hall. He had a brief glimpse as the chamberlain delivered the tray to the group of women gathered in a tight cluster. Then the crowd pushed forward and his view was completely blocked.

Beside him Dan made an effort to distract him. 'Wonder how that coin got all the way here?' he said.

'Probably sent from New Spain to Manila to pay for the China trade and then onwards,' Hector replied, trying to conceal his concern. It occurred to him that Maria would choose the side with the shield, because it was the emblem of her country.

The chamberlain was coming back, tray in hand. He went straight to the Sultan, gave a low bow and murmured a few words and proffered the tray. The old man lifted the cloth and looked beneath it and gave a barely perceptible nod. Beside him, Prince Jainalabidin broke into a wide smile. Mansur turned back to Hector. 'His Majesty the Sultan approves,' he announced.

Hector's heart leaped and he took a pace towards the palace women, until Dan's hand on his shoulder restrained him. The old Sultan was being helped to his feet, and the spectators were waiting in respectful silence while he tottered from the audience chamber. The old man and his son finally passed from view and

Hector turned back to find that Maria and her companions had vanished. The audience was at an end, and everyone was leaving the audience chamber. They streamed out through double doors that led to the rear of the palace. For as long as he dared, he waited, but still there was no sign of Maria. Soon he and his comrades were the only guests remaining in the room, and one of the palace guards appeared and insisted that they rejoin the rest of the company. As they emerged from the Kedatun sultan and out into the fresh air, the reason for the crowd's enthusiasm was evident. Carpets had been spread on the ground and large green leaves set out as plates. On them were piled fish and shrimps, yams, sweet potatoes, bananas, coconuts, unknown vegetables. Sago was offered in every form imaginable: buns, cakes, porridge, biscuits, skewered on bamboo sticks or wrapped in leaves, fried and steamed. The crowd of the Sultan's guests were already seated and helping themselves to the feast.

Musallam had kept a space for them. He was in great good humour. 'I'll be happy to purchase your bird skins from you. They're very valuable,' he said as Hector and his friends joined him cross-legged on the carpet.

Hector found it impossible to concentrate on the food or the bantering conversation of his companions. Only the Omoro menfolk sat down to eat. Their wives had withdrawn to a discreet distance and were standing, looking on. Occasionally one of them might come forward to help the women from the palace kitchens, who were replenishing the piles of food.

'Hello, what's this?' said Jacques. He reached forward and picked up a dark-purple fruit from a pile in front of him. It was the size of an apple and had a smooth, glossy skin. He turned it over in his hand and looked enquiringly at the Malaccan.

'Don't eat the rind,' advised Musallam. He beckoned to one of the servants hovering in the background, took a short knife from her and cut the fruit in half. 'Here, try the white part in the middle,' he said, using the point of the knife to prise out a chunk of creamy-white pulp.

Jacques popped it in his mouth and chewed thoughtfully. 'Remarkable. Sweet and sour at the same time. Somewhere between a peach and a lemon.'

'Mangosteen,' said Musallam. He leaned back with a contented sigh. 'The four of you have proved the truth of an old saying that we have at home, "When the junk is wrecked, the shark gets his fill", though in your case you wrecked your ship deliberately.'

Hector was aware that serving women were passing behind the line of guests, offering bowls of water in which to wash their hands and a towel to dry them. He wondered where and when he would be allowed to meet Maria.

'We say "It's an ill wind that blows nobody any good",' he remarked. The silk sash around his waist was uncomfortable. It had ridden up his waist when he sat down, and he paused to adjust it. A serving woman was at his elbow, kneeling, and had placed a bowl of water before him. Absent-mindedly he rinsed his fingers and then she handed him a small towel. As he took it, his fingers felt a small, hard object within the cloth. He shook it out and the two-real coin fell into his palm. Startled, he swung around. The serving woman was modestly dressed in Omoro style in a plain green sarong and a short overjacket, her features concealed by a long white veil. He reached out tentatively and, when the woman did not withdraw, lifted aside the veil.

Maria's eyes regarded him, mischievously.

He lurched to his feet, his heart pounding. His mouth was dry and he felt unsteady, as if he was not in full control of his legs. The others looked up from their meal, and Jacques waved his mangosteen, the juice leaking down his chin. 'Off you go. You have your whole future to discuss,' he grinned.

Hector took Maria by the hand. He held on as if she would disappear again if he released his grip. By unspoken agreement they slipped away from the assembled company and, with Maria leading the way, hurried through the Kedatun sultan and out on to the portico in front of the palace. The guards ignored them as they made their way to the edge of the hill and stopped at last, looking out at the harbour. Hector could see Musallam's jong far below.

'I should have recognized you sooner,' he confessed, turning towards her. 'The costume suits you.'

'As does yours,' she said with a smile. He glanced down at his own white pantaloons and silk belt, and realized he was still holding the Spanish silver coin in his other hand.

'How did you know which side to select?' he asked.

'At first I nearly chose the side that had the names of the rulers, Charles and Johanna. I imagined you'd have picked them because you thought them to be a couple, King and Queen, man and wife as you want us to be. Then I realized and changed my mind.'

'Realized what?' he asked, though he had a shrewd idea.

'Charles and Johanna were not man and wife, but son and daughter. She was Johanna the Mad and he ruled in her name while she was still alive.'

'So you chose the two pillars?'

She looked at him seriously. 'For a good reason.'

For a moment Hector was at a loss. 'You mean "Spain and the Indies" because we find ourselves in the Orient?'

She shook her head. 'Every child in Spain knows that the two pillars are those that Hercules set up at the Straits of Gibraltar to mark the end of the world. But Charles, when he came to the throne, changed that. He took the two pillars as his emblem, and added the motto "plus ultra" – "more beyond".' She paused. 'I thought there could be no better watchword for our future.'

Hector looked at her admiringly. Maria was so calm and so certain. 'That ship down there,' he said, 'it sails tomorrow for Malacca. The captain has offered to take us with him.'

'I know,' she said simply. 'There's not much that escapes the ears of the harem.'

'In Malacca we'll be able to find someone who can marry us properly, if that's what you want.'

'And what happens then? Where do we go?' Maria asked softly.

'I don't know,' Hector answered truthfully.

Maria regarded him with her large dark, solemn eyes. 'If you're caught and identified in the Spanish territories, you'll be arrested, tried and executed as a pirate. My testimony won't save you a second time.'

'I'm willing to take that risk.'

She gave a small, tender smile. 'But I love you too much to let you.'

His heart went out to her. He gazed over the harbour. The sea beyond had turned a deep indigo-blue in the afternoon sun, and on the horizon a procession of low clouds, touched with grey, drifted southwards. He thought of the impending monsoon winds, which Musallam had promised would carry them to Malacca. 'Somewhere out there must be a place where we can live together, where we'll be left alone,' he said.

Maria lifted her chin defiantly. 'Together we can find it. When I was a child back in Andalusia, my father used to encourage me by translating the words on the coin as "ever further". Let that be our private motto.'

Hector slipped an arm around her waist and held her closer. Already, in the back of his mind, an idea had begun to take shape. He squeezed the silver coin tightly, felt the edge bite into his palm. 'The waves beneath the pillars represent the vastness of the ocean,' he said. 'It will mean another voyage and, this time, to sanctuary.'

HISTORICAL NOTE

Several of the sea robbers whom Hector Lynch encounters in his Pacific adventure are known to history. So too are three of the ships on which he sails. The *Bachelor's Delight* was particularly notorious, and her picture has been identified on an early eighteenth-century map of the Americas. Originally a Danish slave ship, she was seized in 1684 off the West African coast by John Cook, a seasoned buccaneer. The *Delight* was then adapted as a pirate raider by reducing her upper works so that she sailed more handily. Under Cook she was taken round the Horn and into the Pacific to begin four years of piratical cruising. When Cook died of scurvy off the island of Juan Fernandez, Edward Davis took command. He had already taken part in the overland raid into the South Sea in 1680 (see Hector Lynch's adventures in *Corsair*) and proved to be one of the most competent buccaneer captains. In May 1688 Davis brought the *Delight* to Philadelphia, where she was sold, only to begin a second stint as a pirate ship. She reappeared in the Indian Ocean commanded by yet another sea robber, John Kelly. Based in the pirate havens of Madagascar, the *Delight* cruised for prey off the African coast before returning to New York.

The *Cygnet* also appears in the public records. Spelt *Signett*, she was 'a ship of 180 tunns and 16 guns, formerly called the Little England' and on 1 October 1683 sailed from the Downs bound for the South Sea with a cargo worth £5,000. Her captain, as Hector finds, was Charles Swan, who intended to open trade with the Spanish colonists in Peru. They rebuffed him at Valdivia when there was a skirmish and two members of the landing party were killed. Thwarted and aggrieved, Swan and his men eventually turned pirate and looted and pillaged the Spanish colonies and shipping until, in

April 1686, the *Cygnet* headed west across the Pacific. On board was William Dampier, later renowned for his circumnavigations and scientific observations on the winds and ocean currents. The *Cygnet* visited the Thief Islands and then went on to Mindanao in the Philippines. There her crew mutinied. They deposed Swan and left him behind. The *Cygnet* spent some time voyaging in South East Asian waters – Dampier left the ship in the Nicobar Islands – and made her final landfall in Madagascar. There she sank on her moorings, her hull eaten through by teredo worm, in St Augustine's Bay.

The *Nicholas*, twenty-six guns, was also a real vessel. Commanded by John Eaton, she reached the Pacific in January 1685 and operated with little success until her captain decided to head west and try to intercept the Manila Galleon. When she called at Guam in the Thief Islands, there was a brush with the Chamorro. As in Hector's fictional adventures, a letter was received in French, Spanish, Dutch and Latin from the Governor of the Ladrones, Damian de Esplana, asking who they were. A brief alliance was formed between the pirates and the Spaniards, with the *Nicholas* supplying the Spanish garrison with gunpowder (not the other way round, as in Hector's adventure). The *Nicholas* sailed on to China, but her poor luck continued. She chased (but failed to catch) a Chinese vessel laden with silver, and the ship's master deserted in Timor. The *Nicholas* was last reported near Jakarta, Indonesia. Then she vanishes from history.

Swan, Cook, Dampier, Eaton – all were true-life sea robbers. Damian de Esplana, who governed the Thief Islands from 1683 to 1694, gained a reputation as an excellent soldier, but was less honest than he appeared. He accumulated so much wealth by selling government stores at 500 per cent mark-up, and investing the profits in shady commerce with Manila, that his heirs spent ten years quarrelling over the division of his fortune.

Hector's adventures on the unnamed island subject to the Satsuma clan and then among the Chamorro are purely fictitious, but with regard to the assistance rendered to the Sultan of Omoro (an imaginary petty kingdom) it is worth noting that several late seventeenth-century sea robbers finished up as professional gunners in the armies of eastern potentates.

The bizarre story of the ice-shrouded vessel entombed on an iceberg is adapted from a later, nineteenth-century tradition. The *San Telmo*, a seventy-four-gun ship of the line, was purchased from Russia by the Spanish government in 1819 and sent to Peru by way of Cape Horn. Most of her escorting vessels arrived safely, but the *San Telmo* vanished. Her fate was a complete mystery. Then, according to one report, an Italian vessel negotiating Cape Horn met with a huge iceberg on which was observed the stranded hulk of a great black ship, dismasted. Going on board, the visitors were able to identify the *San Telmo*, and found the ship's commander frozen to death in his cabin. Beside him lay the corpse of his dog.